"I think you s[hould stay] with me tonight," Bannon said. "You can have the bedroom. I'll sleep out here."

I didn't bother to object because I knew I was in for a rough night. I'd be awakening at every little noise, if I got any sleep at all. I wasn't a happy camper. These close encounters with bullets and knives were beginning to wear on me. For that reason—and that reason alone, I told myself—I could live with the notion of Bannon sleeping outside my door, even if it was tempting fate.

I told Bannon I wanted to go to my room to get my things. He went with me. The door to my room was not easily missed; it was the one with the bullet hole in it.

"You know what worries me the most?" I said. "I'm running out of lives. Soon I won't have any left."

By Lynn Montana

RUNNING FOR COVER
RUNNING ON EMPTY

LYNN MONTANA

RUNNING FOR COVER

AVON BOOKS

An Imprint of HarperCollinsPublishers

This is a work of fiction. Names, characters, places, and incidents are products of the author's imagination or are used fictitiously and are not to be construed as real. Any resemblance to actual events, locales, organizations, or persons, living or dead, is entirely coincidental.

AVON BOOKS
An Imprint of HarperCollins*Publishers*
10 East 53rd Street
New York, New York 10022-5299

Copyright © 2006 by Lynn Montana
ISBN-13: 978-0-06-074257-7
ISBN-10: 0-06-074257-7
www.avonromance.com

First Avon Books paperback printing: March 2006

Avon Trademark Reg. U.S. Pat. Off. and in Other Countries, Marca Registrada, Hecho en U.S.A.
HarperCollins® is a registered trademark of HarperCollins Publishers Inc.

Printed in the U.S.A.

10 9 8 7 6 5 4 3 2 1

RUNNING FOR COVER

Chapter
1

My mother and I have always had differing opinions on whether a girl could drink, cuss, and sleep around, yet still be considered a lady. To tell you the truth, I don't think she cared all that much about the drinking and cussing part, but as a genteel Southern woman, Mama figured broadening the definition was important.

Actually our differences weren't so much about my willingness to occasionally test the waters with an attractive guy as they were about Braxton Cooper. Brax, I should explain, was the reason I was in New York on a Friday morning in May instead of at home in Atlanta.

Though the nominal purpose of my trip to the Big Apple was to buy diamonds, I came this particular weekend because at six o'clock tomorrow evening Brax—the only man I'd ever loved—would be marrying Mary Beth Alden at the Cathedral of Saint Philip in Buckhead with the cream of the social register of Fulton County, Georgia in attendance, including my parents. Therein lay Mama's and my differences.

The pivotal conversation had come a month ago, right after I'd returned from a buying trip to South America. "Lexie, you will be goin' to the weddin', won't you?" she'd asked rhetorically.

"Not on your life. Former fiancées are about as welcome at weddings as lepers at a bathhouse."

"They invited you, Alexis Chandler."

"They invited me because I'm your daughter, and you've been Mrs. Cooper's best friend since kindergarten."

"That may be true, but I'd think you'd want to be there with your head held high."

"Mama, *I* broke the engagement, not Brax. So I don't need to hold my head high. That part of my life is history. I wish you'd accept that and move on."

But poor Mama couldn't. Brax was not only the son of her lifelong friend—the two of us all but betrothed from the age of three—she considered him a true knight in shining armor. And he was, in his way. Which also explains why I'd accepted his ring, a quite nice two-carat oval diamond with no bow tie, VVS F color, set in platinum.

Long story short, after six months I returned the ring. Love, I decided, was not reason enough to marry if it meant being untrue to myself. And that being the case, I saw breaking up as a singular act of bravery. But to Mama it was utter insanity and certain to damn my romantic life for all eternity.

Be that as it may, I'd opted for adventure and independence rather than marriage and family. I deal in precious stones for a living, you see. My passion is gemstones—rubies, emeralds, sapphires, and diamonds. I travel to the far corners of the earth in search of them. Never tire of looking at them. Cut or uncut—doesn't matter to me. I just love gems. Always have. Probably always will.

I came by an interest in gemstones honestly. My grandfather, Edward Rutledge, Mama's daddy, was a giant in the industry, a larger-than-life figure who'd been known as the

"Indiana Jones of the Gem Trade." Much to my mother's chagrin, I'd taken over the business when he died a few years ago, which had been Granddaddy's and my plan all along. Of course, my mother had never regarded the gem business as a proper pursuit for a lady, hating the fact that we tromped through jungles and traveled to the remote outposts of the world—whatever it took to find that extra special stone.

New York was anything but primitive, though the guys in the Diamond District on 47th Street can be as cutthroat as any gemstone hunter in the outback. But I liked mixing it up with them almost as much. The language employed in the Diamond District could be colorful, though not so crude as what I run into in South America, where deals are often cut in a dusty bar over a bottle of tequila. Nor did I have to pack heat in New York or get physical the way I sometimes did out in the provinces.

Here I could work in heels and a business suit and not worry about some asshole trying to paw me. Which was not to say I didn't mind occasionally having to kick a little ass, if only to keep 'em honest and to maintain my reputation as Edward Rutledge's granddaughter. Like Granddad, I was considered shrewd and tough. It wasn't very ladylike, maybe, but it was me.

I was in a testy mood that morning as I dressed in my room at the Florentine Hotel in Midtown. I guess I was feeling nostalgic about Brax—I'm not an insensitive bitch, after all. And yeah, I truly had loved the guy. I bailed because I'm not the housewife, soccer mom type, no disrespect to anybody intended. Actually, I'm not even the have-a-nice-little-career-on-the-side type of girl. I'm a woman who has to have the freedom to do her thing, which didn't fit into Brax's plans for us. So, when it comes to men, my options are, shall we say, limited.

But, hey, that's the price of freedom. And it was exactly

what I told myself as I looked in the mirror, double-checking my makeup. Tomorrow wasn't going to be easy for me, even if I'd long since made peace with myself over Brax. But there was another wrinkle to the situation I'd been trying to ignore—mostly without success.

In a few days I would be turning thirty, which, according to Mama, had me on the threshold of spinsterhood. I didn't like thinking in those terms. Though I've been told I'm attractive, I don't focus on that. I'm a physical person—tall like my brothers and in great shape due to a vigorous regimen of martial arts training. I get attention from men, but not for the right reasons and not always from the right ones. That's the life of a modern woman, I guess. The point is my life was working.

Having gotten myself into as positive a frame of mind as I could, I headed for the elevator, ready to do battle with the boys over on 47th Street. Down in the lobby, I was greeted by the energy of New York. Horns sounded outside. I could see a couple of guys yelling at each other on the sidewalk out front—or maybe they were discussing last night's Yankees game. With New Yorkers, it wasn't always easy to tell.

In any case, I'd trained myself to be observant, aware of everything going on around me. I took note of men in particular, knowing a girl could never be too careful, especially one who carried around a lot of cash and valuables. Out of habit, I stay on my toes, keeping track of who's looking, who's following, which faces keep popping up.

That's why I happened to notice a guy sitting in the lobby, facing the bank of elevators. It was a weekday, so the place was fairly crowded, but to my trained eye, this guy really stood out. First, he was reading a newspaper while wearing sunglasses. If it was LA, I might have bought it, but this was Manhattan. Second, I'd noticed him earlier when I'd come down to the coffee shop for breakfast. Third, he seemed familiar. I wasn't sure, but I thought he may first have appeared on my radar screen when I'd arrived at JFK the previous evening. Faces stick in my mind. This one certainly did.

The guy was neatly dressed in a dark suit and looked respectable enough. He wasn't a bum. So why was he spending the morning hanging out in a hotel lobby, with seemingly nothing to do? And if I was right about him having been at the airport, wasn't it awfully coincidental that he'd show up at my hotel?

I didn't have to carry cash in New York, so I only had about sixty or eighty bucks on me. Any diamonds I bought today would be shipped to Atlanta, so I wouldn't be carrying valuable stones later. If I was being stalked by somebody intending to rob me, they were in for a rude awakening. But I still didn't like it.

I headed for the revolving doors, intending to walk to the Diamond District since it was such a lovely day. I was interested to see if Mr. Hollywood would follow, or if my imagination was getting the better of me. With Brax getting married and the big birthday just around the corner, maybe I had a subconscious need for a man to obsess over me a little. I have my pride, after all, so if a guy's going to pay special attention, I'd rather it be because of my legs than my wallet.

I walked the half block to Fifth Avenue and saw no sign of Mr. Hollywood, or anyone else, following. I guess I was relieved, though I admit I took perverse pleasure in giving some pestering jerk the what-for.

I came to 48th Street and, while waiting for the light to change, I glanced back at the spires of St. Patrick's Cathedral. I wished the damned bells would stop ringing because, of course, they reminded me of Brax's impending nuptials. That's when I noticed a man peeking around the newsstand on the corner. He had on sunglasses and a dark suit. Yes, it was Mr. Hollywood, and he was watching me. Damn.

Chapter 2

Two hours later I stepped from Herman Sable's shop, the last of the four I'd visited that morning. There was no sign of Mr. Hollywood now, nor had there been earlier when I'd gone up and down the street visiting my diamond merchant friends. I wasn't concerned, but I elected to take a taxi back to the hotel rather than walk, just the same. No sense inviting trouble.

What I really wanted was to go for a nice long run. It was the best antidote for stress, but I wasn't big on running on sidewalks. Instead I planned to pay a visit to the hotel's exercise room. My fondness for fitness came naturally, having grown up with three brothers. My mother thought martial arts were fine for my brothers, but couldn't understand what good a black belt in karate did for me. Mama didn't understand that getting knocked around gave you backbone and put callouses on your psyche.

The taxi got stuck in the middle of a traffic jam, so I had the driver drop me off a block from the hotel. There was an entrance off the side street and a secondary bank of elevators

I could access with my room key. It saved me the trouble of going all the way around to the front and through the lobby.

When I reached my floor, I walked down the long hallway toward my room. As I passed the main elevator lobby, I saw a man sitting on one of the straight chairs. It wasn't Mr. Hollywood—this guy was bigger and fair. He was in a suit, but wore no tie. He did not seem to be waiting for an elevator, which, though odd, wasn't as remarkable as his reaction on seeing me. First his eyes rounded, then he stood abruptly.

"Excuse, me," he said, calling to me as I passed by.

I stopped. "Yes?" When he began moving toward me, I coiled my muscles.

"I have a problem," he said. "I'm waiting for my wife, but there must have been a mix-up and I have a feeling she's expecting me someplace else. You wouldn't have a cell phone I could borrow to call her, would you?"

"Why not use a house phone or talk to the desk clerks? I'm sure they can help."

The guy seemed momentarily at a loss, but then he said, "I suppose I could, but I don't want to miss her coming up the elevator."

"Talk to them downstairs," I said, not wanting to prolong the encounter.

As I turned and headed down the hall I thought I heard him say something, though the comment didn't seem to be addressed to me. Was he talking to himself or was he just nuts? A moment later, I saw a woman coming out of a room several doors down—my room. She was in a pantsuit and fairly young. She did not look in my direction, but began hurrying toward the stairwell at the far end of the hall.

"Hey!" I called, but she didn't stop or look back.

I was about to take off after her when the guy grabbed me from behind. I reacted instinctively, stomping his foot with my spike heel. He howled, his grip loosening enough so I could drive an elbow into his gut. I finished him off with a knee to the face, knocking him flat on his back.

The guy wasn't my main concern, though—it was the woman who had ducked into the stairwell. I jogged down to my room. The door was ajar. Pausing long enough to pull it closed, I took off down the hall as fast as my high heels would allow. When I reached the stairwell, I could hear footsteps a couple of floors below.

Being in heels and a skirt, I was at a disadvantage, but I followed her anyway. We must have gone down five or six floors before I heard a door slam below. She apparently exited onto a floor, but I couldn't be sure which one. Stopping, I listened, but there was total silence. I'd lost her.

I climbed back up to my floor, having no idea what I'd find once I reached my room. Except for a little blood on the carpet in the hallway, there was no sign of the guy I'd decked. Clearly, the two were in cahoots—he hadn't been talking to himself, he'd warned her by radio I was coming.

I was surprised to find everything intact in my room. There weren't even signs of a search. This didn't make sense. I picked up the phone and dialed hotel security. After reporting the incident, I called reception and told them I wanted a new room.

A bellman showed up as I finished talking to the two hotel security people who'd been apologetic but had no explanation for the incident, not that I expected they would. They promised to post someone on the floor and the bellman took me to my new room. After unpacking I changed into my workout clothes, grabbed my room key and cell phone, then headed for the hotel gym, wondering if fate was trying, in some bizarre way, to get my mind off Brax and Mary Beth.

Forty-five minutes later, while my former fiancé was

standing at the altar of the Cathedral of Saint Philip in Buckhead, practicing his vows, I was in the weight room doing bench presses with a hundred-pound barbell. I was sweating like a pig, knowing that if Brax could have seen me and Mary Beth side-by-side then, he'd have thanked his lucky stars I walked when I did. The plain truth was that Mary Beth was exactly what he needed in a wife in the way that I was not.

No sooner had I congratulated myself for my generosity of spirit than fate stepped up with its final surprise of the day. My cell phone rang.

I wiped my hands with my towel, then picked up the phone. "Yeah?"

"Alex?" A man's voice.

"Yes . . ." I said, dabbing my face with the towel.

"It's Martin Sedley, love. And I have glorious news."

Martin was my man in Thailand, a fifty-something Brit expatriate and trusted associate, who had worked closely with my grandfather. "Where are you?"

"In Bangkok, of course."

I glanced at the clock. "What time is it there, anyway?"

"The time bloody well doesn't matter, love," he cried gleefully from fifteen thousand miles away, "how'd you like a go at the Heart of Burma?"

I was so stunned, I don't think I took a breath. I'd been waiting to hear these words for more than two years. If I wasn't so tough, I probably would have broken into tears. Instead I did what I could to calm my pounding heart and said, "Martin, you haven't been drinking, have you?"

"Heavens no," he replied. "I'm dead serious. I think I can get you a crack at the stone, but you'll have to act quickly."

I glanced at the clock again. "I should be heading for the airport the moment I hang up the phone, in other words."

"You should be here within the week," he replied. "Let me put it that way."

I pondered that. "Martin, tell me this isn't just a barroom rumor."

"It's the most definitive lead I've had yet, I promise you. I've been given ironclad assurances from a reliable source that it's doable."

My little heart was beating like a bongo drum, workout sweat dripping off me. "It's been a while since I've been down your way," I told him. "A trip to Thailand wouldn't be a bad idea, regardless."

"This, I assure you, is anything but routine. I don't use the term 'chance of a lifetime' loosely, Alex."

His obvious excitement added to my own. Thoughts were moving through my head at lightning speed. "Who will I be dealing with?" I asked.

"You remember the name Chung Lee?"

"You've mentioned him. He's Thai, but ethnic Chinese, an older guy, right?"

"That's correct. Uh . . . and . . . uh . . ."

I could tell from his hesitation that something was wrong. "What's the matter?"

"Well, I've only just learned that there may be a third party in the mix."

We seemed to be getting to the point. "Who?"

"His name is Cole Bannon. He's an American business-man here in Bangkok."

I ran the name through my mind, but it wasn't familiar. "And?"

"Well, to be perfectly frank about it, Chung Lee has in-sisted that you and Mr. Bannon work together on this."

"Martin, I work alone, you know that."

"Yes, I tried to explain that to Chung, but he was insistent.

And he does hold the cards, Alex. I know it's not ideal, but we're talking about the Heart of Burma, after all."

That, I realized, was the point. The bigger the prize, the more you had to be willing to compromise. "Okay, fine. I'll come talk to them."

"Splendid," Martin chirped. "Splendid."

I told Martin I'd call back with my flight information once my plans were set, then ended the call, crying "Yes!" as I pumped my fist in the air. That brought some curious glances from the chubby couple walking side-by-side on treadmills, but I didn't care. Martin's call had transformed me from a girl who'd run away from home into one ready to conquer the world. Good old fate had come to the rescue.

Chapter 3

Thanks to Martin's call, I didn't mind eating a boring room service meal while the wedding rehearsal feast was going on in Atlanta. In fact, it was all I could do to contain my joy, knowing I was on the trail of an incredible Burmese ruby, one rumored to be the most magnificent find ever.

Nobody outside Myanmar had seen it, but the "Heart of Burma" had been whispered about for years by gemologists around the world. Could it really be within my grasp? Would I be the one to land it?

My grandfather was one of the first to hear about the famous gemstone because of his extensive connections. The day he told me about it stands out in my mind so vividly I shiver every time I think about it. It was late afternoon, and I'd just returned from a buying trip to Colombia with a rather nice collection of emeralds. I went straight to the office from the airport to stow the gems in our safe and found Granddaddy sitting in his desk chair, staring out the window at the falling darkness. He looked so unhappy I dropped into the chair across from him, knowing he needed to talk.

"I've found my ruby, Sparkle, the only piece missin' from my collection," he said.

I should explain that "Sparkle Plenty" was the nickname my grandfather had given me when I was a little girl. Other family members occasionally called me "Sparkle" as well, but it was Grandad's pet name for me.

On that night, though, happy as he was to see me, he sounded terribly sad, more so than usual when he talked about his incomplete collection. Not finding his ruby was the greatest disappointment of his professional life.

Granddad had procured some of the finest gemstones in the world—one of the most famous, not to mention largest, cornflower blue sapphires ever found in Ceylon before it became Sri Lanka, an incredible Colombian emerald now on display at Tiffany's in New York, a perfectly matched strand of fifteen-millimeter South Sea pearls and many fabulous white and canary diamonds. There was even one pink diamond so magnificent that it ended up as the centerpiece in a new diamond tiara commissioned by the House of Windsor. And all of those gems had Edward Rutledge's stamp on them. Some wonderful rubies had passed through Granddad's hands, but never the exceptional, one-of-a-kind "masterwork of God," as he called his special finds.

That evening in his office he looked at me and said, "It's a perfect pigeon-blood uncut ruby, and they call it the 'Heart of Burma.'"

The secret of my grandfather's success was his willingness to go to the source, to take chances, risk danger, do whatever it took to be standing there when the raw stone was taken from the ground, or when it arrived in some provincial town on the back of a mule. In the old days Granddad had gone to Burma in search of his ruby, and he was one of the few people allowed into the country to purchase gemstones after it had become the Union of Myanmar. But his special ruby had always eluded him. Until now.

"How about if we go to Burma together?" I'd said.

Granddad considered that for a while, then muttered, "It'd be an adventure, all right, but I'm afraid at this point it'd be a pipe dream."

"Between your brains and my brawn we can do it, Granddaddy. I know we can."

My grandfather had developed heart trouble and was getting up there in years. But he had me to do the heavy lifting.

"Word is the ruby's still in Burma," he said, "but I'll make some calls and see."

I was thrilled to think we might team up to get that final jewel in the Rutledge crown, but the venture never got off the ground. A few weeks after that conversation, my grandfather's quest for the crown jewel of his career was cut short by another heart attack. He died soon afterward, leaving me in charge of the company and the family legacy. The last words he said to me were, "Sparkle, it's in your hands."

I felt greatly honored that my grandfather had left the company to me. My mother and brothers had gotten the lion's share of his other assets, but Granddad knew I was the only one willing and able to carry on the family tradition. I considered it a sacred trust.

But my grandfather had died with unfinished business. His obsession to complete the collection was now mine. I wanted the Heart of Burma just as badly. Whether it was true or not, I still felt I had a lot to prove and a lot to live up to. I'd sacrificed a great deal for this life, and I wasn't going to settle for just getting the job done. I wanted to be a legend in the industry, the same as my grandfather. I wanted to be worthy of the Rutledge heritage.

As I went to bed that night, I had a deep sense of transition from one phase of my life to another. It had proven to be a special day. The upcoming wedding in Atlanta and the bizarre events here in New York paled aside Martin's news. What I had no way of knowing was that the adventure which lay ahead was much more than I could possibly have imagined. It was more, even, than the Heart of Burma itself. Fate, I later discovered, was a rascal.

I returned to Atlanta feeling a curious blend of euphoria and dread. On the up side, I was jazzed about finally having a crack at the Heart of Burma and eager to get to Thailand. But I also knew there were a few issues I had to contend with first—Mama, the aftermath of Brax's wedding, and my birthday, to name a few.

Birthdays were huge in my family, and milestone birthdays gargantuan. Meaning, I was not looking forward to telling the parents that I'd be on the far side of the world when I turned thirty. I soon discovered that was the least of my problems. The mysterious man following me in New York, and the couple who'd broken into my hotel room, proved to be only the tip of the iceberg.

That became apparent when I pulled into the drive of the big house I lived in in Peachtree Park, only to see my landlady, Miss Tippet, who'd been sitting on the porch, go scurrying inside at the sight of me. This was extremely unusual because normally she'd pounce on me when I returned from a trip to catch me up on everything that had happened in my absence—all the important stuff from which cat had been hit by a delivery truck to whose vegetable garden had become overgrown with weeds.

Miss Tippet was your prototypical old maid, though not all that old in point of fact—probably my mother's age—but she had the spinster's mentality of my grandmother's generation and was stiff and proper right down to her carefully-trimmed-but-never-painted toenails. It wasn't at all characteristic of her to avoid me, unless I was in the company of a man, in which case she'd peek through her curtains, taking notes.

Much of what she heard and saw got reported to my mother, whom she knew, but couldn't exactly call a friend. I guess Southern ladies of a certain age felt it incumbent to look out for the moral rectitude of the coming generation. Mostly Mama didn't recount what pieces of intelligence were passed on to her by Miss Tippet, but my best guess was that she had more inside knowledge of my social life than mothers normally did.

Deciding I'd be finding out what was going on soon enough, I went upstairs to my second floor flat, opening the windows to let in a little spring air. I'd no sooner finished going through my mail when my mother called. "How was New York, Lexie, honey? Did you find some lovely diamonds?"

I decided it was best to discuss the hard issues face-to-face, so I obfuscated. "Nothing I couldn't live without."

"Did you have a good time?" Mama had never fully understood that business travel was mostly a pain in the ass and not intended as an opportunity for fun.

"It was interesting . . . let me put it that way." I wasn't about to tell her about my run-in with the couple at the hotel, and I'd save my conversation with Martin for later.

"Well, why don't you come to the house for supper this evenin', so we can catch up. I'm sure you'll want to hear all about the weddin'."

I didn't want to wallow in it for sure, but I was more than a little curious. Mostly, though, dinner seemed like a good idea because it would give me the opportunity to tell my parents I'd be in Thailand for my birthday.

I arrived at my family home that evening at the appointed hour, and while I had a gin and tonic with my father—by custom, Mama made her entrances a tad late—I told him about my escapade in New York. My dad, Reece Chandler, and I had never been close the way some fathers and daughters were, probably because he'd been a military man—retiring as a brigadier general—and hadn't been around much when I was growing up. I think he regretted that as much as I did, so we'd been working on our relationship the last several years, spending what time we could together, enjoying shared interests like shooting—both skeet and trap—sports, fitness, and the outdoors.

"I assume you don't intend to share that story with your mama," my father said after I told him about the hotel episode.

"No way."

"Garnet's old school and New York remains enemy territory," he said, nodding.

Daddy understood Mama better than any of us, so I decided to heed his advice, though I did ask for a second drink, which was rare for me when in my parents' home.

Mama made her entrance a few minutes later, looking, as always, as though the governor were on the guest list. We sat down to dinner almost immediately and, while my father ate his chicken and dumplings, Mama and I dished about the wedding, the reception, the guests, Mary Beth's dress, her mother's dress, the music, the food, the cake, the helicopter—everything but Brax. Perhaps she thought she was being considerate, but Mama had a way of making loud points in a very soft manner.

She did manage to work the conversation around to what probably had been a major reason for the invitation. It started out with a comment delivered with her trademark lilt filled with sugar and honey. "You know, Lexie, I had the most curious conversation with Gladys Tippet last evenin'."

I glanced at my father, who shrugged as if to say he had no idea this was coming.

"Curious conversations with Miss Tippet are a common

occurrence," I said. "The poor old dear has gone around the bend. I wouldn't take anything she says seriously."

"Then there's nothin' to the story of you becomin' the gun moll of a gang of Middle Eastern terrorists?"

I blinked. "Pardon me?"

"I swear that's what she said."

I caught my father's eye, and we exchanged smiles before I returned my attention to Mama. "You're not joking?"

"Gladys admitted there was a good deal of speculation on her part."

"No kidding. I don't suppose she explained where she got that notion."

"Well, she did say something about being questioned about you by the FBI."

"Huh?"

"That's what she said, Lexie."

I put down my fork. "I don't believe it. Trust me, she's old and getting senile."

"I would be most grateful if you didn't refer to Gladys as old. She's about my age, thank you very much."

"But you're getting younger each year, Garnet," my father said, coming to my rescue, "and she's not."

"That little bit of chivalry has earned you a piece of pie, dear," my mother replied, "and I sincerely thank you for the kindness."

"Mama," I interjected, "all I can say is I don't have any idea why the FBI would investigate me, assuming it's true, which I doubt. But I will have a word with Miss Tippet and report back to you, if that would make you feel better."

"Actually, it would."

It was while we were having dessert that I dropped the bomb that I'd be leaving for Thailand in a few days. Mother's fork slipped from her fingers, clanking on her plate. She stared at me with dismay.

"You're goin' to be in Thailand for your birthday? Your *thirtieth* birthday?"

"Mama, this could be my shot at the finest ruby in the world. I can't pass it up."

My mother chewed on her lip, trying to maintain control, but her big dark lashes fluttered and her hands trembled. Daddy, who'd seen it before, continued to eat his pecan pie. "Lexie, darlin'," she said after a moment, her tone controlled, but only barely, "I was hopin' you'd be spendin' your special day with your family."

"I would if I could, but this is an incredible opportunity. Something I *have* to do."

"I see," she said, lowering her eyes. She sat in silence for a bit, a slight but wounded smile on her peach lips. "If you'll excuse me, I think I'll lie down for a while. I have the most terrible headache you can imagine. I'll ask Dora to serve your coffee."

My mother, the true, genteel Southern lady she was, smiled at me, got up from the table, and left the dining room. There'd been no harsh words, no tearful accusations, but she'd made her point. After she was gone, my father and I looked at each other.

"Why does she always have to do that?" I asked. "I mean, I'm almost thirty years old, not sixteen. Why can't she understand I have a life of my own?"

"I believe she does understand, Lexie," my father replied laconically. "If I interpret your mother correctly, and I believe I do, she's lamenting the fact that she'll be missing Gray's thirtieth birthday, as well as yours."

My father's words, though not so intended, cut through me like a sword. My twin brother had been killed in Iraq shortly after Granddaddy died, bringing a double tragedy to the family. Gray's death had left a scar on us all. My brother and I had not been close like many twins, but we were closer to each other than either of us were to our two older brothers, Heath and Austin. It was my mother, though, who'd suffered most, and I hated the thought of adding to her sorrow by being away on our birthday.

After we'd had our coffee, Daddy and I played a game of chess, though I had trouble keeping my mind on the game. Having gone down to a quick defeat—unusual because normally I beat my father—I bowed to the inevitable and went upstairs to talk to Mama. If I didn't get things out on the table, I knew it would eat at me for days. I found her lying on her bed, listening to the Chopin nocturnes she favored as she stared wistfully out the window at the falling twilight.

"Mama," I said, "I'm really sorry about being away for my birthday."

"Lexie darlin', I know your work's important. You've got your granddaddy's blood in your veins. He loved his family, but there was adventure in his soul. There was no repressin' it for love nor money. You're exactly the same."

"I wish I could be the daughter you wanted, but it's just not me, Mama. A girl has to be true to herself."

"Yes, and I've come to accept that."

It was sort of true, but not completely. I knew my mother. She was not one to let go of anything important to her, and my future remained her pet project, no matter what she said. It was something I just had to live with, like it or not.

Chapter
4

A couple of days later I boarded my flight to Thailand, leaving behind a somewhat murky situation. Brax was on his honeymoon, and that chapter of my life was closed, but the incident in New York and Miss Tippet's story about the FBI continued to haunt me.

My landlady didn't want to discuss the matter at first, I think out of fear she might compromise some important national security interest, but eventually she opened up and told me what they'd asked her—which turned out to be fairly routine-sounding, even by her account. Had she seen any unusual, recent signs of conspicuous wealth? Did I use drugs? Who did I associate with? I suspect her answer to the last question included the names—or license plate numbers—of every man who'd called on me the past three years. Not that there were all that many, but if they'd been there, Miss Tippet wouldn't have missed them.

Leaving nothing to chance, I paid a visit to the FBI Atlanta Field Office, but they wouldn't talk to me. It had occurred to me that Mr. Hollywood and the couple at the Florentine were with the FBI, but I had no way of proving it.

The bottom line was, the FBI's intentions with respect to Alexis Chandler of Atlanta, Georgia remained unclear.

I didn't like it, but what could I do? If it was serious, the problem would be there when I got home. In the meantime, I needed to concentrate on the Heart of Burma.

By the time the plane began its decent into Don Muang Airport in Bangkok I was more than ready to disembark. Transpacific travel is exhausting, especially when you don't sleep well on airplanes, which I don't. It was twilight when we touched down and dark by the time I came out of customs.

The first surprise came when Martin wasn't there to greet me. Instead there was a pretty Thai woman waiting for me. She was dressed much like me in a crisp khaki shirt and pants and wore light blue tinted designer sunglasses. Between her beauty and élan, she might have been a Bond girl.

"Khun Alex," she said, using the formal form of address, followed by a *wai,* the traditional greeting with her palms pressed together and her slender fingers pointing at her chin, combined with a little bow, "welcome to Thailand. I am Joy, and I come in Martin's place."

Her name struck me as ironic considering her formal demeanor. I offered my hand, which she shook, her grip surprisingly firm. "How did you know me?"

"Here there are not many lovely tall *farang* with ebony hair and blue eyes. Also, I have seen your picture."

"I see. What's up with Martin? Is he ill?"

"No."

"Will he be at the hotel?"

"Yes," she replied, "I think so."

I wasn't getting much information, though it was hard to tell whether it was by design or because of the limitations of language.

"Do you work for him?"

"No, just doing favor."

Joy insisted on taking my suitcase, though it had wheels. We piled my carry-on bag on top and headed to the exit of the terminal building. I kept my satchel.

For a while she didn't speak, then, "Your flight, it was good?"

"Good, but long." Not knowing exactly how Joy fit into things, I remained circumspect.

Early evening was a magical time of day, especially in the tropics. A silver-blue Mercedes sedan stood waiting for us at the curb. Joy opened the rear passenger door for me. I climbed in and she put my suitcase in the trunk. Then she got in the driver's seat. Reaching over, she opened the glove box and removed an irregularly shaped package, which she handed to me. "Martin say to give this to you."

I removed the cord and plain brown paper. As expected, it was the 9 mm automatic I carried while in Thailand. Considering I dealt in cash and jewels, a weapon was not just good insurance, it could be life-saving. Her handing me the gun also reassured me on one point—she knew Martin well enough for him to have entrusted my weapon to her.

No conversation passed between us on our way into town, but I found myself wondering about Joy. Martin usually worked alone, and a stylish woman did not seem the sort of person who'd do him a favor. The whole thing seemed a little fishy to me.

Sitting in the plush leather seat of the Mercedes with the air-conditioning blowing in my face, I could have fallen asleep. But my instincts told me I had a possible situation on my hands, so I needed to stay alert. I lowered the window beside me an inch to savor the pungent, tropical air.

Most of my adventures occurred in exotic locales that were opulently sensual, poor, sometimes decadent, and often dangerous. But places such as this were also where treasures like the Heart of Burma were to be found. I was excited, despite my fatigue.

"I don't want make you too nervous," Joy said, bringing me from my dreamy state, "but maybe we have trouble."

I sat up, instantly alert. "What do you mean?"

"Car follow us since airport. You carry lots of money, maybe?"

"No, I don't have an unusual amount of cash," I said, not mentioning that I had a letter of credit that was substantial, though useless to any thief. I turned to look out the back window. There was a fair amount of traffic on the expressway into the city, but it was moving well. Mostly I saw headlights. "Is it the one right behind us?"

"No, behind that one."

"Are you sure he's following us? It could be he happened to leave the airport at the same time."

"No, I change speed. He always stay behind."

I tried to think who it might be. No one I'd noticed either on the plane or at the airport had shown a particular interest in me. If I was being stalked now, it had to be a stranger because I didn't know anybody of note in Bangkok other than Martin. Certainly nobody who was aware I was coming— apart from Chung Lee and Cole Bannon, that is. And I hadn't actually met either of them.

If I felt more paranoid than usual it was because of the events in New York and the crazy business with the FBI in Atlanta. It made no sense that either of those problems would have followed me to the Orient. More likely, this concerned the ruby.

"Joy, do you know Chung Lee?"

"Yes, very much," she replied. "He is my uncle. This his car."

"Oh, I see."

Now things were starting to make sense. Maybe Joy was

doing double duty—a favor for Martin and spying for her "uncle." I was sufficiently attuned to Chinese culture to know that the term "uncle" meant there was some familial or close social connection. Regardless, it seemed unlikely that somebody associated with Chung would follow me if I was already with Joy. And if she knew who the tail was, she wouldn't have brought it to my attention.

"How about Cole Bannon?" I asked. "Do you know him?"

"Also yes," she replied vaguely.

"But he's not your uncle."

Joy giggled at this and perhaps blushed. "No, Khun Alex, he is not my uncle."

She seemed to enjoy the touch of humor, but quickly grew serious again. I saw her keeping a close eye on the rearview mirror.

The best explanation for the tail remained the ruby. It could be a competitor for the Heart of Burma—somebody who found me a threat to his or her interests. There was no shortage of possible candidates, because there wasn't a gem dealer in the world who wouldn't love to get his hands on the stone. And, unfortunately, some people would stop at nothing to do just that.

"I think we should try to find out who it is," I said to Joy.

She looked at me with surprise.

"Serious?"

"Yeah, I'd like to nip this in the bud."

"Okay, maybe I leave highway and go in quiet neighborhood, see if he follow."

"No, let's just find a place to pull over. If that car is following us, he can't very well stop behind us without being obvious."

"Okay, I stop."

I took my automatic out of my satchel and Joy pulled the Mercedes over at a layby. I looked back and saw the car she'd referred to. Seeing us parking, the driver seemed to hesitate, then continued on. The vehicle was a late-model Japanese import. As best I could tell there was a single occupant, a man, though between the darkness and glare of headlights, I didn't get a good look at him.

"Let's follow him," I said.

Joy pulled back onto the roadway and accelerated to catch up. Our man sped up. Soon we were engaged in a highspeed chase, weaving through traffic and coming close to a collision on two occasions.

I've never been a speed demon and the caper was making me pretty damn nervous. A bad accident would be a hell of a price to pay for my curiosity. Joy was a skillful driver, thank goodness, but our prey was determined. When he made a sudden exit off the motor way, we missed the turn and he eluded us.

"Very sorry," Joy said.

"Don't worry about it. It may be just as well. I'd hate to be in an accident without good cause."

I was trying to be blasé, but the truth was I'd been gripping the door handle. In fact, it wasn't until we were approaching the Old Farang Quarter where the Oriental Hotel was located that my heart calmed down.

Granddad hadn't made a point of it, but subsequent to his passing I'd learned that the Heart of Burma had a bloody history. The pursuit of it had resulted in more than one death and a good deal of suffering. It was beginning to appear I wouldn't be given a free pass, which meant I had something else to worry about as well. My life.

Chapter
5

I intended to talk to Martin about
Chung Lee and Cole Bannon, since one or both of them
could be connected with—or might be able to explain—who
the tail was. And, though Joy was unlikely to provide much
useful information about Chung, considering their relationship, the same might not be true of Bannon. I decided to
probe.

"What can you tell me about Mr. Bannon?" I asked her as
we neared the hotel.

She gave me a quick glance. "He very hot," she said with
a flick of her brow.

The colloquialism made me smile, especially with the accent. "He's hot, huh? Lady's man?"

"Depend on which lady, I guess," she said, smiling.

I gathered Joy was impressed. But I didn't care what he
looked like or how he was regarded . . . except as a businessman. "What does he do, exactly?" I asked.

"He buy and sell things to send to America and other
places."

"He's an exporter, in other words."

"Maybe yes. I don't know the business questions."

"Is he a friend of your uncle?" I asked.

"Not good friends, but they do some business," she replied, circumspect as always. "I don't know what."

I'd gotten as much as I'd likely get. Anyway, the hotel was just around the corner.

"Here we are," she said, pulling into the drive.

I liked the Oriental and, like my grandfather, usually stayed there when I was in Bangkok. It was located on the Chao Phraya River in the original foreign commercial district of the city. The French Embassy was next door.

Joy and I said goodbye, shaking hands, and I entered the hotel, heading straight for the registration desk. Between the long flight and the car chase, I was exhausted, but I needed to talk to Martin.

As the clerk did the paperwork, I glanced around the lobby with its huge potted plants and enormous wooden bells hanging from the ceiling. No sign of Martin.

"Is there a message for me from Mr. Sedley?" I asked the clerk.

"He asked to be notified of your arrival," the young man replied. "I already sent the bellboy to fetch him."

I was relieved at the news, but still found all this drama rather curious. Did Martin have some sort of surprise in store?

I had just gotten my key and arranged for my bags to be taken to my room, when I spotted Martin coming out of the bar. He was a slightly overweight, over-the-top Old World gentleman who was normally fastidiously dressed. But he looked as if he'd allowed himself to go to seed in the nine months since my last trip to Thailand. His white tropical suit was rumpled, his gray hair slightly mussed, his gait more wobbly than usual. The last bit I'd seen before—especially

after he'd had a few gin and tonics—but even then he usually maintained a dignified air.

"Alex, my love," he said, reaching me, his bushy brows
arching as he gave me a painful smile, "so good to see you."
Taking my hand, he kissed it.

This performance was a bit extreme, even for Martin. I
had a funny feeling.

"Sorry not to make it to the airport," he said, "but I was
engaged in work on our project. I trust Joy took care of you
properly."

"She was very accommodating, though not everybody in
Bangkok seemed happy to see me." I told him about our little car chase.

As he listened, he grew more sober, punctuating my tale
with interjections like, "Good God!" "Surely not." "How ex-
traordinary!" "Good gracious me!" "Have you ever?" "How
positively rude," and finally, "What a bloody nuisance, Alex.
Thank God you were unharmed."

I looked him dead in the eye and said, "Martin, you'd
know as well as anyone, who do you think was behind
this?"

"I haven't a clue, love. Honestly."

"Is anybody else on the trail of the stone?" I asked Martin.

"There is no shortage of chaps who'd dearly love to lay
their hands on it, as you well know, but I can't name anyone
in particular who's on the case."

"No rumors, then?"

"None whatsoever. I've spoken to no one about this but
Chung Lee. Who he might be talking to is another matter altogether, though it can't be in his interest to create problems
for you. Simply can't."

That made sense, but after New York, Miss Tippet, and
now this car chase, I no longer trusted reason.

"What's the deal with Joy?" I asked. "Is Chung providing you with drivers?"

"No, we were in negotiations when the time came to pick you up. Chung volunteered to send someone."

"I see. So what were the negotiations about?"

"I've been ironing out wrinkles," he replied. "It appears matters are settled."

"What's been settled and with whom?"

Martin scratched the back of his head and shifted his weight. And he did not look me in the eye. "There's been a bit of a problem," he said sheepishly.

I knew it. I'd come all this way for a stone that mattered so much to me, only to have things fall apart. "The deal's fallen through," I said glumly.

"Oh, good heavens, no. Nothing like that. No, no, not at all. Gracious."

I was as frustrated as I was relieved. "What then?"

"Why don't we finish this discussion over a drink? No point in standing in the bloody lobby. Come," he said, taking my arm, "let's repair to the lounge."

"Thanks, but I'm bushed, and I want to go to bed. Just tell me what's going on."

"Can we at least sit?" He led me over to a couple of up-holstered chairs. Giving me a woeful look, he said, "I'm afraid we're up against a bit of a delay."

"What do you mean, a delay?"

He leaned close and I could smell the alcohol on his breath. "Bannon's been out of town and won't be returning until tomorrow. Chung leaves for Hong Kong tomorrow and will be gone a week. He wants to delay things until his return so that the three of you can sit down and work things out."

"A *week*?"

"Yes, I know. I told him you'd arranged to be here for a meeting tomorrow."

"So, it's on or not?"

"It depends on Bannon's availability."

"I still don't understand his role in this. He's that essential?"

"I'm afraid so. In Chung's view, in any case. Don't ask why. It's been foisted on me, and I've had no say in the matter whatsoever. I don't know any more than do you."

I wasn't sure whether I was getting the straight story. Martin had a tendency to put the best light on things and, like most middlemen, he had to soften the parties' most extreme positions. Still, I didn't like it that I'd flown halfway around the world to be given the runaround. Maybe I wasn't a grizzled veteran in this business, but I'd been buying stones for over a decade, I was competent and respected, and I ran Rutledge's. Besides, this was Asia, where saving face mattered.

I stared hard at Martin, wanting him to know I wasn't pleased. "Tell them the meeting's tomorrow or not at all. And now, I'm going to bed."

We both stood and Martin took my hand. "Bloody unfortunate things have gotten off to such a rotten start. I hope it hasn't been too upsetting."

"After a good night's sleep, I'm sure I'll be fine."

"I'll ring you up in the morning with their response."

"If it's not what I want to hear, I'll be on the first flight home."

I bid Martin goodnight, then headed toward the elevators. If I'd come off as severe with Martin, it was intentional. If he wasn't concerned, Chung wouldn't be. Middlemen were supposed to get it from both sides.

My room was in the modern tower rather than the original white-shuttered structure containing the famous Authors' Wing where Granddad and I once had high tea. The lounge was noted for being the place where Somerset Maugham held court, and being there with my grandfather remains one of my favorite-ever memories of Bangkok.

I was tempted to crawl directly in bed but had a shower instead. The warm water relaxed me and made the cool sheets feel extra welcoming, but I no sooner turned off the lights than my mind began working.

Instead of being poised to embark on my quest for the Heart of Burma, I was in a Mexican stand-off with my so-called partners. I was also being stalked. And if all that wasn't enough, tomorrow was my thirtieth birthday. I had no significant other to share it with, no friends or even family. That was enough to depress any girl.

I couldn't let that bother me, though. I was where I wanted to be, doing what I wanted to do. And I had the challenge of a lifetime to occupy me because somewhere out there, probably locked in a strongbox in a jungle camp, was the Heart of Burma, the final jewel in the Rutledge crown.

Chapter 6

I'd slept in and was having a conti-
nental breakfast in my room when Martin called. "Spectacular news, love. We'll be meeting with Chung Lee at eleven."

I looked at my watch. That didn't give me much time.
"I've got to hurry then."

"Chung will send a car for you. It'll be out front at half
past ten. And, if you don't mind, Alex, I'll go directly to his
office and meet you there."

"No problem."

I made the mistake of having a third cup of coffee while
doing my makeup, then compounded the problem by not
making a final visit to the john before leaving my room. I
was so eager to get started on my quest that I didn't think of
my bladder.

The Mercedes with Joy at the wheel was waiting outside
the hotel. She got out of the car and greeted me with a smile
and a *wai*, which I returned.

"You feel better this morning, Khun Alex?"

"Yes, thank you," I said. "A good night's sleep does won-
ders." I didn't mention that it was my birthday, which tended

to be a good day for most people. In this instance, the jury was still out.

"I like your clothes," she said, opening the door for me.

I'd decided to wear camouflage fatigues and boots—my preferred mode of dress in the back country. True, Bangkok wasn't the bush, but the macho look had a practical value in certain cultures. Military garb brought an air of caution, if not respect, from the men I encountered—though I had to be able and willing to back it up, which meant kicking butt, if the need arose. With Chung I knew I'd be facing sexism, and if my proposed role involved slogging through the jungle to secure the ruby, I wanted to look like I could do it. Sissy girls need not apply.

Joy pulled the Mercedes into the street and we were on our way. I asked where her uncle's offices were located and she told me in Chinatown. I'd been there before. It was a district in the old city and had once been the financial center of Bangkok. Now it was home to the sizable ethnic Chinese population. Significant commerce and many financial transactions still took place in Chinatown because of the importance of the Chinese community to the trade, business, and banking of the country.

Chung Lee was essentially a middleman, a deal arranger, a high-level version of Martin, who was more of a deal finder. In the Chinese culture, a guy who knew everyone of importance and was well respected wielded a lot of power and had influence. That was Chung Lee. In the American context, he'd fall somewhere between a consultant, a lobbyist, and a Mafia don.

Joy took Charoen Krung all the way to Chinatown, turning onto Soi Isara Nuphap, a crowded alleyway that passed for a street. The first block was lined with gold shops, a profusion of Chinese herbal medicine stores, snack stalls and noodle shops. Every other business in the next block seemed to be a spice shop, and the narrow sidewalks were crowded with vendors selling fresh and preserved foods of every imaginable sort.

When we reached Songwat Road Joy turned right, and we went a short block before we parked behind a truck that could easily have been older than me. A gang of porters was busy unloading large barrels filled with God-knows-what.

Chung's offices were located in a nineteenth-century wooden warehouse. There were a number of these old relics down near the river, and they were of significance mostly for their historical, rather than economic, value.

The building looked dilapidated, its wooden facade bleached by the sun, weathered and streaked by the tropical rains. There was a rather interesting pediment gracing the front of the building and decorative carved wooden finials that must have been wonderful when new. Now they were chipped and broken. But I had learned during my numerous trips to the Orient that the external appearance of a thing, whether a building or a person, was not a reliable indicator of what was inside.

Joy walked with me to the heavy wooden entry door, and rang the bell. Giving me a smile that could have been reflective of our growing friendship, she offered her hand. As we shook, the door opened and Joy headed back to the car.

The glare of the afternoon sun was so bright that I could barely make out the shadowy figure inside until he stepped into the light. It was a man, stocky and round-faced, sporting a bristly crew cut. He gave me a nod and said, "Come, please."

I followed him inside. The vestibule we entered was windowless, dank, and cool. A large lightbulb hung in the middle of the room. On the rear wall were a set of heavy double doors, which I assumed accessed the warehouse. A young man sat to one side of the vestibule on a straight chair. Leaning against the wall next to him was an automatic rifle. I gathered he was a guard.

On the other wall was a large window-like opening and behind it an office where four women worked among piles of papers and files on cluttered tables and desks. In the front right corner of the vestibule was a narrow staircase. My guide headed upstairs and I followed him to the second floor and into a long corridor with low ceilings. Though stark, the walls were painted and the wood floor was polished and clean.

I followed him halfway along the corridor to an elegantly carved wooden door where we stopped. My escort knocked and, in response to a command from within, he opened the door and motioned for me to enter.

My heart beating nicely now, I stepped into a large room which had the feel of a paneled wood study or library, Chinese style. There was a blue and white carpet on the polished hardwood floor, built-in bookcases containing books, *objet d'art* and artifacts. In front of the large, arched window lighting the room was a huge teak desk and behind it an elderly Chinese gentleman in a short-sleeve white shirt and a shock of thick white hair. He was bone thin, his face gaunt, almost skeletal. He had a wispy, white mustache and goatee that struck me as Confucian.

"Alex," came a voice from the other side of the room, "you're here. Jolly good." Martin, seated in a Ming scholar's chair, rose and came over. He was in another of his white suits, not so rumpled as the one he wore the night before.

"Allow me to present you to Khun Lee," he said, taking me by the arm. Martin and I approached the desk and Chung rose. "This is Alexis Chandler."

I did a *wai*, keeping my hands high up under my chin and holding it until Chung had responded with a *wai* of his own. I thought I noted a flicker of satisfaction on the old man's stoic face upon seeing my courtesy. My grandfather had always tried hard to be respectful of the peoples and cultures he visited and taught me to do the same.

"Please sit down, Miss Chandler," Chung said in surprisingly good English. He motioned toward the Ming chair opposite Martin. Once I was seated, he said, "I understand your reception in Bangkok was hectic."

"That's very true, Mr. Chung. Joy is an accomplished driver, though."

"Well, you're here, and that's what matters."

I noticed the remaining chair in the room. "Are we waiting for Mr. Bannon?"

"Unfortunately, he won't be here," Chung said. "He had another obligation."

"I hope that won't be a problem."

"No, we thought perhaps you could meet with him later. It's just as well. Better that you and I speak in private first."

I was glad because Bannon's involvement bothered me from the start. Maybe I was overly sensitive, but I didn't like the implication I *needed* the help of a man.

"May I offer you some tea?" Chung asked. "Perhaps something to eat?"

I wasn't hungry, and the last thing I needed was something to drink. I had to go to the bathroom but was reluctant to ask to use the facilities because it was something a girl would do. I decided to tough it out. "No, thank you," I replied. "I've had too much coffee already." I decided to get right to the issue that was bothering me.

"I have a question, Mr. Chung. What's Mr. Bannon's role in this?

Chung reflected. "The idea of including him was mine, Miss Chandler. I wanted someone who has local connections, and it seemed that dealing with a countryman might make it easier for you. It struck me as a good compromise."

"Are you saying you don't think I can do this on my own?"

I saw Martin shift uncomfortably. Okay, I knew I was being direct, which was not the Asian way, but I was in no mood to be patronized, either.

"I know you Americans have a fondness for direct speech," Chung said, "but I think to best answer your question, I need to give you a little background. There is a Burmese gentleman with control of the ruby. For the moment, let's call him Mr. X. He and I have agreed through intermediaries that I will purchase the ruby. Unfortunately, I have no idea what the Heart of Burma is worth."

"I didn't come here to be an advisor," I said. "I assumed we'd be partners."

"Yes, that's the intention."

"Will there be a senior partner?"

"Hmm. If I'm not mistaken," Chung said, "you're asking who will be in charge."

I glanced at Martin, who seemed to be holding his breath. "That would be one way to put it," I said to Chung, "yes."

He tapped the tips of the fingers of his two hands together, his eyes never leaving me. "Let me save us both time and face by suggesting we become equal partners. My investors and I will provide half the capital for the acquisition, and you will provide half."

I considered that. "Who markets the stone?"

"That will be your responsibility," Chung said. "We share the profits equally."

"After my expenses on both the acquisition and marketing ends."

Chung conceded the point with a nod of his head. "If you wish."

Chung Lee was proving easy to deal with, though taking a partner was not my preferred way of doing business. On the other hand, if he was a silent partner, then to the world the

Heart of Burma would still be my stone. "What about Bannon?" I asked.

Our host stroked his chin whiskers, looking thoughtful. "May I be direct again?"

"Please."

"Mr. X, shall we say, operates . . . what is the expression? . . . on the margins."

"And?"

"Mr. Bannon has experience in dealing with such people, and he knows the territory, both in the geographical and sociological sense. Plus, we will probably be bartering for the stone. Mr. Bannon, being a trader, has experience in such matters."

I wondered what wasn't being said. "I have a feeling there's more to it than that."

He smiled. "Miss Chandler, you're most astute. There *is* another problem."

"And that is?"

Looking embarrassed, Chung Lee said, "The problem is you're a woman."

Chapter
7

I gave him a level look. "Presumably the fact that I'm a woman isn't a problem for you, or I wouldn't be here."

"Most assuredly."

"So the party who has a problem with my gender is Mr. X."

"This is correct. But please don't misunderstand. Mr. X is fond enough of women—some might say too fond—but his appreciation of the fairer sex does not extend to the realm of business."

"And Bannon is the solution."

"He seems the best choice, if only because they speak the same language."

"And have the same plumbing," I muttered.

"Pardon me?"

"Nothing, I was just thinking out loud."

"So, what do you think, Miss Chandler?"

My need to get back to the Oriental for the sake of my bladder was growing more urgent by the moment, so I wanted to conclude this conversation quickly. Yet we were at a sensitive stage of the negotiations, and I had to be patient.

"As long as Bannon's just a front man and maybe advises on trading issues, I suppose I can live with it," I said. "The next question is, who pays him?"

"This we must decide."

The way Chung hesitated, I sensed we might be coming to our first snag. "Did you have something in mind?"

"Mr. Bannon will be working with you on the operational side, Miss Chandler, contributing to your effort. It seems appropriate that he be paid from your half."

Martin gave me a little nod as if to say, "I told you he was a sharp cookie."

"I can see how you might feel that way," I said to Chung, "but if I'm putting up half the capital and doing the physical work, it seems only fair that Bannon's compensation come off the top."

Chung stroked his goatee again. "I agree that you will make the greater effort, but on the other hand, without me there is no deal. I am the connection to Mr. X."

"And . . . there are other gemologists."

He did not say, "Exactly!" but it was written all over his face. I had a hunch, though, that Chung also knew there were damned few gemologists of stature who would trek into the jungle to deal with some lowlife who worked "on the margins." Even so, the old man gazed at me like he was staring down a bear.

We were at that point in every negotiation where the first to speak after a silence was the one who'd lose. Chung Lee, I judged, could sit there looking at me all day. I had patience, but I also had a full bladder. Time was not on my side. I needed to act.

"Tell you what, Mr. Chung," I said. "Why not think about it, and if you'd like to call me before you leave town, I'll be at the Oriental." With that I stood, did a *wai*, picked up my satchel and headed for the door.

"Miss Chandler," Chung said, stopping me. "I'll give you sixty percent of the deal, and you make whatever arrangements with Mr. Bannon that you wish. If you can get him to do it for a fixed fee or at less than ten percent, you could come out ahead."

"And if he wants more?"

"You strike me as a skilled negotiator," he said.

I considered that. "Let me feel him out and get back to you."

"His car is waiting for you downstairs."

"He wants to meet with me *now*?"

"I'm told he's completed his business, and I'll be leaving for Hong Kong in a few hours," Chung said, meaningfully. "We can put further discussions off until my return at the end of the week, if you prefer."

Ball back in my court.

"Okay, fine, I'll see him now," I said, motivated equally by a desire for the deal and a desire for a bathroom. "Call me later, Martin," I said. Then I went out the door.

As I hurried down the hall, I realized that Mother Nature had done me a huge favor. Granddad had always said that if you get up from the negotiating table and make a statement by walking away, you'd better be damned willing to go out the door. Chung had tipped his hand as to how important I was to the deal.

Now I had to contend with Bannon. But not until I paid a visit to the facilities.

Downstairs in the vestibule there weren't any doors with figures of men and women on them, but there was a young man leaning against the wall, talking to the guard. I went to the window that looked into the office where the women were working.

"Excuse me," I said to the woman who was nearest, "where is the bathroom?"

"Go through doors to back of warehouse." She pointed.

Pushing the big doors open, I peered down the huge, barn-like structure that was crammed to the rafters with boxes, barrels, and large crates. The musty air was filled with aromas, some spicy and pleasant, others less so. This did not look promising. I decided to wait. Wherever I was to meet with Bannon, it had to be more civilized than this.

Closing the doors, I turned and the young man who'd been leaning against the wall, talking to the guard, came to attention. He looked at me quizzically.

"You really Khun Alex?" he said, sounding incredulous.

"Yes, Alex Chandler. Are you Mr. Bannon's driver?"

He did a *wai*, looking bewildered.

"Listen, is it far to where I'll be seeing Mr. Bannon?"

"Maybe twenty minutes."

It would be the longest twenty minutes of my life. We went out of the building. The vehicle parked outside was a battered twelve-year-old Toyota. This was a bad omen.

I saw no point in getting in back. At some point, pretension became laughable. The driver climbed in behind the wheel and put his key in the ignition. The engine turned over, but didn't start. He tried again. Same result. Wouldn't you know? But then the engine started and we took off.

"Do you work for Mr. Bannon?"

"Only sometime."

"Does he speak Thai?"

The question brought a toothy smile to the young man's face. "He think so."

I had to chuckle at that. The comment could very well be indicative of Bannon's entire persona. Normally I'm not the prejudiced sort, but I'd gleaned just enough about Cole Bannon to have doubts about him. This was unfortunate, considering he now stood between me and the Heart of Burma.

Fifteen minutes later we came to a stop in front of a modern, fairly classy-looking multi-story building. The ground floor was a restaurant. I thanked the young man for the ride and went inside the building.

It being the lunch hour, there were customers seated at the tables in the restaurant, though it wasn't crowded. Not a good omen. A severe middle-aged woman in a high-neck, black *chong-sam* stood behind a podium. She regarded me over half-frame reading glasses as I approached.

"May I help you?" Her English was good, but stilted.

"I'm here to see Mr. Bannon," I said, "but I would very much like to use your restroom." I looked back in the direction I thought they might be located.

"I'm sorry, there are workman making repairs," she said.

I couldn't believe this. "Please, there must be someplace I can go."

The woman frowned. "What is your name?"

"Alex Chandler."

She looked down at her schedule. "*You* are Alex Chandler?" She, too, was incredulous. I was beginning to see a pattern.

"Look, I really need to use the facilities," I said impatiently, "could you please direct me somewhere?"

"Yes, yes, there are toilets in the suite," she said, perplexed. Turning, she called to one of the girls seated on the carpeted steps behind her and said something.

I noticed half a dozen scantily clad girls lounging on the plush carpeted steps nearby, and it hit me. This was a brothel. In Thailand, sex was available in all sorts of businesses ranging from bars and beer gardens to coffee shops, discos, massage parlors, and bathhouses. The legendary Patpong area, which was not far from here, was famous worldwide for its nightlife. But when an establishment like this one was located outside the nightclub districts, you never could be sure what it was until you walked in the door.

An attractive Thai woman in a skimpy tank top and mini-skirt came forward. "Come with me, please."

I was more annoyed than disconcerted, my mind jumping back and forth between my pressing physical problem and the fact that Bannon had chosen to meet in a brothel. Maybe the guy was even worse than I feared.

We waited at the elevator for a car to arrive. She pushed the button, then looked me over, her expression disapproving, as though I had just crawled out of the jungle. I suddenly regretted my choice of attire.

"What's the name of this place?" I asked.

"Nakhon Spa," she replied. "Bath and massage."

I was in one of the infamous upscale Bangkok bathhouses, which I'd heard about, but never seen up close and personal. They were known for the Thai body massage—where the girl runs her naked, soapy body over the customer. It was supposed to be a wonderfully sensuous experience. It didn't necessarily involve sex, though in most cases it did. Female tourists sometimes had body massages purely for the sensual experience, though not in a place like this. The usual locale was in the privacy of their hotel. I had my sensual side, but this was outside my range of experience.

"This best bath and massage in all Bangkok," the girl said proudly, as the elevator stopped. We stepped out. "You American?"

"Yes."

"I never see American lady here," she said as we walked along.

"No, I imagine not."

I was beginning to understand what had happened. Between everybody being surprised at my name and the choice of meeting site, Bannon must have thought Alex Chandler was a man. It was the only explanation. But I had to go to the bathroom so badly I wasn't able to sort out the implications, let alone decide what to do.

We reached our destination, one of the many highly decorated doors with fancy hardware. The girl knocked, then opened the door. Opposite us was an ornate Chinese screen which blocked the view. I heard giggles over loud music. My escort announced our arrival, but I wasn't about to stand on ceremony. I wanted that bathroom. But stepping around the screen, I came up short.

Two slender Thai girls, naked as jaybirds, were dancing in front of a man seated on a plush sofa. He was clothed, wearing a polo shirt and trousers. But he wasn't just a guy. He was a damned fine-looking man. Despite everything, I stared.

That wasn't like me. It was out of character. I guess it was a combination of the circumstances and my state of mind. I mean, I was in a brothel, for crissake.

Everyone in the room seemed to be frozen in place, me looking at them and they looking at me. Finally, Bannon pointed the remote control in his hand at the stereo, plunging the room into silence. I heard the door close behind me, my escort having left. The three people across the room continued to stare at me, but nobody spoke or moved.

"Please forgive the interruption, but I'd like to use your bathroom."

Bannon lifted his hand and pointed to the door on the other side of the enormous elevated tub that dominated the room. Without further ado, I nearly skipped past the huge heart-shaped bed to the door. Inside, I made a beeline for the commode.

Chapter
8

Never had relief felt so sublime.
But then the reality of what awaited me in the other room
sank in. I wasn't sure whether to be amused or angry.

In fairness, I decided that Bannon had to be as embarrassed as I, so tolerance was called for. And while I was
hardly a prude and knew all too well how men behaved—
having lived through my brothers' single years—I still did
not relish the thought of cavorting in a Thai bathhouse just to
be sociable. Nor, I suspect, was Bannon jazzed with the idea.
But I was trapped in his bathroom while he and two naked
women awaited me and an explanation.

Steeling myself, I went out to find Bannon seated on the
sofa as before, but the two women had put on short little cotton robes as a gesture of modesty. One sat on the platform of
the tub, the other on the arm of the sofa. Again all three
gazed at me.

"Please don't tell me you're Alex Chandler," Bannon said.

"Sorry, but I am."

He glanced heavenward as if to say, "God, why me?"

Then, shaking his head, he gave me a bemused smile. "Welcome to the Nakhon Spa."

Bannon was not only handsome as hell, he was cute, a Troy doll. That was the term my best friend, Macy Nesmith, and I invented in high school. Our sophomore year there was a senior, a boy named Troy Caradine, who was the school's big heartthrob—tailback on the football team, homecoming king, and every pimple-faced girl's dream. Shaggy blond, with wide shoulders, a big, super white-toothed smile, and the self-assurance that comes with being irresistible to the opposite sex. Such guys were the stuff of spring break flings, and every girl seemed to run into one somewhere along the way.

I'd had mine—Rob—on the Costa del Sol in Spain during a summer when I was in college. He took me to a bullfight, to the beach, then to bed. Bannon, though, was the adult version, which probably made him more dangerous. I pegged him at thirty-seven or eight, the party boy who never grew up.

"I take it this was intended to be some sort of male bonding ritual," I said.

"Euphemistically speaking, yes."

"Sorry to spoil your fun by being a girl."

"You know," he said, wagging his finger, "I never thought it possible that someone being a girl could spoil my fun, but you may be the exception."

He laughed and so did I.

Bannon had a sense of humor, which I appreciated, and he wasn't a dolt, which helped, because the stereotypical Troy doll always loved the image in the mirror best. Of course, conceit remained a very real possibility.

"Not that you're going to believe this," Bannon said, "but when you came in we were holding a dance contest. I got drafted into judging."

I repressed my smile. "Tough duty."

"Yeah, right. Well, since you're here, care to join us?"

We were speaking from across the room, but the man's aplomb was evident, even at a distance. That said, we were still in a brothel, and he was cavorting with two naked women when I came in. That pretty well defined who I was dealing with.

"You know," I said, "maybe we should reschedule."

"Why not talk now? Things could hardly get any worse, and who knows, they might get better."

The question seemed to be, was I up to socializing with a reprobate and a couple of prostitutes? It was a challenge of the first order. But I wasn't about to shrink from it, though I knew dear sweet Mama would have already passed out cold.

Bannon gestured for me to join him. The closer I got, the better appreciation I had of his rugged good looks, his thick, slightly mussed tawny hair, his shoulders and muscular build. My gaze rested on his remarkable blue eyes—lighter than mine, a clear aquamarine, and absolutely stunning. He had one of those ultra-short beards of only four or five days of growth and a crooked smile—more of the isn't-this-fun sort of smile, rather than the one you'd call cocky or arrogant. My initial impression was that he was a man who found everything amusing, taking nothing that happened too seriously. And he was definitely of the alpha male variety, not unlike my father and brothers.

"I'm Cole, if you haven't figured that out," he said, offering his hand, which I shook. "That's Mai Soo over there on the tub, and this is Ree. She won the dance contest and the five hundred *baht* prize, in case you're wondering."

"Congratulations," I said to the girl.

She was the prettier of the two, her black hair shoulder-length with red highlights. Mai Soo's hair was much shorter, her face rounder. Both had nice figures.

"Thank you," Ree said, lowering her eyes and blushing.

Both young women were lovely, delicate creatures. Many people consider Thai women the most beautiful on earth. They did have a gentle grace that made me feel like an Amazon in my boots and fatigues.

"How fortunate I am to be in the presence of three such beautiful women," Bannon said as though belying the thought that had just gone through my mind. "I think this calls for a celebration. Mai Soo, why don't you get us some beers?"

"I really don't think I should stay," I said as the girl went off.

"Nonsense," Bannon said, taking my arm and guiding me down onto the sofa. "No one in Atlanta will hear you were cavorting in a bathhouse in Bangkok, I promise you. What happens inside these walls, stays inside these walls. You've got my word on that." He sat beside me, grinning and resting his hands on his knees. "So, this is your first time in a massage parlor, but not your first time in Bangkok, I gather."

"That's correct. I've been here on business many times."

Bannon scratched his head. "Now, how could I have been under the misconception you were a guy?"

"My name."

"Yes, but you'd think the fact that you're not only a female, but an exceedingly attractive one, would have come up along the way."

"Didn't you talk to Chung Lee about me?"

"A very brief conversation. Mostly I spoke to his assistant."

"In English?"

"No, in Thai." The explanation seemed to hit him. "Ah, that's what happened. A communication snafu. Languages aren't my strong suit. Must have missed a nuance."

"Nice to hear a man referring to gender as a nuance."

Bannon gave me a wink.

Mai Soo returned with four beers on a tray. We each took

one, but I didn't intend to drink much of mine, not on an empty stomach.

"What do you think, ladies, shall we drink to our celebrated guest? This lady is a world-famous gemologist, you know."

The women nodded their assent.

Bannon game me a crinkly-eyed smile. "Is it Alexandra?"

"Alexis, actually. My friends and family call me Lexie."

"Do your drinking buddies at the Nakhon Spa count as friends?"

"Sure, why not?"

"To Lexie, then," Bannon said, "on this very special day."

His choice of words was ironic, considering it was my birthday, which I'd all but forgotten until his remark. What a hell of a birthday. Great material for cocktail party conversation down the road, though. "What did you do for your birthday?" "Went to a brothel in Bangkok." Of course, Mama came to mind. What would she think if she could see me now?

Everybody drank. I took a ladylike sip that would have made Mama proud.

"We do have business to discuss, Lexie," Bannon said in a more serious tone. "The plan . . . when I still thought you were a guy . . . was to have a few beers, a massage, relax a bit first. You being a gal changes things, of course, but there's no reason we can't have a good time." He glanced at the women, then back at me. "These girls can give one hell of a great massage. I don't know how uptight you are, but this *is* the land of sensuality. What do you think? Care to try something a tad different?"

Chapter 9

The thought of Rob and the Costa del Sol went through my mind fleetingly in response to Bannon's proposition, sugar-coated though it was. How many men who'd known a woman for ten minutes would have the guts or the gall to suggest such a thing? Only a libertine far from home, living a decadent life, I surmised.

When you knock around in a man's world, you don't want to come off as stuffy or puritanical. I'd engaged in sport and drinking bouts with the best of them, but never the erotic and sensual. Nor was I about to start now. The Heart of Burma was a very serious matter as far as I was concerned, and I intended to make that clear.

"You know, Cole," I said, "tempting though the notion is, I think I'll pass."

"Fair enough. Don't want to step on toes."

"You're not stepping on toes. This is just not me."

"Understood." He turned to the women. "Well, ladies, I'll catch you next time."

They each did a brief *wai* and headed for the door, taking their beers with them. After they were gone, Bannon took a

long drink from his bottle. "So, Khun Alex, is there somebody special back home? Not that it's any of my business, of
course. I don't mean to be impertinent, but it's always good
to know who you're dealing with."

"There is somebody I care for, as a matter of fact. Brax
happens to be in the Caribbean at the moment." I did not like
to mislead, even if it wasn't technically a lie, but when you
are a single businesswoman, you do and say what is necessary to keep the wolves at bay and the man-woman thing
outside the equation.

True, I dated when I found someone who interested me.
But it was also true that Brax had set a pretty high bar. I
wasn't so needy—either emotionally or physically—that I
had to get laid on a regular basis, which was damned fortunate considering my relationships tended to be brief and
sporadic. I can't honestly say I was content with the romantic side of my life. I knew something was missing. But that
was the price I had to pay to realize my dreams.

"I take it you're single," I said, relying on the obvious
signs, though with a man like this, you never knew.

"I'm unattached in every respect," he replied. "My lady
friends tend to be of the sort you just met."

"An amazingly candid admission," I said. I took a hasty
sip of beer.

"Well you know, Lexie, this is a culture with different
values and sensibilities. I admit to having embraced it ea-
gerly. I don't see sensual pleasure as a moral issue. Actually, it's more a part of the social fabric of everyday life
here."

Cole Bannon was surprisingly intelligent and well-
spoken. That did not mean he was a grownup, however. A
man could still be a boy at almost any age. Troy dolls were
equal opportunity in that respect.

"Not to get into polemics or sexual politics," I said, "but

do you think those girls feel the same way about the sensual side of Thai life as you?"

"We're talking about exploitation, are we?"

I shrugged and drank more beer.

"Almost anything I could say would come across as rationalizing," Bannon said, "but I'll give you my take anyway. The Thais are a pragmatic people. Those girls made more money in a couple of hours this afternoon than the average worker makes in a week or two. Each of them supports an extended family back home in the countryside and are damned proud of it. The attractive ones can name their price and working conditions. There's poverty in this country and exploitation because of it, but not across the board. There are cultures where any woman working outside the home is being exploited."

"Sorry, Cole, but you *are* rationalizing."

"Okay, I won't argue. But let me say this: if you're going to live and work in a country like Thailand, as I have for years, you're well advised to look at the situation through the prism of the Thai experience, not the one you bring with you from home."

"I'll keep that in mind."

He gave me that wry grin again. "I think there's something else you're a lot more interested in discussing than Thai sexual mores," he said.

"Quite true."

He took a long pull on his bottle of beer. "So, apparently you and I are going after this rock they call the Heart of Burma."

"That's what I'm here to talk to you about."

He surveyed me. "Let me guess. Chung left it up to you to negotiate my action."

I could see that Bannon wasn't stupid when it came to business, either. "My deal with Chung depends on whether you and I can reach an accommodation," I said.

"I see. And he's left you little wiggle room, if I know good old Khun Lee."

Bannon knew what he was doing, all right. I shrugged in response.

"Okay, Lexie, how do you want to do this? Do I say we split everything fifty-fifty, you counter eighty-twenty, and we end up somewhere in the middle, or what?"

I stared at him, trying to decide whether it would be better to knock him down or take the patient, reasonable approach.

"You seem hesitant," he said.

"I don't think we can talk numbers unless we agree what it is you'll be doing."

"Fair enough."

I fiddled with my beer bottle but didn't drink more because the little I'd had had gone to my head. "Look, I'll be honest with you," I said. "I don't even know why your services are required . . . except that I'm told our Mr. X . . . the guy we'll be dealing with is . . ."

"Is what?"

"A sexist pig."

"That's what I've heard, too, but it's only part of the story. I don't know the man personally, mind you, but we have . . . let's say . . . mutual acquaintances. In this culture, who you know is very important."

"Okay, you're saying you'll be more than just a beard."

He smiled at that. "Believe it or not, Lexie, I have more to offer than just this mug. I'll admit, though, that being a guy serves me in this particular instance."

I half chuckled, half scoffed. "The way I see it, plumbing is only worth so much."

"In other words, my gender contribution doesn't justify a big piece of the pie."

"I might have put it more diplomatically, but basically that's it, yes."

"Let's be specific," he said.

"Okay, I consider twenty percent of my side of the deal to be ridiculous under the circumstances. In fact, I was thinking more in terms of a salary, a daily wage."

"Oooh," Bannon said, making an O with his lips, "you are a tough cookie." Lifting his hand he added, "And I mean that as a compliment, so don't get pissed."

"I'm a realist," I told him. "I look at the facts."

He finished off his beer, the cords of neck rippling as he drank. I'd been aware of the physical man I was dealing with almost from the moment I'd walked in the door. But after going at him *mano-a-mano*, I realized that Cole Bannon had more going for him than his looks. He was clever and he had charm. But his character was still in doubt. I didn't have a lot to go on, but in that department he seemed questionable at best.

I'd grown up a lot since Macy and I had first figured out the male mystique, but the Troy dolls had apparently grown up too. The question going through my mind now was if it was just a coincidence that Chung Lee had chosen to pair me up with a Lothario, or if he thought that was the way to control me.

"Forgive me if I sound immodest," Bannon said, "but I'm very good at what I do. I've been operating in this country for years. More importantly, I know the border area and the people up there."

"I'm sure you're qualified. But price is determined by what the market will bear."

"I'm not irreplaceable, in other words."

"Surely you aren't saying that you are."

He grinned. "The most accomplished great white hunter still wants the very best guide available. I may not be irreplaceable, but you'd be hard-pressed to find someone better suited for the job."

"You obviously believe in yourself. But I'm the one who has to be convinced."

"Do you think Chung Lee would want less than the best?"

"Okay, let's assume your qualifications. What are your services worth?"

"We're talking risk and danger, in addition to my time. I could make the difference between success and failure. What's that worth to you?"

Damn if I wasn't starting to like the guy, and that wasn't good. Not in a negotiation. And yet, if we did work together, trust would be essential. I was torn.

"You know," he said, when he didn't get an answer to his question, "we could sit here all day, debating how useful or essential I am to the project. To save us both time, why don't you tell me how much leeway Chung Lee gave you to make our deal."

"That's like asking what I paid for something I'm trying to resell at a profit."

"Look, sweetheart, if we're not in the same ballpark, then we're wasting each other's time. Give me your bottom line, and I'll tell you whether I'll do it for that."

I studied Cole Bannon, who I decided was most definitely dumb like a fox. "I've got sixty percent of the deal to play with," I said.

He nodded. "Meaning twenty percent of the pie is ear-marked for me."

"Twenty percent if Chung Lee and I end up with an equal take. I intend to come away with fifty percent."

"You're saying I should accept ten points, and it's coming out of Chung's half."

"Right."

Bannon leaned back in the sofa and stretched his arm out behind me, crossing his legs. He stared off, reflecting. I was aware of the furry tuft of hair at the neck of his polo shirt. Brax had a hairy chest, and I'd always loved it. Bannon, I could see, had a chest on him, too, one the girls must love snuggling against.

"You know what makes sense," Bannon said, "is that we split this three ways."

I had to laugh. "I might as well go to the airport, get on a plane, and go home."

"You're that greedy."

"I know what I'm bringing to the table."

"Okay, I'll make this easy. Give me the twenty points and we've got a deal."

"Ten."

"Fifteen," Bannon said.

"Twelve and a half."

"Twelve and a half and you take me to dinner to celebrate our new partnership."

"When we sell the stone."

He gave me a big, wide smile. "You know what, Lexie? I may have to marry you. No other woman I've ever met has been half so delightfully challenging as you."

I had to admire his pluck even if he was prone to overconfidence. Standing, I offered him my hand. "It was nice meeting you, Cole."

He stood as well, and we shook hands.

"I'll finalize things with Chung," I said. "One of us will be in touch with you."

"Sedley knows how to get hold of me."

"Thanks for the beer," I said. "*And* the use of your bathroom."

"Always happy to accommodate a lady." Then he gave me that grin of his. "Even one in combat boots." His expectant look said, "What? No retort to that, sweetheart?"

I looked down at my boots. Jimmy Choo's they were not.

But that's all right, I had forty-seven and a half percent of the deal, and he had twelve and a half. No need to rain on his parade. Giving him a smile, I headed for the door.

As I reached the screen, a thought occurred. I stopped and, turning abruptly, I caught him staring at my derriere. "Oh, by the way," I said, "Some guy followed me from the airport. Would you have any idea who could be that interested in me?"

Bannon shrugged, then said, "Well, this is only an opinion, but if I had to guess, I'd say it's somebody who likes the lay of those trousers on your sweet little behind."

I flushed, then spun on my heel and got the hell out.

Chapter
10

    Okay, so Cole Bannon was good with the quip, but he was still a Troy doll. The only thing that mattered was if he would be useful in my quest for the Heart of Burma. That didn't keep my cheeks from burning as I marched out of the building, though. He was, after all, a man, and they could get to you. The key was not letting him become a problem.

Bannon's car and driver were waiting. The way the young man looked at me, I could tell he was trying to read what had transpired inside. When I climbed in without saying anything he said, "Big surprise, huh?"

"Mr. Bannon was surprised, yes."

"Me too," the driver said with a laugh. "I like to see boss's face."

I realized I was lucky there hadn't been an even greater embarrassment, like walking in on Bannon unclothed or worse.

During the drive to the hotel I contemplated where things stood. The deal was workable. The main thing was I had a crack at the ruby. That's what I cared about.

Arriving at the Oriental, I went straight to my room and phoned Martin.

"Smashing!" he enthused when I told him I'd come to terms with Bannon. "You've done it, Alex, congratulations!"

"Until I have the road map to the ruby there's nothing to celebrate, Martin. And I still have to figure out how I'm going to finesse Bannon."

"Not to worry, love. Small beer. I'm sure you'll have no trouble with the gentleman."

"What makes you so sure?"

"I've seen you at work, Alex. And I've also seen the way fellows like Bannon react to you. You'll have him eating out of your hand nicely, I'm quite certain."

"Martin, if you're saying what I think you're saying, you're as delusional as he is. I have no intention of indulging the man. He either plays the game my way or he's out. And I'd like you to make that clear to Chung, by the way. I don't care what his Mr. X thinks."

Martin cleared his throat. "As you wish, Alex."

I might have overreacted a bit, but the ruby was an emotional issue for me. Dispassion wasn't an option when it came to the Heart of Burma.

"I do have request of you, Alex," Martin said.

"What's that?"

"I should like you to do me the honor of accompanying me to dinner this evening. If I'm not mistaken, we have a birthday to celebrate."

"That's sweet of you, Martin, but don't feel you have to entertain me. Honestly, spending a quiet evening alone is fine. A birthday is no big deal."

"To you perhaps, love, but to me it's exceedingly important. You have to eat, so you'll dine with me, and you can have your alone time later. Shall we meet in the lobby at, say, eight o'clock?"

I could see he was determined, so I decided to humor him. It was easier than fighting it. Plus I could get a report on his conversation with Chung Lee. "Okay," I said, "let's have dinner, but I do want to make it an early evening. And no gifts, all right?"

"Nothing?"

"Bring me good news from Chung. That's the only present I want."

"As you wish, Alex. And, speaking of Chung, I'd better give the old boy a tinkle before he heads for the airport."

"Good. I'd like to set up a schedule and begin planning the operation."

"Right you are. See you tonight at eight then, love. Cheerio."

I decided to have a nice hot bath to relax. The day had been hectic, and I needed to unwind.

It was good to get out of the jungle fatigues. In retrospect I could see they hadn't been the correct choice of attire. Bannon must have laughed up his sleeve at the sight of me. Not that I really cared what he thought.

Recalling his suggestion of a massage, I had to smile. What did he think? That I'd get in the tub and play footsie with him and the girls?

Sinking deep in the tub, I continued to reflect on my first-ever visit to a bathhouse. Cole Bannon was entertaining, I had to give him that, and if I was obsessing now, well, I was entitled. I was alone on a milestone birthday, Brax was on his honeymoon, and I was more needy at the moment than I was willing to admit.

The upshot was that I was slipping into one of my "Rob moods" which, I suppose, was a polite way of saying I was horny. But a chance to indulge my libido would not be coming anytime soon. Sure, Cole Bannon fit the bill in the looks department, but we'd be working together, and that made it a *very* bad idea. Still, he was good fantasy material.

* * *

Martin, looking the spiffiest yet, was waiting in the lobby when I stepped out of the elevator. There was a faint smell of alcohol about him, but his eyes were clearer than they'd been in the past day or so.

"Don't you look smashing!" he said, delighting in my appearance.

In keeping with my whimsical mood, I'd worn the only formal thing I'd brought with me, a black silk chong-sam I'd had made on a trip to Hong Kong the year before. I never wore it in Atlanta because the thigh-high split seemed a bit pretentious, if not *outré*. But it worked fine in the sensuous Orient. Besides, what the hell. I was thirty.

"And I like your earrings."

They were Imperial jade, a gift from my grandfather, which he bought for me during our last trip to Thailand. Though I didn't wear them often, I always felt close to him when I did. "Thank you."

He took my hand, stepping back to admire me. "So regal and elegant," he said. "I don't feel worthy."

"Now you're being silly."

"Not in the least." He made me turn around, embarrassing me. "And so authentic."

I guess he was referring to the ebony hair sticks I'd stuck in my chignon. "Not really. It's more the mood."

"Well, you're gorgeous, love, trust me."

"My, but you're in good spirits, Martin," I said as we headed for the entrance. "You must have good news for me."

"Nothing special. Everything's on track, mind you, but it's not that. If I'm a bit beside myself, it's because I do enjoy a do."

"This isn't really a party, it's dinner."

"Oh, but the occasion makes it very special."

Martin's blush was so vivid and his eyes twinkled so that

it made me wonder what was going on. "What aren't you telling me?"

"Not a thing, love." Then he trilled with laughter.

Perhaps he was more into his cups than I'd allowed. Fortunately the China House was a few steps from the entrance to the hotel and just around the corner from the French Embassy. The hotel's premiere restaurant was located in an old colonial style house that was adjacent. Grandad and I had eaten there on one or two occasions. He was especially fond of Cantonese cuisine, which was their specialty.

The lovely old structure with its rick-rack gingerbread trim was all lit up, glowing white against the night sky. The building was surrounded by a low, wrought iron fence, the entrance and garden adorned with large urns and exotic plants. A warm glow shown through the tall palladium windows as we approached the entrance.

The white-clad doorman did a *wai*, bowing as he opened the door. Inside, waiters in dark silk pantaloon-like trousers shaped like jodhpurs and worn under white Nehru jackets, scurried about. The *maître d'*, a squat man in a tuxedo and black tie, approached.

"Good evening, Mr. Sedley," he said. "Madam. We're ready for you, sir. Please follow me."

The way Martin beamed made me wonder again what was up. My curiosity increased when we went up the stairs. "Given the occasion, I thought a private room would be more appropriate," Martin explained.

"That's thoughtful, but you're making far too much of this," I said. "Really."

"I wouldn't have it any other way, love."

The *maître d'* led us to a door which he opened with a flourish. "Madam, please."

I stepped into the dimly lit room, just noticing the large circular table in the center of the room was set for several persons, when the lights went up and I heard cries of "Surprise!"

Looking around I was shocked to see my parents—Mama beaming, her hands clasped together at her throat, my father in a white dinner jacket behind her, smiling broadly. On the other side were my brother Heath and his pregnant wife, Julie. Heath was in his Army dress uniform, grinning like the cat who'd swallowed the canary. Julie, nearly five months into her pregnancy, was so rosy-cheeked she was florid.

"My God!" I cried, my hands at my mouth, incredulous. "I can't believe this!"

"How could we allow our baby to celebrate her big birthday all by her lonesome?" Mama asked rhetorically as she gathered me into her arms. "It just wouldn't be right."

As I hugged my mother, my eyes filled with tears, I saw another person at the back of the room. Like my father, he was in a white dinner jacket, though it hung open insouciantly. His hands were thrust in his pockets, a lazy grin on his handsome face. It was none other than Cole Bannon.

Chapter
11

Seeing Bannon was an even bigger
shock than seeing my family. I was only a few hours removed from my last glimpse of him, but his presence in the
bosom of my family couldn't have been more unexpected
than, say, Brax without Mary Beth.

After I'd gotten hugs and kisses and birthday wishes from
my family, Bannon ambled over. "Happy birthday," he said
with the calm assurance of an old family friend.

He extended his hand and I went to shake it, but he drew
my hand to his mouth and kissed it. "And many happy returns of the day."

"Thank you. What a nice surprise to see you here."

It was more a shock than a nice surprise, but what was I
going to say? I glanced at Martin, hoping for an explanation,
but Mama beat him to it.

"It was the most uncanny thing, Lexie," she said, "but
when the four of us were talkin' to Mr. Sedley this afternoon, he happened to mention Mr. Bannon by name and
Heath asked if it could possibly be the same Cole Bannon
he'd known in the Army Infantry School down at Ft. Ben-

ning. Naturally, we made a call, discovered it was indeed the same Cole Bannon, and, considering the two of you are working together, how could we not invite him to our little party?"

"My, that is a coincidence," I said, wondering who was to blame for this.

When my mother slipped her hand through Bannon's arm and beamed up at him like a teenaged girl with a crush, I knew I was in for trouble. Had he seduced her, she seduced him, or was it a little of both?

"We've been havin' the most delightful conversation while waitin' for you, sugar," Mama went on. "Cole has lived such an interesting life."

Bannon smiled at me with obvious self-satisfaction, and I thought, *Mama, if you could only have seen the fine gentleman this afternoon the way I did.* It was unlikely that had even crossed his mind, but the smile on his face was certainly understandable. He'd had a good day—he'd gotten a decent chunk of my deal and he'd ingratiated himself with my family. I was sure he was gloating underneath, thinking he had a nice insurance policy and maybe some leverage to boot. That remained to be seen, of course, but there was no doubt he'd managed to complicate my life. The question was, did I blame him or circumstance?

My mother instructed the waiter to open a bottle of champagne so they could toast me. Bannon aside, it was a thrill to have my family here. While the wine was being poured, Mama explained how she'd laid her plans for my surprise.

"Austin would have been here, as well," my father added, "but he is on a training maneuver and couldn't get away. We were pleased Heath and Julie could come, though."

"And the baby," I said, taking my sister-in-law's hand.

"I was planning on taking a few days of leave anyway," Heath explained, "and Julie and I wanted to see a little of

Thailand before we leave Japan at the end of summer, so here we are."

"I'm so happy you did," I said, giving my brother another hug.

The waiter distributed glasses of champagne, and my family toasted me. I was touched that they'd gone to all this trouble, just so I wouldn't be alone for my birthday. If I felt at all strange, it was because of Cole Bannon.

I can't say I resented his presence, but it was a little creepy, I think because he was getting a glimpse of the private side of me that I kept separate from my business. To his credit, Bannon fit in surprisingly well. He had his military background in common with my brother and father, though he hadn't been career military. As for my mother, well, I could see he had her number right out of the chute. The man was as adept with a genteel Southern lady as he was with the hookers.

At one point, while the men were talking war, Mama pulled me and Julie aside for some girl talk. "What a nice young man your friend Cole is," she said. "He's so urbane and debonair."

It was all I could do to keep from laughing. "Mama, he's a business associate, not a friend." I wanted to add, "I only met him today, in a whorehouse, as a matter of fact." I didn't say that, of course. Why disillusion her? Besides, it would have caused me more grief than it would have Cole Bannon.

"He thinks very highly of you, I can tell," Mama said.

"What makes you think so?"

"He said as much, for one thing. Isn't that right, Julie?"

"Yes," she agreed, "he said you have a way with the Thais and really fit in well."

I colored at that, knowing he could only be referring to Mai Soo and Ree because he never saw me with anyone else. I shot him a wicked glare, only to find him smiling at me.

The bastard probably knew exactly what was going on in our little gossip session.

"You don't know him well enough to draw any conclusions. I certainly don't."

"Well, no surprise there," Mama replied. "You're not as experienced as I, Lexie. I've been sizin' up men for the better part of half a century . . . not that I necessarily want you girls remindin' me of that fact. But I assure you of this—I can read a lot in a man's eyes and in his manner that goes right over many women's heads."

"Mama, I'm not naive when it comes to men. I've seen his type before."

"Oh, don't get me wrong. I'm sure Mr. Bannon's cut a pretty wide swath in his time, but a man should. Look at him. How can he not be attractive to the ladies? I suspect his wilder days are mostly behind him, though," my mother said. "He is a widower, after all."

"He is?"

"Yes, didn't you know?"

I shook my head, looking at him. "No, I didn't."

"Well, then you see that I am accomplished at gettin' to the bottom of things."

"You've always been the family's social maven, Mama."

"Be that as it may, what matters in these situations is what's in a man's heart, the side of him that shows when the chips are down."

"And you know what's in his heart?"

"I know he's most admirin' of you, young lady. And for very good reason. Some things can't be faked. A man's admiration for a woman is one." Mama sipped her champagne and looked over toward the men. "Not that it's any of my business, but I do wish you didn't resist every opportunity that comes your way."

"Opportunity for what, Mama?"

"Don't be obtuse, Alexis, you know exactly what I mean."

I drew a slow breath, but I wasn't going to argue. Not on my birthday, not after my parents had come halfway around the world to be with me. My mother's delusions didn't really matter, anyway. They'd soon be on their way home and her "orchestration" would be behind me. I preferred that word to "manipulation," because my mother could no longer manipulate me, but she sure knew how to set the table.

About the time we were summoned for dinner, Martin came over and, taking my hands, said, "I'm going to have to take my leave. I've another engagement, I'm afraid."

"No," I said, "you have to stay for dinner."

"My job was to get you here, and that's been accomplished. Anyway, I destroy the symmetry of the group, if you haven't noticed. Mr. Bannon will serve as an able dinner companion, I'm quite sure."

"You never did tell me how things went with Chung Lee except to say that everything's on track."

"And it is, but what I didn't realize was that his trip to Hong Kong is partly to finalize arrangements with Mr. X. Now that he knows our side is in order, he plans to press ahead with the other side."

"Meaning we're delayed until he returns."

"Yes, but at least we've got our deal. The time in the interim can be put to good use. I understand Mr. Bannon has a suggestion to share." Martin looked at my mother and Julie in turn, smiling. "I do apologize for talking shop, ladies, but it's my job."

"Not a problem, Mr. Sedley," Mama said.

Martin turned to me again. Leaning forward, he kissed me on the cheek. "Happy birthday, Alex. Have a wonderful, wonderful evening. Talk to you soon."

My mother rewarded Martin with a kiss of her own. "Thank you so much for everything, Mr. Sedley."

"Not at all." Then to the others he called, "Ta-ta!" And he was gone.

"Now there's an amiable man," my mother said as we made our way to the dinner table, "though I think he may be a bit too liberal with the spirits for his own good."

"You have that right."

"And I'm right about our other guest, too, Lexie," Mama said with a glance in Bannon's direction. "You'll see."

Chapter
12

The champagne flowed freely, and I wasn't holding back. Turning thirty justified a champagne hangover. Besides, the bubbly made it easier for me to cope with Cole Bannon. Not that I need Dutch courage to feel comfortable with a guy, but drink and laughter made it easier to slip out of my businesswoman mode.

The meal turned out to be a regular feast—pot-roasted pigeon with lemongrass and soya paste, Peking Duck, sauteed beef tenderloin in black pepper sauce, among other dishes. I ate like I hadn't eaten in weeks, I suppose because *all* my inhibitions were affected, not just my wariness with men.

Not surprisingly, Bannon was the perfect gentleman, the urbane, debonair charmer Mama professed him to be. "You're pretty adept at changing hats," I said in a private aside while the others were engaged in conversation.

"You mean from my business persona to the real me?"

"That's what you call it, your business persona?"

"People are not themselves in a bathhouse, on a cruise

ship or in a gambling casino, I've discovered. The essential person is to be found *en famille*."

"This is *my* family, not *yours*."

"But I'm empathizing and feeling very comfortable among you." He winked.

I'd had enough champagne that I didn't mind him, even though I knew he was full of shit. But if he was a con, he was an amusing con, and it was okay for me to be amused tonight of all nights.

My father tapped his water glass with a spoon, bringing the party to a silence. Then he got to his feet.

"I purposely waited until now to do this," he said, "after having sufficient amounts of champagne to do the job right or not notice if I haven't."

Everybody laughed.

"Seriously, though, my purpose is to toast to our little girl on her thirtieth birthday, a very big day in every person's life. But it seems to me we can't fully honor her and do the day justice without first looking back over the past thirty years. Garnet and I are the only ones who can do that with authority, so we'd like to share some of our fonder memories of our lovely Sparkle Plenty, as her grandfather called her."

"Here, here," my brother cried.

"Just so you don't embarrass me, Daddy," I said.

"Oh, but that's the fun of it, honey."

My father proceeded to recount my most embarrassing childhood experience, the time he took my brothers and me mountain climbing in Colorado—it was more like a hike in the mountains, but to an eight-year-old, it seemed a daring adventure. The long and the short of it was we'd gone halfway up the mountain when I had a call from Mother Nature. Naturally, I crept off into the woods to relieve myself. Squatting there by a tree, my butt hanging out, I heard gales of laughter coming from below. I'd done my business above a switchback in the trail in full sight of a troop of Boy Scouts.

Everybody laughed, including me—I'd long since come to terms with my *faux pas.* I was red in the face, though. Some things time can never completely heal.

Bannon patted my hand. "Bathroom incidents seem to be a recurring theme."

I could have kicked him under the table and very nearly did. My mother, as was usual for her, caught the remark.

"Do you have a story about our Lexie, Mr. Bannon?"

He started to reply, but I spoke for him. "Mr. Bannon, being a gentleman, has no intention of saying a word."

"He has license on your birthday," Mama returned.

"Not if he wishes to live to see the morning."

"Then I guess we're left to speculate," my mother said, clearly pleased.

My family wouldn't let me off the hook that easily. Everybody had a story to tell, not all of them embarrassing. Even I had to admit they tended to be revealing of who I was. Heath recounted the time I was mad at Austin and short-sheeted his bed. "She was only ten, Cole, but she got him good."

"Don't remind me," Mama said, "I can still see your brother's broken toe."

"And he'd have killed me," I said, "if he'd been able to walk."

Everybody laughed.

My father brought the storytelling to a poignant end when he said, "In all seriousness, it's hard to talk about Lexie without mentioning two of the most important people in her life, her grandfather, Edward Rutledge, and her twin brother, Gray. Neither of them are with us any longer, but they were very special to us all." He held up his glass. "To the memory of Edward and Gray."

Daddy's words brought tears to my eyes, and Mama wiped a few away as well, but we drank to my grandfather and my brother.

Coffee was served, and I was glad. I'd been the center of attention for too long. With my parents still recovering from jet lag and starting to mumble about making it an early evening, Bannon stood, obviously intending to make a speech. I cringed, but it wasn't what I expected.

"As it turns out, Lexie and I have a few days before we set off on our mission," he began. "And since you've come all this way, I'm sure you'd like to see a little of the country, as well as more of her. Accordingly, I'd like to invite you all to be my guests at the little hotel I own on the island of Ko Samui. It's a modest place, but the setting is nice and the price certainly right. Anybody up for an island adventure?"

"How thoughtful and generous, Cole," Mama enthused. "But we couldn't impose. There are too many of us."

"No, this is the slow season. I've called down and made sure the availability. There will be enough rooms for two nights beginning tomorrow, which will make it a brief trip, but even a little tropical sun, some rest and relaxation, is good for the soul. Having you as my guests would be a pleasure."

I was astounded and not quite sure what Bannon was up to. Was he simply cementing his position with me, or was there more to the story?

Fifteen minutes later as we left the restaurant, Bannon looked up at the moon and said to me, "It's a beautiful evening, how about a stroll along the river walk?"

"I'm awfully tired," I said.

"A little exercise will help you sleep. Anyway, we have a few things to discuss."

I glanced at my mother, who looked to be on the verge of giving me a big shove into Cole Bannon's arms. "Why don't you go ahead and enjoy the evenin', sugar?" she said.

"Your daddy and I are tired. We'll get to bed early and see you at breakfast." With that she took my father, brother and sister-in-law and headed off to the hotel, leaving me with a fait accompli.

"You outmaneuvered me again," I told Bannon.

"Again? When was the first time?"

"Our negotiations this afternoon. I gave you far too much."

"Just the opposite. Before we're done, you'll admit you got a real bargain."

"You don't lack for confidence, Mr. Bannon."

"You either. Which is why we'll make a great team."

I shook my head, laughing. "So, why did you invite my family to your hotel?"

"Honestly? Because I knew you wouldn't go down there with me alone."

"It's about me, in other words."

"Exactly."

"Your motive being . . ."

"The long and the short of it is, I've got a crush on you."

I laughed. "You are so full of it."

"You don't think that's possible?"

"On the basis of a few hours?"

"Hell, on the basis of the first five minutes," he said.

I caught the glimmer of his pale blue eyes in the moonlight. He actually sounded credible. But I knew better.

"So, why didn't you tell me you were a widower?" I asked.

"It never came up."

"You told my mother."

"She asked."

I figured that was probably true, knowing Mama. "Was your wife Thai?"

"Yes. Damari and I met soon after I arrived in Bangkok

and married several months later. We'd been together for three years when I lost her."

"What happened?"

"Nobody's quite sure. She disappeared, and several days later they found her in the river. Foul play was considered a possibility, or it could have been an accident. They never were able to decide."

"How awful."

"Yeah, Damari was young and beautiful and full of life, then she was gone."

Having heard his story, my heart softened. I saw his cavorting with the prostitutes in a different light. Maybe he used relationships like that to deaden the pain.

We'd come to a spot halfway between the Oriental and the Shangri-La Hotel with a nice view of the river. Stopping, we leaned against the railing and watched the small boats traversing the dark water in the moonlight. Bannon stood close to me, and I was very aware of him. Thoughts evocative of my summer romance with Rob on the Costa del Sol again tripped through my mind. I was thirty, and a part of me yearned for connection and excitement, if only a little kiss.

I could have let that happen, but being thirty also meant I was no longer a girl on a summer adventure. Bullfights and bikinis on the beach were a thing of the past.

Noticing Bannon had been silent for a while, I glanced his way and caught him staring at me. He touched my cheek with the back of his fingers. Knowing he was about to kiss me, I turned away, looking at the river.

"You're fighting yourself," he said. "Is it that guy in the Caribbean?"

I didn't want to lie, but I did anyway. "Yes," I said, "it's Brax."

Chapter
13

 When we resumed walking, we left
the river.

"How about if I show you where I got married," Bannon
said.

Assumption Cathedral was just a few blocks from the
waterfront in a quiet neighborhood in the Old Farang Quarter. The streets were nearly deserted as we approached the
edifice between two long rows of trees. Bannon strolled at
my side, thinking of his wife and their wedding day, I imagined. How could he not?

I continued to agonize over our near kiss—what it meant
that he intended it, and what it meant that I wouldn't let it
happen. This was not a normal day by any means, and I
knew that feelings in such circumstances were not to be
trusted. All I had to do was stick to business and I'd be fine.

With the mood so poignant and melancholy I don't know
how I came to notice, but I became aware of another presence. I felt like we were being watched or followed. The
hairs on the back of my neck standing up, I glanced over my

shoulder and, sure enough, saw a man walking along the row of trees behind us on the right.

We went a bit farther, and I took another peek. The man was still there and being careful to stay hidden in the shadows.

"Cole," I said, "don't look back, but I think we're being followed."

He seemed a bit disconcerted by my news. "Can you see by who?"

"A man. I think he's alone."

We were within twenty yards or so of the main porch of the cathedral, and Bannon stopped and looked up at the facade of the structure, taking my hand as he did so. "I'm going to embrace you," he said. "As I do, take a look and see what our friend is doing."

Bannon took me into his arms then, kissing my hair as I pressed my face against his shoulder and stared back down the row of trees. At first I saw nothing, then a slight movement at the edge of a tree trunk.

"He's hiding behind a tree and watching us."

Bannon lifted my chin and stared into my eyes. "Doesn't seem innocent, does it?"

"No, it doesn't."

"This may call for action, sweetheart," he said. Then, lowering his mouth to mine, he kissed me.

I was momentarily taken aback, not certain if the gesture was part of his act or a cheap way to steal a kiss. I couldn't risk shoving him away, but discreetly withdrew. His grin told me it was an opportunistic gesture. I wanted to slap him, but our stalker was the first consideration and definitely not a joke.

Before I could say anything, Bannon took my hand again and led me toward the entrance to the cathedral. "We'll go to the door and I'll kiss you again," he said. "If he ventures closer, I'll go after him."

"Fine," I said, "but I think we can skip the kissing part."

"It adds an air of authenticity."

"Unless the guy's a voyeur, authenticity doesn't matter."

"You can't fault me for trying."

"Actually, I can."

That elicited a smile.

We'd reached the huge, carved wooden doors, when Bannon again took my hands. "Okay, take another peek," he said.

I did. The guy had advanced to the nearest tree.

"He's behind the first tree on the left."

"Wait here," he said. "I'll be back shortly."

Turning abruptly, Cole Bannon walked smartly toward the guy who, seeing what was happening, took off at a run around the east side of the cathedral. Once he was in the open, I could see that he was slightly built. Bannon ran after him.

I was not a woman given to waiting for a man to slay dragons for me, and, though I wasn't exactly dressed for a run in the park, the slit in my chong-sam did allow for the free movement of my legs, so I took off in the other direction around the west side of the cathedral. I figured I could intercept the guy if he chose to circle around the building.

Running in heels was like trying to sprint on stilts, so I kicked off my shoes, then I took off again, able now to run full speed, though the hard cobbled pavement didn't do my feet any good. When I reached the back of the cathedral, I stopped and peered around the corner, hoping to see the stalker coming my way. Instead, I saw Bannon in the middle of the deserted street, talking to the guy. I couldn't hear what was being said, but I did hear them laugh. I couldn't believe it.

Then, as the Thai lit a cigarette, Bannon slapped him on the shoulder. They shook hands and ambled off in different directions. What was going on?

I knew I'd find out soon enough but decided not to let

Bannon know what I'd seen. Running back the way I'd come, I found my shoes and returned to the porch of the cathedral. I'd just gotten my shoes back on when Bannon sauntered up.

"What happened?" Perspiring, I discreetly wiped the sweat from my brow.

"The guy got away," he replied. "He was either too young and swift, or I'm too old and slow. Guess I'd better get my butt down to the gym."

I was shocked by his perfidy, but the darkness apparently hid the surprise on my face because Bannon seemed not to notice. "Do you have any idea who it was?" I asked. "Or what his intentions were?"

"Haven't a clue."

That told me all I needed to know about Cole Bannon.

It was only a few blocks to the Oriental, but it would take forever to get there. I kept running possible explanations through my mind, not liking any of them.

Bannon made small talk as we walked, and I said enough to make it seem nothing had happened. But in truth, I was upset and concerned. The real Cole Bannon wasn't just the womanizing ne'er-do-well I'd seen at the spa, he was also a liar.

The question was, what to do about it? I considered confronting him, but that would put everything on the line and risk the loss of the ruby. With the project at a critical juncture, I couldn't afford to throw a monkey wrench in the works. Better I get everything lined up with Chung, then have a conversation with him about Bannon. But that would have to wait until Chung's return. What did I do in the interim?

My family's presence now was a complication I didn't need. And the trip to Ko Samui could be a disaster. I could envision my mother gushing over someone I knew to be a snake in the grass. And worse, it would be galling to watch

Bannon lapping it all up while giving me his little winks and smiles. The bastard.

When we finally reached the hotel, I stopped at the entrance, making it clear this was the end of the road. Brannon took a shot at extending the evening, though. "Can I buy you a drink?" he asked.

"Thanks, but I'm tired. I'm calling it a night."

"I understand. Plus, there's your friend Brax to consider."

I felt the blood rush to my cheeks. "Right."

"I enjoyed meeting your parents. They're lovely people. And it was great seeing Heath again."

I wanted to slap him across the face, but I smiled instead. "They are lovely, and they mean the world to me."

"Then we should have a wonderful time on Ko Samui."

I thought, *Yeah, a regular festival of deception and lies.* Instead I said, "It was very generous of you to invite us."

"A small token of my regard for both you and your family. Listen, I'll work out travel arrangements first thing in the morning and call you with the details."

"Could I ask a favor? Would you mind doing the coordinating with Heath? He's good at that sort of thing, and to be honest, I feel like riding in the back of the bus."

Bannon, I could see, wasn't sure what to make of that. "Whatever you want."

I extended my hand. "Thanks. I enjoyed the walk." I gritted my teeth as I said the words, but managed somehow to get them out.

"Yeah, the first day of our acquaintance was an eventful one, wasn't it?"

Bannon was such an accomplished fraud that he sounded completely sincere. I was within an inch of telling him just what I thought of him, but I again reminded myself of the Heart of Burma. I had to keep my eye on the ball or risk losing everything. "*Very* eventful," I replied. "Well, good night, Cole."

"Good night, Sparkle."

I'd already started for the door, but stopped, facing him. I couldn't help myself. "If you don't mind, I'd prefer you not call me that. Alex or Lexie is more appropriate, considering our relationship."

"Absolutely."

"Thank you."

He winked and, not being able to take any more, I went inside, directly to the elevators. I was so indignant I could scream. What a phony. And a sneaky one at that.

I did have one regret, though. I was sorry I'd brought Brax into it. I'd taken the easy way out when I should simply have made it clear I had no interest in getting involved with Bannon in any way, regardless of my circumstances.

When I reached my room, I found the message light on. I checked my voice mail and heard my mother's dulcet tones.

"Alexis, that man is not only charmin' and adorable and smart as a whip, but he loves the international life, the travel and all that, just like you. And he has a thing for you, sugar. I'm certain of that. In my opinion, you'd be a fool not to grab that young man. Again, happy birthday, baby girl."

I looked over at the bedside clock. It was eleven-thirty. In half an hour this day would thankfully, mercifully be over. It was obvious to me now—turning thirty had been a very bad idea.

Chapter
14

I awoke the next morning horrified to discover that I'd been having a sexy dream featuring Cole Bannon. In it, he'd been sweet as pie and sexy as hell, which, I guess, goes to show that even your subconscious mind is easily fooled.

Ten minutes later I was climbing out of the shower when Heath phoned to say he had worked out the arrangements for the trip with Bannon and that the family would be assembling in the coffee shop for breakfast to receive their marching orders. Growing up in a military family had definitely been a formative experience.

"By the way," my brother said. "Bannon is a good guy. I didn't know him real well when we were at Benning, but I had a very favorable impression of him."

"Heath, did Mama put you up to saying that?"

"No, it's something that I thought, as a big brother, you ought to know. Honest."

I wasn't so sure of that, but decided a man could pull the wool over the eyes of other men as easily as women. But it didn't matter. The object would be to get through the next few days with as little pain and discomfort to me and my family as possible.

I was the last one to arrive at the coffee shop, my father and brother having already devoured orders of crepes. Julie's breakfast, I noted, was faithful to her pregnancy regimen, and Mama was savoring her coffee and eyeing me as I approached the table. The look on her face was the one I'd seen countless times at the family breakfast table on a Sunday morning after I'd been on a date the previous night. It spoke volumes—a combination of, "I trust that your virtue is intact, young lady," and "So, was he nice and do you like him?" Naturally I never volunteered a thing, always making Mama ask. Now, at the ripe old age of thirty plus a day, I held to the same strategy.

After greeting everyone and exchanging a few words on the effects of all the champagne we'd consumed, I sat in the empty chair next to Mama. The waitress immediately took my order. She was scarcely gone before my mother fired her first question. "Did you have a nice walk last evening with Mr. Bannon, Lexie?"

"It was okay. We mostly talked business."

"Business?"

"Yes, Mama, that is what I'm in Thailand for, after all."

"I know, but . . ."

"Garnet," my father said, "Lord knows this isn't my field of expertise, but isn't it time we leave Lexie's social life to her?"

Mama gave him a look. "You're right, Reece, it's not your field of expertise."

"What'll you do if you don't like her answer?" Heath asked. "Ground her?"

"You can watch your mouth as well, young man," my mother rejoined. "What I say to my daughter is my concern and nobody else's."

"Yes, ma'am." Heath gave me a wink.

"Actually, I'd prefer not to be the topic of conversation," I said, pouring myself some coffee from the pot that was on the table. "I think everybody has enough worries of their own without taking on mine. But since you're obviously curious, Mama, I'll just say this: the prospects of me becoming involved with Cole Bannon are thin to non-existent, so thin in fact, you'd be hard-pressed to find them with an electron microscope. And that's being optimistic."

As I put the coffeepot down, I noticed a curious silence had come over the table. Scanning the faces of my family, I noticed they weren't so much looking at me as they were looking behind me. I didn't have to turn around to know who was standing there, nor did my genteel Southern breeding stop the words forming on my lips. "Oh, shit."

"Optimistic is an odd choice of word," the voice behind me intoned. "My first thought is from whose perspective?"

Everybody laughed and I wanted to crawl under the table. But he put his hand on my shoulder and gave it a squeeze. "Don't worry, Sparkle. I know you were just having a little fun in recognition of my high regard for you. Fear not, though, I'm a good sport."

Leave it to Mama to find the right words at the right moment. "Mr. Bannon," she said, "why don't you pull up a chair and join us?"

"I wouldn't want to intrude, ma'am. Just came in to let you know the minibus is out front whenever you're ready to head for the airport."

"Have a cup of coffee with us," Mama insisted. "Please."

Bannon ended up sitting across from me, between Heath and my father. I only managed fleeting eye contact. More would have turned my pink cheeks flaming red.

"All kidding aside," Bannon said, addressing the entire party, "I should probably explain that Lexie and I share the same commitment to our business venture. It's just that I've been in the Orient so long that I've fallen into the habit of the social ritual, which Westerners sometimes misconstrue. Here in Asia it's an essential part of doing business. Lexie knows I respect her relationship with Brax, and you should all know it too. So, my request is that you all relax and not worry about a thing."

It was a generous gesture on Bannon's part and, had it not for the fact that my whole family was staring at me with question on their face, I would have thanked him. But damn if I hadn't been trapped by my own damned lie.

Miracle of miracles, Mama held her tongue. I had to thank my lucky stars for that. God only knew how long it would be before my perfidy came back to bite me in the ass.

After getting our luggage, we Chandlers assembled outside the hotel where Cole Bannon waited for us with his driver and minibus. Unable to come up with a good strategy for dealing with the problem, I withdrew into my shell and quite literally sat in the back of the bus. Mama and Daddy were in the second seat, and Heath and Julie were in the third. Bannon sat in front with the driver and regaled my family with a virtual tour guide commentary as we made our way to the airport. He noted points of interest as we drove through the city, but mostly he talked about Ko Samui and how he'd come to own the hotel as a settlement for a business deal gone bad.

"It was run down and worth little more than the land it sat on when I got it," he explained. "But with a bit of capital and some sweat equity, it's become a nice little operation. I don't make much money on it, and I regard it more as a hobby than a business, but it gives me a lot of pleasure."

I listened to what was being said, but mostly I sat under a dark cloud, bemoaning the fact that I'd been outmaneuvered again. And worse, even, I'd shot myself in the foot. My

mother had yet to say anything to me about the reference to
Brax, but that hardly made me optimistic. The old girl was
sharp, and nothing ever got past her. I'd bet my best emerald
earrings she'd figured out what had happened. But would she
let sleeping dogs lie? That was the real question. I could see
I needed to have a chat with her.

"I've arranged to borrow a friend's plane," Bannon explained as we neared the airport, "so we'll be traveling in
style."

Heath and my father had both been airborne, my dad
jump-qualified until the day of his retirement, so they had a
lot of interest in planes, though neither were pilots. Flying
was one passion I didn't share with the men in my family
and so I tuned out the conversation that followed. I knew
Julie wasn't interested either, so I tapped her on the shoulder
and invited her to come back and talk to me. The baby, my
parents' first grandchild, was a hot topic of conversation in
the family, and I hadn't yet had much of an opportunity to
dish with Julie about the big event.

She gave me the whole story in vivid detail, as expectant
mothers are wont to do, her cheeks glowing as she talked.
Given where I was in life, babies weren't at the top of my list
of favorite subjects, but I was happy for her and Heath.

"You don't know what a big favor you're doing for me by
having this baby," I told her. "Mama was counting on me for
grandchildren. She still won't be letting me off the hook, of
course, but this takes a little of the pressure off."

"I wasn't eager for children, either," Julie said, "but when
you're with the right man, things seem to change. Now I
couldn't be happier."

I watched Bannon talking to my father and brother. He
was animated, expressive, entertaining, a regular storyteller.
Con artists definitely had a gift. When you could wrap peo-

ple around your finger with little effort, I suppose it was hard to resist the temptation to take advantage of the situation.

It was hard not to admire the man's gift, though. I wondered how I'd feel about him if he really was the man my family thought him to be. I learned the hard way that my career ambitions made a traditional marriage impossible with Brax, but was that true of every man? There was no way I could abide a liar, a hypocrite, a fraud, and a sneak, but what if a man like Bannon were to come along who was an ethical, upstanding guy?

Why was I even asking myself these questions? I wondered. Was this what happened when you reached the big 3-0? Lordy, if so, that didn't augur well.

We arrived at the airport, and Bannon surprised me when he mentioned he would be piloting. Apparently he'd told the others while Julie and I were talking, because the rest of the family wasn't surprised.

The plane accommodated eight passengers and there were five of us, plus Bannon, so there was plenty of room. I boarded first, again going to the back so I wouldn't have to sit in the copilot's seat. My father sat with me, and Mama sat in front with Bannon, thinking she was salvaging the family's pride, I'm sure.

I felt more like an idiot all the time, but reminded myself the humiliation was well worth the Heart of Burma, which was what this was really about. I'd made a decision, though. When Chung Lee returned from Hong Kong, I'd tell him it was either me or Bannon, because I couldn't work with the guy.

Once airborne, my father took my hand. Leaning close, he said, "Honey, I know you're in a difficult position, but can I give you a little friendly advice? I think you'll get further

and end up where you want if you humor your mother a little. And for that matter, Bannon. A frontal assault on the enemy position is one of the available tactics in combat, and
sometimes it's the best. But deception, disguising your true
intentions, can be just as effective in the right circumstances.
Lord knows your mother is a master at being sweet to people
she hates. The ability to do that has served her well. In the
end you must do what you think is right, but it doesn't hurt to
use a little diplomacy in the interim." My father gave me a
wink. "A word to the wise."

Chapter
15

You'd think a person entering her fourth decade of life might already have figured out what my father had just told me, but it wasn't until he said it that I realized diplomacy, not self-righteous indignation, was what was called for. The choice I faced wasn't between spurning Cole Bannon or marrying him and having his children. It was between open hostility and muddling through. All I had to do was get through the next few days as pleasantly as possible, then work out a solution to the problem.

By the time we'd completed the three-hundred-fifty-mile flight to Ko Samui, I was a new woman, armed with a new attitude. Thanks to my father, I felt much more at ease, which was a benefit in and of itself.

Bannon, ever the good host, circled the island so that we could get a good perspective, pointing out its principal features. Ko Samui was in the Gulf of Thailand, off the Western Seaboard, and larger than I expected. It was known for its coconut palms, white sandy beaches and rugged, mountainous interior. Chaweng, on the northeastern coast, boasted a three mile-long beach, the most beautiful on the island.

"Chaweng has become the principal tourist center," Bannon said over the roar of the plane's engines. "That's where you'll find the fancy resorts. My place is just south of there, near the village of Lamai. You can see the sun reflecting off the metal rooftops in the trees, just below that point of land jutting into the sea."

We all craned our necks and were able to see the village.

"Lamai is not so upscale and caters more to budget-minded Europeans," he continued. "I think it's more lively and colorful, the nightlife more interesting than Chaweng, but you can judge that for yourselves."

Rather than dreading our arrival, I actually found myself looking forward to it. A little fun and relaxation would be the quid pro quo for what Bannon had put me through. And to give the devil his due, maybe that was what he'd been thinking when he proposed the trip.

Bannon made a very nice landing, and I heard my brother telling Julie he was a damned good pilot. That was encouraging because good pilots tended to be responsible individuals. But then, like everything having to do with Cole Bannon, I had very limited experience to go on.

We were greeted at the airport by a man named Thep Mandary and his daughter, Chinda. They ran the hotel for Bannon. The Mandarys had come to meet us because the hotel didn't have a vehicle large enough for the six of us, plus our luggage. Thep drove my parents, Heath and Julie in the car and Chinda drove Bannon, me, plus most of the baggage in the jeep. In observing the byplay between Bannon and Chinda as we loaded up, I sensed some chemistry between them, if only on the girl's part. Of course I wasn't surprised. Bannon had already proven he had a way with the ladies.

He insisted I ride in front with Chinda and wedged himself in next to the suitcases piled on the backseat. The drive down the coast to Lamai was pleasant. The beach at

Chaweng was gorgeous and the resorts sumptuous. "Don't look too closely," Bannon chided, "or you'll be disappointed by your accommodations."

He continued pointing out the sights while Chinda drove silently, though from time to time she cast an occasional jealous glance my way. If she understood what was going on, she'd realize I posed no threat, though she may have been reacting more to Bannon's attentions to me than the other way around.

We weren't yet at the hotel, but I was already realizing that the trip had been a good idea. Ever since New York, I'd been the object of scrutiny and I still wasn't sure by whom. Twice in Thailand somebody had followed me. And after seeing Bannon yakking it up with the guy behind the cathedral, I figured he was somehow mixed up in whatever was going on, if only tangentially. But I wasn't overly concerned about that now. We were on a remote island, far from Bangkok, and I was with my family. If Bannon had an agenda, he'd most likely have to change tactics for the next few days. What he didn't know was that despite my new, more friendly veneer, I was ready for him.

Bannon had named his place the Blue Lagoon Hotel. As we drove through the village of Lamai, which contained a number of older teak houses with thatched roofs in addition to the newer structures, Bannon told me that the name had been inspired by the Brooke Shields movie. "That was the seed of my tropical adventure fantasy that brought me to Thailand," he said. Recalling the sensuality of the film, and knowing what I knew of the man, I believed him.

The Blue Lagoon was one of the few colonial-era buildings on the island. It had originally been built by a coconut plantation baron and was subsequently converted into a hotel. There were five guest rooms in the main building, plus half a dozen thatched roof cottages or huts. Thep, his wife Anura, who was the cook, and Chinda lived on the ground floor of the hotel. Bannon lived in one of the cottages when he was in residence. The rooms we were given were all in the main house.

Anura had prepared a lunch for us which we were to eat on the veranda, in the shade of the coconut palms, overlooking the sea. We had twenty minutes to freshen up and unpack before lunch was served. The rooms were hardly sumptuous, the furniture and decor dated, but the hotel had a certain authenticity about it. My mother pronounced it suitable, which was a veritable stamp of approval considering Mama was a woman who enjoyed her luxuries and was not easily pleased.

I'd decided to change out of the shorts and tank top I'd worn for the flight into a little summer dress and ankle strap sandals. I'd just freshened my cologne when Mama knocked on my door. She looked me over with signs of approval.

"I'm glad to see you've come to your senses, Lexie."

"I'm trying to make it as pleasant for everyone as I can."

"Good." She sat on my bed. "Sugar, can I just say that I know mothers can be a pain in the rear, and I'm undoubtedly among the worst offenders, but seein' that you're makin' an effort, I realize I should too. I'm goin' to try to keep my mouth shut and let you handle things as you choose. That's the way it should be, but you're entitled to hear it from me. And I want you to know I'm sorry if I've stepped on toes."

"Mama, you're right, you can be a pain in the butt, but I do love you."

We embraced. Taking me by the shoulders, she looked into my eyes. Hers were swimming. "Let me say one final thing before I seal my lips. You've only just met Mr. Bannon, and Lord knows I don't know him as well as you, but I can see the two of you together. Those are pretty strong words, considering I'd much rather my grandchildren be across town than halfway around the world, but certain realities can't be denied.

"I realize he might not be the right one. But the gentleman proves to me that there is someone out there for you, Lexie. All I want is that you keep an open mind."

"Believe it or not, Mama, I've come to very similar conclusions."

My admission pleased her immensely, I could tell. "Okay, I've had my say and now," she said, running her fingers across her mouth, "my lips are sealed."

We hugged again and went off to have our lunch.

The ocean air was balmy and Anura Mandary's cooking sublime. I couldn't recall a more relaxed, enjoyable meal I'd shared with my family. If Austin had been there, not to mention Gray and Granddad, it would have been perfect. Bannon, while continuing to play the good host, was a bit more reserved than before. I think it was the soft, balmy air and the sensuousness of the setting as much as anything else.

If there was a fly in the ointment, it was Chinda. She did not like me. She was polite to a fault, but her jealousy was not hard to spot. I wondered if Bannon had said something to her, though it was hard to imagine what.

For dessert we had homemade coconut sorbet, which was fabulous. While clearing the dishes Chinda spilled tea on my lap. She apologized profusely, of course, and ran to get a cloth, but the damage was done.

"Now you have an excuse to change into your swimsuit," Bannon said. "Anybody else up for some time on the beach?"

Julie wanted to rest, and my parents were more interested in taking a stroll in the village. Bannon looked at me, the question on his face.

"I could use some beach time," I said.

"You mind company?"

In keeping with my new attitude, my reply was as chipper as I could make it. "No, Cole, not at all."

Chapter
16

Not being one who spends a lot of
time at the beach, or even the swimming pool, I didn't have
a huge collection of resort and swim wear. A few years earlier I'd attended a conference on the French Riviera, and
while I was there I'd picked up a little black string bikini
which I kept in my suitcase in case I needed a swimsuit
while traveling. It wasn't often that I wore it, but this was
one occasion where I wished I had something a bit more
modest.

It wasn't that I didn't have the body for it, the problem
was it showed a little too much of what I did have. I knew I
could be sending the wrong signal, but then I decided Bannon wasn't the issue. Besides, I did have a filmy little
coverup which helped. When I went downstairs I encountered Anura at the foot of the stairs.

"You need hat," she told me. "Sun much too hot."

She showed me the hotel collection, and I picked out a
straw hat with a black ribbon that matched my suit. Anura
checked me out.

"Very pretty lady," she said approvingly.

I thanked her, thinking that could be part of the problem her daughter had with me. Cole Bannon was waiting at the edge of the veranda with a couple of beach towels under his arm. He was in brief, European cut trunks, also black, and sexy sunglasses. He had a great physique, muscular without being bulky, firm, broad shoulders, great chest. I did like a man with a chest.

He checked me out as I approached, showing definite signs of approval. "You look terrific," he said. "I'm going to have to give Chinda a bonus for spilling that tea."

"I don't think she needs any encouragement, Cole."

"Oh?"

"I don't mean to state the obvious, but she has a thing for you."

"Think so?"

I gave him a look. "Yeah, I'm sure you never noticed."

"Well, she needn't worry about you because you're taken, right?"

I groaned inwardly. "Taken is too strong a word."

"We'll have to talk about that." We set off, strolling through the palms toward the sea. "Bring your sun block?"

"I put some on in my room."

"You can never have too much in the tropical sun." He said it like a man who would be more than willing to assist in lathering on some more.

"I'll keep that in mind."

The beach adjacent to the hotel was practically deserted. Market umbrellas had been set out, and I was glad, since the rays reflecting off the sand and water alone were enough to burn you.

Bannon spread out the beach towels under a large umbrella, and we lay down side-by-side. I was with a hunk I couldn't trust any farther than I could throw, but that didn't matter because my objective was to be pleasant and diplomatic. End of story.

"So, where are you from originally, Cole?" I asked.

"California."

"LA?"

"No, Santa Barbara."

"I've been there. With my family when I was a teenager. We were on vacation, drove all the way up the coast to San Francisco. Santa Barbara was pretty wealthy, as I recall."

"Yeah, lots of old money in Santa Barbara."

"Not to be presumptuous or anything, but any of it yours?"

"Since we're among friends, I suppose I can tell you my mother's people were quite well off and so is she, as a result."

"Ah, then you're a little rich boy."

"Who's been more or less disowned."

"Why's that?"

"Mom never approved of my lifestyle or my choices."

"Because?"

"I think because it reminded her of my father who was . . . well, to be blunt, a fortune hunter and a reprobate."

That explains it! I thought. Not that anybody should be painted with the sins of his father, but certain characteristics did run in families.

"My mother's people basically ran him out of town," Bannon continued. "I was just a little kid at the time, so I never really knew the guy. The last I heard he was living in Mexico off the money he'd filched over the years. Not the ideal role model."

"That's actually very sad."

"Well, you don't mourn the loss of what you never had."

"Do you see your mother?"

"Haven't for years. The last straw was when I married

Damari. Mom did not approve. Not that things were wonderful before that. She'd remarried when I was six and had a second family. I became the odd man out, an unpleasant reminder of the past, as far as my mother was concerned."

What kind of mother would turn her back on her child? Could it be true, or was it a tall tale, designed to elicit sympathy? I hated to be suspicious of everything he said, but I'd been burned by him once.

I studied Bannon, who was propped up on his elbows, staring out at the sea. He was full of contradictions. And so confounding. My feelings about him kept swinging from one extreme to the other.

Chinda arrived with some cool drinks, her face sober and expressionless. The poor thing had to be heartbroken. I wanted to tell her she had nothing to fear from me because I had no interest in her heartthrob, not that it would necessarily make a difference. When it came to emotion, the facts were often secondary.

He said something to the girl in Thai and she scampered off, which struck me as odd. Bannon handed me a drink.

"You probably won't even notice, but these drinks have a little kick. I don't want you to think I'm slipping you a Mickey Finn."

"That's very thoughtful," I said. Rolling on my side, I took a sip. I couldn't tell what was in the drink, but it was fruity and quite tasty. The main thing was it went down easily. I had to give Bannon credit for warning me of the hidden danger.

A few minutes later Chinda was back. She had a pair of binoculars in her hand, which she handed to Bannon. He sent her on her way. Then, sitting cross-legged, he looked through the binoculars out at the water.

"Hmm, very interesting," he muttered.

I sat upright. "What are you looking at?"

"See that yacht a couple hundred yards offshore?"

"Yes."

"There are two guys in it, both with glasses, and they've been watching us. Either they're as admiring of your bikini as I am, or they're up to something." He handed me the binoculars. "Recognize them?"

I was able to see the men clearly. They were both Asian, one rather tall and thin with a mustache and goatee. Judging by their behavior, they did appear to be spying on us. Thinking of the incident at the cathedral, I almost said, "You're more likely to know who they are than I." But if he was in cahoots with them, he wouldn't have brought them to my attention. "No," I said, "they don't look familiar."

I handed the binoculars back. A moment later the yacht headed up the coast.

Bannon watched it go, then said, "They saw us looking at them and spooked." Then he added, "You certainly attract attention, sweetheart."

I was very tempted to say, "Even by your friends." Instead, I sipped my drink, wishing I knew what was going on. Was someone trying to scare me, or were they just keeping me under surveillance? Bannon, I decided, had to be involved in it—whatever *it* was—he just had to be. Maybe he'd pointed out the men on the boat to bolster his credibility.

Then it hit me. Of course. He was purposely trying to frighten me to prove he was needed. The more threatened I felt, the more receptive I'd be to his protection. He'd put the guy up to following us last night, and he'd probably arranged for the men in the boat, as well. It was a simple ploy to drive me into his arms—figuratively, if not literally. I should have caught on sooner.

"I wonder if we should report this to the authorities," I said innocently.

"Lexie, they'd take one look at you and ask for a pair of binoculars themselves."

"You really think that's it?"

"No, but the point I'm making is that a pretty girl attracting attention is not exactly a crime of scandalous proportions."

"So, do we just ignore it?"

"No," he replied, "we stay alert."

"You don't think this could have anything to do with the Heart of Burma, do you?" I asked, throwing out the bait.

"That's exactly what I think . . . unless your friend, Brax, is the jealous type."

"He isn't."

"Then it's got to be the ruby."

"Probably a not-so-friendly competitor."

"Makes sense," Bannon said. "Have any candidates in mind?"

I sipped my drink again. "No, I don't. So, I guess we'll have to grab one of these guys the first chance we get and beat the truth out of them."

"Sounds like a plan."

"Well, I'm counting on you, Cole."

He didn't catch the irony, of course, and I laughed to myself. But the good news was I'd finally figured out what Mr. Bannon was up to. My father was right. Diplomacy could be a very effective weapon.

Chapter
17

The thing about men was that once you had their number they pretty much lost their mystique, meaning now that I'd pegged Bannon, he wasn't quite so disconcerting. True, he still had the physical thing going for him—the guy was a primo Troy doll, no disputing that—but psychologically speaking, I was in control.

Not that I'd let him know that, of course. To the contrary, I'd allowed him to think he had the reins, though maybe I overdid it a bit. My first mistake was accepting another of those drinks. To his credit, Bannon had warned me they were lethal, but between the alcohol and the heat, I was feeling pretty sloshed.

Handing him my empty glass, I said, "Now what?"

"What do you feel like?"

A fleeting recollection of Rob on the beach in Spain went through my mind, which I instantly dismissed, though it did produce a tipsy grin. "You decide."

Bannon stroked his jaw. "How about a swim?"

"That sounds like fun," I agreed, tossing aside my sunglasses and hat.

He removed his sunglasses then, taking my hand, he pulled me to my feet. I practically fell over, but he caught me before I took a header.

"Boy, you weren't kidding about the drinks, were you?"

He put his arm around my waist to support me. "I wouldn't let you go in the water in your condition if the sea weren't so calm. Be assured, though, you're in the company of a gentleman."

I hooted. "You? A gentleman? Bannon, from the minute I saw you with those hookers I knew you were anything but a gentleman. But you *are* cute, I'll give you that."

"Come on," he said, leading me toward the sea, "the water will clear your head."

I staggered along with him, my arm around his waist, knowing despite my drunkenness that I was making a fool of myself. This was not what Daddy meant by being diplomatic. But that was okay. It was broad daylight and my family was nearby. Nothing terrible was going to happen.

The section of the beach by the hotel was near a spit of land that jutted into the sea, protecting the shoreline from the larger waves. Small ones lapped up onto the sand, the water relatively calm. It felt refreshing as we waded in, cool even, but only compared to the hot air. In fact the temperature of the water was like a warm tub and, by the time we'd waded out to shoulder depth, it felt sensuous and heavenly. There was nothing so arousing as warm water, particularly in combination with an attractive man.

Bannon still had hold of my hand, and we faced each other, only a couple of feet apart. I was aware of his shoulders, those incredible pale eyes, the wry twist of his mouth, all of which aroused me.

"So, feel better?" he asked.

"Define better." Though I hated myself for it, I gave him a coquettish grin.

"More clear-headed?" he said with earnest innocence that was as phony as he was.

"No."

"More comfortable?"

"No."

"You don't feel sick, do you?"

"No."

With each "no" I found myself drifting a bit closer to him, not resisting the gentle nudge of the waves. Now our faces were only inches apart.

"I hope you realize I'm about to kiss you," he said.

"Yes, I know."

"You aren't going to be offended and slap me?"

"I don't intend to."

"Then I best strike while the iron is hot."

With that he lifted my chin and kissed me softly on the mouth. It was a tender kiss, but also sensuous. The man knew what he was doing. No surprise there.

Instead of ending, the kiss deepened. I put my arms around his neck and Bannon drew me firmly up against him. All the sexual energy I'd been repressing, all the yearning and hunger, came boiling out.

Bannon took my butt cheeks in his hands and pulled me hard against him, the bulge in his loins pressing against my mound. I'd never made love in the water before, but I was seriously considering it now. That's how much I wanted him.

But then it hit me this wasn't gamesmanship. It had gone far beyond that. We were practically having sex when all I'd intended was to let him think he was in charge.

Gathering myself, I gently pushed him away. "Whew," I said, "what do they put in that drink? An aphrodisiac?"

"I warned you."

"That's true," I said, trying to catch my breath, "you did."

Bannon touched my cheek tenderly. "I hope you aren't upset."

I had trouble looking into his eyes. "More like embarrassed." I glanced toward shore, only then realizing anyone in the hotel could have seen us kissing—anyone from Chinda and her parents to Heath and Julie.

"Embarrassed because . . ."

"Because I let things get out of hand," I said, suddenly feeling very sober. "Obviously, I'm attracted to you. But that's no reason to . . ."

"No reason to what?"

"To lose control. I might have wanted to kiss you at the moment, but it's not what I want for the relationship."

"You're saying it was a mistake."

"Most definitely."

"I see." He sounded hurt, though he could as easily be faking it.

"Look, Cole," I said in a reasonable tone, "it's not your fault this happened. I take responsibility. I won't even use the alcohol as an excuse. I simply made a mistake." I managed to look him in the eye. "Can you accept that?"

He shrugged. "If that's the way you feel. So where do we go from here?"

I looked out to sea. "Can we just go back to where we were before?"

"Pre-kissing cousins, you mean?" He sighed. "Okay, if that's what you want."

"It *is* what I want." I was sobering up quickly now, and the longer we stood there, the more embarrassed I felt. "I'm going to go in now and rest," I announced.

"May I escort you to make sure you're okay?"

"It's not necessary, thank you. I'll be fine."

"Then maybe I'll go for a swim," he said.

"Cole, I'm sorry this happened. I really am."

"Forget it. You're not the first woman who had a change of heart."

It wasn't so much a change of heart as simply coming to my senses, but I didn't feel the need to rub that in. Bannon needed to save face as much as I did.

I began wading back toward shore. As I came out of the water I realized I was still woozy, but I could walk. Nearing the veranda, I found Chinda leaning against a palm tree, glaring at me. She'd seen.

It meant that I'd not only stubbed my toe, I'd also broken her heart.

Chapter
18

Back in my room, I showered, took a couple of aspirin, and lay naked on the bed, relishing the feel of the cool sheets. If my skin was feverish, it was as much a result of that kiss as it was the sun and water.

Despite what I knew about the man, I couldn't help fantasizing about having sex with him—even though I fully intended to have a chat with Chung about getting rid of him. But assuming that didn't pan out and Bannon stayed in the deal, I wondered what the chances were of the two of us having a little extracurricular fun.

Theoretically, I owed him dinner once the ruby was sold. Dinner could easily turn into a sexy weekend somewhere. Could I do that, knowing what I knew about him? I'd never been in a situation like this before. Even Rob, on the Costa del Sol, was a decent guy. I'd been under no illusions about him or any other man with whom my intentions were short-term. The reason was simple. When a guy was Mr. Tonight, as opposed to Mr. Right, a little of him usually went a long way.

The damned trouble was I felt horny now. And despite my resolve, if Cole Bannon had come walking in the door that very minute, I'd have trouble resisting. It was terribly honest of me to admit that, but it was also scary. Disaster was born of moods like the one I was in, and I could only say thank God for Mama and Daddy. What if I were alone on the island with the man?

Fortunately, my sexual fever cooled down and I fell asleep, only awakening when there was a knock on my door. Squinting at the window, I could see it was dusk. I sat up on the edge of the bed, then turned on the lamp.

There was more knocking. "Lexie?" It sounded like Bannon's voice.

"Yes?"

"Are you ready?" he asked. "We'll be leaving for dinner in about ten minutes."

I felt self-conscious talking to him while naked, even with the door between us. "Did you say in *ten* minutes?"

"Yes, didn't Chinda give you the message? She said she knocked on your door."

"I must have slept through it. I'll hurry and try to get ready."

"How about if I take the others to the restaurant and come back for you?"

"Whatever's easiest."

"There was also a call for you from Martin Sedley while you were asleep. They took a message. I've got the slip here."

I glanced around, but my coverup was in the bath and there was nothing handy to slip on. I opened the door partway, hiding myself behind it. Bannon was in a green and beige Hawaiian shirt and slacks. He looked tanned and handsome, sparking recollections of our sexual titilation that afternoon. He handed me the message slip, which was folded in half and sealed with a piece of tape.

"You feeling okay?" he asked.

"Yes. A little groggy, that's all. You woke me, actually."

"I'm sorry there was a snafu. I'll have a word with Chinda."

"No, please don't, Cole. I'm sure she knocked. I just went back to sleep."

"If you say so."

"I'd better hurry," I said.

"Lexie, a suggestion, if I may . . ."

"What's that?"

"If you lounge around in the buff at night, you might want to draw the drapes."

"Why? There's nothing out there but the ocean, is there?"

"It's not what's outside, Lexie. That window makes a perfect mirror."

I spun around and there I was reflected in the glass, naked as a jaybird with Bannon's smiling face in the crack in the door. Bumping the door shut with my butt, I stood there, my hands covering my mouth.

"Don't worry," he said through the door, "I've seen it before. I'll be back in fifteen minutes or so, but don't feel you need to rush."

After drawing the drapes, I sat on the bed and tore the tape so I could read the message. Scrawled in clumsy block letters were the words. "Alex, I have information, return to Bangkok immediately. Martin."

My heart did a back flip. Why was Martin so vague? I wondered. Was it intentional, or was it the limited English of the message taker?

Given the limitations of a traveling wardrobe, I only had a couple of choices of attire. Knowing Mama and Julie would almost certainly wear dresses, I decided on the second most dressy thing I had with me after the chong-sam—a little red, backless silk dress with a short, flouncy skirt, which the salesgirl in Atlanta had described as "sassy." Sass seemed to be what was called for, though a nun's habit was more in keeping with my plan.

I'd just finished doing my hair when there was another knock on my door. "Cole?" I said, before opening it.

"Yeah, it's me."

I'd already girded myself, knowing there was no avoiding facing him, and pulled the door open with a flourish. Bannon looked me up and down.

"Good Lord, but you're beautiful. You look fabulous."

"Thanks, but a stitch of anything would be an improvement."

"It is impossible to improve on your backside, Miss Chandler."

"High praise, Mr. Bannon, but also impolite. A gentleman wouldn't have drawn attention to what he'd seen, either at the time or now."

"I felt the need to express my delight. Besides, I was able to see practically as much at the beach, and I enjoyed that too."

"You're unrepentant."

"Guilty."

I put my hands on my hips to show my disapproval. "The subject is closed. I don't want to hear any more about my rear end. Now or ever."

"Never? But that's such a long time."

"Cole!"

"Okay, okay. Whatever you wish. Ready to go?"

"Yes, except I have a problem."

"What's that?"

I showed him the telephone message slip. "It's hard to believe Martin would be so cryptic. Is there any chance whoever took the message didn't get the whole thing?"

Bannon studied the note. "It looks like Chinda's writing. We could ask her, except that she's gone for the evening."

That was convenient. Had the message been bungled intentionally? Could the girl be jealous enough that she'd pulled a fast one? "I'm going to call Martin," I said.

There weren't phones in the rooms, so we went downstairs to the office where Thep sat reading a paper. Bannon asked if he knew anything about the message Chinda had taken, but he said he didn't. I gave Bannon Martin's number and he dialed it for me. I got an answering machine.

"Martin, it's Alex. How urgently do you need me back in Bangkok, and why can't you give me the information over the phone? Please call again, and if I'm not available, ask for Cole." I hung up and glanced at Bannon. "I suppose that's all I can do."

"If necessary, I can get you on a flight in the morning. And if that doesn't work out, I can fly you back myself."

"It would be a shame to ruin everybody's holiday."

"We'll work it out. But come on," he said, putting his hand at my waist and guiding me toward the door, "I've got a great evening planned. Do you like to dance?"

As we drove through the village of Lamai, I was in a quandary, which pretty much had become the norm for me when it came to Cole Bannon. Every positive feeling I had about the guy either came from the gut or was a rationalization. The objective facts and common sense told me he was a charlatan. Which meant I had to get through this island visit, put him out of my mind, and focus on the Heart of Burma.

We were dining at Giselle's, a French restaurant on the beach which, not surprisingly, was owned by a Frenchwoman named Giselle. The lady herself, in a wrap-around Tahitian-style skirt and tank top, greeted us. Early forties, thin and tanned within an inch of her life, Giselle was earthy and sensual without being truly pretty, which was typical of

French women, who for my money had more style than any other nationality.

The kiss she greeted Bannon with was a degree more enthusiastic than what you'd expect from a fellow member of the Lamai Chamber of Commerce. I estimated the chances at better than fifty-fifty that at some point the two of them had shared a bottle of Pouille Fuissé and ended up in bed, though I probably could have said that about Bannon and almost any attractive woman.

Giselle took us out on the torch-lit lanai where my family was happily ensconced, sipping tropical drinks, save Julie, who was having fruit juice. I opted to join her, being in no mood for the hair of the dog.

The meal was rather pleasant with Bannon playing the dual role of host and family cousin. The kissing part of the equation, as best I could tell, remained secret, but there was no question he'd done a bang-up job of ingratiating himself with the people closest to me. This was confirmed along about dessert when Mama mentioned that she and Daddy had invited Bannon to visit us in Atlanta over the holidays. Noticing I received the news with less than total ecstasy, Bannon gave a little shrug as if to say, "What was I going to do, turn her down?"

Of course that was exactly what he should have done, knowing my intentions to keep the relationship strictly business—with the possible exception of a sexy weekend getaway after everything had been wrapped up. I could hardly blame him, though. Fault had to be laid at the feet of my mother.

I had the opportunity to give her the what-for in the ladies' room before we left the restaurant. "I considered it the polite thing to do," Mama said a bit more indignantly than was usual. "After all, the man has treated the entire family to a couple of lovely days at his hotel. What would you have me do, Lexie? Send him a thank-you note?"

I wondered if maybe this, or something like it, was what Bannon had been angling for all along. But to what end? Surely he wasn't seriously interested in me. No, more likely his act was designed to give him some kind of leverage in our deal. I hadn't yet figured out exactly how, but I would before I was through.

"Besides," my mother added, "Mr. Bannon's interests may extend beyond you. It just might be that he enjoys the company of the rest of us, as well. He never had much of a family life growing up, you know."

I could see Mama had been thorough in her intelligence-gathering, which made me wonder if it might not be time to disabuse her of her illusions. On the other hand, it would make things awkward for everyone. So I decided to leave her with her delusions about Cole Bannon until I got home. The plan for the holidays could easily be changed, not that Bannon was likely to be interested in us by then anyway. In all probability he'd be on to his next scam, the Chandlers long forgotten.

Leaving the ladies' room, we returned to the stage, which meant resuming our roles—Mama the assumptive mother of the bride, me the diplomat and coquette stalling for time. Cole Bannon, all smiles, was waiting, eager to continue his charade.

"And now," he said with what seemed like genuine enthusiasm, "we're off for a taste of Ko Samui's celebrated night life. I think you'll love the place I'm taking you."

Chapter
19

The Stork Club, half a mile down the road, was owned by a Swedish gay man named Hank Öberg. Everything about Hank and the place was incongruous. The club was neo-American in style, the decor a mélange of Art Deco—Hank was a big fan of vintage American films—and Thai. The clientele was almost exclusively European. The DJ was a black Jamaican, the music ranged from Big Band Jazz from the 40s to Reggae and Hip Hop. Mostly, though, it fell in the middle—Sinatra, Martin, Streisand, Fitzgerald, Presley, Aznavour, Iglesias, the Beatles, the Stones, and plenty of disco.

For reasons I refused to speculate about, we were seated at the table of honor in a huge booth next to the dance floor. Hank gushed, but didn't flirt with Bannon, which came as a relief. A scantily clad cocktail waitress with fake boobs served our drinks. There was to be no more tropical stuff since we were now engaged in the serious business of clubbing. Daddy and Heath had scotch on the rocks, Bannon vodka straight up, Mama a gin and tonic, and Julie and I had our Shirley Temples.

On the heels of Bannon's toast to the "Chandler Clan," Benny Goodman and his Band of Renown lit up the room, and our host asked Daddy if he could dance with his lady fair. Naturally Mama, who was not only an exemplary hostess in her own right, but fully capable of being the life of any party, simply glowed.

The two of them put on quite a show doing the swing. They had all the moves, everything in the Hollywood repertoire of dance short of the throws—in deference to Mama's age—and delighted the crowd so much that the DJ was compelled to play a few more Big Band tunes, until Mama finally cried uncle and staggered back to the table.

"Mr. Bannon," she said, fanning herself with the drink menu, "I don't believe I've ever had a dance partner so proficient and exemplary as you."

"What would Fred Astaire have been without Ginger Rogers, Mrs. Chandler?"

Of course Mama beamed, then said, "And don't forget Ginger did everything Fred did, only she did it backwards and in heels." It was one of my mother's favorite lines, which, I guess, she felt proved her feminist credentials. Ha!

A couple of rock and roll tunes from the 50's were next, which gave us a breather. Then, when the DJ played "Moon River," from the movie *Breakfast at Tiffany's*, Heath asked Julie to dance. Bannon gave me an imploring look.

"I promise I won't step on your toes," he said.

Ever the diplomat, like the lady my drink was named after, I went off to slow dance with Cole Bannon under the approving eyes of my mother. He wasn't about to let my parents' scrutiny get in the way of a chance to feel my body, however, drawing me as close to him as possible.

"So," he said, his cheek against my temple as we swayed to the music, "are your recollections of our swim this afternoon as fond as mine?"

"I haven't thought about it much, to be honest."

"I don't believe you," he said.

I pulled my head back, intending to give him a withering look and found him grinning. "Lexie, you enjoyed it as much as I did. Why can't you admit it?"

"I was drunk."

"All drink does is lower inhibitions, it doesn't make you like what you hate."

"How vain and immodest of you to point that out."

"Am I wrong?"

"You're physically attractive, Cole. I'm sure that doesn't come as a surprise. All I'm saying is that turning me on when my inhibitions have been lowered doesn't prove a thing. But why are we discussing this? Your ego doesn't need stroking."

"It's not *my* feelings I'm concerned about," he said, "it's yours. I sense hostility, which I'll be damned if I can understand."

So much for my diplomatic skills—or more apropos, perhaps, my acting skills. "Not every woman on earth is going to fall in love with you," I said dryly.

"I'm not concerned about the other three billion females on the planet, Ms. Chandler. It's you I care about." With that he spun me around a couple of times, drawing me close again. Folding me in his arms, he inhaled my scent as though he had every right. It was all part of his act, but I shivered just the same.

When the song ended Bannon kept me on the dance floor, holding my hand, looking at me like a man who was completely infatuated.

"Allow me another dance," he said.

"You're stubborn as a mule, aren't you?"

"I'm pleasing your mom, if not you."

"Look, I don't mean to be unkind, but seducing my family

is really a waste of your time. Better we both face the reality of the situation."

"Which is . . ."

I was about to answer the question honestly, but a man sitting at the bar caught my attention. He was a tall, thin Asian guy with a mustache and a goatee. I was certain it was one of the men we'd seen that afternoon on the yacht off shore from the hotel.

"Cole . . ." I started to point the guy out, but then thought better of it. Sure, Bannon could chase the guy out of the club, just like he'd run after the man we'd seen at the cathedral, but once they were out of sight they could laugh and slap each other on the back. "I'd like to sit down," I said. "And it's not because of you. My feet hurt."

"Sure," he said, leading me by the hand back to the table.

I slipped into the booth next to Julie and Bannon sat next to me. I checked to see if the guy was still at the bar. He was.

"Mrs. Chandler, you did well training Lexie in the social graces," Bannon said to my mother, "but not as well as your mom did with you. She's an excellent dancer, but not quite up to your standard."

"You flatter me, Mr. Bannon," Mama said, "but it's Alexis you need to impress."

I only half listened to Bannon's response, my mind on the guy at the bar. He was watching me almost defiantly as he smoked. I decided it was time to take action.

"Cole, will you excuse me for a moment?" I said, indicating I wanted to get up from the table. "I need to talk to someone."

Bannon slid off the banquette, as did I, heading directly toward the guy. He didn't get up, as I expected. Instead he continued to sit on his barstool, looking bored.

Coming up to him, I put my hands on my hips and gave him my fiercest glare. "What do you want?" I demanded.

"I beg your pardon?"

"You've been watching me. Both tonight and this afternoon at the beach. You were in a boat with another man."

The guy drew on his cigarette then, after blowing smoke toward the ceiling, he stubbed out the butt in the ashtray at his elbow. "Since when is this a crime?" he asked.

"I didn't say it was a crime, I want to know what your intentions are."

He stared at me for several moments through narrow eyes as though he was considering how to respond. "If you must know, I'm working."

Someone came up next to me, and I glanced over. It was Bannon. I also saw Hank Öberg approaching. My concern, though, was with the man on the barstool.

"Doing what?" I demanded. "And for whom?"

The man reached into his pocket and presented a leather case. It held some sort of official badge or identity card. "I am a police officer, madam," he said, "and you are no more under my scrutiny than any other tourist. Be grateful we are here to protect you."

"Is there a problem, Narong?" Hank said, coming up.

"The lady has mistaken my intentions," the officer said. "It's nothing important." He stood, taking some money out his wallet.

"No," Hank said, stopping him. "You don't pay in my establishment."

The officer nodded his gratitude. "Thank you." Then, addressing me, he said, "Good evening, madam." He walked out of the bar.

Red-faced, I glanced at Bannon. "Well, that was embarrassing."

"He's a cop?" Bannon asked Hank.

"Yes, a detective. Usually we only see him when there is serious trouble."

"I guess I qualify," I said.

"I think you were within your rights," Bannon said.

"I don't believe his story about protecting tourists."

"Me neither. It was bullshit."

For the first time, I actually felt like Cole Bannon and I were on the same side. "What could it be, then?"

"Lexie, you got me."

This was a twist I didn't expect. There were enough bad guys to keep me plenty busy, but now I had to deal with the police, too? It was like the FBI all over again. Something was definitely wrong, and the hell of it was, I had no idea what.

Chapter 20

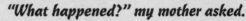

"What happened?" my mother asked.

"A case of mistaken identity," Bannon replied, answering for me. "Lexie and I were under the same misconception."

I was impressed. Bannon managed to be misleading without actually lying. I was afraid, though, it showed just how practiced he was at the art of deception. But being the beneficiary, I wasn't going to quibble.

Thanks to the scotch, Mama got Daddy on the dance floor to foxtrot, which was pretty much the beginning and end of my father's dance repertoire, and Heath and Julie had another go as well. Bannon and I watched them from our table.

"It has to be connected somehow to the ruby," I said. "And maybe it doesn't even have to do with you, me or, for that matter, Chung Lee. It could be Mr. X."

"It's a theory," Bannon allowed.

I studied him. "Cole, tell me the truth. Is there something you aren't telling me?"

"There's lots I'm not telling you," he said. "But none of it is to your detriment, so it doesn't matter."

"Are we talking personal stuff or the Heart of Burma?"

"Both."

"What about the ruby are you keeping from me?"

"You're nothing if not tenacious, Lexie."

"Just tell me."

"Well, for one thing Chung Lee and I played you. We'd pretty much worked out our deal in advance as to my compensation, but he thought you should have to negotiate with me, so that it would be your doing."

"Then you expected me to come walking into the spa."

"I expected a guy named Alex Chandler. As I told you, it was Chung's assistant that provided me the details of your visit and we had a little communication problem."

"So, what's your arrangement with Chung? He's paying you on the side?"

"A little."

"You sneaky bastard."

"You wanted honesty, I'm giving you honesty."

"Well, since we're in an honesty mode," I said, thinking this was the time to confront him with his deception, "I want to ask you something about last night."

"Lexie, excuse me," he said, "but that's one of my all-time favorite disco tunes. You've got to dance with me. But hold that thought."

I sighed and went off with him to dance. We ended up staying out on the floor for three numbers and, by the time we returned to the table, the opportunity for frank discussion was lost. Julie wanted to call it a night, as did Heath and my father, who insisted on picking up the tab, nearly threatening fisticuffs to get his way.

Back at the hotel, the others went to their rooms, and Bannon and I checked with Thep to see if I'd had a call from Martin. I hadn't. Nor had Chinda returned. Her father said she might not come back until morning because she would be staying over with a friend.

"I don't know what to do," I said to Bannon. "Do I head back to Bangkok, or wait to hear from Martin?"

"Until you hear from him you won't know where to find him anyway, so you might as well stay."

"That makes sense. Good point."

"You'll find I'm prone to making sense." He gave me his Troy doll grin.

"Maybe you are more than just a pretty face, after all, Cole."

He pinched my cheek. "So, can I talk you into a stroll on the beach? There's nothing like a little sea air before retiring. You'll sleep much better."

"Okay, there's something we still need to discuss."

We stepped out onto the veranda.

"What's it regarding?" he asked.

"Last night."

We went down the steps and headed for the beach.

"I have a feeling I'm in trouble," he said.

"I think you probably are."

He stopped. "If it's a capital crime, I'd like to be granted a final wish."

I shook my head. The man was incorrigible. "I haven't told you what it was yet."

"That's okay. A dying man has his rights."

The moon shone through the palm fronds, casting dappled shadows on his face. I looked into his eyes. "What's your wish?"

"A kiss, Lexie. That's all, a simple kiss."

I chuckled. "You deserve to be shot, not rewarded," I said.

Bannon kissed me then. It was like the kiss in the water, starting slowly and building. I accepted it passively, but he got me going and I started kissing him back. His fingers dug into my bare back as he crushed me against him, the kiss deepening. I was getting so aroused that I knew I either stopped him or we'd end up making love.

Separating myself, I said, "That's really unfair." I turned to face the sea. "You're trying to spike my guns."

"I'm hoping you'll commute the sentence."

"What I want to discuss is very serious."

"All right then, let's have it."

I turned to him. "I like you. I really do. True, I'm not thrilled about you being in the deal because I don't think it's necessary. But others do, so I have to live with it."

"I'm not as bad as you think, Lexie."

"No, that's where you're wrong. You're dishonest. To be blunt, you're a liar."

"What are you talking about?"

"That man who followed us to the cathedral. You pretended to chase him and you told me he got away. It wasn't true. I went around the building the other way, thinking I could intercept him, but what I found was the two of you standing in the street, laughing and talking. You've lied to me, Cole. And because of that I can't trust you."

"Are you going to let me explain, or are you going to hang me without a trial?"

"You deny you lied to me?"

"No, I wasn't straight with you, that's true. But I had a good reason. The guy was my wife's brother-in-law, her sister's husband, Suthin Supeepote. He was upset over a family matter and wanted to discuss it with me. He'd been waiting for me outside the hotel and when he saw me leave with you he didn't want to interrupt."

"So why did he run?"

"He was embarrassed and didn't want us to think he was

spying. He was waiting for a chance to talk to me alone, that's all."

"Okay, then why didn't you just tell me that? Why did you have to lie? You could have put my mind at ease by being truthful."

"Honestly? I didn't *want* to put your mind at ease. Just the opposite. I wanted you to feel threatened and needy."

"So you could be my protector."

"And it seemed romantic. The point is, my intentions weren't bad. If anything, it shows how much I like you."

"Well, I've got news for you. Honesty is important in personal relationships."

"Oh, you mean like that business about you and Brax? Somehow I think you forgot to mention he was in the Caribbean on his honeymoon."

I flushed. Mama had done it again. "Well, that's different. I was trying to discourage you without hurting your feelings."

"And I was trying to be encouraging, spice things up a little. Is that less noble?"

I could see I'd fallen into my own trap. "Is he really your brother-in-law?"

"Lexie, if I overdid it, if I hurt you, I apologize."

"Well, I do feel a little better," I admitted. "I hated thinking you were in cahoots with whoever's been hassling me."

"Is that what you thought?"

"Maybe I'm paranoid, but outside my family I don't know who I can trust."

"I don't want you to be distrustful of me," he said. "We've both been operating under misconceptions. Can I suggest we start over?"

As he said it, he reached out to touch my cheek. I took his hand and kissed his fingers. "Okay, but can I ask a favor?"

"I'm afraid to ask what," he muttered.

"I think we should cool it a bit until the ruby is in my safe deposit box."

"You really think that's necessary?"

"Cole, you may be good at separating things, but I'm not. To do this right, I've got to focus, and so should you."

"You're asking me to ignore my feelings for you."

"It won't be for long. And, if it's any consolation, it won't be easy for me, either." I gave him a quick kiss on the mouth and hurried back inside the hotel.

Chapter
21

I was awakened early the next morning with an insistent knocking on my door. It was Anura, saying I had a telephone call from Mr. Sedley in Bangkok.

Because of the heat, I'd slept nude and hastily slipped on a light robe, hoping I wouldn't encounter anyone on my way to the public phone. My chances of not being seen were good. Aside from our party, Thep had said that only one other guest room and one cottage were occupied.

Bannon and Thep were working in the office, so Anura directed me toward the small sitting room where there was an extension. Sitting in the armchair next to the phone, I picked up the receiver. "Martin?"

"What's this business about needing you urgently back here in Bangkok?" he said.

"I had a message saying you wanted me to return to Bangkok immediately because you have information."

"There must be some confusion," Martin replied. "I called to say Chung Lee will be returning to Bangkok a day sooner than expected. I wanted you to know so that you didn't go off on a cruise or something. I believe I said you need to return as scheduled, but I didn't say it was urgent. Just keeping you informed, love."

"There was a misunderstanding then."

"No harm done, I trust."

"No." I thought for a moment. "Would you hang on a second, please?" I went over and closed the sitting room door, then returned to the phone. "Martin, do me a favor, would you? I'd like you to track down the brother-in-law of Bannon's late wife, her sister's husband. I can't remember his name exactly, but it was strange. Something like Super Pot. The first name began with an S, too. Sounded like Southern, but that wasn't it."

"What would you like to know about him?"

"Any information you can get, and maybe a way to contact him if need be."

"I'd be delighted, love."

"And be discreet, would you?"

"Absolutely."

When I came out of the sitting room, Bannon was at the registration desk, speaking to another guest, a hefty middle-age woman who, judging by her accent, was German. Seeing me, Bannon checked out my legs, approving of the short robe, I was sure. I made a dash for the stairs.

"Morning, Miss Chandler," he called out. "Are your drapes working okay now?"

"Just fine," I replied as the German lady turned to see me scampering up the staircase. He really was a devil.

I arrived at the landing breathless, only to encounter Heath who was on his way downstairs to get Julie a banana. "A sudden overwhelming craving," he explained.

"Soon you'll be changing diapers and thinking that chasing after bananas is nothing."

"Isn't that the truth."

I started to go on and Heath stopped me.

"By the way, who was the man you and Bannon talked to in the bar last night?"

"A police detective named Narong."

"Oh, really?" my brother said, sounding surprised.

"Yeah, why?"

"I woke up early this morning and went for a stroll around the grounds of the hotel. As I neared Bannon's cottage, I saw the two of them on the deck, talking."

"Bannon and the cop?"

"Yes, the same guy you confronted last night."

I took a moment to digest that. "Did you hear what they were discussing?"

"No, I wasn't that close."

"Did they see you?"

"No, when I spotted them, I turned around and went another way."

This gave me pause. As I thought about it, though, I realized it didn't necessarily mean they were colluding. The detective could have dropped by to question him further. It did concern me, however, that Bannon hadn't mentioned it to me. In fairness, though, he hadn't had much of a chance. It would be interesting to see if he would, even as I dreaded the thought that he might not. Why, I asked myself, was nothing ever easy?

After having breakfast with my family, I politely declined invitations to explore the island with my father and my brother and to shop with Mama and Julie. I was curious what, if anything, Bannon would say about the detective, Narong.

As it turned out, my would-be partner had left the hotel even before my family. Thep said he'd gone out on business, which could mean anything from visiting his accountant, his linen supplier, his local girl, the police, or even a crook or two. I had no confidence about the probability of any of the alternatives.

Left to my own devices, I went for a long walk and ended up having lunch at a beach restaurant in the village of Hin Ta, surrounded by French tourists. One of the single men in the group, a doctor from Paris, tried to hit on me, though he was very respectful. I talked to him for a few minutes out of courtesy, then left after politely declining to go clubbing with him and his friends that evening.

When I got back to the hotel there was no sign of Bannon, so I took a shower, read for a while, then lay down to rest before dinner. I hadn't learned a single thing about Bannon today, and I was still troubled by his conversation with the police detective, not to mention wary what would come of the brother-in-law connection. Meanwhile, I had to go back to being the good actress.

There was still no Bannon by the time the Chandler clan gathered on the lanai for cocktails. Everybody shared their day's adventures while I brooded.

Bannon arrived minutes before we were scheduled to leave for our *soirée*. He was his usual friendly self, though he made no special effort to single me out for a hello-how-was-your-day. On the one hand I was grateful, since I'd requested we cool things down, but I was also miffed he could turn it off so easily. My mother alone seemed to notice the distance between us. I responded with an indifferent shrug to the what's-going-on looks she sent my way.

The plan for the evening was a traditional Thai meal and then a floor show at one of the big hotels in Chaweng. There would be no dancing, which was just as well because I didn't want to have to deal with my conflicted feelings.

Bannon and I rode in different vehicles on the way to the hotel and hardly spoke during dinner or the show. When we gathered for the return trip to the Blue Lagoon, Mama all but deposited me in the jeep with Bannon and made Heath get in the backseat of the car with her and Julie, so my father could ride in front.

As our little caravan set off, I said to him, "Thanks for indulging Mama. Under the circumstances it's not easy."

"Garnet's a delightful lady."

"Wait until she offers you my hand in marriage, then we'll see how delightful you think she is."

"I'm flattered she'd think of me in those terms, Lexie."

"Not to bust your balloon, but her standards aren't as high as they once were."

He chuckled. "Okay, then it's back to being humble."

"So, did you have a good day?" I asked, deciding to probe. "It must have been a relief to get away from your demanding guests."

"I had lots to do," he replied.

He was being enigmatic, and my subtlety wasn't working. I switched to a frontal assault. "You know, all day I've been thinking about that detective at the night club. It's got me bewildered."

Bannon hesitated, then said, "I wouldn't worry about it. There are a thousand innocent explanations."

My heart sank. It wasn't irrefutable proof of a lack of candor, but he was certainly passing up an opportunity to put my mind at ease—assuming he could, of course. Trust, it seemed, was not destined to play a big role in our relationship.

Once back at the hotel, Bannon bid me a cheerful goodnight. There was no suggestion of a walk on the beach.

Chapter 22

Bannon and Heath had arranged the schedule so there'd be some beach time in the morning before we had lunch and then headed for the airport. We'd arrive in Bangkok in plenty of time for my family to catch their flights home. Seeing them had been a treat, but it was time for me to get back to work.

Mama was the first to leave the beach in order to get packed for our return flight. In time the rest of us drifted back, then dutifully assembled first for lunch, then for the trip to the airport.

Thep and Chinda, who had been keeping a low profile, drove us. Bannon spoke to her more than me during the drive, which was just as well. Her relationship with him, if only as an employee, would be more long-term than mine.

When we arrived at the airport, the police detective, Narong, was waiting for us with a couple of uniformed officers. He approached me and said, "Miss Chandler, please come with me."

I was shocked. "Why?"

"We have some questions we'd like to ask."

I glanced at Bannon for a reaction, but saw neither surprise nor alarm. "Am I under arrest?" I asked the detective.

My question elicited a gasp from my mother but hardly a blink from Narong.

"Not unless you refuse to cooperate," he replied.

I was more than a little upset, though I was loathe to show weakness, much less fear. Bannon, taking compassion on me, intervened.

"Detective, I'm taking Miss Chandler and her family back to Bangkok so the other family members can catch their flights home. Is this essential?"

"I'm afraid it is, Mr. Bannon. But you and the others are free to go."

I listened to the conversation with deep suspicion, knowing that Bannon and Narong were better acquainted than they were letting on. Was Bannon simply going through the motions of defending me? I wondered. Could he be in complicity? And more to the point, what was this about?

"We can wait half an hour at most," Bannon told the detective. "Will you be through with her by then?"

"I can't promise," Narong replied. "Miss Chandler . . ." He indicated I should follow. ". . . please come with me."

Narong led me toward the general aviation building. Inside I was taken to an office where two middle-aged Thai officials waited. One was burly and gray, the other small, dour, and mousey. They introduced themselves as senior officers in the national police force. The burly one was named Commander Suchitta, the other Haing.

"I'd like to see your identification, please," I said.

"Certainly," Suchitta replied. "And we wish for your passport."

We exchanged documents. Their identity cards were in Thai script, but looked official. I handed them back, but Haing kept my passport. He motioned for me to sit in the straight chair near the desk. After he made a gesture, Narong and the uniformed cop left the room. The two police officials remained standing as they scrutinized me.

"Why am I being held?" I demanded.

"We wish to talk to you about your affairs in Thailand," Suchitta said. "Please tell why you are here, Miss Chandler."

Suchitta's English was not nearly as good as Narong's who, oddly enough, had been excluded from the conversation. Haing had yet to speak in English.

"I trade in gemstones," I said.

"Who, in Thailand, do you have business with, please?"

"No one, yet. I haven't made any purchases."

"You talk to no one?"

My dealings with Chung Lee were not exactly secret, but no businessperson liked advertising who they were in negotiations with, and I could not see how it was anybody's business, so long as what I did was legal. On the other hand, since they seemed to be so thick with Bannon, they probably already knew the answers to the questions. I decided I might as well get credit for being candid.

"So far I've spoken with Chung Lee, a businessman, and Mr. Bannon."

"No others?"

"No."

"Any other possible partner?"

The other possible partner they were alluding to was most likely the mysterious Mr. X. I now saw why Chung Lee hadn't shared the name with me. I could be totally honest and not compromise anything or anyone.

"There's one other," I told my interrogators. "There's an exceptional ruby known as the Heart of Burma which, I've been told, is in the possession of a foreign gentleman. My hope is that Mr. Chung will be able to arrange for me to meet with the man so that I can negotiate the purchase."

"What his name, please?"

"He's been referred to as Mr. X. That's all I know."

Suchitta studied me as though he was trying to determine my credibility. "I will say something very direct to you. We can have you deported immediately, if we wish. Send you on same plane with your family."

"But why would you do that?"

"Maybe yes, we do this, maybe no. It depend on if you cooperate, Miss Chandler."

"I've answered all of your questions. What more can I do?"

The two men exchanged looks and a few words of Thai passed between them. Suchitta cleared his throat. "You will become informer, Miss Chandler."

"Informer? You mean you want me to spy?"

"We must know everything you know about all people you talk to, please. Especially, Mr. X."

It finally hit me what this was about. Chung had told me that Mr. X operated "on the margins," so naturally the police would have an interest in the guy. They apparently saw me as a potential insider who could obtain intelligence about the man. A sobering thought. If the police had this much interest in Mr. X, he had to be a big-time criminal. Why else would they go to these lengths?

"My proposal very simple," Suchitta said. "If you agree, you stay in Thailand. If not, you must leave immediately. What is your decision, please?"

I was dealing with a man who didn't like to waste time. He also had leverage.

It put me in a very awkward situation, but at least I finally knew what was going on. I couldn't help feeling relieved. But I also wanted to get as much out of the situation as I could.

"I'm not opposed to your request," I said, "but I have a few questions. How did you know about me and my reasons for being in Thailand?"

"This I cannot discuss."

"Can you at least tell me Mr. Bannon's role in this? Is he already an informant?"

"I cannot talk of police business," Suchitta replied. "But I insist you will not talk of this to any person, including Mr. Bannon and Mr. Chung. If too many people know, then the secret is lost. You must trust no one but us. Do you agree?"

I reflected, asking myself what Granddad would do. He'd always said that my conscience was my best guide. I could see no harm in cooperating with the police so long as I didn't have to compromise my integrity.

"Okay, I agree," I told the police officials, "so long as I can do it honorably. If not, I reserve the right to withdraw."

"This is acceptable," Suchitta said, "so long as you understand we have the right to deport you. We return your passport, but watch everything you do."

I took that to mean they would be keeping me on a pretty short leash. Haing handed me my passport.

"So, am I free to leave?"

"This further word, please. You only talk with the agent who is your contact."

"And who would that be?"

"A woman. We thought that best. You already know her. Her name is Joy."

"Chung Lee's niece?"

He smiled. "Miss Chandler, life in Southeast Asia is very complicated."

Chapter
23

Complicated, indeed. That, I realized
as I hurried toward the plane, was the understatement of the
year.

What a bizarre turn of events. A brand-new partner had
been added to the mix—Thai National Police—but since I
could only confide in Joy, essentially I'd be on my own. It
wouldn't be the first time that had happened, but it would be
nice to be able to get Granddad's advice.

Everybody was aboard the aircraft, and Bannon had already started the engines when they saw me coming. He
opened the door so I could board, offering his hand.

"Thank the dear Lord," Mama said once I was inside and
the door was again closed. "I've been worried sick. What did
they want with you, Lexie?"

I knew that would be the first question out of everyone's
mouth, so I was prepared with a story. Of course, had Bannon not been there, I'd have gone with the truth.

"I had lunch in a beach restaurant yesterday," I explained,
"and there was an incident involving some French tourists.
Apparently one of them has been arrested and the police

thought I might be able to provide evidence. They were able to get my name from the credit card receipt."

"The way that detective was acting," my father said, "you'd have thought you were engaged in espionage. As soon as we got back to Bangkok, I was going to pay a visit to the American embassy."

"It's resolved," I said, hating the fact I couldn't be truthful with my own parents.

I reached back, patted Daddy's hand, giving him a meaningful look.

I ended up sitting in the co-pilot's seat, Heath having moved back a row when they saw me coming. As I watched Bannon going through his preparations for takeoff, I realized how the tables had suddenly turned. I'd spent the last day convinced that he had been in complicity with the police; now I was an informant and obligated to keep that secret from him.

We were soon airborne, which gave me the opportunity to gather my thoughts. My new role added a wrinkle I hadn't anticipated. Bannon hadn't been forthcoming about Narong, but I now realized he could be under the same constraints as I. What a mess. But things could be worse. I could have gone to bed with the guy.

When we landed in Bangkok there was just enough time for my family to make their connecting flights.

"I know I'm not supposed to say this," my mother lamented as we were all saying our goodbyes, "but I'm worried about you, Lexie."

"Mama, this is my job, my life."

"Take care of my baby, Mr. Bannon," she said. "That's a condition of sharing our Christmas dinner."

"It's my top priority, Mrs. Chandler."

My mother gave me a big hug. "Give this young man serious consideration," she whispered in my ear. "I have a good feeling about him. A very good feeling."

Poor Mama, if she only knew.

I kissed and hugged Heath and Julie, and they went off to catch their flight.

Before my parents left, Daddy hugged me and whispered in my ear. "I know something's going on you can't discuss, but if you need help, honey, don't hesitate to give me a call."

That touched me and I teared up. "Thanks, Daddy."

Mama and I embraced again, then they took off. I was left with Cole Bannon.

"You're a lucky lady," he said as we walked back down the concourse, "but I suppose you already know that."

"I do."

"Don't worry about me showing up in Atlanta at Christmas, by the way," he said. "Your parents were trying to be polite, and I was being as gracious about it as I could."

"You were very generous and hospitable, Cole, and I appreciate it."

"Enough to have dinner with me tonight?"

"You're putting me on the spot. If I say no, I'll seem like an ingrate."

"I wouldn't want you to do it unless you'd really like to, Lexie."

"I think you know how I feel about things."

"Is it that, or something the police said?"

I gave him a sideward glance, thinking he had to know what had transpired during my interrogation with the police officials. "Like what?"

"I don't know, I'm just trying to understand."

"Actually, I think you do know, Cole."

"What do you mean?"

"Yesterday morning you met with that police detective at

the hotel. Heath was out for a walk, and he saw the two of you together."

"What are you suggesting? That I was conspiring with him?"

"You didn't tell me you'd seen him."

"I didn't see any point in raising your anxiety level," Bannon replied. "Narong just asked routine questions. Wanted to know what I knew about why you were in Thailand."

"And what did you tell him?"

"I was vague. I told him you were a gem trader and that we hoped to do a deal."

"Did you discuss the Heart of Burma?"

"No."

I was in the same position vis-à-vis Bannon as before—I wanted to believe him, but I couldn't. "I still don't understand their interest in me," I said.

"Obviously that story you told about the French tourists wasn't true. Or was it?"

Ball back in my court. Unable to help myself, I blanched, knowing I had no choice but to lie. "Yes," I told him, "it was true."

"Okay."

We left the terminal building and headed for the taxis stand. The driver took our bags and put them in the trunk. We got in the cab. Not much was said as we rode into town. In point of fact, there was nothing to say.

"Am I the only one who finds this sad?" Bannon asked as we neared the Old Farang Quarter.

"What's sad?"

"It feels to me like we just broke up."

"You can't break up something that never really existed."

"There's something you're not telling me," he said.

"Well, welcome to the party, Mr. Bannon. That's been my

feeling about you from the very beginning. The truth seems to be a very elusive quality in Thailand."

"Or for that matter, the Caribbean."

"Oh!"

"Well, am I wrong?"

"I believe I explained that," I said.

"Haven't I explained, as well?"

I looked out the window. "This bickering is getting us nowhere," I said. "Unless we both back off, there's no way we'll be able to work together."

"All right. Fine. I've already agreed we'll do it your way. I thought the friendlier things were, the easier it would be, but if you aren't of the same mind, so be it."

"Thank you."

"Anything to oblige."

Fortunately we were only minutes from the Oriental, and I couldn't wait to get away from him. When we pulled up at the entrance I was out of the taxi like a shot. Bannon got out as well and came around while the driver got my case out of the trunk.

"Lexie, I'm sorry if things have gotten uncomfortable between us, but I want you to know I have the highest regard for both you and your family. Whatever you may think, that's one-hundred-percent honest."

"I appreciate you saying that. And I am grateful for your kindness to my family. That's one-hundred-percent honest, too."

"Maybe we both have something to be thankful for." With that he leaned over and gave me a kiss on the cheek.

There was nothing for me to say, so I turned and went inside.

When I reached my room, I found the message light on my phone blinking. There was a voice mail from Martin. "Alex, I obtained the information you wanted, and I think you'll want to talk to me soonest. You can reach me at my office until six."

I immediately dialed his number and got him.

"I don't think you'll like the news, love," he said. "Mr. Bannon's brother-in-law was killed in a traffic accident over a year ago."

Chapter
24

"Are you certain, Martin?" I asked.

"Quite."

"Could he have more than one brother-in-law?"

"No, his wife had only one sibling, a sister. And her husband's name was Suthin Supeepote. Is that the name you heard?"

"Yes, it is."

"Then the gentleman you inquired about is deceased."

"Jesus, the bastard has lied to me again. Martin, I could just kill him."

"Could there be an explanation?"

"Oh, he'll come up with something, you can be sure of that," I muttered.

"I have an address for the sister, if that would be of use," Martin said. "Her name, by the way, is Sumgi. She lives alone with her children. Do you have a pencil?"

I took down the information, not sure what I'd do with it. But I did know one thing for sure—this time Cole Bannon wouldn't wiggle out of his lie. I'd had it with him. When I met with Chung Lee, I'd make it clear that I couldn't work with Bannon, even if it meant losing my shot at the Heart of Burma.

I hoped Chung would consider Bannon expendable, rather than me, and the prospects of that happening would be greater if I built a solid case. If anybody would have the goods on him, it would be his wife's sister. I decided to pay the lady a visit, preferably unannounced.

Early evening, right after the dinner hour, seemed the best time to call on a mother with young children. Without knowing Sumgi's feelings about Bannon, it would be difficult to know what kind of reception I'd get, but I wanted to nail the bastard so badly that I figured it was definitely worth a try.

I had just finished dressing for the evening when there was a knock at the door. Looking through the peephole, I saw the bellman. I opened the door. The man had a huge bouquet of flowers in his hand.

"Please, miss, these arrived for you."

I tipped him and carried the flowers into the room. There was a card. I opened the envelope. The card read, "I should have been more understanding. Please forgive me." It was signed, "Cole."

I gave a hoot. "Ha! Not on your life, buster!"

But before leaving the room, I did call housekeeping and ask for a large vase.

Martin had told me about a little restaurant a few blocks away that specialized in curries, which I adored. I was especially fond of coconut, peanuts, ginger, basil, lime, lemongrass, and green chiles, all of which were prominent in Thai cuisine. A personal favorite was green curry, though Phanaeng, a dry curry with chicken and shrimp, was wonderful too.

The restaurant, called Captain Mike's for some unknown reason, was only a step up from a noodle shop, the Thai answer to fast food. I hadn't realized it until Martin told me, but most Thais prefer to eat five or six snack meals during the day. "Popping into a noodle shop for a bite is a way of life here," he told me.

My curry was excellent, though not enough to fill my Western-size stomach. I decided to make up for it by having two desserts—mango and sticky rice with coconut cream and a coconut custard.

Right after the waiter placed the desserts on the table, a voice behind me said, "One of those for me, maybe, Khun Alex?"

I turned to see Joy beaming from behind her designer sunglasses. She was in a trimly tailored safari outfit with the sleeves rolled up. It was a sexy yet macho look.

"Hi," I said, happy to see her. "Sit down and join me."

Joy took the chair across from me.

"Take your pick, whichever dessert you want."

"No, thank you, Alex. Just joking. I eat little while ago. But maybe I have beer." Getting the waiter's attention, she ordered a Chang, one of the premium Thai beers. "You, too, Khun Alex?"

"Yeah, why not? I'll have a Singha." The only reason I knew the name was because it had been Grandad's favorite.

Joy said. "So, you very busy, yes?"

"I've been busy, and I've had lots of surprises. You being an example, Joy."

She smiled. "I know what you mean."

"So, how did it happen that you work for the police?"

She gave a half shrug. "Woman who not have rich father or rich husband better find own money. Since I smart, don't have to work in bath house. Not too many Thai lady strong like me."

Joy was certainly living up to her Bond girl image, at least in my mind. "I can see that," I said. "Seems like *I'm* working for *you* now."

She blushed, shaking her head. "No, Khun Alex. I help you, that's all. You tell me things, and I help it go smooth."

She was certainly diplomatic. "I don't have anything to tell you at the moment."

"Yes, I know. But sometime, maybe."

Our beers arrived without glasses. As was the custom, we were to drink out of the bottle. We tapped the necks of our bottles together.

"To a good working relationship," I said.

"Yes, I agree very much."

We both took long pulls. It wasn't too ladylike, but we were a couple of macho women and unafraid to act like it.

"One little problem," Joy said, her tone sober.

"What's that?"

"Two men follow you from hotel."

"Really?"

She nodded solemnly and drank again from her bottle.

"You have any idea who?" I asked.

"No."

"Could it be police?"

She shook her head. "Not police."

"Thai or Caucasian?"

"Thai."

"You know, Joy, I'm starting to feel like Alice in Wonderland."

"Alice? That man or lady?"

"Never mind, it's just an expression. Crazy world."

"This true."

"I discovered one thing while I was away," I said, figuring I'd see what kind of reaction I could get from her. "Cole Bannon might be a nice guy, but he's also a world-class liar. I don't think he's told me the truth yet."

"He's a man, Khun Alex. All men liar."

"Some are worse than others."

"Maybe he like you."

"You and I both know what men like, Joy."

She grinned at that. "Yes, very much."

Joy, I realized, was also dumb like a fox. But I also sensed a genuine concern on her part. "What do you think I should do about the men following me?"

"Be careful. You still have gun?"

"In my purse."

"You be okay then. You go someplace, take taxi. Don't walk in street."

"Okay."

"Now I go out back door, so men not see. I tell restaurant to call taxi for you."

"Thank you, Joy, I appreciate it."

"You strong woman, too, Khun Alex. You be fine." She took a roll of bills from her pocket to pay for the beer, but I wouldn't let her. Giving me a little smile, she did a *wai* and left the dining room.

I sat alone, finishing my beer and wondering who was after me now. These cat and mouse games were getting old, but if someone was trying to discourage me from going after the Heart of Burma, it wouldn't work. I was more determined now than ever.

Chapter
25

Cole Bannon's sister-in-law, Sumgi, lived in a modest but quiet neighborhood in the Thon Buri District, across the river from the Grand Palace. The taxi crossed to the west bank on the Taksin Bridge, then headed north to the Wong-wian Yai traffic circle. After circling the imposing Taksin Monument, we followed one of the major boulevards which paralleled the river.

I tried to keep an eye out for a tail but, given the density of the traffic, I found it almost impossible. The upside was that anybody following would likely have a difficult time keeping us in sight. By the time we reached our destination, I was confident we'd lost anybody who'd tried.

Sumgi's house was at the end of a long narrow street that was fairly dark. That was unfortunate, but with the taxi taking me to the door, I didn't have to walk more than a few steps. I told the driver it might be only a few minutes or it could be a long time, but that he was to wait for me, regardless.

I could see light coming through cracks in the shutters of the front window of the house, giving me hope that Sumgi was home, but there was no porch light. Standing in the shadowed entrance, I knocked on the door.

There was no immediate response, so I knocked again. After a few moments, I heard a woman's voice calling through the heavy door.

"Sumgi?" I replied, hoping the use of her name and a woman's voice would prompt her to investigate.

A few more moments passed before the door opened a crack. A face peered out into the gloom. "Yes, please?" she said.

"Hello," I said, "my name is Alex Chandler. I'm a business associate of your brother-in-law, Cole. Could you answer a few questions for me?"

The expression on the narrow slice of face was wary. "Cole sent you?"

"No, I'd like to talk to you about him, and about your husband."

There was more uncertainty, then the door opened wider. Sumgi, in traditional pajama pants and a long-sleeve top, peered at me inquisitively. Behind her were two little girls, aged four or five. They were similarly attired.

"Is there a problem?" Sumgi asked.

"There's no problem, and I apologize for interrupting, but it's very important that I speak with you."

Stepping back, she opened the door wider and said, "Come inside, please."

I did a little *wai* before entering, which she seemed to appreciate.

"You are American," she said.

"Yes."

"And you work with Cole?"

"Just on one project."

Sumgi was not a great beauty, but she was attractive in a

plain, unassuming way. Her styleless black hair was pulled back off her face into a ponytail and her teeth were a bit crooked, but her features were even and fine.

"Come please," she said.

Sumgi led me into the main room which was dominated by a large table. On the far wall was a sofa and two chairs, which faced a little TV on a stand. The floor was tiled. A few colorful posters decorated the walls.

She motioned for me to sit at the table, and she took the chair opposite from where I sat. The little girls with eyes round as kittens hovered at her side.

"Do you wish something to drink?" Sumgi asked. "Soft drink? Beer?"

"No, thank you."

Glancing around, I noticed a side table against one wall. There were a number of framed photographs on it. I couldn't see the subjects of the photos because they were too far away, but making note of family photos struck me as a good icebreaker.

"Do you have a picture of Cole and your sister?" I asked.

Sumgi dispatched one of the little girls, the fairer of the two, to fetch a photograph, which the child dutifully brought back, her eyes on me as she tucked her head and handed the picture to her mother. Sumgi passed it over to me.

The man in the photo was Cole Bannon, though a slightly thinner, slightly younger version of the man I knew. The woman beside him was petite, not quite reaching his shoulder. But she was lovely, more attractive than her sister, but quite similar in appearance. She was holding a baby.

"Is the baby one of your children?" I asked.

"No, it is Damari's baby," Sumgi replied. "This one." She put an arm around the shoulder of the little girl who'd fetched the picture and drew her against her hip. "She named Dru."

"She's Cole's child?"

"Yes."

The girl's hair was more brownish than black, her features sharper than most Thais. She could easily be Eurasian, though I hadn't noticed until now. "Hello, Dru," I said.

The child tucked her face into Sumgi's arm.

"She's lovely. They both are."

The woman introduced her daughter, also a very cute little girl.

"Cole mentioned your sister, but he never said they'd had a child."

"I raise them like sisters," Sumgi said proudly.

"Does Cole ever see her?" I asked.

"Yes, many times. Because he loves Dru very much, he comes often. Tonight, I think. When you knocked, I think maybe it was him."

My stomach tightened at her words. "He's coming *tonight*?"

"Maybe. It's never sure. I thought maybe he asked you to come here."

"No, I came on my own."

Sumgi nodded. "What do you want to ask, please?"

Seeing Cole Bannon's child and hearing him portrayed as a loving father had thrown me off balance. But I knew with him arriving at any time, I had to cut to the chase.

"A few evenings ago when Cole and I were in the street, a man was following us," I explained. "Cole talked to him privately and later told me it was your husband, Suthin Supeepote, but isn't your husband dead?"

"Yes, for a year."

"Then Cole lied to me. Why would he do such a thing?"

"I don't know," Sumgi said. "Perhaps there was something embarrassing and he spoke of my husband to save face."

That was an Eastern way of looking at things, but Bannon

and I were American. "He told me they discussed family business. Do you have any idea what that could be about?"

Sumgi shook her head. "Do you wish for me to ask?"

"No, no. That's all right. Maybe I'm making more of this than I should, but I'm concerned about Cole's truthfulness. Do you consider him an honest person? Was your sister satisfied with his character?"

"Oh yes, very much," Sumgi said. "My sister very happy. And Cole also. He is very generous. He pays me to stay home with the children so I must not work."

"And his reputation is good?"

"I know nothing of business, but with family, Cole is a most excellent man. Our family loves him very much."

A loving testimonial was something I neither expected nor wanted to hear. This was not at all helpful. On the other hand, Sumgi admitted she knew nothing about the way Bannon conducted business. Even Mafia dons could be loving fathers and husbands, so her glowing testimonial could mean nothing for my purposes.

"I've taken enough of your time," I told Sumgi, deciding to get the hell out of there, "so I should be going. You've been very kind to allow me to interrupt your evening this way."

"It is no problem," she replied. "Why don't you wait for Cole to come? I think he would be surprised to see you."

"He'd be surprised, all right," I muttered. More directly I added, "Thank you for inviting me to stay, but I really must go."

I got up and headed for the door, eager to be on my way. I prayed to God for just two more minutes. Anything to avoid having to face him. After patting each little girl on the head, I shook Sumgi's hand, did a *wai*, then stepped out into the night.

Looking up at the street, I was horrified to discover that my taxi was gone.

Chapter 26

As I studied the street for signs of a
hostile presence, I considered going back inside and phon-
ing for a taxi, but that would increase the likelihood that
Bannon would catch me there. It was a fairly long walk to
the nearest boulevard where taxis would be abundant, but it
struck me as the best alternative, Joy's warning notwithstanding. I had my automatic, so it wasn't like I was without
resources.

I set off at a brisk pace. Mostly the street was deserted,
though occasionally I'd encounter a family group sitting on
their doorstep. I was maybe a quarter of the way to the
boulevard when I realized two men were behind me, maybe
twenty or thirty yards back, one on either side of the street.
My heart began pounding, and I picked up my pace.

Glancing over my shoulder, I saw that the men were keeping up. I clutched my purse to my side, discreetly opening it
so I could quickly grab the automatic, if need be.

I was halfway to the boulevard when I noticed a *samlor*
coming my way. *Samlors* are the Thai version of a three-
wheeled bicycle rickshaw. Though not practical in a city, the

locals used them when traveling relatively short distances within a district.

I considered hailing the driver, but there was a passenger seated in back, which meant I wouldn't be getting a ride.

"Lexie!" a voice called as the *samlor* passed by.

It was Bannon. Cringing, I continued on without replying. When I glanced back, I saw the *samlor* turning around.

"Shit," I said under my breath and began a slow lope. It was the best I could do wearing heeled sandals.

Before long the *samlor* pulled alongside me, the driver huffing and puffing.

"Lexie, what are you doing here?" Bannon asked.

"Taking a walk."

"You're practically running."

"I'm in a hurry."

"What are you doing in this neighborhood?"

"Actually, I came to see your brother-in-law, but it turns out I was too late to catch him . . . a year too late, to be exact."

"I can explain that," he said.

"I'm sure you can, Mr. Bannon. You have a lie ready for every occasion."

"That isn't fair."

"Yeah? Well, I've caught you red-handed, so save your breath."

"Lexie, get in the rickshaw and let me explain."

"I don't want to hear it, so butt out or I'll have you arrested for stalking me."

I was so exasperated I wanted to throw something at him. Ahead I saw the opportunity I needed. There was a small alley off to the right, probably leading to the adjoining street. The *samlor* couldn't easily follow, which would solve my problem.

As soon as I got there, I ran down the narrow passage, nearly tripping over some crates in the darkness. But I hurried, knowing I'd likely get away before Bannon could pay the driver and follow, assuming he was so inclined.

Unfortunately the alley didn't make a straight shot to the next street. It began twisting and turning into other passageways. Soon I was in a virtual maze. Between that and the darkness, it was unlikely anybody would be able to track me. That was the good news. The bad news was that I didn't know where the hell I was.

I decided the thing to do was to return the way I'd come. I'd almost reached the last intersection I'd passed when I heard voices and footsteps. Ducking into a doorway, I peered out and saw two men enter the intersection. There was just enough moonlight for me to see that they were the two who'd followed me from Sumgi's place. "Shit," I muttered under my breath.

One of them, a smallish guy with a shaved head, started in my direction. If he walked past me and proceeded up the alleyway, I'd be caught between them.

I decided to make a run for it. Coming out of the doorway I accidentally kicked a pail across the cobblestones. That set a dog barking, drawing the attention of the men.

I took off at a dead run, hearing shouts behind me as the men joined the chase. I hadn't gone fifty yards before I reached one of the many canals that criss-cross Thon Buri. The alleyway dead-ended there. Now I was trapped.

There were a number of large containers stacked along the dock that fronted the canal. I slipped into a gap between two of the containers, breathing hard as I tried to regain my composure. Seconds later, the men came out of the alleyway and peered up and down the canal.

They were breathing as hard as I was, so they couldn't hear me gasping for air, though they were only twenty feet away. I reached into my purse for my gun, doing the best I could not to make any noise. I was surprised when one of them yelled to someone across the canal. Moving to the back of the crate, I saw a small pedestrian ferry that connected the alleyways on each side of the canal.

Whatever had been said, it brought a call in response from the ferryman. My best guess was that my stalkers had asked him if he'd just transported a female *farang* across the canal. I didn't have to speak Thai to know the answer to that question.

Certain now that they had me, the two men began to methodically search the dock. In seconds I'd be discovered, so I decided to take the initiative. Gun in hand, I stepped out into the open and leveled the automatic on them.

"Hold it right there, boys," I said. "Don't move!"

The men froze, lifting their hands.

"Who are you and why are you following me?" I demanded.

"We don't know what you mean, miss," one said.

"Don't give me that crap. You've been following me all evening."

"We just going home, okay?"

"Bullshit. Let me see your identification. One at a time. You first," I said, indicating the larger of the two men. "Slowly. No fast moves or I shoot."

The man took out his wallet and started to extend it toward me.

"Put it on that box and move back."

He did as he was told.

"Now you," I said to the other man, the one with the shaved head.

When he'd set his wallet on the box, I motioned for them to step away, then I moved forward. Just as I picked up one of the wallets I heard a voice in the alleyway.

"Lexie!"

Recognizing Bannon's voice, I turned my head. During that split second of distraction, the bald guy leaped forward, grabbing my gun hand and sending the automatic skidding across the cobblestones. The other guy lunged for me. I spun the smaller man into him and they clunked heads. The bald guy staggered away dazed, but the other one tried to grab me by the throat. Taking his arm, I ducked and flipped him. He landed flat on his back on the pavement. Rolling over, he got up on his hands and knees, and I kicked him in the stomach, flattening him. I went for my gun.

"Dammit, Lexie!"

I had the automatic in my hand when Bannon came running up. I wanted to shoot him, but instead I clobbered him with the gun, knocking him to the ground. I looked down, seeing he was out cold.

It only then occurred to me that I might have overreacted. What if I killed him?

But then he moaned and I realized he was okay. Glancing up, I saw the big guy snatch the wallets from the box then stagger off toward the alleyway after his friend.

"Hey!" But it was too late. He disappeared into the shadows.

Bannon groaned. I looked down at him, feeling bad, but also disgusted. Time after time he'd conned me, and I wasn't going to let it happen again.

"Bad luck, your pals deserted you. You've got to start keeping better company."

I heard a thud and a clank behind me and, looking over my shoulder, I saw that the ferry had crossed back to the nearside of the canal. Having no desire to go back into the dark maze of alleys, I went over and stepped onto the barge. The ferryman looked at me with uncertainty. Then, rising on his toes, he craned his neck to get a look at Bannon, who was getting to his hands and knees.

"Let's go," I said to the ferryman, indicating I wanted to cross the canal.

He shook his head, pointing at his watch. I gave him a large bill.

"Let's go *now*!"

He pushed off and we headed across the canal. We'd just cleared the dock when Bannon came staggering over.

"Goddamn it, Lexie," he called, holding his hand to the side of his head, "why'd you hit me?"

"First, because I don't like you, and second because I don't like the company you keep," I called back.

"You've got it all wrong."

"No, Mr. Bannon, *you* do."

Chapter
27

If I learned anything that evening it was that you can't trust taxi drivers and that it was a bad idea to wander around Bangkok without a map. It took me forever to find a cab, but when I finally did, I settled into the seat with a heavy sigh and took inventory. I'd lost a button on my blouse, tore a strap on one of my sandals and chipped two nails. The top of my foot was sore from kicking the guy, but all-in-all, casualties on the friendly side were light.

I still had no idea who the men were, or how they were connected to Bannon, but at this point it didn't matter because Bannon was history. If this cost me my shot at the Heart of Burma, I'd hate him even more, but at least I'd gotten in one good lick.

When I reached the Oriental, I dragged myself to my room. The ceiling light in the entry to my room wasn't working, which gave me pause. Removing my gun from my purse, I felt my way to the bed in the dark. I fumbled for the bedside lamp. Once I had it on, I glanced around, and, seeing nothing amiss, I tossed the gun and my purse on the bed and took off my blouse, annoyed to see that the scam around the arm was partially torn. Then I took off my trousers. As I reached behind me to unfasten my bra, I sensed a presence. Somebody was in the room.

Spinning into a crouch position, my hands up, ready for combat, I saw him standing in the bathroom doorway. Cole Bannon held an ice bag to his cheek.

"It's about time," he said, ambling over to the armchair. He dropped into it.

I snatched the automatic and, with one knee still on the bed, I pointed the gun at him. "You bastard!"

"For crissake, Lexie, don't shoot me on top of everything else."

"That's exactly what I'm going to do, you sonovabitch!"

"Okay, so a gentleman would have stopped you from undressing, but dammit, you owe me."

"Cole Bannon, if you aren't out of here in ten seconds, I swear to God I'm going to blow your head off."

"Be warned, Lexie. This is a patriarchal society. In Thailand, females who commit crimes of passion don't get much sympathy."

"You arrogant bastard! Get out of here! Now!"

"Look," Bannon said, "if you won't hear me out, then you might as well shoot me and have hotel security remove the body. That's the only way to get me out of here without allowing me my say."

I was so angry I could barely control myself. Plus I was humiliated, posed there in front of him in my underwear. Needless to say, Bannon took advantage of the opportunity to check out my body.

"So lovely, yet so lethal," he mumbled.

"Whereas you are a horse's ass," I said, striding to the bathroom where I snatched my bathrobe from the back of the door and slipped it on. I returned to the bedroom and sat on the bed, crossing my legs. Resting the gun on my knee, I said, "I'll give you five minutes to spin your next tall tale, Bannon, then I want you gone and I mean it."

"Thank you."

"You're welcome. Now start talking. You've got four minutes and fifty seconds."

He sighed and glanced at the vase of flowers on the table next to him. Reaching over, he snatched a blossom and smelled it. "These weren't cheap, but they didn't do a damned bit of good, did they?"

"Say what you want and make it quick. The sight of you makes me nauseous."

He had a pained look on his face. "This rift between us isn't going to heal anytime soon, is it?"

"Bannon!"

"All right," he said, throwing up his hands. "I lied about that guy at the cathedral being my brother-in-law."

"No kidding."

"But I had a good reason."

"Why am I not surprised?"

"I'm serious, Lexie."

"No, you're a dishonest, conniving, bald-faced liar."

"But you're a fair-minded woman who'll listen with an open mind, right?"

"Just spit it out!"

"All right. When you told me you'd seen us chatting behind the cathedral, you put me in a terrible dilemma."

"Yeah, it was either tell the truth or tell a lie, and you chose the course most befitting your character."

"I was trying to save our deal so you could get your ruby, dammit!"

"Oh, I see. It was an act of sacrifice to lie to me."

"I lied because if I told you the truth, the deal would have been dead then and there. And it didn't have to be. I knew I could save it, and that's what I tried to do."

I scoffed. "You sacrificed for my sake. How noble. And I suppose you have some swamp land you'd like to sell me at a very reasonable price."

"You're using up my five minutes with your sarcastic remarks."

"Just get on with it."

Bannon shifted the ice pack, wincing. If the bastard was expecting sympathy, he wasn't getting any from me.

"The guy at the cathedral is named Santa."

"Santa? As in Santa Claus?" I shook my head, laughing. "And the two guys tonight were the Easter Bunny and the Tooth Fairy, right?"

"You're being sarcastic again."

"Give me a break, Bannon. Santa? You're either insulting my intelligence, or that knock on the head did more damage than I thought."

"His full name is Santa Noonwongsa. And, by the way, Santa's not an uncommon name in Thailand. He's a deal maker, a middleman, very much like your friend Martin. Anyway, several weeks ago Santa got wind of Chung Lee's line on the Heart of Burma. He contacted me about it even before Chung did. His plan was to partner with me and go after the stone. But Chung had something else in mind, namely you. This left me in an awkward position vis-à-vis Santa. Being an honorable person—contrary to popular opinion, at least in this room—I didn't want Santa to think I'd double-crossed him, so I leveled with him, explaining it was out of my hands and that Chung was calling the shots. I asked him to talk to Chung and confirm what I told him."

"If this is true, why didn't you just tell me?"

"First, because our relationship was shaky enough already, and I didn't want to open a can of worms. I'd made my deal with you and Chung, and I was committed to it, so why upset the applecart? Besides, I had no idea you'd seen me talking to Santa. It seemed best to let sleeping dogs lie."

"You know what, Bannon, I almost believe you. Almost."

"Why only almost?"

"Ever heard the story of the boy who cried wolf too often?"

"In retrospect I should have handled it differently, I grant you. But at least my heart was in the right place."

"Yeah, I've heard that before."

"So, if I were to tell you I think those guys tonight may have been sent by Santa Noonwongsa to scare you off the project, you wouldn't care."

"Were they?"

"I honestly don't know," Bannon replied, "but one of them looked familiar, and I do know Santa is taking this hard. All I can say for sure is that it's possible."

I hated it that Bannon sounded so logical and reasonable. I hated it even more that my resolve was cracking. The guy could charm the socks off a rooster.

Then a thought occurred, the flaw in his logic. "Let me ask you something. If the guy at the cathedral was really Santa Noon . . . whatever-his-name-is, why claim it was your brother-in-law? I'd already caught you in a lie, why not come clean?"

"Mainly because you caught me off guard. I wanted to keep Noonwongsa out of the equation, hoping that Chung would set him straight and that would be the end of it."

"Falsehoods have a funny way of biting you in the ass, Bannon."

He shifted the ice pack again. "Yeah, I noticed."

"You deserved what you got, and I don't for a minute regret decking you."

"Well, call me a fool, but the truth is I'm innocent. And for all the mistakes I made, I always had your best interests at heart. Always. I wanted you to get your ruby. And I wanted you to take me to dinner once the sale was made."

"No way that's going to happen."

He looked crestfallen. Damn, if I didn't want to believe him, and that really, really pissed me off. "Cole, you are the slickest, most accomplished fraud I've ever met."

"But I'm a good kisser, right?"

"Irrelevant."

"Surely you can find it in your heart to forgive me."

"How can I forgive you if I don't believe you?"

"You don't believe me?"

"No!"

"Not even if I drag Noonwongsa in here and make him tell you the truth himself?"

"You could phony that up."

"If you won't believe me, who will you believe?"

That gave me an idea. "Hang on, I think I know how to get to the bottom of this." I went to the phone and called Martin at home.

"Hello?" he mumbled, sounding like I'd awakened him.

"Martin, sorry to bother you so late, but I've got an important question. Have you ever heard of a guy called Santa . . ." I covered the mouthpiece. "What's the guy's last name, again?"

"Noonwongsa," Bannon replied.

"Santa Noonwongsa," I said to Martin.

"Yes, I know the little creep. Don't tell me he's decided to hound you as well?"

"Well, I don't know. I heard he had an interest in the stone, and I want to find out whether I should be concerned or not."

"It's hard to say, love. Santa is a little weasel. Not a man I'd ever do business with, that much I can say with certainty."

"Has he bothered you?" I asked.

"He's been having a go at me for weeks, trying to cut himself into the deal."

Suddenly Bannon's story didn't seem quite so outrageous. In fact, Martin almost made it sound plausible. "Martin, do you think this guy Santa might try to use Bannon to get to the stone?"

"I wouldn't put it past him."

"Let me ask you something else. If you were me, would you trust Cole Bannon?"

"With regard to what?"

"Anything. Everything."

"I honestly don't know the man that well, Alex."

"Do you think he's a liar?"

"Well, I think you can handle him, regardless. You've dealt with more than one scoundrel in your time, love."

Martin was not giving me what I needed. "Perhaps you're right. Thanks, and again, I'm sorry to disturb you."

"Not to worry."

"Good night then."

"Ta-ta."

I hung up. Again, I looked at Bannon and he looked at me.

"Well?" he said.

"The jury's still out," I replied.

"Do you still want to shoot me?"

"I may commute the sentence to simple banishment."

"Then it probably isn't a good idea to invite you to have a nightcap with me."

"No, dammit! Just go home, will you? You're lucky to be alive."

"Since I am among the living, may I ask a favor?" he said.

I shook my head in disbelief. "You have nerve, I'll give you that."

"Well, when you're on a roll . . ."

"What's the favor?"

"Come with me and my daughter, Dru, on an outing. To the zoo. She's never known an American lady before. I want her to see a genuine, first-class female American close up. When will I have another opportunity like this?"

"You're kidding, right?"

"No, I'm dead serious. It's important. For her sake."

I sighed. "Let me think about it. But now, I want you to leave."

He got to his feet. "I'm sorry about the misunderstanding, Lexie. I really am."

"And I'm sorry I hit you."

That pleased him. "Let's call it even then, shall we?"

"Good night, Cole."

Indicating the ice bag, he said, "I'll just take this with me, if you don't mind."

Chapter 28

I awoke the next morning feeling more equivocal about Bannon than when I'd gone to bed. But I didn't have the luxury of sorting everything out. Chung Lee was due back in town tomorrow, which meant I either made him choose between me and Bannon, or I let Bannon stay on. My pride was at stake, but so was the Heart of Burma. Emotion and reason. Why did it always seem to come down to that?

When Joy phoned, asking if I had plans for breakfast, I was pleased. I could get her take on Santa Noonwongsa and maybe pressure her some more about Bannon. My instincts told me that she had been holding something back when it came to him. I'd had a funny feeling about that right from the very beginning.

Half an hour later I found Joy waiting in the lobby, looking ready for a *tête-à-tête* with 007 himself. She really was an original, and though I hardly knew her, I liked her, perhaps because we were, in a sense, kindred spirits.

"You like fruit, Khun Alex?" she asked. "We go to juice bar. Very healthy. Nice weather outside, we walk."

With our breakfast plans decided, we headed off on our stroll to the juice bar.

"As it turned out, I could have used you last night," I told her.

"What happen?"

I told her about my little adventure. Joy shook her head, looking very somber.

"This very bad."

"It wasn't a lot of fun. What can you tell me about this guy, Santa Noonwongsa?"

"Only know what people say. Not very good man. You don't see him no more."

"I hadn't planned to put him on my Christmas card list. But I've done my duty reporting in to you, which was the deal." I paused a moment, then continued. "Can I ask you a personal question, Joy? Off the record, which means I don't want it to go in your report to your superiors."

"Sure. We friends."

"I know you've been reluctant to talk about Cole Bannon, but if you were in my shoes, would you allow a personal relationship to develop?"

"What you mean? Have sex?"

I blushed. "No, I mean he wants to be friends, for me to get to know his daughter. I don't normally do that. I try to keep my personal life and my business life separate, so I'm not sure what to tell him."

"I see what you mean."

We were so focused on the problem, really connecting as women who were trying to help each other do, that we weren't as alert as we should have been when we crossed Soi 36, just up the street from the French Embassy.

We both glanced back down the street as we stepped off the curb, but the first sign of trouble was the awful roar of an engine as a car bore down on us at high speed. The driver seemed determined to hit us.

And he did.

Joy, who was closest to the vehicle, fell backward when trying to get out of the way, but she was hit and violently thrown into a parked car up the street. Having a split second more time, I managed to dive toward the gutter. Even so, something hit my foot—I'm not sure whether it was Joy or the vehicle—and sent me tumbling.

For a second I lay dazed on the pavement. Hearing shouts, I lifted my head in time to see the big car disappear around the corner.

From where I was lying I couldn't see Joy, so I got up, so numb I wasn't sure whether I was hurt or not. People were converging from all directions, crying out in Thai. About thirty feet up the street, half a dozen people were gathered around Joy, who lay motionless on the pavement. I staggered toward her as a little woman ran along beside me, I suppose trying to comfort me.

When I reached Joy, people stepped aside. My friend's eyes were closed, her face bloodied and her body mangled. I dropped to my knees beside her as the gathering crowd buzzed. I looked up and said, "Somebody call an ambulance. Get a doctor, the police."

"Yes, yes," one man said, and ducked from the crowd.

I couldn't tell if Joy was breathing, so I bent closer, remembering when I was a child and tried to cross the street on my bike against my mother's orders. A car hit me, though it was scarcely more than a tap, but it was enough to knock me to the pavement. I recall Mama running from the house, dropping to her knees beside me, desperation on her face. I felt the same desperation for Joy.

"Can you hear me?" I whispered, just as my mother had to me all those years ago.

Joy's eyes fluttered open, though one was so badly battered I couldn't see more than a slit. Her lip quivered as she tried to speak. I lowered my head closer still.

Blood oozed from the corner of her mouth. She gave a little cough, then said, "You can trust Bannon, Khun Alex." The expression in her good eye seemed to say, "Really, you can." Then it closed.

Two policemen arrived moments later and an ambulance not long after that. They put me in the back of a police car where I waited until an English-speaking officer arrived. Joy had been taken away in the ambulance by then. I told the officer what had happened.

"It intentional, I think," the cop said. "You know who would do this?"

I didn't know whether to mention Noonwongsa or not. I had no reason to believe he was responsible other than what had happened last night, and that was thin grounds on which to accuse someone of attempted homicide. "No," I told the officer.

They took me back to the Oriental. I asked after Joy, but no one seemed to know her condition. If I'd been in shock earlier, I was okay now, though I had bumps and bruises plus one hell of a headache. Over my protests the house doctor came. He thought I had a mild concussion but was otherwise fit.

I'd asked the hotel to contact Martin. He was there within half an hour. Entering my room, he gave me the sad news that Joy was dead.

I cried, partly because I mourned every death, especially senseless ones. But I also cried because I had identified with Joy, a young woman whose family name I didn't even know. In an odd way we were sisters as much as we were strangers.

Martin had the hotel staff bring me a light meal, which I ate with indifference. Then he sat with me to talk, looking less rumpled than he had, perhaps because it was still early in the day. We speculated about who could have been responsible for the hit and run and whether I was the likely target.

After I finished my meal, a couple of police detectives showed up to take a formal statement. I didn't tell them I was a police informant, figuring someone else would. I did, however, relate what had happened by the canal the previous evening, mentioning Santa Noonwongsa by name.

Once the interview was over, the detectives got up to go. When they opened the door to leave, I saw Cole Bannon standing in the hall. He was holding the hand of a little girl, his daughter, Dru.

Seeing Bannon, Martin picked his Panama hat up from the table and headed for the door himself. "I'm off, love," he called over his shoulder. "If you need anything, don't hesitate to ring me up." Giving Bannon a little bow, he said, "Good morning," then disappeared down the hall.

Bannon stayed at the door. I got up from the table where I'd been sitting.

"We took a chance on catching you at home," he said, "but it looks like you've been busy already this morning. Were you holding a convention?"

"Worse, I'm afraid. Come on in."

He led Dru inside and closed the door, his expression questioning. "What happened?"

I felt shaky again and drew an uneven breath. "I think someone tried to kill me."

Chapter
29

"I'm going to track down Santa myself," Bannon said, clearly upset after I told him the story.

"You think he was responsible?"

"That's what I intend to find out."

We were seated at the table. Bannon's cheek was swollen and discolored. The fact that he didn't complain made me feel terrible—especially after Joy told me I could trust him.

Dru, who'd been watching cartoons on the TV, came over and climbed on her father's lap. Seeing her eyeing the bowl of fruit left over from my meal, I pushed it over to her. She looked at me shyly, then up at her daddy. Bannon took an orange and began to peel it for her.

"I've heard that ruby has a bloody history," he said somberly. "I'm wondering if it hasn't claimed another victim in Joy."

"It's not the stone that's responsible," I said. "It's greed."

"Look what it's done to us."

"I don't think our problems had anything to the with the Heart of Burma, Cole," I said. "Unless you're trying to tell me something."

"I'm not. I don't have any better idea what's going on than you."

"Is that true?"

"Yes."

"What's the story with you and Joy? I don't think you fully leveled with me."

He'd finished peeling the orange and tore off a wedge, which he gave to his daughter. Smiling at me, the little girl bit off a chunk. She was so adorable I had trouble taking my eyes off of her.

"I don't recall saying much about her," he replied.

"Let me rephrase that. When I asked her about you, she was always vague, and I sensed she was holding something back."

He tore off another wedge of orange and put it on the table in front of Dru, looking uncomfortable. "I don't want to lie to you anymore, Lexie," he said. "I promised myself I wouldn't. I'm hesitating because your question puts me in an awkward position."

"Okay, but now that she's dead, there's something I feel I need to tell you. She was working with the police."

"I know that, Lexie. In fact, I know everything."

"Even that they asked me to be an informant?"

"Yes. And that you weren't supposed to tell me."

"I figured you were in deeper with them than you were letting on. There's a reason I brought it up, though. Before she died, Joy told me I could trust you. I'll be honest, a person's dying words carry a lot of weight with me. I considered her a friend."

Bannon reached over and took my hand. I don't know why—unless it was because of what had happened to Joy—but I teared up. Dru noticed.

I was hardly an expert on children, but despite having little understanding of the world, they always knew when something was wrong. A half-eaten wedge of orange in her hand, Dru looked back up at her daddy with concern as if to say, "What's wrong with this lady?" He kissed her hair.

Call me a sucker, but my heart crumbled.

"Where does all this leave us?" Bannon asked.

"I don't know about us, but I do know I'm confused. I have no idea who the good guys are and who the bad guys are."

"I'll clarify things, if I can."

"Were you and Joy working together?"

"Yes and no. She was brought into the deal shortly before you arrived. But we knew each other before that."

I searched his eyes, knowing the answer to my question before I asked it. "Were you lovers?"

Bannon gave his daughter another wedge of orange. She was too young to follow our conversation, but Bannon chose his words carefully just the same. "I won't parse, Lexie. Joy and I had a fling. It was brief, it didn't mean a great deal to either of us."

I nodded, understanding. "Joy was a vibrant and beautiful woman. She had great energy. I'm surprised your feelings for her weren't deeper."

"They were what they were," he said.

"Did you remain friends?"

"We didn't see each other. I suppose there was lingering admiration and respect."

I looked at Dru, who had been eyeing me with curiosity. Reaching out, I brushed her cheek with my finger. "You seem to make a habit of getting involved with the women you work with," I said casually, doing my best to hide any edge to my voice.

"If that's an indirect reference to you and me, it doesn't apply. The two situations are apples and oranges."

"Well, I didn't . . . you-know-what with you, that's true."

"I don't make a habit of sleeping . . . or trying to sleep . . .

with the women I work with," he said. "You're a special case, and my feelings about you are unique."

"Don't feel you have to sugarcoat it, Cole. I'm not accusing you of anything, nor am I offended. It's just that in this new atmosphere of candor, I'm trying to understand you as best I can."

"Well, today you've heard the bald truth," he said.

"I sense that."

"Does that mean I'm back in your good graces?"

"I don't know if I'd go that far."

He laughed. "Come to the zoo with Dru and me and we can discuss it further."

"It's been a rough day. I don't know that I'm up to it."

"This may be our only chance. Besides, some fresh air and some lions and tigers and peanuts will cure what ails you. Getting your mind off what happened is important."

"You make it very tempting," I said.

Dru reached up for her daddy's face and Bannon had to grab her sticky little hand, kissing the back of it.

"Here, Dru," I said, dipping the corner of a napkin in a water glass. Taking her hand, I washed it off, the way my mother did when I was a child.

"You're a natural," Bannon said.

"A natural what?"

"Mother."

"Wash your mouth out with soap," I said.

"You're offended?"

"No, it's just not the way I think of myself."

He studied me. "Has something to do with Brax, doesn't it?"

"No, it has to do with me. But why did you bring him up?"

"Something your mother said."

"I might have known," I said, shaking my head.

"Parenthood doesn't have to be conventional," he said.

"Children have well-defined needs."

"And they all begin and end with love."

"I would never have taken you to be a social philosopher," I said.

"There's a lot you don't know about me," he replied. "And not all of it is bad."

I smiled and he reached over and pinched my cheek.

"You need a change of scene, sweetheart," he said, "come with us to the zoo."

The Dusit Zoo, Bannon told me, had once been the private botanical gardens of Rama V, a nineteenth-century Siamese king. It was a lush and beautiful place, the setting park-like. As we strolled, Dru between us, holding our hands, I marveled at the situation. The guy I'd first seen in the company of a couple of naked prostitutes had charmed my mother into inviting him into the bosom of our family, and now here he was playing the role of loving father and family man.

Braxton Cooper had envisioned the two of us strolling in a park with our kids just like this, and I'd recoiled at the notion. Yet, here I was with Bannon, doing practically the same thing and feeling okay about it. Of course, there was a big difference between going on an outing with a friend and having your life defined for you by the man you planned to marry.

But what if this new and gentler Cole Bannon turned out to be something more than just a friend? Not that I had aspirations along those lines. There were several reasons I remained wary. First, I was slow to jump on any man's bandwagon—there were just too many ways things could go wrong. And second, I wasn't so naive as to think that a leopard could change his spots. Sure, I might have been overly critical of Bannon, and perhaps had misunderstood his intentions, but it was still true he'd been less than honest. The best policy, I decided, was to wait and see how things developed.

Dru's favorite animal was the tiger, and we spent quite a bit of time watching a couple of yearlings at play. Bannon reminded me that they were native to this part of the world, though they were few in number and pretty much stayed clear of humans. "It's been a while since one's been seen walking down the streets of Bangkok," he joked.

"The way things have been going for me recently, I wouldn't be surprised if it happened," I replied.

"From what I've seen of you, sweetheart, the tiger would be smart to run."

Chapter
30

The three of us had a late lunch at an outdoor café, and Dru became more confident chatting with me in English with a little Thai thrown in here and there for good measure. We'd found a children's book in English about the zoo animals in the gift shop, and I bought it for her as a remembrance of me. After lunch we sat on a bench in the garden, and I read it to her while Bannon sat back, listening.

"Don't try to make anything of this," I said to him as an aside. "I regard it as a pleasant diversion, that's all."

"Whatever you say."

Dru got impatient and made me turn the page, pointing to the picture of an elephant. "Mommy rides one like him," she said.

I glanced at Bannon.

"I told her how Damari rode to our wedding on an elephant. It was in her native village in the north. It's become a family folktale."

"Sounds pretty romantic to me."

"It was, actually."

He sounded wistful. "It's been painful for you, hasn't it?"

"I try not to dwell on it," he said.

"How is it you haven't remarried? With all these beautiful Thai girls, you certainly have plenty to choose from."

"That's not where I am," he said. "Nobody can be replaced. Instead, you go on to other things, new life experiences. It's much healthier."

I was beginning to see that Bannon was wise as well as charming. It was a nice combination.

"Lexie," Dru said, exasperated now, "talk about the elephant."

"Well, I like elephants a lot. Do you?"

"Uh-huh," she said, nodding.

"If you two like elephants so much, what do you say we have a ride on one?" Bannon interjected.

"Oh, Daddy!" Dru said giddily. "Can we? Can we?"

"Are you serious?" I said.

"Yeah, they have elephant rides. It's a good way to see the park."

We went off to find an elephant, and Dru was beside herself with joy. I was a little amped myself. "I've never seen an elephant up close and personal," I told him.

"Well, here's your big chance."

The elephant station was a big platform which the passenger climbed onto so they could step right onto the seats situated on either side of the animal's back. The turbaned driver sat astride the elephant's neck. As we arrived, one elephant was leaving with a full compliment of passengers. There was just one other couple waiting as a second elephant came up to the platform. Bannon paid the attendant extra so we could go without having to wait to fill the remaining places.

It was amazing how far above the ground we were, and how fortunate that the animal was so docile. We took off, the ride surprisingly steady despite the huge beast's lumbering gait. Dru, who sat between us, was bouncing in her seat, but she gripped my hand tightly, as fearful as she was excited. Her glee alone was worth the price of admission.

Bannon watched his child with the loving eye of a proud father, toying with her silky hair. When our eyes met, we exchanged smiles and he reached over, drawing the back of his fingers along the line of my jaw.

"Thanks for doing this, Lexie," he said warmly. "You've made it a special day."

"The pleasure is all mine, seriously."

Our route took us around the larger of the lakes in the park and into a wooded glade. There were a few people strolling along the path. It wasn't exactly like being in the jungle, but maybe as close as you could get within the confines of Bangkok.

With the dappled sunlight coming through the canopy of trees, and Dru smiling up at her father and me in turn, it struck me as an idyllic moment. *Wouldn't Mama love to see a picture of this?* I thought. She would have been as gleeful as Dru.

But the moment didn't last. Just when things seemed about as perfect as they could be, evil again reared its ugly head. This time, though, instead of a car bearing down on us, aggression came in the form of a slight man dressed in a white shirt and khaki trousers who stepped out from behind a big tree. He was Thai, and his head was shaved bald like the smaller of the men I'd fought at the canal the previous night. He looked a lot more ominous with an assault rifle in his hands.

Bannon and I were ducking under a low-hanging branch when the man made his appearance. It may have been that small movement which saved my life, because at that very instant our attacker squeezed off a burst. I felt at least one round cut through my hair at the nape of my neck.

The gunfire spooked the elephant, which made a sudden lurch forward. He also swung sharply away from the direction of the shots, which caused a second volley of rounds to miss us, at least one of which, we later learned, struck the huge beast in the haunch.

The elephant was no more in the mood to stick around than we were. His trunk in the air, trumpeting, he charged up the path at full speed, bouncing us around so violently that we nearly fell from our seats. Dru and the woman on the other side of the animal were both screaming, though you could hardly hear them because of the elephant's terrified screeching.

Bannon grabbed Dru, and I held on for dear life as we raced along, the occasional tree branch swatting at us as though we were flies. I looked back, but there was no way a man on foot could keep pace. I had no idea elephants could move so fast.

We must have gone a couple hundred yards, all the while the driver yelling and trying to get the animal under control. Our pace eventually slowed to a brisk walk, and finally the elephant stopped. He wasn't about to let the incident go, however. Lifting his trunk high above him, he let out a trumpet blast that might have broken windows had there been any nearby. I suppose it was an instinctive warning to the non-existent herd. Either that or he was in pain.

The rest of us took inventory and determined that no one was hurt. Dru was crying, though, and climbed into her father's arms. For the first time Bannon spoke.

"We may be sitting ducks if we stay on this thing," he said. "No telling if there are other snipers around. I think we should climb down and get out of here on foot."

I saw the elephant lifting its right rear leg, and that's when I noticed the spot of blood on its haunch. The driver seemed to be trying to get the beast to move, but our mount was in no mood to cooperate. Short of waiting for a rescue party, walking seemed the only alternative.

"How are we going to get down?" I asked.

"I'll drop to the ground," Bannon said, "and you can lower Dru to me."

The little girl continued to sob, clinging to her father's neck. Bannon had to separate himself from her, handing her to me.

"It's okay, sweetie pie, you'll be fine," I told her, pressing her face to mine. All the confusion and excitement aside, I heard my mother's voice.

Bannon dropped to the ground as the elephant threw back its ears and trumpeted again. I lowered Dru, holding her by the arms, and Bannon caught her. Then I crawled to the edge of the seat and let myself drop. Bannon caught me by the waist and eased me to the ground.

Dru clawed at his leg, and he lifted her into his arms. "We've got to get back to the main part of the zoo and the crowds," he said, wiping the tears from his daughter's face. "But I don't think we should walk back the way we came."

"Maybe we should avoid the paths altogether," I said, opening my purse. I took out my automatic. "And if there is another ambush, this time there'll be return fire."

Fortunately I had on shoes that were decent for walking. We struck off into the brush. I led, my gun at the ready, and Bannon followed, carrying his daughter. Dru had stopped crying, which was good—no point in advertising our presence.

I figured our assailant had fled, but the woods afforded a certain amount of cover, which meant it was possible our man would stick around for a while, looking for another opportunity to shoot me. I had to be the target. This time, though, I'd be ready for him.

Chapter
31

   *We chose an indirect route to mini-*mize the chances of another encounter with the bad guys and, by the time we reached civilization, there were police everywhere and the woods had been cordoned off.

Bannon said something in Thai to the first cop we encountered, and we were taken to the zoo security office. There we talked to more senior police officials. Bannon did most of the talking, and I held Dru on my lap. After a while an officer who spoke excellent English came into the office to question me.

"I'll take Dru out and get her a soft drink," Bannon said, lifting his daughter into his arms. "Back in a few minutes."

The officer asked me to tell him what happened. About the time I finished the story, another man entered the office. It was Suchitta, one of the senior police officials I'd talked to on Ko Samui, the burly, thick-haired guy.

"Hello, Miss Chandler," he said with a slight bow. "You have more trouble."

"There does seem to be a trend, doesn't there? First Joy, now this."

"Ah, yes, very sad. Much trouble."

"I don't suppose you know who has it in for me."

Suchitta motioned for me to sit, and he drew up a chair across from me. "No, but I hope you can say who, Miss Chandler."

"I don't know any more than when we last talked," I said, though that wasn't exactly true. Bannon had told me more, and I'd taken him into my confidence, but I wasn't about to share that with Suchitta.

"Well, Miss Chandler, they tell me you see before the man who tried to shoot you," he said, getting down to business.

"I think he was one of the two men who followed me last night. In fact, just before Joy was killed I told her about it. I was reporting in, as you asked."

"This is most appreciated, Miss Chandler."

"What happens now that Joy is dead?"

"We will find somebody else."

I saw an opportunity and decided to snatch it. "Couldn't it be Mr. Bannon? He's been in Thailand so long, surely you know him and trust him."

A funny look passed over Suchitta's face, then he said, "Perhaps."

"There's one other thing," I said. "I told Joy I was suspicious that a man named Santa Noonwongsa could be behind the attacks on me. She was concerned."

"Noonwongsa? This is not possible, Miss Chandler, because he has not been in the country for some days."

I didn't expect that. "Really? How long has he been gone from Thailand?"

"I think maybe two weeks."

Yet another surprise. And a rather upsetting one. If it was true, it meant that wasn't Noonwongsa at the cathedral. "So Mr. Bannon couldn't have met with this Mr. Noonwongsa here in Bangkok earlier this week?"

"He says this?"

"Yes," I replied.

"Excuse me, please, Miss Chandler. I must make inquiry."

Suchitta got up and walked out of the office, leaving me wondering what was going on. Had Bannon lied to me again? I hoped not because the bullet that had whizzed through my hair wasn't a joke.

Anxious, I got up and paced, deciding I might have a cup of tea after all. As I made my way to the table, I happened to glance out the window and saw Cole Bannon standing under a tree in front of the building. Dru was at his side, and she was holding a soft drink as she leaned against her daddy's leg. But that wasn't what grabbed my attention. It was the man with them—a lanky Caucasian guy with dark hair and a sharp angular face. He and Bannon were having a pretty intense conversation.

Moments later two men approached them. One was Suchitta, the other the officer who'd questioned me earlier. As they conversed, I saw Bannon shaking his head, looking upset. More conversation followed, then Suchitta headed back to the building.

Sipping the tea so as not to arouse suspicion, I returned to the chair where I'd been sitting. Moments later the police official entered.

"So sorry, Miss Chandler. I made inquiry and my officers tell me that Santa Noonwongsa has been in Bangkok many days. I was mistaken."

"I see. So, Mr. Bannon could have met with him, after all."

"Yes," he replied, "this is true." He steepled his fingers and continued, "Also, I have given thought to your question about Mr. Bannon. I have decided you can speak with him as you would to Joy."

"Then he's my new contact?"

"Yes. We know him well, as you say yourself."

"Hmm. Out of curiosity, when we spoke in Ko Samui, why did you ask me not to tell Mr. Bannon I was cooperating with you?"

"It was . . . how do you say? . . . a test. We wish to see if you can be trusted."

"It seems I passed the test."

"Yes, it is true."

I wondered at that. It was apparent to me that Bannon and I badly needed to talk. Much as I hated to say it, I'd been misled yet again. The question was, by whom? If I could take comfort in anything, though, it was that Bannon seemed to be in league with the cops, rather than the robbers.

After thanking me for my cooperation and expressing his regrets about my difficulties, Suchitta had me look over the statement which had been prepared, then asked me to sign it.

Bannon and Dru returned just as we were finishing. The cop left the room.

"I see your daddy found you a soda," I said to the little girl.

"One for you too," she said, handing me the bottle she held behind her back.

"Oh, how thoughtful," I said. "Was it your idea or your daddy's?"

"Daddy."

"My, what honesty," I said, glancing at Bannon.

He opened the bottle for me. I was thirsty and took a big sip.

"And we have some good news," he said. "Our friend, the elephant, was not seriously wounded. They told me he was more annoyed than actually injured."

"I imagine Dru was especially happy to hear that."

"Yes," Bannon said, stroking her head, "we're trying to minimize the trauma. Speaking of which, how would you like to come home with us for a family dinner? Just the three of us."

"You think I'm safe for your daughter to be around, Cole? One of those bullets could have hit her, you know."

"We're getting a police escort. And tomorrow I'll be sending Sumgi and the girls to the country for a week or so. I share your concern about Dru's safety."

"And all because somebody's mightily annoyed with me and wants to do me in."

"That's not the only reason I'm sending them away, Lexie. You and I'll be leaving town to go after that ruby in the next day or two anyway." He took my hand. "I'd really like you to join us this evening. Dru would love it. You're right up there with the tigers and the elephant, as far as she's concerned. That's almost as good as it gets."

It was not until we were driving through the streets of Bangkok, a police car leading the way with another following, that I learned about Bannon's housing accommodations. He had two places. The first was a condo in a modern high-rise off Ratchadamri Road, near Lumphini Park, which gave him easy access to the Central Business District. His other home was an old teak house in the suburb of Muang Thong Thani, which offered easy access to the airport and the high-tech industrial parks to the north. "Believe it or not, proximity to work is a factor. I really do conduct business from time to time," he told me with a laugh. "It's my practical side."

The man was more substantial than I thought. And maybe an accomplished businessman. In addition to his import-export business, he had the hotel on Ko Samui and two homes in Bangkok. That didn't seem the typical lifestyle of a con artist. So, why hadn't some things been ringing true? And why so much conflicting evidence?

I couldn't help wondering what his intentions were for the evening. Dru's presence meant there was need for a certain decorum, but she was a child and she would be going to bed. Perhaps I'd been kidding myself about the innocence of the situation. The goodwill he'd garnered when I'd clunked him on the head and when he'd received Joy's endorsement had limits.

Chapter
32

We arrived at his building, which wasn't luxurious, though it was quite nice. It had a wonderful view of the park and downtown from the terrace. And though it wasn't large—just two bedrooms, living area, kitchen and bath—it was well appointed with teak furniture, hardwood floors, and lots of Thai art and artifacts.

Bannon had a ton of books, which surprised me a little. I knew he was bright, but I didn't take him to be cerebral. Sides of him I hadn't seen kept popping up. There were a number of family photos on the book shelves as well—one of his mother, several of his wife, and lots of Dru. The women in his life seemed to be of major importance.

Dru ran off to the room she used when she was there. Bannon poured us each a glass of wine and went to work on dinner while I sat on a barstool to watch.

"I'm not a great cook," he said, "but I do a couple of Thai dishes. Unfortunately, you're going to see pretty much my entire repertoire the first night. God only knows what I'll do for an encore."

The man seemed to have little doubt there'd be other such occasions. I sipped my wine without comment.

"So, do you like to cook?" he asked.

"Not a lot, and I'm not very good at it."

"Hmm, you too, huh? That either means we're meant for each other or we're hopelessly mismatched."

"Cooking skills have little bearing on our ability to work with each other, Cole," I said. "But I was encouraged by the way we handled things today at the zoo."

"Which means . . ."

"Just that it augurs well. It'll take teamwork to land the Heart of Burma. I've been concerned about how workable our partnership is, as you know."

"I hope your doubts are behind you," he said.

"Well, the proof is in the pudding."

"The pressure is on, in other words," he said with a grin.

Bannon began chopping vegetables, and I continued to sip my wine as I admired him. I decided this was the time to press him, when his guard was down.

"Cole, who was that white guy you talked to outside the zoo security office?"

He stopped mid-chop. "White guy?"

"Yes, tall, thin, dark hair. You were standing under the tree in front of the building. I happened to look out the window and saw you."

"Oh, you mean Elliot Webster. He's an old friend."

There was something in Bannon's tone and manner that said it was the beginning of another lie. I had the same awful feeling as before. "So, he just happened by?"

He put down the knife and faced me, leaning against the counter. "Not exactly. Elliot works in the American Consulate."

"Doing what?"

Bannon looked uncomfortable. "Among other things he's

the liaison with the local police. I met him in connection with a fraud problem I had in a business deal."

"Why was he at the zoo?"

"He was in the police station when word came that some American tourists were involved in an assault, so he went with them in case he was needed."

"I see." I'd traveled abroad enough to know that consular officials did not monitor local police activities.

"What did you think when you saw him?" Bannon asked.

"Nothing in particular. I was just curious. It is odd, though, that he didn't speak to me. I'd been assaulted, too."

"I explained what was going on and that you were in good hands."

"That makes sense."

He returned to his chopping. My unsettled feeling grew worse. I didn't want more distrust and decided I needed to get to the bottom of things sooner rather than later.

"Cole, was that man at the cathedral that night really Santa Noonwongsa?"

He stopped chopping again. "Pardon me?"

"Commander Suchitta told me Noonwongsa's been out of the country."

"Yes, I know. He told me."

"So, what's the story?"

"The commander was mistaken about Noonwongsa being out of the country, and I told him so. He wasn't aware I'd seen Noonwongsa."

"You discussed it with him, then?"

"Yes, outside the security office at the zoo."

"And that's what that conversation was about?"

"Yes."

That rang true. "Did he tell you I'd be reporting to you now that Joy is dead?"

"It was my idea, actually."

"Then you're tighter with the police than you let on to me."

"I didn't make as much a point of it as I might have, that's true."

I drank more wine. "So, what part of the story haven't I heard, Cole?"

"What do you mean?"

"Bits and pieces keep coming out. It makes me wonder what I haven't heard."

"You have nothing to worry about."

"I notice you didn't answer the question."

"Daddy, Daddy!" Dru exclaimed as she came running into the kitchen with a stuffed elephant in her hand. "See!" She pointed to the elephant's behind where she'd put red marks with a crayon. "It's bleeding, but it doesn't hurt."

"Elephants are pretty tough, angel," Bannon said, giving me a wink.

"Me, too." She pointed to her leg where she marked her skin with the crayon.

"You're pretty brave, all right. Just like the elephant."

Dru nodded and smiled shyly at me.

"Where's the new book Lexie bought you?" he asked the girl. "Maybe she can read you some more while I fix our dinner."

"How come she doesn't cook, like Sumgi?"

That made Bannon chuckle. "How would you like to handle that one, Lexie?"

"Yeah, it seems your daughter needs her consciousness raised a little. They can't get their education on being a modern woman too young."

"And who's better qualified to instruct her?"

"Which is why I'm here, right?"

"Not entirely," he replied.

"No, Cole, that *is* the reason. You wanted her to know an

American woman, so here I am." I took Dru's hand. "Come on, sweetie, it's time for some girl talk."

"What does that mean?"

"It means there are some things boys don't need to hear."

"A secret?"

"More like the cold, hard truth, Dru."

As we headed for the front room, Bannon called, "Let me fill your glass."

"No thanks. The last time I drank too much around you, I got myself in trouble."

"Trouble's a relative term."

"We'll go with my definition."

Chapter
33

The three of us ate by candlelight out
on the balcony in the balmy evening air. The meal was tasty.
I told Bannon he could open a restaurant, and he said, "The
menu would be limited. I'm a one-note Johnny."

Putting my chopsticks down, I leaned back in my chair,
relaxed for the first time that day. The mood was pleasant.
Dru's presence made the atmosphere seem familial. The kid
tweaked my maternal instincts, probably because I wasn't
around children much.

The important thing was that Dru weathered the trauma
with no adverse effects we were aware of, though it remained to be seen how she'd handle being alone in her dark
room. That's when the goblins tended to arrive.

But if Dru was unaffected, I wasn't sure I could say the
same. I caught myself brushing my neck where that bullet
had whizzed through my hair. It was the first time I'd been
shot at in the line of duty. Granddad had had a few armed encounters, which he claimed came with the territory. "Everything has its price," he'd say, "and the bigger the prize, the
greater the danger."

If things had changed, it was because in Granddad's day a good deal of the world was untouched by modernization. Nowadays you could go into the deepest jungles and find satellite phones in the hands of the bad guys. It was a whole different ball game.

For dessert, Bannon served coconut ice cream, always a favorite of mine. Afterward, Dru slumped in her chair with a big yawn.

"I think the Sandman has signaled it's time for bed," Bannon said.

"I don't want to," Dru protested, though her heart wasn't in it.

"Maybe this is a good time for me to go, as well," I said.

"You can't leave, Lexie," Bannon protested. "At least stay until Dru's in bed and we can have an after-dinner drink."

I'd let him talk me into more wine during dinner and, as a result, I felt pleasantly high—not a good thing in the presence of a man as seductive as Cole Bannon. And while it was true he was still the man who'd been cavorting in the company of a couple of prostitutes when I'd met him, he was also a widower and Dru's daddy. He'd gotten Joy's endorsement as well, making it harder for me to be critical of him.

"One drink," I said, "then I really am leaving."

Bannon had a not-if-I-can-help-it look on his face, but said nothing. He took his daughter off for a quick bath and to get ready for bed. I stayed out on the balcony where I stood at the railing, staring at the lights and marveling at the events of recent days. The Heart of Burma had turned into a far bigger challenge than I'd anticipated. And I hadn't yet set foot into the jungle!

There'd been plenty of danger and lots to be concerned about, but what made the trip unique and exciting was Cole Bannon. I'd never known a man who was seductive and confounding at the same time.

As I stood there, the sounds and smells of the Orient rising from the streets below, I couldn't help wondering if the life I was leading was enough. In a few minutes, I'd be joined by a sexy man who'd gladly take me to bed, if I let him. But to what end? For the pleasure? Was that what I wanted? Was it enough?

In the past the occasional fling seemed to fulfill my needs. And yes, I recognized that one's love life could be more than friendship, affection, and a little sex when the need became overwhelming. I'd made a conscious decision to sacrifice certain things for other advantages and, until now, I'd been content. So, why was I suddenly questioning everything? Was it my milestone birthday? Was it Bannon? Dru? The emotional vacuum I'd been living in? Or, was it a combination of things?

I wondered if I needed to go to bed with the guy if only to get it behind me. I've had women friends tell me they'd get so obsessed with the should-we-or-shouldn't-we dilemma that they couldn't function, and the relationship didn't evolve. Was that where Bannon and I were headed, or was I rationalizing?

The trouble with a sexual relationship was that while reducing tension, it added complications. To know what was right, a woman had to be in touch with her feelings and her needs, but she also had to be smart, especially if she was engaged in serious business. And I was engaged in serious business.

"I've always liked this view," Bannon said from behind me, "but I must say it's much improved with you in it."

I turned to face him, leaning my elbows on the rail. "Is that your standard line?"

"No, I've been saving it for the right occasion and the right woman."

"Those are pretty strong words, Mr. Bannon."

"And pretty strongly felt."

I gave him a wary smile.

"You look skeptical."

"I know men, Cole."

He came to the railing and stood beside me, staring out at the tropical night. "No doubt, but you don't know me."

"Truer words were never spoken."

"What I'm saying is that you don't give me enough credit for the genuine respect and feelings I have for you."

"You just want to get me to bed."

"You think that's my objective?"

"Yeah," I said, feeling brazen, "I do."

"I won't deny I feel that sort of attraction, but I have certain misgivings, too."

"What sort of misgivings?"

"I don't want to create problems for you. I know how you feel about your work, and the Heart of Burma, and I'm trying to respect that."

Naturally he was saying all the right things. Could I reasonably expect less from the guy? He knew how to seduce a woman. Hell, a warning to that effect might as well be tattooed on his forehead. And yet I was tempted to accommodate him. I'd halfway decided to have a fling with him, though not until after the operation. Would it be that big a deal if it happened sooner? Bannon was a big boy. He'd be able to handle me telling him, "Okay, we've scratched the itch, now let's get back to business."

"You've got me curious what's going through that pretty head of yours," he said.

"Some thoughts are meant to stay private."

"I thought so."

"What?"

"You're torn," he said. "But that's okay, so am I."

"What are you torn about?"

"Believe it or not, the same thing you are."

I drew a breath. "I'll say goodnight to Dru. Then I'm going."

"But not until after our nightcap."

I gave him a look and started to move past him, but he took my arm, stopping me. "I want you to stay with me."

"I thought you were torn."

"The devil is getting the upper hand."

"No surprise there."

Again, I tried to go, but he wouldn't let me. He kissed me instead. Tenderly.

After the kiss I said, "I want to see Dru."

"She'll be asleep," he said, letting me go.

Bannon knew his daughter. She lay in bed, her eyes closed, out like a lamp. I went over and kissed her head, thanking the Lord that she'd escaped the day unscathed. If she'd been hurt because of me, I wouldn't have been able to bear it.

I returned to where Bannon waited at the doorway. We looked back at the child.

"Ever yearn for one of your own?" he asked.

"It's not in the cards," I replied. "At least not for the time being."

He leaned on the doorframe behind me, his arm next to my head, his face near mine. "What's the guy who finally snags you going to have to do?" he asked.

"I don't know," I said with a shrug. "Be the right person, I guess."

Bannon's face moved toward mine. "He'll be one hell of a guy, that's for sure."

His lips were just inches from mine.

"True."

I knew I should duck under his arm and escape, but I didn't move until his lips met mine and we kissed again.

"The guy will be a lucky bastard," he murmured. "He'd better appreciate you."

Bannon ran his fingertips down the side of my neck. My heart began to race.

"I'm not the jealous type," he said, "but I envy him."

"There's nobody to envy," I said, playing with the buttons on his shirt.

"Somebody will claim you. It's a matter of time."

"You make it sound like a raffle and I'm the prize."

"You're the prize all right, Lexie." His lips grazed my ear. "More wine?"

I took a deep breath. "Is that a euphemism for sex?"

"Is that what you want?"

I considered that for a long while. "Will it make tomorrow easier or harder?"

"I don't know about you, but I'll like tomorrow much better," he replied.

"It's always nice to score."

He ran the back of his fingers across my cheek. "That's not why."

I shuddered under his touch, suddenly wanting him, wanting to be with him. "Why will you feel better?"

"Because I've thought of this since I first saw you. Because it feels right. Because it *is* right."

I gave him a gentle nudge out the door and closed it behind me. Then I went into his bedroom and undressed in the faint light coming from the front room. Bannon watched me, his arms folded over his chest as he stood at the door.

"Is it like being with one of the girls at the spa?" I asked.

"Not at all."

"How's it different? Other than I'm using you as much as you're using me."

"Don't say that," he said.

"Why?"

He moved toward me and I tensed, though I wasn't so much afraid of him as of the situation. This was about sex, yes, but it was also about me. Bannon was about to find out who I was, and so was I.

Chapter
34

He took my face and looked into my
eyes. "You're a crazy-maker, Alex Chandler, you know that,
don't you?"

"I don't mean any harm," I said.

"I know that, but you're a crazy-maker just the same."

Bannon kissed me deeply. I got excited, especially when
he cupped my buttocks and pulled me hard against him. I
didn't want to think about what was happening, I just wanted
it to happen.

"I'm going to have to get out of these clothes if this is going anywhere," he muttered as I kissed his mouth.

"Well, do it quickly," I said, reaching down and pressing
my hand against the bulge in his pants.

Bannon kissed the end of my nose. "Get in bed."

I did and moments later he was there beside me, naked,
caressing my breasts, gliding his hand between my legs. I
needed this even more than I realized. I needed to be a
woman.

I took him in my hand. He was hard, and I was already
wet. "Take me," I said.

Bannon moved between my legs, entering me. My heart pounded so hard it hurt. I arched, taking him deeper. We kissed, biting at each other's lips.

Our bodies merged seamlessly, our being the focus of everything—his pleasure and mine. I didn't want the feeling to end, yet at the same time, I knew I was rushing toward an end I both wanted and dreaded.

My excitement surged one last time, then I came, crying out. Bannon shuddered, then collapsed on me. For a few moments, he was mine. I felt more the conqueror than the conquered. After he recovered a bit, he kissed my neck. "Jesus, Lexie."

"We really got it on," I said.

"Tell me about it."

Then it happened—the little voice from the door. "Daddy, why is Lexie crying?"

Once I was dressed, I went to Dru's room where I found Bannon sitting on the edge of the bed, reading to her from the book I'd bought.

"Lexie!" she exclaimed.

"Hi, sweetie pie," I said. "I have to go home, so I came to kiss you good-bye."

"Don't go," she protested. "Read with us."

"I can't, honey. Next time I will, though."

I gave her a kiss, then brushing Bannon's shoulder with my fingers, I said, "Thanks for the nice evening."

"It shouldn't end this way," he said.

"Actually, it should. Did you call me a taxi?"

"Yes."

"See you in the morning, then."

"Let me walk you down."

"No, stay with Dru. I'm fine. Really."

Bannon insisted on going downstairs with me, saying Dru

would be fine for a few minutes. All the way down in the elevator he held me, kissing my forehead and lifting my chin so he could kiss my lips.

"I'm glad Dru is as young as she is," I said as we stepped into the empty lobby.

"Most families in this country live in one or two rooms. Sex is part of life."

"Yes, but I'm not her mother."

"But she's really fond of you, Lexie."

I looked up at him. "Don't make too much of this," I said.

He touched my chin with his finger. "Do you regret the fact that we made love, or are you preparing me for the future?"

"My, you believe in getting right to the nitty gritty, don't you?"

"To me, tonight wasn't about getting laid."

I didn't say anything.

"Was that all it was to you?"

"Cole, I really do believe we're better off keeping things professional, at least for the time being. And I know, that sounds hypocritical considering what just happened, but making love with you tonight was necessary, just as not making love with you from now on is necessary, too."

He shook his head. "If I said something like that to a woman she'd call me a cad."

"I understand why you might be upset. But I figured you could take it."

He playfully tapped my jaw with his fist. "I can hardly complain, I guess."

"Think of me as one of the girls at the spa. I can be your favorite girl, if you like, but that's the way to regard this."

"Does it make you feel safer?"

"Yeah, actually it does."

I said good night and went out to the taxi and the waiting police escort.

* * *

I awoke the next morning determined to give my full attention to the Heart of Burma. If all went well with Chung Lee, we'd be launching the operation at long last. As far as I was concerned, it couldn't be soon enough.

In his last letter to me before he was killed in the Gulf, my brother, Gray, said that far and away the worst part of war was sitting around waiting for it to begin. As it turned out, he was wrong, but I could understand his anxiety during those long hours before the attack began. Action did bring a feeling of relief, even if it meant going into danger and facing the possibility of death.

The plan was that Bannon and I would meet Chung Lee at the docks near his office where we'd board Chung's boat and cruise the Chao Phraya while we conferred. Chung had left word that a car would be outside the hotel at nine to transport me to the rendezvous point. During dinner last night Bannon and I had discussed arrangements, and he'd told me that we'd likely leave directly for the airport from our meeting and that I should be packed and ready to roll when I left the hotel.

I was glad to see he'd put the welfare of his child first, having made arrangements to send her away with her aunt and cousin. If my mother had seen him with Dru, it would have melted her heart. I could almost hear her—"See, sugar, didn't I tell you? That young man's a keeper."

Well, I was a long, long way from anything like that, but I had to admit yesterday was an eye-opener. Now, if the man could only refrain from letting me down.

Chapter
35

I left the Oriental dressed in beige cotton pants, a white T-shirt and low boots. I had on my aviator-style sunglasses but looked a step less macho than I had the day I'd first met Chung and Bannon wearing my jungle fatigues. I was a little older and wiser now, and I'd used up a couple of my lives, but despite the intervening distractions, the Heart of Burma remained my top priority.

Chung Lee had not only sent a car and driver, but a security man to ride shotgun, plus another vehicle with three more security people. It made me wonder if I had underestimated the depth of the danger I was in.

"You seem to be expecting a coup d'etat," I said to the man who greeted me. He was about my age, his steely countenance masked by dark glasses.

"We can't be too careful, Miss Chandler."

He was undoubtedly right.

We took a circuitous route along secondary streets to Chinatown, arriving at the dock located opposite Chung Lee's warehouse. The excitement and the intrigue appealed to me. Maybe I was addicted.

But it wasn't just the ruby and the adventure. I was excited because I would be seeing Bannon. This was the morning after. One of two things would follow—either we'd advance or we'd retreat. Rarely did things remain as they were before, which was what I actually wanted. But the decision wasn't mine alone. I'd have to wait and see how Bannon reacted before I could be sure how things would go.

Chung's "pleasure boat," as he called it, was easily as old as he was, an ancient sixty-foot wooden yacht designed for plying the tranquil waters of the river. The old man stood on the deck smoking when our entourage arrived at the dock. A young man stood at his side. Other security men were on the dock, looking as steely as my escort. I did not see Cole Bannon.

One of the men took my bag and followed me up the gangplank to the polished deck of the boat. I gave Chung a *wai*, which he returned.

"Miss Chandler, so good to see you alive and well," he said, managing a smile.

"I've been fortunate."

Chung took a drag. "So they tell me. I'm very sorry for your troubles."

"I hope my ordeals of the past few days haven't been in vain."

"No, be assured I have good news, if that's your concern."

I was relieved. Still, with so much up in the air and the specifics murky, there was a chance of the deal going sour. Chung hadn't indicated where things stood when he'd gone to negotiate final details with Mr. X, but I figured nothing could be taken for granted. Be that as it may, my sense was that the burden was about to shift from Chung's shoulders to mine. That's what I wanted.

Glancing around I said, "I gather Mr. Bannon hasn't yet arrived."

"No, but I expect him at any time," Chung replied, the slits of his eyes even narrower in the bright morning sun.

I was disappointed, but at the same time relieved.

"Perhaps you'd like a coffee while we wait," Chung said.

"That would be nice, thank you."

Chung took a final drag on his cigarette and flipped the butt into the water. Then he led the way to the rear deck where a table and three chairs were set up under a canopy. It was still early enough that the air was quite pleasant. One of Chung's retainers held a chair for me, and the old man and I sat down.

"You have a lovely boat," I told him. "Have you had it long?"

"For many years, Miss Chandler. I have many pleasant memories. Beautiful ladies and lovely old boats go well together, don't you think?"

I smiled, though my thoughts were on the empty chair as much as my host.

"Have you had breakfast?" Chung asked. "I can have them bring some cakes."

I'd run late that morning and never did get around to ordering breakfast. "I would like something to eat," I replied, "thank you."

Chung gave the signal to a steward, who stood by.

"So, the unpleasantness of the past few days hasn't dampened your desire for the ruby," Chung said.

Noticing a smudge on my sunglasses, I took them off and cleaned them on my shirt. "No, I'm eager to get started."

"Your courage is most admirable, Miss Chandler. There are many men who would already have been on the first plane home."

"Some men have courage, others don't. The same is true of women. Your niece, Joy, for example, was strong and courageous. I'm very sorry for your loss."

"Thank you. Her death was most tragic. Very sad indeed."

I put my sunglasses back on, wondering if he knew about Joy's complicity with the police, but saw nothing to be gained by asking. It no longer mattered, except perhaps as an indication of how informed Chung himself was. But if he was unaware, the news would be unsettling and add to his grief.

"I'm distressed to think she died because of me," I said.

"Please don't believe this," he replied. "She lived a dangerous life and accepted the consequences. She earned the respect of everyone many times over."

The coffee and some small cakes were served by the steward. I added some cream to my coffee and took a sip. I popped a cake into my mouth, as well. Chung sat stoically watching me.

"So, who do you think is responsible for all the mischief?" I asked.

"The common wisdom is Noonwongsa, as you know. My sources confirm this."

"Do you expect he'll be arrested?"

"If he returns to Thailand, perhaps."

"He's fled the country?"

"He's been gone for many days."

I blinked. "*Many* days?"

"More than a week," Chung replied. "He had a strong interest in the ruby, and was vexed when I chose not to do business with him. I can only surmise he found out about our relationship and tried to eliminate the competition."

"You're saying he directed the attempts on my life from afar and hasn't actually been here in Bangkok?"

"That's correct. My sources tell me he's been in Cambodia for a week at least, I think to insulate himself from the events of recent days. Noonwongsa is ambitious and bloodthirsty, but not as bright as he needs to be for this business.

However, he does have connections with certain criminal elements, and that makes him dangerous. This is why I would have nothing to do with him."

I was speechless and took another sip of coffee. "I assume Mr. Bannon wouldn't want anything to do with Noonwongsa either," I said innocently.

"I'm sure not," Chung replied.

"Then I wonder why he told me he'd been in contact with Noonwongsa."

"Mr. Bannon has been talking to Noonwongsa?"

"He told me he had a brief conversation with him a few days ago. It was here in Bangkok, in the street. At the time, Bannon dismissed it as incidental, saying Noonwongsa was pestering him because of his interest in the ruby."

"You must have misunderstood, Miss Chandler, because I'm quite sure Santa Noonwongsa has been out of the country. Mr. Bannon couldn't have met with him here. Not in the last ten days."

It was another blow, and it sent a jolt through me. *Not again*!

"Perhaps it was a miscommunication," Chung said, reflecting. He picked up his cup and took a sip.

I had another cake, but my mind was spinning. It was no miscommunication. His story about the man at the cathedral being Noonwongsa was utter bullshit. I was inclined to believe Chung because Suchitta had said virtually the same thing—that Noonwongsa was out of the country when the encounter at the cathedral took place. True, the police official had changed his story later, but now I assumed Bannon had prompted him to do so.

It was a good thing I'd arrived before Bannon and was able to get the truth from Chung. That was the good news. The bad news was I had to contend with Bannon's deceit yet again. Why couldn't I have found this out before I'd gone to bed with him?

Chapter 36

I leaned back in my chair as I considered what I'd heard. Bannon had worked his way back into my good graces largely because Joy had told me he could be trusted. I couldn't imagine that she would lie with her dying breath, which meant that Bannon had duped her too. The sad part was I might never know. But I was certain of one thing—I wouldn't go off into the jungle with a man I couldn't trust.

"You seem distressed, Miss Chandler," Chung observed.

"I am distressed, Mr. Chung."

"Why?"

The time had come to lay my cards on the table. If I had to pick someone to confide in, it would be Chung. He alone could give me access to Mr. X and the stone.

"May I speak frankly?"

"Certainly."

"I don't think Cole Bannon can be trusted."

Chung could not hide his surprise. "Why do you say that?"

"He's lied so often I doubt he himself knows the truth. Several times I've caught him, but he managed to wiggle out of it. Not anymore. Earlier I mentioned Bannon claimed to have talked to Noonwongsa in Bangkok only days ago. I in fact saw Bannon talking to someone suspicious in the street. When I questioned him about it, he at first denied the encounter, then he gave me two different accounts of who it was. The last name he gave me was Santa Noonwongsa, which we know is a lie. The police also told me Noonwongsa was out of the country, but changed their story after talking to Bannon."

"Hmm," Chung said, stroking his chin, "this is a complication."

"It's far worse than that, Mr. Chung."

"Are you suggesting Mr. Bannon has ulterior motives?"

"I don't know what he's up to unless he's simply looking for advantage any way he can get it. He'll say and do anything it takes, including using his own child."

"I heard about the incident at the zoo," Chung said, "but surely you aren't suggesting Mr. Bannon is in complicity with Noonwongsa."

"No, I don't think he would risk his child's life, but we'd be foolish to trust him."

Chung had a ponderous expression on his face. His hands folded on his lap, he sat like a statue. "You put me on the horns of a dilemma," he said after several moments.

"I'm sorry. It's not what I intended, but the one thing I do know is that I can't work with Cole Bannon after what I've been through with him. I hate to do this to you, but you're going to have to choose between us."

"You're certain his transgressions are that serious, Miss Chandler?"

I could see the deal crumbling before my eyes, and, since

I'd likely be on the first plane out of Bangkok anyway, I didn't have a lot to lose. At a minimum, I'd be able to walk away feeling good about myself.

"Bannon deceived Joy, and I know for a fact he's a police informant. They pressured me into being an informant as well, I'm sure at Bannon's suggestion."

"To what end?"

"I gathered their objective is your friend, Mr. X. I was supposed to keep all this secret, but things have become so bizarre, I can't continue the charade. The only way to hold the deal together that I can see is to get rid of Bannon. Otherwise, we may as well shake hands and say good-bye."

Chung studied me. "You are indeed a very courageous woman, Miss Chandler, and you have earned my respect."

"This is the only way I know to do business."

"Your candor has earned candor in return. It's time you know the whole story."

I was surprised by the remark and even more by Chung's ominous tone. I took a big sip of coffee. "It would be a pleasant change of pace to get the truth, that's for sure."

Chung smiled. "You have good reason to be suspicious of Mr. Bannon because he has not been truthful with you, as you allege."

I nodded, though it hurt having my suspicions confirmed. I would have much preferred that the man I'd been with last night was the real Cole Bannon.

"So, what's his angle, Mr. Chung?" My tone was as even and unemotional as I could make it, but the fact was my gut was in a knot and I felt sick. Had I been alone I might have cried.

"In fairness," my host continued, "I haven't been fully honest with you either."

I blinked.

"Let me start at the beginning," Chung said. "But I must

ask that everything I tell you be held in the strictest of confidence. Do I have your word?"

"Yes, certainly."

"Mr. X is in fact the legendary warlord, Colonel Than Lwin. Perhaps you've heard of him. In the press he's often referred to by his nickname, the 'Burmese Tiger.' "

"Isn't he the one involved in the opium trade?"

"Yes, opium was the basis of his power. He rules the Golden Triangle. But with the government crackdown, the drug trade has been stymied, which created problems for Lwin. But that's not all. He's been at war with the Myanmar government for many years, which means he has supporters among those opposed to the regime in Rangoon. He's a scoundrel, but he has sympathizers around the world. I am fortunate to have his confidence. As a result, many people who want to do business with him come to see me first."

I had a hunch what was coming. "And that's how you and Bannon got together."

"Yes, in fact, it was Mr. Bannon who came to me, not the other way around."

"What's his game?"

"Simply stated, Mr. Bannon is an arms dealer and he wants Lwin's business."

"You're kidding."

"I'm afraid not."

The image of Bannon and me together in the throes of passionate love came to mind, and I quailed. I hated to think I'd gone to bed with a gunrunner, a merchant of death. Things were getting worse by the minute. I cleared my throat. "Then he's a phony businessman, as well as a liar."

"Not exactly. He's in the import-export business. That part is true. He keeps his arms trade activities well disguised. I was unaware of his clandestine operation myself until recently. The point is Colonel Lwin needs arms to continue his resistance against the Myanmar regime. With less cash available because of the fall-off in the drug trade, Lwin decided to use one of his most valuable assets to barter arms."

"The Heart of Burma."

"Precisely, Miss Chandler. The colonel needs arms, and he asked me to handle the sale of the ruby. Rumors of this began circulating, and Mr. Bannon came to me, eager to make the trade. There was one thing missing that prevented us from progressing."

"A reputable gemologist and gem trader."

"Right again. Finding the right person was my job. Mr. Bannon felt that whoever I chose should be kept in the dark about the details and that his or her exclusive function would be to deal with the stone. He felt it was important that his own role be made to seem secondary. He felt he would be more effective if he took a low profile."

His low profile wasn't so low that it excluded seducing me, I thought. The man was a cynical opportunist on top of everything else. I hated him!

"As I indicated at our first meeting," Chung continued, "Mr. Bannon has special knowledge and expertise to offer over and above being able to provide Lwin with the arms he desires. You see, everything must be done inside Myanmar in a region of the country controlled by Lwin. It will mean secretly crossing into Myanmar territory and doing business surreptitiously under tense and difficult circumstances. Needless to say, it's a dangerous undertaking. Mr. Bannon has deceived you, but he did so only because he couldn't risk telling you the truth."

"For good reason," I said.

"Yes, and I understand your unhappiness. But if I may, Miss Chandler, I believe I was right when I said you and Mr. Bannon would make an excellent team."

That mental image of our lovemaking again came to mind, and I could only hope I wasn't as red-faced as I felt. The irony was excruciating.

I took a calming breath. "The danger doesn't bother me so much as the legality."

"Minor customs and security violations are involved, it's true. But the transfer of the ruby is perfectly legal in Thailand. Granted, in Myanmar it's a different matter, but everything is done under the table there. The plan we concocted was designed to keep you isolated and . . . well, in the dark. For your own protection as much as anything else."

"You kept me in the dark, all right."

Chung lowered his eyes. "You have my apologies, Miss Chandler. But that's in the past. Circumstances have changed. What has not changed is that you and I can still do exactly what I proposed from the beginning—sell the gem and take our profit."

"But not without Bannon's involvement. He's the necessary evil in the equation."

"Unfortunately."

"The point is I'm in bed . . . figuratively speaking . . . with a conscienceless pirate."

Chung gave a helpless shrug.

"Frankly, I don't like the idea of doing business with Lwin," I said. "How many lives has he ruined? How many people have died at his hands?"

"He's a man of war, there's no denying that. But you should understand that, Miss Chandler. You come from a military family, do you not?"

"Yes, but the military I know doesn't tyrannize people. And by doing business with Lwin, we're going to enable him to keep going."

"A buyer never has control over what a seller does with the proceeds of a sale, Miss Chandler. Nor is it our responsibility. Colonel Lwin has a wonderful gem, and he wishes to barter it for arms. The world bought diamonds from South Africa when it was under the yoke of apartheid, did it not? This is no different."

I pondered that for a while, wondering what Granddad would say about my deal. Sometimes the gem trade brought you into contact with some pretty unsavory characters. I knew that. I'd done deals with men I would not want within a mile of any child's school. And Chung did have a point about having neither control nor responsibility for what a seller did with his money. But Lwin didn't concern me as much as Bannon.

"I'm curious why you've told me this," I said. "It surely wouldn't please Bannon to know you've confided in me."

"You're quite right," he replied. "I told you because you were about to walk away. Colonel Lwin gave me a very narrow time frame to do this deal and, to be frank, I can't easily replace you at this late hour. Besides, we're not the only ones who want the ruby. Noonwongsa is pursuing it. Lwin told me that Noonwongsa contacted him from Phnom Penh asking to bid on the stone. Lwin said we were first in line and that he wanted our negotiation to run its course before he talked to anyone else."

"Bargaining tactics," I said.

"Of course."

"But it also explains why it would be convenient for Noonwongsa if I were dead."

"And why it would be convenient for us, if you were not," Chung rejoined.

"Which is why Bannon is so protective. If they get me, he's out in the cold."

"Yes, there is a great deal at stake for everyone."

I shook my head, amazed that I'd gotten myself into such a mess, especially with the likes of Cole Bannon. All along the guy had played me for a fool, manipulating me any way he could to keep me on board, so he could do his dirty deal. I wondered if the sex had been as false as everything else. Oh, he was happy enough to get his rocks off, and the fact that I was naive may have added to his enjoyment, but I had little doubt that when push came to shove, I was no different than one of the girls at the Nakhon Spa.

I wanted to wring his neck with my bare hands—shooting him would be too good. Then a thought occurred to me.

"There's one thing I don't understand, Mr. Chung. If Bannon is running guns, how is it that he's so thick with the police? They can't approve of his activities."

"I can only surmise that it's because he's careful to make sure his customers are not in Thailand and that no toes are stepped on locally. This is the base of his operations, and he runs a reputable import-export business here. That's clearly by design. Additionally, this is a Third World country, where influence and indulgence are for sale."

"You're saying he has the police on his payroll."

"It's conjecture, but the sympathy of a few key officials is all he'd need."

That made sense. Suchitta and Haing came to mind. Bannon had them in his pocket. He wasn't their informant, he owned them. That business in Ko Samui and at the zoo was a sham. The assault may have been real, but the way the police handled the matter was directed by Bannon—the police escort to his condominium, the show of concern, it was all to protect his interests.

But how was it Joy hadn't seen through him? She'd known him far longer than I. Was he that slick, that heartless, that cruel?

I was so disgusted that I wanted to head straight for the airport. I couldn't get out of Thailand fast enough. "What a shame it's come to this," I said, shaking my head.

"It's unfortunate the way things have played out," Chung concurred. "But it needn't end this way."

"After what you've told me?"

"Think about it, Miss Chandler. What's changed? Colonel Lwin has the Heart of Burma, and he wants to sell it. You and I can find a buyer and make a handsome profit. All you have to do is get the stone. I've already arranged with Colonel Lwin to get you into Myanmar and safely to his camp. He will receive you because I've vouched for your reputability. All that remains is for you to examine the gem and negotiate a price."

"What about Bannon?"

"He will provide the arms Colonel Lwin wants, but what affair is that of ours? I will tell you frankly that the arms will be consigned to me and delivered to an overseas location, then transported to Lwin. None of that is your concern. Once you have negotiated the price and have the gem in hand, our funds will be placed in escrow so Mr. Bannon can pay his suppliers. While you're reselling the stone in the open market, Mr. Bannon and I will arrange for the delivery of the arms. If there is blood on anyone's hands, it won't be on yours, Miss Chandler. The point is, you need not be concerned about Mr. Bannon. Leave him to me."

That was easy for Chung Lee to say, but I was the one who'd have to slog through the jungle with him. I'd have to look him in the eye and recall how I'd been used.

"If it helps, think of it this way—Bannon used us and now we can use him."

I hadn't thought in those terms, but the notion of using Bannon had appeal. As long as I was able to acquire the Heart of Burma, I'd be content. Success was all the revenge I needed. Once the stone was in my hands, I could tell Bannon to go to hell.

"You like the idea?" Chung asked, sounding hopeful.

"A lot."

"Excellent. But a note of caution, if I may. It seems to me this would work best if we leave Mr. Bannon with his illusions."

"You're saying . . ."

"I'm saying there's nothing to be gained by making him aware you know the whole story. Things will go more smoothly if he's under the impression you believe he'll be bartering foodstuffs, electronic equipment, and heavy machinery. There is power in knowledge, Miss Chandler. The more you know and the less he's aware of it, the better for everyone, especially you and me."

"You have a devious mind, Mr. Chung."

"No, I'm being practical. Why let Mr. Bannon's concerns get in our way?"

Maybe I'd been seduced by the devil, but damn if Chung Lee wasn't making sense. It wouldn't hurt to turn the tables on Cole Bannon, and, what's more, turning the tables on him would feel pretty damn good. "Okay, I'm convinced," I said. "Let's do it."

Chapter
37

For the first time since my arrival,
I felt in control. Chung Lee and I had been candid with each other, and we'd established trust. My preference would have been not to have to deal with Cole Bannon, but there were benefits to the plan Chung and I had worked out, not the least of which was the opportunity to give good old Cole the comeuppance he deserved. It would be profitable, perhaps even fun.

My host and I had finished our coffee, but there was still no sign of Bannon. Chung began consulting his watch with regularity. I felt a spark of concern myself. Bannon was as much a target as I, and Noonwongsa could upset our apple-cart by eliminating either of us. A painful death was too good for Cole Bannon, but the truth was I didn't actually want to see him hurt. I was pissed, but not heartless.

As I squirmed in my chair, wishing Bannon would show up so I could stop worrying, one of Chung's aides approached with a cell phone. I didn't understand what was said, but Chung was courteous enough to tell me the call was from Bannon. I was relieved, if only because I could start hating him again.

"Ah, Mr. Bannon," Chung said, "I take it you've been delayed." He listened for a few moments then said, "I see. Well, let me have my captain speak to you and together you can make arrangements." He handed the phone to his aide, uttered instructions, and sent him on his way. To me he said, "It seems Mr. Bannon is having difficulties with the travel arrangements for his family. Since he's upriver, we agreed to meet at a more convenient location to save time. We'll be shoving off shortly. Meanwhile, is there anything you need? Anything that would make you more comfortable?"

"No, thank you, I'm fine. It's a lovely morning, I'll just enjoy the voyage."

"Please make yourself at home," Chung said. "But if you'll excuse me, I have business inside to take care of."

Chung left and I glanced around, noticing preparations were being made for our departure. I went over to the railing to watch. As I stood there, the boat's engine came to life, the lines were cast off. Moments later we were under way.

The big pleasure boat moved against the current, slowly at first, but gradually gaining speed. I watched the Chinatown waterfront slip by, realizing this was my chance to work out a plan for dealing with Bannon.

The easiest thing would be to act as though nothing had happened, but it would be a test of my acting skills to keep Bannon happy and his suspicions at bay without going to bed with him again. The Heart of Burma was important to me, but using sex to get it made me no better than the girls at the Nakhon Spa. Just more expensive.

After a while I moved to the bow of the boat for a better view. Though the river was busy with lots of boat traffic, the overall mood was relaxed. I suppose the tropical sun and rising temperature had something to do with that. But it was still pleasant, and, had I not been engaged in the quest of a lifetime, I might have enjoyed it even more.

Though the biggest challenges lay ahead, it helped to know the score. From here on I'd know what was behind everything Bannon told me, from the smallest fib to the greatest lie. Chung was right. Knowledge gave me power.

As we approached the Memorial Bridge, the security man who'd met me at the hotel approached. "Please, Miss Chandler," he said, "there are many boats on the water. I think it's better if you come inside."

Did he think that I might be shot by a gunman on the bridge or a passing motorboat? On reflection, the notion wasn't outlandish. Now that I knew Noonwongsa's game, I realized anything was possible.

I decided to join the captain in the wheelhouse. He was a cherubic little man with apple cheeks and an authoritative demeanor. He wore a white uniform and white shoes.

"Welcome, Miss Chandler," he said, rising on his toes.

"Thank you."

"Much safer here," he said, beaming. "Beside, you see much better."

"Is it far to where we meet Mr. Bannon?"

"Not so far. Maybe one kilometer. You can see." He pointed to the shoreline ahead, then reached over and took a pair of binoculars that were hanging on a hook and handed them to me. "You know famous temple, Wat Arun, there? We find Mr. Bannon at ferry dock nearby."

I peered through the glasses at the famous *wat* with its remarkable central *prang* or tower that rose a couple hundred feet into the sky. Situated on the riverbank, it was one of the city's more famous landmarks. I'd been to the temple with Granddad on my first visit to Thailand and recalled the colorful porcelain decoration and the incredible sculpture and detail work.

After briefly scanning the elegant and airy profile of the temple, I turned my attention to the riverfront. Sure enough, I was able to spot Cole Bannon on the dock. But he was not alone. Next to him was Elliot Webster, the consular official I'd seen him speaking to at the zoo. What would Webster be doing there? I wondered. Investigating more tourist problems?

Then it occurred to me Webster was likely involved in the arms trade himself. But I wouldn't bother asking Bannon about it because he'd come up with some cockamamie explanation. From now on I'd act as though I was taking everything he said at face value—at least until I had the Heart of Burma in my hand. Then all bets would be off.

Five minutes later we came up to the dock where Bannon waited, now alone. He was beaming as though he couldn't wait to see me. I'd gone down to the main deck to greet him, waiting as they shoved out the boarding ladder so he could embark.

Webster was nowhere to be seen. No need to arouse suspicion, eh, Mr. Bannon?

He looked handsome in a khaki shirt, matching trousers, and deck shoes. He was appealing as ever, the difference—thanks entirely to Chung Lee's candor—being that I now knew an arms dealer lingered under the sheep's clothing. I wanted to scratch his eyes out, but instead I smiled, returning the little wave he gave me.

The boarding ladder no sooner touched the dock than Bannon, a duffle bag slung over his shoulder, jogged up to the deck and stepped aboard. Handing the bag to a crewman, he turned to me and said, "Bet you thought I missed the boat altogether."

"You'd never let that happen, Cole."

"Certainly not when you're aboard, sweetheart," he said, giving me a friendly kiss on the temple and a brief hug.

"How's Dru?" I asked.

"Fine," he replied. "She slept okay and was in good spirits this morning. When we got to Sumgi's, she told her cousin all about her big adventure, which is a good sign, I guess. So, how are you feeling this morning?"

It was time for my first lie. But that was fine; it would take me days to catch up with him and his untruths. "Great."

Bannon looked pleased. "Told you today would be better."

"You were certainly right about that."

We had to move up the deck a bit so the crew could retrieve the boarding ladder.

"Ah, Mr. Bannon, you made it." It was Chung Lee, who came shuffling along the deck, a cigarette in the corner of his mouth.

Bannon shook his hand. "My apologies for any inconvenience caused."

"Were you able to make arrangements for your family?"

"Yes, I had a young fellow who works for me drive them to the country."

"I'm sure they'll be safe," Chung said. He gave a small bow. "Well, we have a great deal to discuss. Shall we make ourselves comfortable?" He took a final drag on his cigarette and flipped it into the water, as before. Then he led the way back to the rear deck.

We took our seats, Bannon holding my chair for me. Chung asked if we wanted refreshments, both Bannon and I declined.

"First, I will brief you on my negotiations in Hong Kong," the old man said. He proceeded to give us an account of his meeting with the "Burmese Tiger." I kept a close eye on Bannon while Chung spoke so I could evaluate his reaction, my sunglasses enabling me to be subtle. I couldn't pick up on anything telling. The guy was a pro. I sure as hell wouldn't want to get in a poker game with him.

Chung went over some of the ground he'd already covered with me, though in greater detail. At one point he had an aide bring out a topographical map of the border area, which we spread out on the table.

"I have no idea where Lwin's camp is located," he said, "but you'll be crossing the border somewhere in this area," he said, pointing. "You'll spend your last night in Thailand in the small town of Mae Hong Son, which, as you can see, is virtually on the border. You'll be met there by a guide provided by Colonel Lwin. He will introduce himself as Myat. From that point on, you'll be in his hands."

Bannon had taken a notebook from his pocket and scratched out a few notes. Between his military background and his knowledge of the countryside, I could see that he would be useful. The operation promised to be exciting—that appealed to my taste for adventure. It was a shame it had to be with Cole Bannon, though, and an even greater tragedy was that I had to pretend to enjoy it.

I studied him as Chung Lee continued to speak. Bannon was so charming, so good-looking, that a person would never take him for a charlatan. But then, that was the reason for his success—probably in selling arms, as well as seducing women. It was too damned bad he was so depraved. I wanted to throw up.

Chapter
38

We continued our trek upriver, discussing the operation, me doing my best to focus on what Bannon was saying, rather than on him. It wasn't easy. His every smile and gesture would take me back to last night. The only thing that saved me was knowing it had been false.

As the morning wore on, it grew hotter, and Bannon and I both accepted Chung's offer of a cool drink. The steward brought tall glasses of lemonade, which hit the spot.

Bannon, looking self-satisfied, reached over and patted my hand. "That ruby is almost within your reach, Lexie."

"Yeah, I know."

"I expected you to be a little more excited."

"I'm trying to focus on the task. I wish I knew more about Colonel Lwin. The more you know about a person, the easier it is to negotiate with him." I turned to our host. "You've met Lwin, Mr. Chung, do you have any insights you'd care to share?"

"The colonel is shrewd, and he rules with an iron fist, Miss Chandler. He understands power, I'll say that for him."

"What are his weaknesses?"

"Hubris. Those with power often let it go to their heads."

"He's got an ego, in other words."

"That's safe to say. I believe I've mentioned he has a fond-ness for women. That, too, may be an Achilles heel."

"How so?"

"What Mr. Chung is saying is that Lwin might find you distracting."

I glanced at Bannon. "He's sexist, but you're saying he's a . . . ladies' man, too?"

"Mr. Chung can answer that better than I."

I turned toward our host who, despite his stony demeanor, managed to look uncomfortable. "Yes, Lwin does have that reputation," he said.

"What are we talking here, exactly?" I asked. "He keeps a harem?"

Chung did not laugh, which I took to be a bad sign.

"He admits to having a weakness for beautiful women."

Chung's embarrassment told me a great deal—he wanted me on board, at least in part *because* I was a woman, not *in spite of the fact*. For a moment I was speechless. Then I said, "Well I certainly hope there aren't any expectations, because I don't charm men to gain advantage in a negotiation."

"Sure you do," Bannon said. "You're an attractive woman, and it's a natural result of any conversation you have. What you mean is you don't use sexual favors to sweeten a deal. They're two different things."

I turned red, partly because I was embarrassed and partly because I was incensed. "Thank you, Cole, I appreciate you making that clear."

"Colonel Lwin has predilections," Chung said. "It's impor-tant that you know this in advance so you aren't blindsided."

"Nice time to bring it up," I said indignantly.

"Is his appreciation of women a problem for you?" Chung asked.

I was already concerned about the guy being a psychopath, but now I find out he's a pervert too. It didn't exactly make my heart sing with joy, but on the other hand, I also didn't want to make too big a deal of it. "I'm sure I can handle him," I said. "But I want to know exactly what he expects."

"When I met with him nothing was said about expectations," Chung said.

"Does he even know I'm a woman?"

"Yes."

"That's all?"

"He inquired about you at our first meeting, and I told him we'd never met. I did, however, have a photograph, and he was eager to see it. He seemed most impressed."

I did not like the sound of what I was hearing.

"Lexie, don't worry about it," Bannon said. "I'll personally guarantee your safety. Even the Burmese Tiger can be tamed."

Wonderful! I thought. I'd been concerned about keeping Bannon at bay, and now he was my first line of defense against a womanizing rake. Talk about the fox guarding the chicken coop.

"You look skeptical," he said.

I gave him a thin smile. "Sometimes I have a little trouble with male bravado."

"You don't believe me?"

"Oh, you're probably sincere, it's just that Lwin has an army and you have . . . I'm not sure what. A gun?"

"Hey, this is getting blown all out of proportion. The guy has a reputation for being randy, but he's not a rapist." He turned to Chung. "Am I right about that?"

"You're right, Mr. Bannon. The colonel may live in a jungle camp, but he's a man of culture and education, if indeed a man with a fondness for women."

I knew that being cultured and educated didn't mean he

wasn't a lecher, but Bannon was probably right, the issue was getting blown out of proportion. My pique had as much or more to do with Bannon, since sex was already a sore point between us.

Bannon and Chung continued to banter, moving on to another subject. I listened quietly, realizing I was in bed with a band of thieves, and I'd been used. Since my arrival in Thailand, I'd been coddled, cajoled, patronized, manipulated, and deceived, and for one simple reason—they needed me. Well, I needed them, too. But the closer I got to the ruby, the less essential they became. As they say, two can play this game.

After about twenty minutes we put in at the ferry boat dock at Wisnut Kasat where a car and driver were waiting to take us to the airport. The steely security man who'd been my guardian angel all day was to accompany us. We said our goodbyes to Chung Lee, then headed for the airport.

Our plan was to fly to the city of Chiang Mai in the mountainous north of the country, which also happened to be one of my favorite towns in the world. "The rose of the North," as it was called, was a beautiful—some people said magical—place with magnificent *wats* and gardens, lovely views, and some great shopping. Usually I went to Chiang Mai as a tourist, rather than gem trader, but this time I was on the trail of the most fabulous stone of my career.

We arrived at the airport without incident. So far, so good. I told Bannon I needed to put my gun in my suitcase, knowing I'd be unable to carry it on the plane. Chung's security guy told us that it was no longer possible to transport a weapon in checked luggage, but that there was an alternative. Arrangements had been made for our weapons to be transshipped to Chiang Mai and delivered to our hotel. I wasn't pleased, but I had no choice. I gave the guy my automatic, and Bannon gave him his gun, as well.

Our man went as far as the gate with us, not leaving our sides until we boarded. I wasn't sure whether to be worried or comforted, but being in the cross-hairs of somebody's scope was beginning to feel like familiar territory.

The plane was only half full, which meant Bannon and I were pretty much alone. This was the first time that had happened since I'd learned who the bastard really was. And I was even more uncomfortable than I'd expected to be.

I avoided interacting with him by staring out the window and watching the ground crew. Sooner or later I'd have to talk to him, it being a given he'd turn the conversation to personal matters. I didn't have long to wait. He got my attention by taking my hand. I gave him a sideward glance, resisting the urge to yank my hand away.

"You okay, Lexie?"

"Sure. Why?"

"I don't know, you seem funny . . . uncomfortable somehow."

Bannon's antennas were too good. "I'm just trying to focus on the ruby. When an operation is about to get rolling, I tend to block everything else out."

"Not *everything*, surely."

"Pretty much so."

"You sure that's what it is?"

He was adamant so I decided this was the time to give him the speech I'd planned. "Cole, if you're alluding to last night . . ."

"I'm not alluding to anything in particular. But is last night the problem? Was it Dru walking in on us?"

"That wasn't one of my prouder moments, but that isn't it."

"What's the problem then?"

I could see it was time for Big Lie Number Two—or Number Three, if you counted the misinformation I'd given him about Brax in the beginning, which, of course, I did not.

"What happened between us is secondary now," I said. "When I'm working on a major acquisition, I try to avoid distractions. Last night was really . . . wonderful," I said almost choking on the word, "but it was a bad idea considering it was the eve of our departure for Myanmar."

"I don't understand," he said. "You still have to eat and sleep and . . . well, live."

"You're a man. Compartmentalizing comes easily for you. I like to devote myself wholeheartedly to my top priority, and I can only spread my emotional energy so thin."

"Let me be clear on what you're saying. You'd like to pretend last night never happened, that we're just business partners."

He was miffed, I could tell. Men never liked being rebuffed. But I also knew I couldn't risk alienating him. I had to be gentle. It was time for my next lie. "I'd like to put our personal relationship on hold," I explained, "at least until we get back from Myanmar. After the ruby is safely in a vault we can go on a romantic getaway to celebrate—assuming you want to, that is."

He chuckled. "You certainly understand the principle of incentive, don't you, sweetheart? Trust me, I don't need to be bribed. It's your deal, you call the shots."

I looked in his eyes, trying to conjure up loving thoughts because I knew that my true feelings weren't easily hidden. To deceive him, I would have to deceive myself.

Chapter
39

Once again Cole Bannon became the
perfect gentleman. I was glad, but attributed his behavior to
his chameleon nature, not to a philanthropic impulse. But it
made things easier for me. For that I was grateful.

Unarmed, I was more wary than usual as we rode from the
airport into Chiang Mai, but I was in good spirits. Chung
had arranged for our accommodations, the Tapae Place, a
modern, middle-grade hotel located in the center of town between the river and the Tha Phae Gate.

One of our rooms was a suite, which Bannon offered me,
but I opted for the smaller room down the hall. As the bell
hop deposited my bag in my room, Bannon said, "I thought
I'd have room service bring tea and a bite to eat to the suite.
Care to join me?"

I didn't want to, but I'd been saying no so much that I figured I'd better throw him a bone. "Okay, but first I'd like to
freshen up."

I closed the door and leaned against it. I didn't want to
think about it, but less than twenty-four hours ago I'd slept
with the man. If I'd only waited one more day . . .

The bath was not elegant, but it was gleaming clean and modern. I took off my shirt, sponged myself off with a damp cloth, ran a comb through my hair, and put on fresh lip gloss, enough to feel good without overdoing it.

I went down the hall to the suite where I found Bannon in the company of a cute Thai girl who was a bit reminiscent of Joy. "Lexie, this is Leean," he said. "She's brought us our pea shooters." He indicated a package on the table.

The girl did a *wai*.

"That was quick," I said.

"I tell Mr. Bannon special delivery," she tittered before heading for the door.

"Cute girl," I said when she was gone. "Are you old friends or just efficient at making new ones?" I couldn't resist the barb.

He wasn't sure whether I was peeved or just making a quip. I wasn't sure myself.

"Your people skills explain your success in business," I added for clarification.

He accepted that as a positive signal. "Well, life is short."

"So, we're armed and dangerous once again," I said, changing the subject.

He went to the table and began opening the package. He took out my automatic and handed it to me along with the extra clips of ammunition.

"Feel safer?"

"Not so naked," I said, pushing the magazine into the butt of the pistol.

I saw Bannon's smile and knew what he was thinking. I hated that we'd had sex.

The room service waiter brought our tea. I sat with my gun resting on my knee, under the table. It was terrible constantly being in fear for your life. After the guy was gone, I put the automatic on the table next to my cup and saucer.

"I'm sorry it's come to this, Lexie," Bannon said, indicating the pistol. "You shouldn't have to be afraid every moment."

"I've had to operate in dangerous circumstances before, but I've never run into anybody quite like Noonwongsa, I have to admit."

"And you haven't even met the guy."

"But I saw him with you, Cole, which I guess is close enough."

The guy was so smooth, he didn't so much as blink. "You still galled that I misled you about that?" he asked.

"No," I said, "you finally told me the truth, and that's all that matters."

Bannon showed no trace of guilt or remorse. To the contrary, he seemed pleased. I wasn't surprised.

"Let's see what we have to eat," he said, lifting the cover off a serving dish. "I ordered a sampler plate, so there's a bit of everything to choose from."

In his shoes, I'd change the subject, too. "Looks good," I said.

We served ourselves and ate with appetite. I had come to understand that there were two Cole Bannons—the surface guy who could lie with a straight face and coolly pretend nothing had happened. Then there was the real one. But that was okay. I would use the smooth phony to get what I wanted. And when this was over and I had my ruby, I'd walk away.

We had some cakes for dessert, and he poured me a second cup of tea. We regarded each other, thinking our secret thoughts.

I rose and said, "I'm going back to my room."

Bannon was taken aback by my abruptness and blinked.

"I'd like to rest," I said by way of explanation.

"Lexie," he said before I could leave. "What's wrong?"

"Flying can be fatiguing."

"That's not what I mean."

"What *do* you mean, Cole?"

"You're acting funny. You have doubts about me. I can tell."

"Of course I do. That happens when relationships change. They're the routine doubts every woman has about every man."

"Is that really true?"

"Yes," I said, the untruths coming more easily all the time.

"Then I shouldn't worry?"

"Not unless you give me reason to distrust you."

"Listen," he said, reaching out and taking my hand, "one of my favorite restaurants in the world is here in Chiang Mai. How about I take you there for dinner, my treat?"

"I don't have anything to wear."

"Not even a little black dress?"

"I packed before realizing charming Colonel Lwin was part of my job description. When you're headed for the jungle, you tend not to think like a *femme fatale*."

"How about if I buy you an outfit?" he'd said. "I'd really like to take you to this place. It fairly demands a gentleman have a sophisticated lady on his arm."

"You're serious, aren't you?"

"How many chances like this will I have?"

Bannon may have been trying to gauge my feelings, but for me the answer was very simple. This would be his one and only shot. He was lucky that I still needed to humor him—though not so far as to let him buy me an outfit.

"*If* I can find something to wear, I'll go," I said, "but only if."

"Would you like company?"

"No, to be honest. If the shopping's serious, men tend to get in the way. But I'll let you know if I find something."

*   *   *

I asked the girl at the front desk where I'd most likely find evening attire in my size. She suggested I try the shops in either the Regent or the Westin, the luxury hotels that catered to Westerners. "Or, maybe you find something in department stores at Tha Phae Gate. Much closer." Since the gate and shopping district were around the corner, I decided to try the department stores first.

I had my gun in my purse as I left the hotel, knowing I had to remain vigilant, even though it was unlikely Noonwongsa's boys were aware we were in Chiang Mai. Crowded city streets could be dangerous places, but they could be safer than isolated spots, where an assassin stood less of a chance of being identified and caught.

I soon discovered there was little to choose from in my size. I ended up buying a red Thai silk sleeveless sheath with a low cut back, the only thing that fit and looked decent. It was sexy without being blatant and not half bad, I decided while examining myself in the mirror. Naturally, I couldn't wear my low boots and ended up buying gold sandals.

I tried to imagine what it would be like months from now if I happened upon the dress in my closet. Would the memories it conjured up be mortifying or pleasant? The answer depended on what happened over the next few days.

Back at the hotel, I found Bannon pacing the lobby. He looked relieved to see me.

"Thank goodness," he said.

"What's wrong?"

"I had a call from Bangkok. There's news about Noonwongsa. The Thai police have been in communication with officials in Cambodia concerning the possibility of an arrest warrant. But it seems our boy has dropped out of sight. They aren't sure where he is, but he may be headed this way."

"And you're concerned?"

"I may make light of things at times, but I take my responsibilities seriously."

"Which responsibilities are those?"

"Keeping you safe."

His expression was grave, and that sobered me. "So, do we hunker down until it's time to leave town?"

"I don't think we have to go to that extreme." He glanced at the sack. "I take it you found something to wear."

"Yes."

"Is it sexy?"

"That wasn't the primary criterion, but yes. So, dinner is still on?"

"Yeah. I've arranged for special transportation."

"A tank?"

He laughed. "No, they're sending a car. But it is unique. You'll see."

I hated saying it, but I did. "Well, I'm in your hands, Cole."

"I'll knock on your door at seven. Meanwhile, I'm going out for a while."

"*Alone?*" I said mocking him.

"I know it's risky, but I need something to wear, too. I'm renting a dinner jacket."

"You're kidding."

"I want this to be a special night, sweetheart. We deserve it."

Chapter
40

It was odd how mental associations work. That evening as I dressed for my elegant dinner with Cole Bannon, two special occasions went tripping through my mind. One was my junior prom in high school—I was a candidate for prom queen and didn't win. The other occasion was the Chandler and Cooper families dinner at the Piedmont Driving Club in Buckhead the night Brax and I formally announced our engagement. On both occasions I wore red. But it wasn't until I stood staring at myself in the mirror that it occurred to me that having chosen red for tonight might be a bad omen.

On the other hand, my relationship with Bannon had already been determined. There was nothing left to go bad unless social events and rubies were affected by the same cosmic forces. If there was any bad karma headed my way, I hoped the gods would direct it at Bannon, not the Heart of Burma.

But fate wasn't the sort to roll over and play dead. About two minutes before Bannon was scheduled to knock on my door, the room phone rang.

"Lexie, darlin', I'm so sorry to disturb you when you're workin', but I'm afraid I have bad news." It was my mother, and her dire tone made my heart stop. I was certain something had happened to my father, or to one of my brothers.

"What, Mama?"

"I tried to reach you at the Oriental, but they said you checked out. So I called Mr. Sedley, and he was kind enough to track down this number in Chiang Mai. Am I pronouncin' it correctly?"

"Mama, for God sakes, what happened?"

"It's Julie, honey. She very nearly lost her baby. She's going to be fine, but she's been hospitalized. Heath told us she may have to keep to her bed until she's ready to deliver. Can you imagine?"

I gave an enormous sigh of relief, certain she was going to say Daddy had had a heart attack or Austin had been run over by a tank or something. Julie's baby was important, but they were both okay, so the news wasn't as dire as it might have been.

"I guess the trip to Thailand was overly ambitious," Mama went on. "And I feel dreadful because I was the one who pushed for them to be there. I so wanted your birthday to be special."

"It's not your fault, Mama. I'm sure her doctor wouldn't have let her make the trip if he didn't feel it was safe."

"It's sweet of you to say that, sugar. And Heath said the same thing, but you know how I am about my babies and now my grandbaby."

"Well, don't worry, Mama. It doesn't help, and it can only wear on you. But I appreciate you letting me know about Julie. Please give her and Heath my best wishes. I'll call them once things have settled down on this end."

"I'll pass that on. And how are things going with our dear friend, Mr. Bannon?"

I realized then that we may have gotten to the real point of the call. My mother was a devious little devil. Knowing her, I was certain she'd been dying of curiosity, wondering what had been going on. There wasn't time to give her the whole story, not when Bannon would be knocking on my door momentarily. But even if I had time, it wouldn't be a good idea to tell her what he really was, because then she'd worry.

"Everything's fine," I said. "We're about to begin negotiations for the stone."

"Then things are . . . friendly between the two of you?"

"Yes, Mama, but there hasn't been much time for socializing." *If you don't count the night I went to bed with him*, I thought. But this was no time for admissions. I pressed on. "I'm focused on the ruby. When I'm working, especially on a challenging project, other things get pushed aside."

"I know you're sincere, Alexis, but how could you ignore that man? Under *any* circumstances? Surely, you're exaggeratin'. Or are you sayin' it's none of my business? Which is your right, of course. It's just that we were all so fond of Mr. Bannon and lookin' forward to his visit, come Christmastime."

"Mama, I know you are trying to—" A knock on the door interrupted me mid-sentence. "Hold on, there's somebody at the door."

I went and looked through the peephole. It was Bannon, as I expected. I opened the door, took one look at him and my teeth nearly fell out.

He wore a white dinner jacket, bow tie, cummerbund, the works. The guy looked incredible. But he was too busy looking at my outfit to notice my reaction.

"Come on in," I said, only then noticing he had a bouquet in his hand.

"You look fantastic, Lexie."

"Thank you. I'm on the phone," I said. "I'll just be a minute." I went back and picked up the receiver. "I'm going to have to get off now," I said to my mother. "I'm going to dinner. Maybe I can give you a call later."

"Lexie, was that Mr. Bannon's voice I heard?"

"Yes. Why?"

"Could I just have a quick word with him?"

"Is it necessary?"

"I just need a moment, sugar. I'd like to thank him again for his hospitality."

I rolled my eyes. "Hang on." I turned to Bannon and extended the phone. "Cole, it's my mother. She'd like to speak with you."

He stepped over and took the receiver, handing me the flowers and, catching me off guard, stole a quick kiss. I blanched, stepping away before he noticed, though I did smell the blossoms.

"Hello, Mrs. Chandler, how are you?" he said effusively.

I knew how the conversation would go without having to hear both sides. There would be mutual flattery, adulation, well-wishing, and thanks. Rather than stand there listening, I decided to go find something to put the flowers in. Snatching the water pitcher from the table, I went into the bath to fill it.

"It was my pleasure entirely," I heard him saying. "I'm only sorry you couldn't have stayed longer. . . . Yes, we'll be leaving shortly. I'm taking Lexie to Le Coq d'Or. It's one of the finest restaurants in the country. . . . That's right, French. You'd love it, by the way. In fact, your next trip to Thailand will have to include Chiang Mai, and you must have at least one meal at Le Coq d'Or. . . . Well, I wish you could see her, Mrs. Chandler. I've never seen Lexie more beautiful than she is tonight. In case you don't know it, you have a remarkable daughter, a lovely, lovely woman. And I mean that sincerely. When she opened the door, I was absolutely spellbound."

I turned on the faucet, rolling my eyes. Bannon had my

mother's number, there was no arguing that. I could almost hear her gushing from the other room.

"You know, Mrs. Chandler, I have been thinking about your kind invitation," he said. "It would be a wonderful trip and great to see you and your husband again, but I really think we should leave it up to Lexie. . . . Oh, I appreciate that, ma'am, but I'd only accept if she wanted me there. The two of you need to talk it over. . . . Yes, we probably should go, I imagine our car is waiting. . . . Thank you, I'm sure we'll have a great time."

Then I heard him laugh.

"Yes, ma'am, I promise you I will. On your instructions."

The pitcher full, I stuck in the flowers from Bannon's little bouquet and carried it into the bedroom as he was saying his good-byes to my mother. I put the pitcher down on the table as he was hanging up.

"Your mama is quite a lady," he said, coming over to where I stood. Then, lifting my chin with his finger, he added, "She gave me strict instructions to kiss you for her."

Before I could utter a word, Bannon leaned down and kissed me softly on the lips.

"I can't very well disobey your mother, now can I?"

"You are a shameless opportunist," I said, giving him a narrow-eyed look.

"Guilty. But hell, it was probably the only way I was going to get a kiss tonight."

"You got that right."

He gave me a quizzical look. "Is a harmless little kiss from me that upsetting?"

I'd been too pointed. "Well, let's just say inappropriate under the circumstances."

"Meaning I'm relegated to my fantasies. At least until you have the ruby."

"Exactly."

His expression was more appraising than disapproving. "Your mother renewed her invitation to visit them in Atlanta over the holidays, by the way."

"I heard. And you were gentlemanly enough to defer to me. That was very considerate. I appreciate it."

"Have you given it any thought?"

"Why don't we discuss that when we get back from Myanmar?"

"We're going to be real busy when we get back, won't we?"

I smiled and thought to myself, *Mr. Bannon, if you only knew.*

Chapter 41

A genuine London taxi cab was waiting for us outside the hotel. "Wow!" I exclaimed. "This is how we're getting to the restaurant?"

"I thought it would be fun."

Cole Bannon had the social graces down cold. The day I'd first seen him at the Nakhon Spa I never imagined he would be helping me into a London taxi, attired in a dinner jacket and taking me to an expensive French restaurant. But then neither did I think I would have gone to bed with him as his child slept in the next room.

Not ten minutes ago he all but had my mother asking him if she should start updating her wedding invitation list, and now he had me as gaga as a sixteen-year-old on the way to the prom. The man's allure was so convincing that I almost felt guilty about condemning him. But he was a gunrunner, for heaven's sake. He'd made a fool of me once. It wouldn't happen again.

I had to keep the guy on the line, though, and that meant being friendly enough to avoid alienating him. It was a balancing act because my natural inclination was either to embrace a guy or shove him away.

From downtown we drove east, crossing the river. The restaurant was located in a colonial-style teak house on Koh Klang Road. Painted white, it was situated in a lush garden. The interior was elegant and formal, influenced by both the Thai and French traditions. There were highly polished dark hardwood floors and crown molding, white tablecloths and teakwood furniture. The *maître d'hôtel* seated us by open French doors overlooking the garden. Bannon and I looked at one another in the warm glow of candlelight.

"With one exception, this has to be the highlight of our acquaintance," he said.

I wasn't about to ask what the exception was. I did not need to be reminded.

The waiter came to discuss the menu with Bannon—it was, after all, a traditional establishment in a tradition-bound country. My escort ordered for us, after consulting with me, though he had strong suggestions as to my choices. His intent was to be amusing, but I wasn't going to object. I'd let this be his fantasy night. To a point.

Watching Bannon in action for two minutes was enough for me to be impressed with his sophistication. I'd always felt that Brax had class and *savoir faire* but my former fiancé was more limited, a Southern gentleman, albeit of the new generation. Bannon, on the other hand, was a man of the world in the truest sense of the word.

The waiter left and Bannon noticed me contemplating him.

"What are you thinking?"

"I'm trying to decide which is the real you," I said frankly. "Was it the guy drinking beer at the spa with the naked hookers or the one in the dinner jacket who just ordered French champagne in French."

"The easiest—and maybe best—answer is both."

"Don't you have a sense that one is more you than the other?"

"I have a hunch you want me to say that this is the real me."

"Not necessarily."

"What *would* you like to hear me say, then?"

"Strange as it may seem, the truth."

A smile touched his lips. "Okay, the closest thing to the real me is the guy with the little girl you had dinner with a few nights ago. I'd like to think that would be your choice, as well."

I flushed and he noticed.

"Sorry, Lexie," he said, "but you asked."

"Okay, fine. I shouldn't have brought it up."

The waiter brought the champagne. I couldn't wait for a big gulp, but I could see he wanted to make a toast first.

He extended his glass. "To your happiness, Alexis." He paused. "To the prize you seek, the Heart of Burma." He paused again. "To your success in attaining both."

"Thank you, Cole. And to you, as well."

He nodded, we touched glasses, and I had my big gulp of champagne.

We dined on pan fried foie gras with a port wine sauce, bouillabaisse, Chateaubriand, and a Grand Marnier soufflé for dessert. We had two different wines in addition to the champagne, and I had to be careful not to get tipsy. Everything was excellent.

The London taxi was waiting to take us home. I let Bannon hold my hand so as not to seem unsociable. Despite everything going on beneath the surface, I had to admit it was a pleasant evening.

As we made our way back to the hotel, I lay my head back and stared out the window. I could feel Bannon's presence beside me and knew exactly what he was thinking. It wouldn't happen, though. I was too smart, too tough, too well informed.

"I know you'll want to get to bed early," he said, "but will you indulge me with one other thing?"

"What's that?"

"I'd like to pick up a little present for Dru. Have you been to the Night Bazaar?"

"Not for a long time."

"Do you mind if I have the driver drop us there? We'd only have a few blocks to walk back to the hotel. But if you'd rather not, I'll tell him to take you in the taxi."

"No, that's fine, I'd like to see the Bazaar again."

"Great," he said, giving my hand a squeeze.

Our London taxi dropped us off outside the main entrance. I'd first visited the Night Bazaar with Granddad and recalled combing the antique booths on the top floor, looking for a present for Mama. He ended up buying her a two-hundred-year-old wedding basket, which she still kept by her dressing table.

Bannon was looking for a smaller gift, so we concentrated on the stalls on the ground floor where there were lots of hill-tribe crafts, leather goods, Lanna textiles, Saa paper, Lacquerware, and silver. He ended up buying a couple of Saa paper umbrellas for Dru and her cousin and some Lanna fabrics for Sumgi. As an extra little gift for his daughter, he bought a hill-tribe doll.

While we were examining the fabrics, Bannon asked if any of them in particular appealed to me. I told him they were lovely, but that I wouldn't let him buy me any.

"What would your mother like, then?" he asked.

I could see he wouldn't be deterred, so I pointed out a fabric I thought she'd like.

"And which of these would she pick out for you?"

I gave him a look.

"Hypothetical question."

"Yeah, sure. I might be naive, Cole, but I'm not stupid."

"She's going to get two and will want to give one to you, so you might as well tell me which it will be."

I pointed to one of the fabrics, which I did like a lot. "But let me pay for it."

"Not on your life."

Rather than having to carry his purchases for the duration of the trip, he arranged to have his family's gifts shipped to Bangkok and the fabric to Atlanta. When we'd finished, we began walking back to the hotel.

Because of the altitude, the evenings could be quite cool in Chiang Mai, and, seeing that I was cold, Bannon took off his jacket and slipped it around my shoulders.

"I can get us a taxi," he said.

"I don't mind the walk, as long as we don't get ambushed."

The stroll was pleasant, in part because of the air, but also the vibrant street life. To me, the streets in almost every corner of the Orient were colorful and interesting. It was different with an escort, and it took me back to when I'd traveled with my grandfather. There was no question that being with a man made for an entirely different dynamic.

We reached the hotel without incident. I returned Bannon's jacket to him, and we went up to our floor in the elevator. I was thirty years old and no longer a kid. I'd slept with the guy once already, but as we walked along the hall to my room, I felt like a girl on her first date. Would he try to kiss me? Should I let him or resolutely refuse?

We came to my door.

"It was a lovely evening and a fabulous meal," I said. "Thank you so much."

"Just to be able to see you in that dress made it all worthwhile." His smile was the benevolent smile of a father, rather than the Lothario and blackguard I knew him to be.

I effected a demure, if false, expression.

"Your mother did say to give you two kisses," he said in a stone sober tone. "Did I mention that?"

"No, Cole, I don't believe you did."

"Amazing I'd let something like that slip my mind."

"And hard to believe," I said.

He had that seductive look I'd so often seen, starting with that very first day at the bathhouse. He said, "I think I deserve the benefit of the doubt, don't you?"

We were playacting—both of us—though with very different intentions. In keeping with my strategy to string Bannon along, I decided to allow him one more kiss. He did not need to be told to proceed. He read my acquiescence immediately, lowered his head, and kissed me on the lips.

I could easily have kissed him back, but I didn't. My heart was thumping pretty nicely, even though I was holding back. Bannon had a knack for arousing me, and, I suspect, a good many other women as well.

After a few moments of growing intensity, I backed off, gently separating myself from him. "Mama might have suggested a kiss or two," I said, "but she brought me up to react to a gentleman's affection with decorum."

"Is that right?"

"Yes, sir, I assure you, it is."

"Then whose daughter were you that night at my apartment?"

I gave him a look. "That, Mr. Bannon, is a very ungentlemanly question. I would have thought you'd have better breeding than to embarrass a lady that way. I'm afraid I must bid you goodnight."

With that, I turned the key in the lock, stepped into my room and, giving him the faintest of smiles, let the door close. I stood in the dark and took a long, deep breath. Cole Bannon was one hell of a challenge, but after tonight I was confident of being able to handle him. All I needed to do was hang on for a few more days.

As I moved forward, feeling for the light switch on the wall, I noticed the air seemed unusually cool. Then I saw that the slider leading to the balcony outside my room was open. I didn't recall leaving it that way.

Just as I found the switch plate with my fingertips I heard a noise behind me. At the same instant an arm wrapped around my throat, a hand clamped over my mouth, and I was arched backward so violently my feet were nearly lifted off the floor.

The light came on and I saw a man wearing a silk ski-mask-like cloth over his head step from the bath, where he'd been hiding. The mask had eye holes and was peaked on top with a little tassel. He held a revolver in his hand. Stepping forward, he pressed the muzzle to my forehead and said, "Silence or you die."

My eyes bulged as the arm tightened on my throat. Nobody moved, the three of us frozen, waiting and listening, it seemed. Then I realized what was happening. They were giving Bannon time to return to his room, out of earshot.

After twenty or thirty agonizing seconds, the gunman cocked the hammer of his revolver. This was it. I was certain I was about to die.

Chapter
42

Acting on pure reflex, I swiped at the man's gun hand, knocking the weapon aside as I simultaneously brought my foot sharply up between his legs. The gun went off, the bullet slamming into the door. Seeing his buddy crumple to the floor, the man with the choke hold wrenched and twisted my body, trying to wrestle me to the floor.

Though contorted, I managed to drive my elbow into his stomach, but I couldn't twist free. I pushed back as hard as I could, ramming him into the door, the impact knocking the wind out of him.

Meanwhile, the gunman struggled to his feet. As he raised his weapon to fire, he staggered forward. I lifted my leg, ripping the seam of my skirt, and shoved him in the chest, sending him flying backwards. The gun went off again, this time the bullet tearing into the ceiling.

As he lay on his back, my dancing partner held onto me for dear life, but a couple more elbows to the midsection loosened his grip. Deciding the man with the weapon was the greater threat, I charged him, stomping on his gun hand with the heel of my sandal before he could fire yet again. He let out a yowl, and I spun around in time to see his pal—also masked—pull out a long-bladed knife and come toward me.

I didn't have time to wrest the gun away, so I turned and ran out onto the balcony. I hadn't checked it out earlier so, when I peered over the railing, I discovered there were no easy routes of escape. It was a four-story drop to the ground. There was a three-foot stretch of wall between me and the balconies on either side. The one and only possibility seemed to be the balcony directly below. But to get to it I would have to hang from the railing and swing onto it.

Knowing I had no time to spare, I threw my leg over the top rail, glad I'd already split the seam of my skirt. Outside the railing now, my toes on the ledge, I looked up to see the guy with the knife at the door. I bent down and grasped the bottom stringer with my hands and let my legs drop until I swung freely. As I hung there, I looked up and saw the knife-wielding assailant take a swipe at me, the blade just missing my ear.

As a freshman in high school I'd taken gymnastics and, though it had been a hell of a long time since I'd been on a high bar, I knew how to coil and thrust to begin a rotation. Despite the intervening years, a gold medal performance was required if I was going to save myself. Lifting my knees till they touched the ceiling of the balcony below, I swung my body out into empty space, then snapped it back and let go of the stringer, landing on the balcony below, a nearly perfect dismount.

A faint light came from the room. I saw a heavyset Japanese gentleman lying on the bed, naked. A slender Thai beauty, also naked, was astride him; they were going at it hot and heavy. I was stunned, never before having seen another couple having sex. I was embarrassed but also fascinated . . . not that I had the luxury of indulging myself. I hated to interrupt them. But I had no choice, considering my life was on the line.

Finding the sliding door unlocked, I stepped into the room. They didn't seem to hear and I wondered if there was any chance I could slip past them unnoticed. But I couldn't. When I reached the foot of the bed, the man spotted me and sat upright so abruptly the girl fell off of him, almost falling onto the floor.

The three of us looked at each other with round eyes. In my shoes, Mama would have come up with the perfect remark, but Mama had never met a faux pas she couldn't handle. The only thing I could think to do was apologize.

"I'm so sorry," I said, "please forgive the interruption." I pointed to the door, mortified, but also acutely aware I was in danger. "I'll be leaving now."

The Japanese gentleman continued to stare, incredulous, his mouth hanging open, his turgid member cloaked with a flourescent lime-green condom, which was a distraction of the first order, I have to admit. Gathering myself, I went to the door just as somebody started banging on it, bringing me back to reality. I looked through the peephole. It was the masked assailant, the one with the gun. He was yelling in a threatening way.

Glancing back at the couple, I saw that the girl was hunkered down, struggling to cover herself with a pillow. The man was standing, his erection less imposing now. He began blustering, yelling in Japanese and shaking his fists at me.

"There's a guy with a gun at your door," I explained, trying to sound both calm and reasonable, though I was neither. "I really don't have much choice. Would you mind if I used your phone?"

With the pounding on the door continuing, I stepped over to the bedstand and picked up the receiver. The man, who seemed not to have understood a word I said, came over to me and started shouting even louder. The desk clerk came on the line.

"Call the police," I cried over the tumult. "Some armed men are trying to break into . . ." I checked the number on the phone. ". . . room 412."

Just then the man in the hall fired into the door, probably trying to shatter the lock. The girl screamed. I handed the phone to the Japanese guy as we heard the door being kicked down. I stepped to the wall by the entry as my assailant charged in. Sticking out my foot, I tripped him, then pounced on him, grabbing his gun hand.

We rolled on the floor and he ended up on top of me, glaring through the eye holes in his mask. Then there was a crash and he fell over, the girl having clunked him with a water pitcher.

Her lover hurried over, wrenched the gun from my assailant's hand, and began yelling again, gesticulating wildly. I tried to explain but he was so angry with me he didn't notice the assailant stagger to his feet. When the girl pointed out the guy was escaping, her lover fired an errant shot, but the Ninja got away.

Really pissed, the Japanese gentleman started berating me. Here I was, sitting on the floor, the hem of my skirt ripped to the hip, two naked people standing over me, one half covered by a pillow, the other holding a gun, his once tumescent organ drooping before my eyes like an overcooked asparagus. I glanced at the girl.

She said, "I think he say, put up your hands, don't move."

I sat curled up on the sofa in Bannon's suite while the police detective took my statement. Bannon was next to me. It had taken a while to sort things out, the Japanese guest insisting I'd been involved in a conspiracy to rob him. It turned out he was drunk on sake and not coherent enough to realize the

Ninja and I hadn't been on the friendliest of terms. The hooker was more helpful and, once the situation became clear, he apologized profusely and sent an expensive bottle of champagne to the suite.

My assailants had made a clean getaway. The detective told us the intruders were likely local thugs who'd been hired to kill me. They hoped to make an identification through fingerprints and the gun.

"It's a good thing they were inept," I said.

"Criminals here not so sophisticated as in city," the detective explained.

"Which means we'll be even safer once we're in the jungle," Bannon quipped.

"Except for tiger," the detective said. "We have incident of tiger eating villager."

"Oh, great," I said.

"Where you going, exactly?" the detective asked.

"Photo safari," Bannon said without blinking. "We leave first thing in the morning."

Damn, but the guy was good. The smoothest liar I'd ever seen in my life.

Once the detective had everything he needed, he asked us to check back with him after our excursion and Bannon promised we would. The hotel's assistant manager, who'd been present and apologetic throughout, told Bannon they would arrange for a policeman to be posted in the hall during the night.

Bannon had some security precautions of his own in mind. "I think you should stay in the suite with me tonight," he said. "Even if you wouldn't sleep better, I would. You can have the bedroom, I'll have them bring a roll-away for me. I'll sleep out here."

I didn't bother to object because I knew I was in for a rough night. I'd be awakening at every little noise, if I got any sleep at all. An adrenaline rush had carried me through the ordeal—my performance having won me accolades from Bannon and the police, despite the comedic interlude at the end—but I wasn't a happy camper. These close encounters with bullets and knives were beginning to wear on me. For that reason—and that reason alone, I told myself—I could live with the notion of Bannon sleeping outside my door, even if it was tempting fate.

Once everybody was gone I told Bannon I wanted to go to my room to get my things. He went with me. The door to my room was not easily missed; it was the one with the bullet hole in it.

"You know what worries me the most?" I said. "I'm running out of lives. I won't have any left should I have an angry encounter with an Atlanta bus."

"This is my fault. I should have anticipated this and insisted we share the suite, but I was afraid you'd think I had ulterior motives."

"And I'd have been wrong?"

"I gave you my word, Lexie."

Well, I knew what that was good for, but circumstances had changed. Now my biggest concern was living to see the Heart of Burma.

"You have been very sweet, Cole," I said, "and I appreciate it."

"Two reasons," he replied. "It's my job and I care."

It was a very nice sentiment. Too bad I couldn't believe it.

Since we were leaving first thing in the morning, I went ahead and cleaned all my things out of the room and Bannon helped me carry them to the suite. When he saw me arraying my toiletries in the bath, he said, "I've forgotten some of the pleasant little details of living with a woman."

"I'm a *very* short-term guest," I said.

"So, where are we going on our sexy getaway to celebrate our success?"

It wasn't my favorite topic, so I demurred. "Let's discuss it when we have the ruby."

"Ooo-kay."

He wasn't too happy being put off. I had to be more careful. "Please don't be upset with me, Cole," I said by way of apology. "I've had a bad day."

"I should be more understanding. I'd like to make you an offer, though. If you get the willies during the night and need the comfort of a warm body, I'm available. No-obligation, no-ulterior-motives. In other words, a teddy bear at no extra charge."

"Thanks, I'll keep that in mind."

"Well, I suppose you'll want to turn in, considering we've got an early morning."

"Yes, I would."

Bannon touched my cheek affectionately. "Good night then, sweetheart."

Not surprisingly, I had trouble falling asleep. But even when I did, I slept fitfully, awakening often. Once or twice I lay there, tempted to take Bannon up on his offer to play teddy bear. But common sense prevailed.

The fact that I would even consider playing footsie with him was cause for concern. I knew what was happening, and it went beyond the fact that there had been yet another attempt on my life. My resolve was weakening. Desire was getting the upper hand. I don't know if that was a tribute to Bannon's innate appeal, or my innate desire to believe his intentions were good, even in the face of convincing and compelling evidence to the contrary.

The fact that he was a charlatan was a given. What I

wanted to believe, though, was that his desire for me was genuine and that he truly cared. I'm convinced that a nugget of neediness grows in the heart of every woman. Clearly, the challenge was to ensure that it wouldn't be my downfall.

Chapter
43

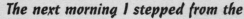 **The next morning I stepped from the** bedroom in freshly pressed jungle fatigues. Breakfast had been delivered and Bannon sat at the table, waiting for me.

"God, Lexie," he said, shaking his head, "this incarnation and the one I took to dinner last night are so different, yet both so appealing. I'm torn over which Alexis Chandler to fall in love with."

"You'd better save your hyperbole for Colonel Lwin," I said. "He's got to become the boy of both our dreams, at least for the next few days."

"You're right, of course, but a guy's entitled to his fantasies, isn't he?"

I put my hands on my hips and gave him a look.

"So," he said, "care for coffee?"

We didn't have a lot of time to spare, so we ate quickly and lugged our bags down to the lobby in the company of the policeman who'd stood guard during the night. The hotel presented us with a complimentary basket lunch along with more sincere apologies and many *wais*. The hotel certainly couldn't be blamed for our troubles, because we had a damned good idea why the assault had occurred. The list of probable culprits pretty much began and ended with Santa Noonwongsa. Because of what had happened the past couple of days, I worried about our drive today. If I could be ambushed in my hotel room, why not on an isolated back road?

Apparently Bannon had been concerned about the same thing because as we tossed our bags into the back of the jeep he'd rented he told me about the plan he'd worked out with the police. "They'll escort us to a road junction ten miles outside of town, then put up a temporary roadblock to make sure we aren't followed," he explained. "Once we're on the maze of back roads, it'll be tough for anyone to pinpoint our location."

"Unless Noonwongsa, or whoever's behind this, has an informant."

"You've mentioned that before."

"Well, it seems to me somebody's awfully good at figuring out where we're going to be. They're always lying in wait."

"I don't know who or how, Lexie. The only explanation is that they've been watching you closely and strike when they have the opportunity. Our coming to Chiang Mai was a pretty good bet, and there are ways of finding out which hotel a particular *farang* is staying in. But I'm confident of this—they're going to need a spy satellite to keep tabs on us from here on out."

"I hope you're right."

I looked behind us a lot, eyeing every approaching vehicle with suspicion. But the scenery was fantastic, the day pleasant, and Cole Bannon good company. After a while I began to relax a little.

Bannon had preplanned our route with more in mind than getting from point A to point B. "There's a waterfall ahead that's half a mile off the road," he said as we sped along. "They tell me it's magical. What do you think of hiking in and having our picnic lunch there?" It sounded like a pleasant diversion, so I agreed.

It took two inquiries and one U-turn to find the trailhead, but we eventually found the jump-off place. I had my weapon with me, of course, but I didn't expect to need it. The sun-dappled jungle did not seem the likely habitat of gangsters and assassins. But my wary mind conjured up other concerns.

"How serious do you think the danger is from tigers?" I asked as we strode along, pushing aside the lacy ferns and occasional vines that had grown across the trail.

"Attacks on humans are rare, Lexie, if only because the tiger population has dwindled so. They're an endangered species."

"Tell that to the man who was eaten."

"I read about the incident in the paper. The circumstances were unusual. He encountered a female with cubs and didn't use discretion."

"Is running away discreet enough?"

He laughed. "If you have a reason to be worried, it's that you're so delectable."

"Shut up," I said. "If there are any tigers listening, they may get ideas."

We reached the waterfall, staring in awe as we emerged from the undergrowth. It was a magical spot, all right, and not because the fall was spectacular or the water volume impressive. It was the poetry of the setting, the loveliness of the cascade. Framed by ferns and the canopy of the jungle, it was reminiscent of a Japanese watercolor painting.

There was nobody else around, fortunately for us, so we were able to spread our picnic lunch right on a mossy patch of ground at the edge of the pool. I was so taken by the scene,

I didn't want to interrupt myself to unpack the picnic basket. Bannon, who I guess was hungry, took care of it instead.

For a while I didn't bother to eat, mesmerized as I was by sunlight playing on the falling water. "There is beauty in the world," I said. "Incredible beauty."

"And not just of the geographical variety," Bannon said. He was staring at me. "But this is awfully special, I grant you."

"You have a silver tongue, Mr. Bannon, I'll give you that."

He gave me a long, ponderous look, then said, "In the interest of good relations, and as a gesture of good faith, I need to tell you something."

His tone, if not his words, elevated my pulse a notch or two.

"There's a little more to my story than I've let on."

"What do you mean?"

"I haven't told you everything about myself, but I intend to the minute we're safely back from Myanmar. I just want you to know I have the best intentions."

"That's not exactly comforting, Cole. Now I'm going to be paranoid."

"There's no reason to worry. I hate being less than fully honest, but I have to for your protection. The less you know about me, the better."

"Now you're making it sound ominous. What am I supposed to think after you say something like that?"

"Lexie, I know you don't trust me. We've been dancing around each other, pretending—me that I'm something that I'm not, and you that you don't know or don't care. I hate it and want you to know that."

"This is a very weird conversation," I said.

"I realize that. But I'm not the bad guy you think I am."

"And I should accept that on faith, I suppose."

"All I ask is that you not write me off until I've had a chance to come clean."

I studied him, not knowing whether I should be heartened or disillusioned. I had to admit one thing—it was the most honest he'd seemed yet. But what I didn't know was if it was more of his act, or if it was the beginning of a new era.

Chapter
44

After our little heart-to-heart talk, qualified though it was, I think we both felt a burden had been lifted. At least I felt that way. Bannon had taken a chance, and I sensed he wanted to do the right thing. That gave me hope, and hope was important.

We ate our lunch with gusto—I had more of an appetite than I'd realized, and the mood was lighter. The ambience of the waterfall and its natural beauty were factors, but mostly it was our newfound understanding that truths remained to be shared.

After we'd finished eating, we decided to take an up-close-and-personal look at the falls. Working our way around the pool, jumping from one mossy boulder to the next, we arrived at the base of the falls. The misty air felt gloriously fresh and cool. We were soon damp, if not wet, and it was exhilarating. Since the last cascade spilled over a protruding ledge into the pool, we were able to move behind the waterfall, thus making a full circuit of the pool. The problem was the moss was slippery, our footing treacherous.

With the water pouring down an arm's length away, we

stepped carefully from one boulder to the next until we came to a big gap in the chain of rocks. It required a leap of six feet, which wasn't that far, but doing it without slipping would be a challenge.

"Shall we try it or turn back?" Bannon asked.

"What the hell, let's give it a try."

Bannon jumped first, his foot slipping when he hit the rock. But somehow he managed to right himself and keep from falling in the water.

"Okay, Lexie," he yelled over the roar of the falls, "now you! Don't worry, I'll catch you!"

Readying myself, I made the leap, clearing the gap without a problem, but my boot slid into Bannon's foot, knocking him off balance. We teetered, clinging to each other before toppling over like a couple of drunk sailors, landing in the pool with a splash.

We surfaced at the same time, inches from the curtain of falling water, shrieking and laughing. Bannon was able to stand on the bottom, but the pool was too deep for me. So he gathered me in, pulling my body against his. I looked up into his eyes. He pushed a strand of hair off my face and kissed me.

This time I kissed him back with as much fervor as the night we'd made love. I was a damned fool, I knew, but a desperately optimistic one, hoping against hope that somehow, some way, Cole Bannon would turn out to be the honorable, if flawed, human being I wanted him to be.

The upshot was that we were back on speaking terms—or, more accurately, kissing terms—and still more importantly, it was probably too late to do anything about it but accept the fact.

The little town of Mae Hong Son was in a valley ringed by jungle-covered mountains not far from the Myanmar border. As we approached the dusty outskirts, Bannon told me that the Burmese influence remained strong, with much of the local population having relocated there from Burma.

"Which means moving back and forth must be easy," I said.

"Depends on who you are."

That again brought to mind Bannon's undisclosed secret. I'd been thinking about it during our drive to Mae Hong Son, wondering if he'd come clean about being an arms dealer. I still wasn't happy with the fact, but if he was forthright about it and willingly faced the consequences of my reaction, it would show he had integrity.

Dusk was approaching as we entered the center of town. The commercial district was not large, the cement buildings mostly two-story, the phone and electrical lines strung overhead, as was typical in most provincial towns. Nor was there the bustle of activity you found even in small cities like Chiang Mai. As I looked out at the people sitting on straight chairs or on stoops, the listless dogs lying at the curbs, the scattered *samlors* and wobbly cyclists riding up the street at a leisurely pace, I realized it was a sleepy town, much like Dalton, the village in the mountains of North Georgia where Granddaddy was born.

The ambience was different at Chong Kham Lake, which was situated in a park-like setting in the center of the town. Bannon said the lake had once been a bathing pool for elephants. Now it afforded locals and tourists alike a scenic spot to stroll and relax.

"Maybe we can take a walk later," he said. "It's really pleasant in the evening."

"You've been here before," I said.

"Yes," he replied. His tone indicated he didn't wish to say more.

The accommodations Chung Lee had arranged for us were considerably more modest than our hotel in Chiang Mai, but they were colorful. We had a room in a guesthouse

situated on the residential side of the lake. It was a traditional Shan teak house that had been converted to commercial use.

"You'll get a taste of the real Thailand," Bannon said.

The tiny woman who greeted us showed us to our room, a
traditional bedroom with mattresses on the straw mat floors.
The walls were rough-hewn boards and there were no windows except for the air vents up near the ceiling. Instead of a
closet, there were hooks on the walls for clothing to be hung,
with large straw baskets in lieu of a chest of drawers. It was
a rather primitive set-up, though authentic and colorful, appealing to my sense of adventure.

"Only one room?" I said.

The woman didn't speak English, so Bannon translated.
"She said she was told there would be two guests," he explained, "so we got a room with two beds. She asked me if
that was a problem."

"And you said?"

"Not for me."

"Well, it is for *me*," I replied. "Tell her we need another
room."

Bannon spoke to her again, reporting to me that there
were no other rooms available. "Looks like we're going to
have to make do."

"Are you telling me the truth?"

"Absolutely."

I didn't know whether to believe him or not. "And I suppose there aren't any other guesthouses nearby."

"I think this may be the last available room in town," he
said, tongue in cheek.

"Yeah, well, you're lucky you're cute, Cole. And you're
also lucky there are two beds. Otherwise you'd be sleeping
on the floor."

The rascal smiled.

It was apparent there'd been a sea change in our relationship, the confession of sorts he'd made at the waterfall having turned the tide. Or maybe it was just that I'd been looking for an excuse to forgive him and once he'd gotten his foot in the door I was toast. But Bannon had one last hurdle to get over. He had to come completely clean with me. By his own admission, that couldn't happen until we'd returned from Myanmar.

Chapter 45

Though our clothing had long since dried, we were eager to change and get cleaned up. My hair was a mess and needed washing. We did not have a private bath, so while I bathed in the communal facilities, Bannon took our clothes to the landlady, who agreed to wash and press them for morning.

I'd changed into my white T-shirt and khaki pants. While Bannon took his turn in the bathroom, I lay on one of the mattresses to see what it was like. Needless to say it was firm, but quite comfortable, even the funny rectangular pillow felt good.

Bannon returned, wearing his pants, but no shirt, his hair wet and mussed. One look at that chest, and I was ready to let him have his way with me. I didn't, though. He'd need to do his *mea culpa* first. My pride and good judgment demanded it.

Since we were in Northern Thailand, Bannon said it was only fitting that we eat in the traditional northern style. He'd arranged for us to have a *khantoke* dinner at a nearby restaurant that was as authentic as our guesthouse.

We were seated in a small, private dining room, our table on an elevated platform in the middle of the room. There were two liquid candles on the table, the only other light coming from lanterns in the corner of the room. It was wonderfully romantic. I was happy that Bannon and I were on better terms and could enjoy it.

Our meal included a spicy dip, pork skin, and a chicken and vegetable curry that was exquisite. To drink we had a potent local beer that went well with the spicy food.

Toward the end of the meal I looked at Bannon, his face bathed in the soft glow of candlelight. Though I had a pretty good idea, I asked, "So, what are you thinking?"

"I think we should forget the ruby and skip ahead to post-mission celebration."

"I was afraid you'd say that."

"I haven't been the same since we fell into that pool at the waterfall," he said.

"To be honest, I haven't either."

"It must be a good omen, Lexie."

"We'll see."

"You're hesitating because . . ."

"Honestly? Because I need to know everything before I sleep with you again."

"You *will* know everything about me. I promised you that already."

"Before the ruby, not after, Cole."

He seemed uncomfortable with that. "Why don't we continue this discussion as we stroll around the lake?"

Bannon paid the bill, and we left the restaurant. It was a lovely evening, but I did need the light jacket I'd brought along. Bannon and I strolled arm-in-arm past the two temples overlooking the lake, neither really ancient. He told me they were less than two hundred years old. Wat Chong Klang looked especially exotic reflected in the water.

As we ambled along in the falling dusk, we came up to a small group of mostly Japanese tourists clustered around a woman and a girl in colorful tribal attire. They sat on a bench, beaming as their pictures were being taken. What was remarkable about the woman was her incredibly long neck.

"They're Padaung," Bannon explained. "They put those brass rings around their necks to elongate them."

I'd seen pictures of African women with elongated necks but hadn't realized they did it in Thailand as well. "Why, for heaven's sake, do they do that? Is it for aesthetics?"

"I hesitate to tell you the explanation I was given."

"Tell me anyway."

"It was originally to protect them from Tiger attacks."

"You mean so the tiger couldn't bite their neck?"

Bannon shrugged. "That's the story."

"I think I prefer my automatic."

Continuing on around the lake, we came to a fitness park not far from the guesthouse. I showed Bannon how strong I was by doing ten reps on the chin-up bar.

"I think you're the first woman I've known who could do more than one."

"I had three brothers and had to keep pace with them or get eaten alive."

He chuckled. "No tiger would risk attacking you, Lexie. And I see now Noonwongsa never had a chance."

"At this point I'm a little more concerned about Colonel Lwin than Noonwongsa."

Bannon was silent. I decided to take the initiative.

"Is there anything I need to fear that you haven't told me?"

"You're really holding my feet to the fire, aren't you?"

"Maybe I'd rather know the truth than go into this thing blind."

"Lexie, I told you, it's in your best interest not to know the whole truth."

I considered my options for a moment, then plunged ahead. "I'm going to make it easy for you, Cole. I know you're an arms dealer and that you'll be bartering with Lwin for weapons."

He didn't look pleased. "Chung Lee told you."

"Yeah."

"I wish he hadn't opened his mouth."

"Well, it would have been better if you'd come clean from the beginning. It would have saved us both a lot of grief. Your lies have been a big problem for me."

Bannon brooded for a while, then said, "I hate to say it, but my fibs are the least of your problems."

"True, I haven't exactly enjoyed all the attempts on my life."

"That was Noonwongsa. I'm talking about what lies ahead."

"You mean Lwin?"

"Yes."

"I know he's no saint, but are you suggesting there's more I have to worry about?"

"Let me put it this way. The less you know, the better off you are. That's why I wanted you focused on the role of gemologist and oblivious to everything else. You shouldn't get mixed up in the dirty work, Lexie. Seriously."

"What dirty work? The arms dealing?"

"Yeah, the arms dealing."

I knew he was lying. Normally he was smooth as hell, but for once, he wasn't the least bit convincing.

"Look, if anybody asks you, you can say I deal in arms, and that's all you know because it *is* all you know."

It was patronizing, and I didn't like that, but I sensed he really did believe it was in my best interests to be kept in the dark. And with things having improved between us, I was reluctant to foment yet another crisis. "Fine," I said, "we'll do it your way."

Bannon put his arm around me. "Admit it, being friendly is much more fun."

He had a point. I'd been out-maneuvered and he was getting his way, but there was benefit in it for me as well. The guy was one hell of a lover.

Once we were back in our room, we kissed once, then couldn't get our clothes off fast enough. Bannon had been redeemed, to a point. True, he was still an arms dealer, and he was holding something back, but now he was at least being honest about it. The lies had been the big problem for me. Like most women, I can deal with the truth, if I know what it is. At the moment, though, I didn't want to think about any of that. We were all that mattered.

I lay on my back, my hands over my head, as he kissed my breasts and belly. I wanted only one thing—to surrender. "You're damned lucky you're irresistible," I purred. "It's actually unfair."

"What's unfair? You're having fun, aren't you?"

He dragged his tongue across my belly button and I shivered. "But how will I feel about this in the morning?"

"Fondly, I hope."

I took his face in my hands and pulled him up so I could talk to him. "You know what I thought the first time I saw you? I thought you were a Troy doll."

"A what?"

I told him about Troy Caradine, the heartthrob at my high school and how Macy Nesmith and I had named a whole class of boys after him.

"So you saw me as a male bimbo, huh?"

"Basically. I still do. But you're fun, so that's okay."

Bannon bit my neck, making me yelp. "You think tigers are fun, too?"

"Quit that!"

He roared and continued nibbling my neck, which tickled horribly. I shrieked.

"Cole, people will hear."

"So what?"

"They'll think you're assaulting me."

"I am, but with good intentions."

"What good intentions?

He grinned at me in the faint light of the lanterns. "Your pleasure, Khun Alex."

He kissed my belly again lightly, his moist lips making my skin tingle. Then he ran his tongue farther south. I could feel his warm breath on me and I tensed. Parting my legs, he kissed the insides of my thighs. My breath grew short. I moaned.

Bannon inched closer, and the nearer he got to the critical point, the stronger the pulses inside me became. When his tongue found my nub, I shuddered. "Oh . . . God . . ."

The pleasure was so intense I couldn't take it. I tried to hold it back, to make it last, but my body wouldn't cooperate. I came.

I never thought of myself as particularly vocal while making love, but I cried out, my body out of control as I crushed Bannon's head against me. When it was over, I melted into the mattress, spent. Half a minute passed.

"Good Lord," I finally said as my heart continued to hammer against my ribs. "I think I'm dying."

"I wish you wouldn't yet," he said, rubbing his cheek against my hipbone.

"That was incredible, Cole. Where did you learn to do that?" I'd no sooner asked the question than I knew it was stupid. "Never mind, I don't think I want to know."

"You inspire me," he murmured.

"Bullshit. But nice of you to say so."

I took handfuls of his tawny hair and pulled him up to me so I could kiss him.

I rubbed my cheek against his. "How do you want me?"

Bannon took the rectangular pillow, placed it in the middle of the bed, and rolled me onto it, facedown, so that it was under my hips. Without a word he moved behind. I extended my arms above my head and grabbed the mattress as he grasped my haunches, entering me.

The thrusts were slow at first, the sensation incredible. His long, even strokes grew determined. I didn't think it possible that I'd come again so quickly, but as his excitement grew, mine did as well. We came within seconds of each other, our bodies moving in perfect syncopation until the moment of release.

We both gasped, then he collapsed on me. Cole Bannon was mine and I was his. We were one.

Chapter 46

I awoke before dawn, still naked and tangled in Bannon's long limbs, fond recollections of our night together coming to mind. We'd made love once more before we fell asleep. Then, in the middle of the night, I had awakened when Cole ran his hand over my breast. We made love a third time then, slowly, quietly, without a word passing between us. I think I fell asleep afterward with him still in me.

Now it was morning and time to get back to reality. In spite of that, I allowed myself to speculate about the future. If sex were the only issue, I could marry the guy tomorrow and it wouldn't be too quick. But a man's skill as a lover was no basis for love, much less marriage. It could justify an affair, but I wasn't even sure I wanted that.

Bannon may have fulfilled me sexually, but he was still something of a mystery. I'd been peeling away the layers of his persona, but how far did I have to go to get to his heart?

He groaned and a few seconds later his eyes fluttered open. I smiled at him.

"What a beautiful sight to wake up to," he mumbled.

"You too."

"We did it, didn't we?" he said, rubbing his face. "I didn't dream that."

"No, we did it, all right. Including once in the middle of the night, if you want to be technical about it."

Bannon closed his eyes and smiled blissfully. I stroked his cheek. He took my hand.

"Lexie, you're incredible."

"You too."

He kissed my fingers.

"So," I said, "you're going to take the jeep to the rental agency before Colonel Lwin's man comes for us, is that the plan?"

"Yeah," he said listlessly, "that's the plan."

I noticed qualification in his voice. "What's wrong?"

He rolled his head toward me. "Are you sure you really want to do this?"

"What?"

"Go after the ruby? Is it really that important?"

"Cole!" I said, rising to my elbows. "After all we've gone through to get this close. Of course I want to go after the ruby."

"We could decide our relationship is more important than a stupid chunk of mineral, and we could get in the jeep and ride off into the sunset together."

"If it wasn't six in the morning, I'd think you've been drinking. What makes you say something like that? You know me well enough by now to realize nothing is going to keep me from the Heart of Burma."

"It could be a lot more dangerous out there than you think, Lexie. Everything we've gone through until now could be a cakewalk in comparison."

"Are you trying to talk me out of it?"

"Sort of."

"There's no 'sort of' about it. What's happened? What's changed?"

"I don't want anything to happen to you," he replied.

"I'm not fragile, Cole, and I still have a few lives left."

He sat up in the bed, facing me. "Seriously, sweetheart, if we return to Bangkok, we can grab Dru and be on a plane to Tahiti or someplace within hours."

"Why are you talking like this?"

"Lexie, I've fallen in love with you and suddenly nothing else seems important. I'm serious about how tough the next few days are going to be."

"You shouldn't use the term love loosely," I said, rubbing his knuckles.

"I didn't. I mean every word."

I bit my lip. He'd caught me flat-footed, and I didn't know what to say.

"But it's early in the relationship," he continued, "and I know we need more time to decide what it means. Don't feel you have to comment. I just want you to know I'm not talking off the top of my head."

I reached out and touched his face, my eyes glistening.

"Believe me," he said, "Lwin is a very serious guy."

"Do you know something I don't?"

He drew a breath. "No, but I think I know better what we're up against. It would be wrong of me to let you go into this thinking it's about some damned ruby."

"That's what it *is* about as far as I'm concerned. I know it's an arms deal to you, but like you said, I can't worry about that. Let's go see the man and, if he's reasonable, we can do our deal and come home."

Bannon grimaced. "You're not easily deterred, are you?"

I smiled. "Congratulations, I think you're finally getting to know me."

"Yeah, stubborn as a mule. Oh well, no woman is perfect." He patted my cheek. "I'd better get cleaned up and on my way."

"Can I just say one thing first? I have very strong feelings for you too."

Bannon kissed me, looking as pleased as I'd ever seen him. Then he left the bed.

The sun was peeking over the mountains when I came out of the guesthouse with our bags. Bannon had been gone longer than expected, though not long enough for me to worry. I was more concerned our guide would arrive before he did.

As it turned out the concern was justified. After two or three minutes, a battered little pickup truck came up the street and pulled into the drive, stopping not far from the bench where I sat. The driver, a man with a gaunt, pocked face, gave me a blank stare that fell short of hostile, though not by much.

He seemed to have no intention to speak to me, and I wasn't sure whether to approach him. Finally I decided to take the initiative and walked over to the vehicle.

"Are you Mr. Myat?" I said.

He gave a nod, his expression stone sober.

"Mr. Bannon's taking back the jeep, he'll be here soon."

Again Myat nodded, but showed no interest in having a conversation. I looked over the vehicle, realizing that there was only room for one passenger in the cab. Somebody would be riding in back and, knowing the status of women in this society, I had a pretty good idea who Myat would expect it to be. I returned to the bench.

For the next ten minutes, the man who was to lead us to Colonel Lwin and the Heart of Burma occupied his world, and I occupied mine. Then Bannon arrived with a driver from the rental agency. He got out of the vehicle and came walking up the drive. Myat climbed out of his truck, greeting him with courtesy, if not enthusiasm. I was beginning to see why Chung Lee felt I needed Cole Bannon for the jungle phase of the expedition. After his professions of love, the business aspects of our relationship seemed less important, but I was glad for his presence for practical, as well as romantic, reasons.

I walked to where the two men stood talking. They were speaking in Thai. If Myat didn't speak English, it could explain his reticence. Bannon glanced at me, putting an arm around my shoulders. I sensed it was time to discuss seating arrangements.

"I'll ride in back with our bags," Bannon said.

"No, I think I should," I said. "When in Rome and all that."

"We'll be on some rough, dusty roads," he said. "It won't be very comfortable."

"At least I won't have to ride with a crate of chickens or a pig. Anyway, why cast doubt about your manhood? Women in the back of the bus. Isn't that the rule?"

Bannon put his arms around me and gave me a hug. "You are a trooper," he said. "But if it gets too bad, I'm going to switch places with you."

"And lose face?"

"I'll tell him you're pregnant."

"Perish the thought."

"Well, maybe not now, granted, but . . ."

"Bannon, shut up and get in the truck."

Loaded up, we took off, leaving Mae Hong Son. We did not head west, toward the Myanmar border, as I expected, going north instead. There being no glass in the back window in the truck, Bannon and I were as close as if we'd been sitting side by side. As a result we could talk.

"Do you know where we're going?" I asked.

"Not exactly. The Myanmar army doesn't know where Lwin's camp is located, and he doesn't want anybody else to know either. Believe me, after a trek through the jungle, we won't have any idea where we are ourselves."

For the first twenty miles the road was semi-paved and, discounting the occasional bone-jarring bump, not too bad. But then we turned onto a secondary road which wasn't quite up to the standard of the gravel roads in the back country of northern Georgia.

After ten miles or so we came to a road junction and stopped. There was a shack nearby, which I realized was a refreshment stand of sorts. Several mountain tribesmen sat under a nearby tree and came over with baskets of handicrafts, hoping to make a sale. I occupied myself looking over their wares while Myat and Bannon went inside the shack. They came out a minute later with beers in their hands. Bannon had one for me.

Beer wasn't the ideal thirst-quencher, but it tasted good under hot, dusty conditions, even if it wasn't cold. Bannon watched me take a long pull.

"Do I look like Ma Kettle?" I asked, pushing my hair off my face.

"Lexie, I find you beautiful under any and all circumstances."

"You feel guilty about me being treated like livestock."

"The roughest stretch lies ahead," he replied. "It's time we switch places."

"Not on your life. I'm enjoying your guilt. But don't worry, I'll find a way for you to make it up to me."

"Like how?"

I smiled innocently. "I have fond recollections of last night."

"Deal," he said with a grin. "Now, get in the truck, woman. I don't want any more lip from you."

"Oh, how I love a masterful man."

He gave me a swat on the behind.

Yep, our relationship had definitely turned a corner.

Chapter
47

The road we traveled on the final ten miles of the journey hardly qualified as a road—two muddy or dusty ruts, depending on the local terrain, would be more descriptive. Twice we encountered logging crews with elephants dragging huge logs along the trail.

We'd gone over a pass, then up a deep gorge, stopping at a small settlement which consisted of half a dozen huts. There were a few men present, but no women I could see. I decided it was more of an outpost than a village. I jumped out of the truck. Myat got our bags, handing them to one of the men who approached.

Bannon, who'd been looking around, said, "From here on, we walk. Our man told me we'll eat here before we head out, but we don't have much time if we're going to make it into Myanmar before nightfall."

We were provided backpacks, machetes, canteens, and individual bottles of insect repellant. Looking at my bottle, I said to Bannon, "Not a good sign, but better than brass rings for my neck, I suppose."

"Fear not, Lexie. No tiger's going to get you, I've already claimed the territory."

"That's comforting to know."

"We'd better get our gear ready."

"I guess we leave our luggage here."

"No bearers in this jungle."

"I didn't think so."

There was a large crate outside one of the huts, which I used as a table to spread out my things and transfer them into the backpack. Three or four of the men sat on their haunches, watching me. Apparently there hadn't been many female *farangs* in this neck of the woods, and I was a curiosity. When I took out my automatic and slipped the holster on my belt, I heard them murmur.

Once Bannon and I had finished packing, Myat invited us into the largest of the huts where our lunch was waiting. It wasn't fancy—a stew of rice, vegetables, fish and spices, which we ate with chopsticks out of wooden bowls. To drink, we had warm beer.

Our lunch eaten and the table cleared by the leathery little man who'd served us, Myat and Bannon engaged in a conversation that sounded a good deal more serious than postprandial banter. I grew concerned as it went on and on. I could tell Bannon was struggling because of his limitations with the language, but they seemed to reach an understanding in the end.

"So, what's going on?" I asked after Myat got up from the table and left the hut.

"There's been a lot of recent activity by the Myanmar Army along the border," Bannon replied. "In short, it's not the best time to be going in."

"That's what you were discussing?"

"That, and strategy. The question was whether we make a

dash during broad daylight or try to sneak in at night. The problem with going at night is it would take a few days and we'd have to hole up someplace during the daylight hours anyway. We decided to split the difference and make the crossing during the evening hours in semi-darkness rather than the dead of night."

"I never have liked that term, dead of night," I said with a shiver. I was thinking about snakes, which I happen to hate, though I wasn't about to bring up my phobias. "To the extent I get a vote, daylight sounds good to me."

He took my hand. "It's not too late to turn back."

"Come on," I said, rising, "let's get cracking before the mosquitos and other critters come out of their holes."

Myat, as somber as ever, was waiting for us with his own pack and machete in hand. He'd added a slouch hat to his attire and had an automatic rifle slung over his shoulder. Myat did not look like the ideal traveling companion. I was thankful for Bannon's presence.

We set off, following a trail up the gorge for a short distance before leaving it for a secondary path that led up one face of the canyon. The climb was steep and rocky, though there were plenty of trees, shrubs and other vegetation. It took us the better part of an hour to reach the rim.

Dense jungle covered the back side of the ridge, which dropped off gradually. The trail was barely visible, overgrown with vegetation. Myatt used his machete to clear the way. At times I wondered if there was a trail at all.

We waded through several streams and crossed a small river on a fallen log as a family of small monkeys chattered and kibitzed in the trees. That was also where I saw my first snake, a big one, which was the main reason I declined Bannon's offer to take a rest break. "I'd rather wait until I'm tired and really need it," I said.

I'd studied maps of the area before leaving home and was familiar enough with the geography to know that we were very close to Myanmar, if we hadn't already crossed the border. The river we'd traversed was likely a tributary of the Salween, which flowed all the way from China to the Gulf of Martaban on the west coast. Lwin's camp had to be in the rugged jungle east of the river, somewhere near the Golden Triangle.

We stopped at the next stream to rest. From here on out, Myat had no intention of consulting me, I could see. In a way I was sorry we hadn't rested at the river, because this spot was boggy and damp and looked to be the home of a hundred snakes, though I didn't see any. There were plenty of mosquitoes though, prompting me to slather on lots of insect repellent.

Bannon watched me applying the oily mixture to my face, neck, and arms while Myat fooled with his gear. "You know, you really are beautiful," Bannon said with genuine admiration.

"Thanks, but if I look half as bad as I feel, you're in the early stages of jungle fever. Do you think the colonel has showers in his camp?"

"Probably with gold fixtures."

"I hope you're right."

Myatt muttered something to Bannon, which was duly passed on to me. "He said we'll be coming to the area where there have been a lot of enemy patrols, so we'll have to move more cautiously and make as little noise as possible."

"What happens if they capture us, Cole?"

He shrugged. "Want me to ask?"

"I won't be turning back no matter what he says, but I might as well know."

Bannon spoke to our guide who looked over at me and

smiled for the first time in our brief acquaintance. He gave a cryptic answer punctuated with a chuckle. I turned to Bannon for the translation.

"You don't want to know," he said.

"Of course I do."

Bannon rolled his eyes. "He said they'd shoot him in the head on the spot and we'd be dragged off and thrown in prison."

"For how long?"

"A few years."

I gave a half shrug. "Well, I'd still be in my thirties."

Bannon smiled and Myat added something else, his comment this time more lengthy. I again turned to Bannon.

"It was nothing," he said.

"Dammit, Cole, quit pampering. Technically, you're working for me."

"All right, Ms. Chandler. Myat just made the point that Westerners doing business with Colonel Lwin are not much appreciated. If you're captured, the entire patrol will probably have its way with you before turning you in."

"He said that?"

"You see why I didn't want to tell you."

Needless to say, it was a sobering comment. Bannon had an I-tried-to-warn-you look on his face. I could see why he thought Tahiti would be preferable to the jungle camp.

I took a long drink of water from my canteen. "Tell Mr. Lightness and Joy I'm ready when he is."

We took off again at a much more cautious pace. Myat didn't hack at vines and undergrowth as much, probably because it was noisy. Our progress was slow and the afternoon wearing on. Once, when I said something to Bannon, Myat, who was right in front of me, turned and gave me a withering look, pressing his finger to his lips.

Myat didn't scare me, but what he'd said about the Myanmar army did. Discretion being the better part of valor, I'd
save my feminist spirit for later, when we were back in Thailand. In places where the law of the jungle reigned supreme,
women were at a distinct disadvantage.

Judging by the fall of the terrain, we seemed to be coming to yet another river. Dusk was approaching, and Myat
was all but tiptoeing along the trail. Every twenty yards he
would stop and listen. I would listen, too, but all I could hear
was the caw and cry of birds, monkeys, and God knows
what else.

But then, just as we entered a small clearing, we heard human voices. Myat signaled us to move off the trail. We hurried to the edge of the clearing and plunged into the
undergrowth as quietly as we could, laying down on the
boggy ground.

The voices grew louder. They were coming our way. But
then I saw something that made my heart stop. On the other
side of the clearing, less than twenty yards away, a tiger
emerged from the jungle.

I reached for my gun. Only then did Bannon and Myat see
the big cat, which stopped in its tracks and turned its head
toward the sounds of approaching humans. I stared at the
sleek beast, my heart in my throat, aware there wasn't a
damned thing between me and him—no bars, no moat, nothing. I thought of the villager who'd been eaten and hoped to
God this guy wasn't the culprit.

For a second I thought the tiger might lope over and take
refuge on our side of the clearing, but after a moment's hesitation it retreated into the undergrowth. I let out a sigh of relief.

Myat, meanwhile, had taken his automatic rifle from his

shoulder and was in a firing position. I don't think his concern was the tiger.

Seconds later a soldier stepped into the clearing, followed by another, then yet another. All in all, a dozen men passed by, oblivious to both us and the tiger. Once the patrol had disappeared into the jungle, Myat told Bannon he would go down the trail a way to make sure there wasn't a larger party following the patrol. We were to stay put until he returned.

Taking his rifle, Myat jogged across the clearing and disappeared from sight.

"What does he expect us to do if he gets captured?" I whispered.

"Lexie, at that point, I don't think he'd care all that much."

"You're right. How selfish of me to wonder."

Myat was only gone three or four minutes before reappearing. He waved at us to come. Bannon and I got up and were halfway across the clearing when I realized that in the excitement and confusion I'd left my backpack behind. There was no time to discuss it, and I couldn't go on without it, so I dashed back without saying anything.

It was only fifty feet—the distance from my parents' front porch to the street—but in the few seconds it took, Bannon had reached the other side of the clearing. He turned about the time I lifted the backpack onto my shoulders. I hadn't gone two steps toward him before the quiet of the jungle was shattered by a bone-rattling roar.

I froze and, glancing over, saw that the tiger had reemerged from the jungle. His green eyes zeroed in on me, and he crouched, his sinewy body coiling to attack. I had my automatic in my holster, true, but I felt as good as naked. First, I had to draw the gun, then fire. How many shots could

I get off before the beast pounced on me? And, given the fact I was trembling like a leaf in a gale, how true would the shots be?

The tiger bared his fangs, roared again, then took a slow, deliberate step in my direction. I about wet my pants.

Chapter 48

I had the presence of mind to pull my gun from the holster slowly, without making a sudden motion. The tiger took another threatening step toward me. I lifted the weapon and aimed between the big cat's eyes.

"Lexie," Bannon said in a low voice from across the clearing, "if you shoot, it'll alert the patrol. They'll be on our ass in seconds."

Easy for you to say, I thought. But he was right. I was in a no-win situation. I either became the tiger's lunch, or I shot him and got raped. This gave a whole new meaning to the phrase, "the lady and the tiger."

From the corner of my eye, I saw Bannon and Myat creeping into the clearing, perhaps hoping to distract the huge beast. The big cat seemed in a quandary of his own. Did he charge and eat, or did he cover his flank first? He snarled, glancing at them, then back at me. Seeming displeased by the new complication, he coiled back on his haunches, giving every sign he'd opted to eat first and deal with the interlopers later.

Ironically, my would-be rapists helped the tiger make up

his mind. Voices could again be heard on the trail. The patrol was retracing their steps. The tiger faced a whole new ball game. The odds had shifted against him.

Snarling with annoyance in the direction of the approaching patrol, the tiger swung his long, graceful body around and loped back into the undergrowth, disappearing as harmlessly as a kitten taking refuge under a bed.

I was so relieved, I nearly dropped to my knees. But there was no time for celebration because of the patrol. Myat gave a low whistle and waved for me to come. I took off at a run. When I reached the men, we lit out, charging down the trail pell-mell. The patrol was behind us and could have already been alerted to our presence, perhaps having seen signs that we'd passed by.

For the next twenty minutes we ran as fast as the jungle would allow, ignoring the vines and vegetation. The patrol didn't have any bloodhounds, to be sure, but I felt like an escaped prisoner fleeing through the swamps of south Georgia, the baying hounds and the law in hot pursuit.

We crossed one stream and splashed a quarter of a mile up another before Myat decided it was safe to stop. I was pretty winded and sweating profusely by the time we slung off our packs and sat on a big log at the edge of the stream. We all were soaked and exhausted. And it wasn't just because of the heat and the exertion. We'd had a damned close call. Myat could have been shot, and I had nearly endured the worst a man-eating tiger and twelve cutthroat men had to offer.

It was dusk, with darkness falling. We'd left the trail, which meant we'd be traveling cross-country from now on. I hoped Myat knew where we were and how we got from here to Colonel Lwin's camp.

Bannon patted my knee. "How you doing, sweetheart?"

"I guess it's too late to change my mind about Tahiti, isn't it?"

He gave me a sympathetic smile. "After a tiger and a Myanmar army patrol, it's hard to believe it could get worse."

"Will it?"

Bannon shook his head. "I wish I knew Lwin by more than reputation."

I glanced at Myat, who was preoccupied. Presumably he couldn't understand a word, but you never knew. Lowering my voice, I said, "How bad can Lwin be?"

"Let's hope he's all business so we can do our thing and get the hell out of here."

"Amen to that."

I smiled, but Bannon didn't. In fact, he was no longer looking at me. He was staring at something behind me, and, judging by the expression on his face, whatever it was he saw, it didn't please him.

"Don't move, Lexie," he said, reaching for his gun.

My heart almost stopped. "Cole, what is it?"

"Don't move a muscle. Don't even twitch."

Another tiger? I had no idea. Worse, I didn't know what to hope for. The list of terrible possibilities was too long.

About the time Cole had unholstered his gun, Myat pushed past him, arm and machete raised. I flinched as the blade went swishing over my head. A second later something clunked on my back and fell to the ground.

I let out a little scream and jumped to my feet, spinning around. There on the ground, I saw what I half expected—a six-foot snake in two three-foot pieces, writhing and gushing blood.

"Oh, my God!" I cried, burying my face in Bannon's chest.

He held me, stroking my back as my body trembled. There was too much adrenaline in my blood for me to cry, but I shook like I never had before.

"Just relax, sweetheart. You're okay."

"The hell I am."

"It was just an overgrown garden snake."

I hooted at that. "You're still a goddamn liar, Cole."

From the corner of my eye, I watched Myat flick the bifurcated snake into the brush with his machete. A tremor went through me.

"I don't suppose there's a U.S. Army helicopter nearby ready to extract us."

"I wish there were." He gave me a sympathetic look which turned puckish.

"Cole Bannon, don't you dare say 'I told you so.' *Ever*."

"Not even at Christmas?"

"No."

"How about on our twentieth anniversary?"

"Bad joke."

"It needn't be."

I gave him a little push away and picked up my backpack. "This ruby had better be worth a hundred million dollars retail because that's what I'm charging the buyer, come hell or high water." I put my hands on my hips as Bannon and Myat both stared at me. "Come on, Cole, tell him I want to see Colonel Lwin."

Myat smiled at me for the second time in our acquaintance, then said something. I glanced at Bannon, wanting a translation. "What did he say?"

"That if you have to go to the bathroom that bad, you should use the bushes. Half a snake, he says, can't hurt you."

I would have flipped Myat the bird, were it not for the fact he'd just saved my butt. Anyway, we still needed his services.

Pursing my lips, I said, "Tell him thanks, but I'd rather wait."

Myat said we'd lost too much time to make it to the camp before morning and that we'd be lucky to find the right trail. We still had some jungle to walk through and, with night approaching, we needed to get a move on.

As it turned out, darkness fell and we were still hacking our way through the jungle. Myat got out a flashlight so he could see where we were putting our feet. It was exhausting work, especially in the dark. Bannon traded off the machete work with Myat to give him a breather. We all agreed this was better than sleeping on the jungle floor, the only alternative.

Eventually we reached the trail and Myat seemed relieved. He told us it wasn't far to a place where we could spend the night. In less than half a mile we came to a shack which Myat said had been built for travelers trekking to the camp.

Myat had some food provisions in his pack—sticky rice balls, dried pork strips, and dried fruit. The three of us sat cross-legged on the floor with an oil lamp for light, dining on Myat's repast, washing the food down with water from our canteens.

After dinner was over we had two options—talk or sleep. Myat had already proven himself not to be much of a conversationalist and, since we were all bone tired, we decided to lie down on the straw mats that were to be our beds. Bannon and I took one side of the tiny room and Myat the other.

After I lathered myself with insect repellent, I snuggled up to the man who'd become my lover. He gathered me to him, kissing my temple. We hadn't been lying there for two minutes before Myat began to snore.

"You suppose we'd wake him?" Bannon whispered in my ear.

"You mean if we talk?"

"I was thinking of your cries of pleasure."

"Look, buster, I had encounters with a tiger, twelve rapists, and a snake today. The only cries of pleasure you'll hear from me will be if I dream about a nice hot bath."

"In other words, this exotic tropical getaway doesn't spark your romantic imagination," he said.

"Let me put it this way, Cole. You're more likely to get co-operation from Myat than me."

He laughed and kissed me. I was soon sound asleep.

I managed to sleep through most of the night. When I awoke, it wasn't to the smell of coffee and bacon. There were shouts outside the hut. Myat jumped up, his automatic rifle in hand, and peered out the door. There were more shouts.

Bannon crawled over and took a peek outside. He glanced back at me, his expression grim. "Bad news, sweetheart. It appears we're surrounded by the Myanmar Army. They're telling us to come out with our hands up."

"Shit," I said, "it wasn't supposed to work out this way."

"Tell me about it."

Myat sagged against the wall, looking defeated, as he mumbled something.

"He says if we try to fight, this little straw hut will be cut up like a *piñata*," Bannon said. "That's a loose translation."

"No kidding."

The three of us looked at each other. Myat had the most to fear, Bannon the least. Once the bullets started flying we'd be dead. That much was certain.

"If there's a senior officer out there, we might get decent treatment," Bannon said.

He was offering what comfort he could, but, basically, the situation was hopeless. Bannon and Myat conferred. I could see by dawn's early light that my dreams about the Heart of

Burma were going up in smoke. And that was the least of my troubles. But the one I was concerned about was Myat. I didn't want them executing him on the spot.

"How about if I negotiate with them?" I said.

"You?" Bannon said.

"Why not? I might be able to get them to listen, assuming somebody speaks English. I'm going to ask them to spare Myat's life."

"If you're going out there," Bannon said, "we're going out together."

"They won't expect to see me, Cole. The shock value alone might make the ploy more effective."

"I'm not letting you go alone," he insisted.

"You happen to work for me," I said.

"Yeah, well you're a woman, and the rules are different here."

I got up and started for the door. Bannon tried to grab me, but I side-stepped him, pushing him away.

"Lexie," he yelled, but I was already out the door.

Chapter 49

I stood in the dust in front of the hut, squinting in the morning sun. I could see armed men standing in intervals at the edge of the jungle. They had us surrounded.

"Who's the officer in charge?" I called.

"Lexie," Bannon shouted, "get your ass back in here."

I glanced over my shoulder. He stood in the doorway. "Let me do this, Cole. Go back inside. Please."

"Who are you, lady?" A voice called from the jungle.

"Alexis Chandler," I called back. "I'm a reporter. I'm writing a story about the rebellion in Myanmar."

A slender man with a mustache and wearing a crisp uniform stepped from the undergrowth. With him were two soldiers with automatic rifles. I didn't know the Myanmar Army insignia, but I'd been around military enough to know a senior officer when I saw one. If I had to guess, a major or lieutenant colonel.

"Come," the officer said, beckoning me toward him.

I started walking.

Bannon said, "You're not going alone."

I heard his footsteps behind me, then shots rang out, cutting up the dust at his feet.

"Get back inside," I hollered at him.

He had no choice but to comply. I proceeded to where the officer waited. He looked me up and down.

"A great surprise, indeed." He smiled, amused. "How many are inside?"

"Two. My American associate and our guide."

"Do you have papers?"

"No, we crossed illegally from Thailand."

"You may be arrested."

"I understand."

The officer seemed befuddled and uncertain what to do, just as I'd hoped. "Tell the others to come out," he said after a moment.

"I will, but I want your promise of proper treatment."

He smiled. "Do I understand that you dictate the terms of your surrender?"

"You seemed to be an officer and a gentleman. I simply want your assurance that you'll behave in accordance."

His smile broadened. "Miss Chandler, is it?"

"Yes."

"You are indeed a refreshing change. Nonetheless, you are under arrest. Now tell the others to come out."

I wasn't sure if I'd done us any good or not, but it was better than being cut up in a hail of gunfire. "Okay."

I turned and was about to shout at Bannon and Myat to come out when shots rang out on all sides. For a second I thought they'd opened fire on the hut, but then I realized the fire was coming from behind the troops that had us surrounded.

Before I could blink, one of the armed men fell to the ground. The officer and the other man sprinted for the bush. I hit the ground, my face sinking into the dust. The gunfire became intense. I was certain that at any moment I'd be shot, what with the way the bullets flew on all sides.

I don't know how long I lay there in the kill zone with the firefight going on around me. It seemed like fifteen minutes, but it was probably only two. As suddenly as it began, the shooting stopped. I lifted my head and saw the bodies of army soldiers all around.

"Lexie!" Bannon came running from the shack and skidded to the ground on his knees next to me. "Are you all right?"

"Yeah. What the hell happened?" I asked, confused.

"I don't know."

I was still on my belly when more soldiers appeared, but they weren't dressed like the others. These men were irregulars—rebels, most likely.

While they began checking enemy bodies, a stocky man in crisp fatigues and a purple beret came toward us. He was barrel-chested, but short. He wore sunglasses and a holstered pistol on his hip, his bearing that of a senior officer. His smile was punctuated with a gleaming gold tooth.

He put his hands on his hips and said, "Miss Chandler, you look like you could use a bath."

"You must be Colonel Lwin," I said.

The man known as the Burmese Tiger grinned. "At your service."

Bannon and I got to our feet. As I dusted myself off, the colonel handed me his handkerchief. "Such a pretty face should not be covered by dirt. Please," he said, giving a little bow.

It was all terribly polite, but my gut told me I could be in for trouble.

"Enemy patrols invade our territory in recent days," Colonel Than Lwin explained to me as we strode along the trail with armed men on all sides. "We hear that larger force moving in, so I decide to put a stop on it. I also concerned maybe they capture you. Good thing I come. Right, Miss Chandler?"

"We're very glad you arrived when you did, Colonel," I said with a glance at Bannon, who was on my other side.

He did not look happy. I knew it was because Lwin had been falling all over himself to charm me, but we were alive thanks to the colonel and, at a minimum, he deserved some indulgence.

"Don't overdo it," Bannon had said earlier as Lwin issued orders to his men.

"Cole," I'd said, "if this man really does have a shower I can use, you're demoted to second most important man in my life until I've had a chance to clean up. Sorry, but hot water and soap is my top priority at the moment."

"The fickle nature of womankind," he groused, shaking his head.

"Don't pout, sweetie. They'll let you wash up and eat too, I'm sure." That galled him. But that was okay. Every man needed a taste of humiliation now and then.

We soon came to a jeep trail where a dozen vehicles were parked. Lwin helped me into the back of the only clean polished jeep in the bunch and told Bannon to find a place in one of the other vehicles. Poor Cole. *Sometimes it does pay to be a woman,* I thought as I gave him a sympathetic look.

But I also knew I had to be careful because of Lwin's reputation as a womanizer. There was a fine line between being friendly and too friendly. Usually it didn't take long to find out where the line was. Few men were subtle.

But I did want that bath.

The ride to Lwin's camp involved traversing more rough terrain. I was surprised how civilized the installation looked. For all intents and purposes, it was a small town spread out in an area half a mile square. There was hot and cold running water, a modern communications system, and even satellite phones.

After helping me from the jeep, the colonel took me aside. "Sorry to ask personal question, Miss Chandler, but what your relationship with Mr. Bannon? Myat say you very friendly."

The purpose of Lwin's question was obvious, and I knew my answer would be critical. I decided to try to split the difference between encouraging and disappointing him. "Cole and I are business associates," I told him, "but we're also good friends. I'm very fond of him."

Lwin wasn't sure he liked what he heard, but I could also tell he didn't know what conclusion to draw. He decided to get more specific and at the same time put me on the spot, as men are wont to do.

"Let me ask," he said. "I have very nice house with guest room where you can stay. Also there is guesthouse for visitor. It has two bedroom and not so nice as my house. I put Mr. Bannon in guesthouse. You wish to stay with Mr. Bannon or you wish to stay with me?"

I could see maneuvering through Lwin's mine field wasn't going to be easy, but I was a woman and, as a result, innately more clever in such matters. "Since Mr. Bannon and I are partners, we need to stick together," I said. "How else can we hope to outsmart you in negotiations?" I gave him my sweetest smile. "So I would like to stay at the guesthouse. But I hope to see your lovely home."

His half scowl turned into a full-blown grin with my final words. "This I promise, Miss Chandler. Tonight you will have dinner with me. And drinks, of course." His brows flicked salaciously under his sunglasses.

I had a sinking feeling. And the more his gold tooth gleamed, the deeper I sank. God help me if the little toad expected sexual favors as part of the deal. I couldn't say I hadn't been warned, but he owned the Heart of Burma, and he'd saved my life.

"I look forward to dining with you, Colonel," I told him, "but until then I'd like to rest. What time should Mr. Bannon and I be at your house?"

Lwin's mouth jaw dropped, seeing I'd outflanked him. He could have told me Bannon wasn't invited, but that would have been too blatant, even for him. The man was obviously used to having his way. He ran his army as though he was God and treated his men like toy soldiers. Women obviously existed for his pleasure. Distasteful as that was, I'd have to deal with it. The issue was the same as it had been from the beginning. How badly did I want the Heart of Burma?

Chapter 50

Cole Bannon slumped in the rattan armchair in the sitting room as I came out of the bath. He had a grumpy expression on his face.

I had a towel wrapped around my wet hair and wore one of the terry robes I'd found hanging on the back of the bathroom door. The robe was short and showed a lot of leg. Bannon was in too foul a mood to notice. Either that or he was making a point.

"Your turn," I said, cheerfully.

Bannon groused.

"The hot water's a little erratic," I said, ignoring his mood, "but otherwise, it's a good shower. And it felt *wonderful*."

"Nice to see you're so easily pleased."

"Why are you in such a bad mood? Things are going well."

"Yeah, for Lwin. Can't you see that the guy's trying to lure you into his web. He took one look at you and flipped. It was written all over his face."

"You're blowing things out of proportion."

"The hell I am. Trust me, you're playing this wrong. With guys like Lwin, you've got to be firm, let him know you aren't interested."

"I tried that with you and look where it got me."

"My point precisely."

My brows rose. "The difference being you're irresistible and the colonel's not."

"My point is you can't give him any encouragement. Think about it, Lexie, we're in the middle of nowhere and this guy's got a thousand armed men at his beck and call. He can do what he wants."

"Now just a minute," I said, putting my hands on my hips. "Wasn't it you and Chung who said Lwin might have a thing for the ladies, but he's a civilized gentleman?"

"That was mostly Chung. Anyway, it's beside the point. We're here now, and the signals you send are what matter."

"Is that really what this fit of pique is about?"

He took a deep breath. "You can be really annoying when you put your mind to it, Alexis Chandler," he said. "Do you know that?"

"You didn't answer the question."

Bannon got up and began pacing. "Maybe it's more complicated than Lwin's character, or lack thereof. Besides, things have changed since we had that conversation."

"How so?" It was catty, maybe, but I was going to make him say it.

"Things are different between us, in case you haven't noticed." He continued to pace, looking positively angry.

"Oh, I've noticed all right."

He stopped abruptly. "And?"

"And what? We have a sexual relationship. Is that what you want me to say?"

He looked wounded. "Lexie, I love you. Doesn't that matter to you?"

I went over to him and took his face in my hands. "Of course it matters to me. It makes me very happy. And I'm very, very fond of you. I can't wait until we've got this behind us and can focus on each other. I've told you that."

"And meanwhile you'll play footsie with Lwin." He removed my hands.

"Cole, I'm not playing footsie with him. I'm trying to be polite, yes. More than polite, maybe. But I know what I'm doing. Lwin wanted to have dinner alone with me tonight, but I worked it so that you were invited, too. I've told him you are a friend and that you're very important to me. Just because I don't spit in his face, doesn't mean I'm encouraging him. I can't afford to alienate him. Can't you see that?"

"It's not *your* intentions I'm worried about. It's *his*."

I gave him an indulgent smile. "You wouldn't be jealous, would you?"

He smirked. "Okay, I might be a little jealous, but I'm not going to stand idly by and watch Lwin take advantage of you. While you were in the shower he sent a messenger over. He wants me to see him so we can go over his shopping list."

"That's good, it shows he's serious."

"They're two separate issues. But the point is that while I'm there I'm going to tell him how things are between us. I'm telling him that you're mine and unavailable."

"You wouldn't!"

"I not only would, I will."

"Cole, you're going to mess everything up. Please don't."

"It's the truth. And besides, if telling him you're not for sale messes up the deal, it only proves he's not serious about doing business with us. What if we were married, for crissake? Could he expect me to share my wife?"

"Well, we aren't married!" I snapped.

"Listen, I've lived here for years; I know how things work."

I took a calming breath. "Okay, I'll make a deal with you. If you will refrain from telling him we're a couple, then tonight at dinner I'll say whatever is necessary to make it clear that my only interest is doing business. You'll be there, you'll be able to see how he's behaving. If Lwin gets out of line, I'll tell him thanks, but no thanks. Is that fair?"

Bannon wasn't satisfied. "Why not tell him the truth up front?"

"Because I know a thing or two about men myself. From a woman's perspective. There are ways to let a man down without hurting his feelings. Friendliness, even a little harmless flirting, can help salvage a man's pride. Granted, I don't know Lwin well, but it's obvious he's prideful. I'll let him know the score, but I need to do it my own way. Allow me that, please."

Bannon shook his head. "You're amazing, Lexie. I'd decided exactly what I was going to do and nothing was going to stop me. Now after sweet-talking me, you've got me backing down."

I gave him a kiss on the lips. "Look at it this way, if I can talk you into behaving reasonably, shouldn't I be able to do the same with Colonel Lwin?"

"Not necessarily. I'm a nice guy, and I happen to love you. That makes a difference, you know."

"Your feelings for me are very important," I said, caressing his cheek, "but I also want your trust. It's just as important that you believe in me as it is that I believe in you."

"Okay, uncle," he said, holding up his hands. "There. You win. But you still have to be careful. In the Orient overconfidence can be deadly. And *that* is a fact."

"I'll keep that in mind. Now go have a shower. You stink."

Bannon cuffed my chin, chuckling, then headed for the bath.

Again, I sighed. I knew from the beginning that I was taking a calculated risk with Lwin. Now I had to hope that I was right about him and Bannon was wrong. Time would tell. As Mama liked to say, everybody's chickens come home to roost eventually.

I took a nap, and when I awoke, Bannon still hadn't returned from his meeting with Colonel Lwin. I hoped that Bannon had kept his promise. I was certain that had been his intent, but men were prideful and that sometimes got in the way of their judgment.

But in another way our little spat was encouraging. He was jealous, true, but I think he cared about more than just winning me at Lwin's expense. Twice now he'd told me he loved me, and I was fairly certain he meant it.

Truth bc known, I had strong feelings about him too. But before I could decide what they meant, we needed to spend a lot of time together—without the ruby to worry about and without bullets flying over our heads.

I heard the front door open and somebody come in. I went to see if it was Bannon and found him at the small refrigerator in the wet bar. Glancing up, he saw me.

"Hi. I was just getting myself a beer, care for one?"

"No thanks."

He removed the cap from the bottle and took a long pull.

"So, how'd it go with Lwin?" I asked.

He ambled over to the rattan chair and sat. "Pretty well.

His list was extensive, but I got the impression he'd be reasonable. It comes down to what the ruby's worth."

"Did he say anything about it?"

He took another sip of beer. "Only that he was looking forward to showing it to you and getting your assessment."

"That's good, right?"

"Yes, but that's not all we discussed. Tonight came up."

I tensed. "Cole, don't tell me you broke your promise."

"No, but I sure wanted to."

"Then what happened?"

"The good colonel has gotten me a date for tonight."

"A date?"

"Yes, with one of the camp floozies. He said she was a special girl, but how special can she be and live out here? The point is, he's counting on you for female companionship this evening, but he didn't want me to feel left out. Bottom line is I've got a date with a woman who will do whatever it takes to please me. I'm sure Lwin's expecting the same of you."

I watched him take another long drink of beer. "Are you serious?"

"Swear to God."

"Well, what did you say?"

"Considering I was under orders to keep my mouth shut, all I could do was smile and thank him. I guess I'm fortunate Lwin cares about my sexual gratification enough to line up a girl. But the truth of the matter is, I came this close to telling him you weren't available for his gratification under *any* circumstances. Being a man of my word, however, I declined to comment. *You'll* have to deal with the bastard."

"Damn," I grumbled. "Are you sure he's thinking in terms of sex? I mean, maybe he just wanted a more congenial dinner party."

Bannon hooted, almost spilling his beer. He wiped his mouth with the back of his hand. "Hey, little girl, would you like to see my puppy? And I've got candy."

"Oh, shut up!"

"Sorry, Lexie, but you're in for a rude awakening."

Chapter
51

I spent the rest of the afternoon worrying, which could have been what Bannon intended. He might have blown things out of proportion, but I had to assume the worst and prepare myself accordingly.

Bannon was in such a grouchy mood that he'd decided to go for a walk, saying he was curious about the layout of the camp. I was glad because if he'd stayed we'd have been at each other's throats. I was sure I could handle Lwin. What I didn't know was whether I could keep him at bay and still do business with him.

Not long after Bannon left the guesthouse a little woman with a congenial smile came to the door. She was in peasant garb and carried a basket. "Need something?" she asked. "You have laundry? Want eat something?" Entering, she put the basket on the table and removed a teapot and cups. She also had some fruit, dried meats, and rice cakes, which she put out. "Where dirty clothes?"

I got the fatigues I'd worn the day before. I had a second set which I planned to wear that night. I'd hung them up to get out the wrinkles, but they didn't look very good.

The woman took the fatigues, then pointed at the set hanging on the wall. "I fix."

"Thank you," I said.

She smiled, doing a modified *wai*. I asked her name.

"Kee," she replied.

"Do you work for Colonel Lwin?" I asked.

"Everybody work for him."

"Are there many women in the camp?"

"Maybe two hundred. Some wife. Some not."

"Is Colonel Lwin's wife here, Kee?"

"Oh, no. In China now. He have many lady. Many, many."

"Here in the camp?"

"They come from city, stay, then go. Many, many. Some have baby too. Today he send away Number One girl."

"Why?"

"She cry because boss want *farang*."

"You mean *me?*"

Kee nodded, beaming. "No lady *farang* come before. You first. Very special."

I swallowed hard. With her limited English, Kee had painted a very vivid picture of Colonel Than Lwin. It made what Chung Lee and Bannon had said about him seem like a whitewash job. Lwin couldn't think I had any interest in becoming his mistress, but Kee sure assumed I was there for sex, since women were brought in for that purpose.

"I'm here for business," I said, feeling the need to correct her misapprehension.

Kee looked uncertain, then nodded. "Money, yes?"

"No, not that kind of money."

Not understanding, she shrugged and gathered the fatigues. "Have pretty dress?"

"No dress," I said. "Just those."

She shook her head, not approving. "You big, but I try to find." After a nod of complicity, she went to the door.

"You're bringing my fatigues back, aren't you?"

"Yes, yes." And she was gone.

I wasn't at all sure I'd see my clothes again.

Bannon was gone a long time. With each passing minute I grew more and more uncomfortable. Here I was in a house in the middle of the jungle with nothing to wear but a bathrobe, and I was to have dinner with a lecherous womanizing dictator. How could this mission have gone so badly wrong?

When Bannon finally showed up, I was relieved. He started talking about the layout of the camp, the facilities. I listened for a while, but finally had to interrupt.

"Cole, I'm afraid you're right about Colonel Lwin's intentions."

"Why? Did he send his doctor over to check you out?"

"That's not funny."

"I'm struggling mightily not to say I told you so. What happened?"

I told him about Kee's visit. "What bothers me most is that he sent his mistress away, apparently because of me. The guy's both serious and determined."

"Well, it fits the pattern," Bannon said with a shrug. "What can I say?"

"It doesn't really change anything because I intend to be firm. I'll get pointed with him if I have to. But I need to get dressed soon. Would you go find the maid and ask her to bring back my fatigues?"

"I'll see if I can find her." He left.

I paced as Bannon had earlier, realizing I'd misread things. But I told myself it wasn't the end of the world. The worst that could happen was that I'd piss Lwin off. If he let that squirrel the deal, then it was unlikely we'd have put it together anyway. But surely the arms were more important than me. I couldn't be *that* special.

A few minutes later Bannon returned with Kee in tow. "She was on her way over when I ran into her," he said.

The little woman had a basket of clothing. Unfortunately my fatigues were not among the items she spread out for me to see. She had some sleazy dresses, probably cast-offs from previous occupants of the royal bedchamber. Looking at them, my heart sank. I thought of the hookers at the Nakhon Spa.

"I can't wear these, even if they fit," I said. "Cole, tell her I want my fatigues."

He spoke to the woman who replied. Then to me he said, "Bad news, sweetheart. They're in the wash and won't be ready until morning."

"Then I'm not going to dinner."

"That's the first sensible thing you've said since we got here."

I gave him a look. "Cole, do something. That man has the Heart of Burma."

"I'm sure he knows that, dear, and the leverage it gives him."

"Well, you don't have to look so damned pleased!"

"Pleased? What did I say?"

"It's not what you said, it's what you're thinking. The hell with it," I said, snatching up the dresses and heading for my bedroom. "If one of these fits, I'm wearing it. I am going to see that ruby, come hell or high water."

"I'll pray for high water," Bannon said.

He'd added another comment, but I didn't hear. I'd slammed the door.

I could only fit into one of the dresses the maid had brought, which made my choice easy. The winner was an electric blue sarong-like dress that only came to mid-thigh. It was suitable for a hostess at a Bangkok disco, which was probably where the original owner was at the moment. The dress was way too sexy, making me look like a slut. But I had a plan. The guesthouse was well furnished, so I looked around and found a Thai silk table runner in a drawer. I would use it as a stole, adding an air of modesty. There were no shoes in the camp that fit me, but Kee found some fancy gold-ornamented flip-flops that some poor woman donated for the cause.

When I came out of the bedroom, I found Bannon in freshly pressed khakis, sitting in his rattan chair. His brows went up at the sight of me.

"I know I look like a whore, so don't say it. Say something nice instead."

Bannon stroked his jaw, then said, "Colonel Lwin is a very lucky man."

"Oh, Cole, did you have to say that? I'm nervous enough already."

"You could have come to Tahiti with me, so I have no sympathy." He frowned. "Well, I do, but I wish I didn't."

In a way I was sorry I hadn't taken him up on the offer, but as I'd dressed I thought of Granddad and what the Heart of Burma would have meant to him. The gem was within a hundred yards of where I stood. How could I not go for it when I was this close, even if it meant fighting off a libidinous toad?

"I'll be coming back with you tonight. That's all I have to say on the matter."

"Well then," he said rising, "in that case it would be my pleasure to escort you to the colonel's abode." He offered me his arm. "But be warned, if the bastard lays a hand on you, I'm going to deck him."

"He'd have you shot."

"I don't care."

"Think of Dru."

He frowned. "Yeah, it would be inconvenient if I did get shot. I not only wouldn't see my daughter again, but we couldn't have our babies."

"Don't worry, I'll handle him," I said. "I promise."

Chapter
52

Colonel Than Lwin's home made the
guesthouse seem like an economy motel. A round-faced
houseboy with spiky hair showed us into a sitting room that
was the rustic equivalent of a Parisian salon, the furnishings
French ormolu replicas mixed with Burmese art. It was gar-
ish and over the top, but then so was Lwin.

The man himself was seated in a wingback chair, a petite
young woman in a red dress sat on a sofa. She looked Chinese, her long black hair piled on her head and held in place
with hair sticks. She smiled nervously when she saw us. The
colonel, wearing a white silk smoking jacket, rose, then
pushed his tinted glasses up off his nose. He beamed, his
gold tooth gleaming clear across the room.

"Ah, our welcome guests have arrived. Good evening,
Miss Chandler, Mr. Bannon." He checked out my legs as he
approached us. "Very beautiful, indeed." Taking my hand,
he kissed it.

I quailed, but forced a smile. "How gallant you are,
Colonel."

He beamed, then shook Bannon's hand perfunctorily. Motioning toward the woman, he said, "That's Miss Woo. Go sit with her, Mr. Bannon."

Bannon gave me a sideward glance and went to join his date on the sofa. I could tell he'd much rather punch Lwin out, grab my hand, and make a run for the border. But he was forbearing because of me. I was so close to the Heart of Burma that I could smell it. All that stood between me and the stone was a little former Army colonel turned warlord, crook, and ladies' man, the so-called Burmese Tiger.

Lwin gestured for me to sit on the facing sofa. As I moved past him, he gave my butt a little pat and muttered, "Very nice."

Anybody else and I might have slapped him. But he had the ruby. Bannon, for his part, turned bright red. No sooner were we seated—Lwin with his pudgy thigh right up against mine—than the houseboy, who was named Han, arrived to take drink orders.

"You like Johnnie Walker Blue Label, Mr. Bannon?" Lwin asked. "I have some."

"Fine, whatever," Bannon said, not looking at the man, probably out of fear of an irresistible urge to leap over the coffee table and throttle him.

"For you, Miss Chandler, a special drink with tiny pink umbrella. American ladies like little umbrellas, yes?"

"That would be lovely." A glance at Bannon told me he'd turned an even deeper shade of red. "So, Colonel Lwin," I said, wanting to take charge of the conversation, "I've been here half a day and you haven't yet told me about the Heart of Burma."

"It is very beautiful and very large. The best ruby in the world."

"That's what I've heard. But all that is known about it is mostly rumor. When will I get to see it?"

"After dinner. First, we get better acquainted." He put his hand on my bare knee.

"No, Colonel, first the stone," I said, removing his hand. "There will be time for getting acquainted after the negotiations."

"In Asia, it is important to have trust before there can be business."

"And I only do business with gentlemen who respect the wishes of a lady. So, the question is, can I trust you to be a gentleman?"

"Ah, very clever, Miss Chandler," he said, chuckling. "Your friend is very clever, Mr. Bannon, yes?"

"Oh, Alex will pick your pockets clean if you aren't careful, Colonel."

"We will see," he said, "we will see."

The drinks were served, and Lwin launched into a self-congratulatory soliloquy about his power and achievements. As he talked he would touch my arm or give me a wink, but he didn't put his hand on my knee again.

Miss Woo, for her part, went into high gear with Bannon, fawning over him, feeding him hors d'oeuvres, brushing crumbs from the corner of his mouth with her cocktail napkin. I wondered at one point if she was going to start undressing him.

At first Bannon mostly ignored her, but after a while he relaxed and seemed amused by it all. He'd accepted a second drink, I noticed, so maybe the alcohol was getting to him. I couldn't believe he was trying to make me jealous. More likely he was trying to numb himself so as not to worry about me and Lwin.

When dinner was announced, we all got up and Bannon nearly fell face first on the coffee table. Were it not for Miss Woo, he would have landed in the hors d'oeuvres.

"Cole, are you all right?" I asked.

He looked at me strangely. I couldn't say he seemed drunk, and he'd only had two scotches, but something was wrong.

"My head feels funny," he said. He gave it a shake.

"You feel better when you eat," Lwin said. "Visitors sometimes feel funny first day or two. Maybe altitude, maybe water."

Miss Woo took his arm, and we started for the dining room, but Bannon hadn't gone two steps before he staggered and nearly fell.

"Cole," I said, rushing up and taking his arm.

He looked at me bleary-eyed. "Sweetheart, I don't feel so good. I think I need to lie down."

"I'll take you back to the guesthouse," I said.

"No, no please," Miss Woo interjected. "I take him. He be okay. I see this before. You have dinner. No problem."

Bannon looked at me, struggling to keep his eyes from crossing. "Get a look at the goddamn ruby, Lexie, then come home. I'll be okay."

Something odd was happening, making me wary. Seeing my skepticism, Bannon got insistent.

"Get it over with so we can get the hell out of here," he muttered.

Lwin summoned Han, who took Bannon's other arm, and they helped him toward the door where one of the guards took over. Lwin shook his head. "So sorry about that. Perhaps I have expert come to check the water. You feel okay, Miss Chandler?"

"Yes, fine." What I didn't say was, that made me all the more suspicious. But if Lwin had doctored Bannon's drink or something, it wasn't going to do him any good.

Taking my arm, Lwin led me toward the dining room. Han held my chair for me. The man they called the Burmese Tiger took his place at the head of the table next to me as the servant cleared the other two place settings. I had no doubt this had all been planned.

"I have talked too much," Lwin said with surprising modesty. "Now you must tell me about your work."

I gave him my cocktail party account of life as a gem trader, and the man listened with rapt attention as the first course of the meal was served. I managed to sneak a bite of food now and then as he listened, eating voraciously.

The houseboy brought the main dishes, putting a serving from each onto our dinner plates. We began eating.

"You are very special woman, Miss Chandler," Lwin said. "So beautiful and so smart. You would make very interesting wife."

"I hear you're married," I said, seeing the opening. "Tell me about Mrs. Lwin."

The colonel guzzled his wine and signaled Han to refill his glass. He'd been eyeing my breasts. I pulled my makeshift shawl across my chest.

"No more Mrs. Lwin," he said. "Divorced now. I looking for new wife."

"How interesting."

"I have very nice house, as you see. Also, I have house in Indonesia. Very big by ocean. Apartment in Paris, too. Wife of Colonel Lwin have very interesting life. Much travel, much luxuries, yes?"

"So it seems."

The way he beamed, I wondered if he thought I was interviewing for the job. But it was his next remark that really set off the alarm. "I like American woman very much. American woman tall, long leg, much breast." He flicked his brows. "Like you."

I almost choked on the bite in my mouth. "That's a generalization, Colonel."

"No, like you, they very beautiful. American movie star best in world. Meg Ryan number one. You know Meg Ryan?"

"Not personally."

"She just like you, Miss Chandler. So beautiful. I have all her movie. I watch almost every night. I marry her tomorrow if she say yes."

"I'm sure she'd be flattered."

"Same for you," he said, his gold tooth gleaming. Reaching over, he seized my hand. "Want to marry me?"

"I beg your pardon?"

"If not for me, maybe you're dead now, Miss Chandler. How do you say? Now you owe me your life."

"There's no question I'm very grateful for what you did, Colonel," I said, trying to extricate my hand. But he held it firm in his viselike grip.

"So now maybe you marry me, Miss Chandler, since I save your life." He howled with laughter, I suppose to show he was joking, but there was a point behind the comment. The toad liked me.

Dinner finally ended. Lwin had a great deal of wine, even finishing the glass I'd hardly touched. With him drunk, things were likely to get worse.

"Now I think you wish to see ruby very much, yes?"

"I'm dying to see it, Colonel," I said, my heart beating nicely.

"Come then."

Lwin jumped up and ran around to help me with my chair, pushing Han away. Then he took me by the wrist, clamping on it with his pudgy fingers as though I was an errant child, threatening to escape. The colonel led me toward the back of the house. I stopped.

"Where are we going?" I demanded, as he continued tugging on my arm.

"To see ruby."

"Where is it?"

"In my bedroom," Lwin said with determination.

"Can't you bring it to the front room?"

"Heart of Burma never leave my room."

"Colonel Lwin, you promised me you were a gentleman."

"Yes, and it is true. Why are you afraid?"

"I'm not afraid. I'm a proper lady, and I don't go to gentlemen's bedrooms."

Lwin reached inside his coat and took out a small revolver, which he weighed for a moment before putting it in my hand. "Now you are proper lady with a gun. Come, Miss Chandler."

The colonel was more clever than he seemed, alternately cajoling and shaming me. A quick glance told me the gun wasn't loaded, so I tossed it on a chair. "I'm telling you right now that all I'm interested in is the ruby."

"Yes, me also."

That was a crock, but if I had to prove it to him the hard way, I would. I went with him, but I did close my shawl over my chest. Once we were in the bedroom the colonel took off his jacket and tossed it on a chair. The houseboy entered moments later with a tray of after-dinner drinks.

"Have a brandy, Miss Chandler," Lwin said.

It was more an order than an offer. I pointedly declined.

"You still don't trust me," he said.

"I came in here to see the ruby."

He went to the door, turned the key in the lock, then put the key in his pocket.

"Why did you do that?"

"So nobody come in."

I knew he was more concerned about somebody going out, but nothing was to be gained by drawing attention to the fact.

"Please sit and be comfortable," he said.

There was no chair in the room, only a huge bed with an extravagant, brightly colored silk spread.

"Thank you, I prefer to stand."

Lwin unbuttoned his shirt partway, but before I could tell him to keep his clothing on or bear the consequences, he went over to the large chest against the wall, took a key ring from his pocket, and unlocked the top drawer. Then he removed an ornate gold box that was about half the size of a shoe box. He carried it to the bed and set it in the center. Looking at me with a self-satisfied grin, he said, "The Heart of Burma inside."

Chapter
53

 Lwin got on the bed, and said, "Come
have a look."

I was reluctant. For all I knew, the box was empty, his intent being to get me in a compromising position.

"What matter, Miss Chandler? You don't want to see ruby?"

"Yes, I very much want to see it, but not on your bed."

"Where else?" he said, looking around. "On floor?"

I gave him a disapproving look.

"Come on," he said, "no problem. I gentleman, and I save your life."

I was torn between a fear of doing something stupid and an overwhelming desire to see the stone. Reluctantly I climbed onto the bed and knelt opposite him, the gold box between us. I held the shawl closed at my neck. He shook his head disapprovingly.

"In movie, Meg Ryan much more friendly."

"A movie is very different from this, Colonel."

"Maybe you lucky one to be here with me."

"Could I see the stone, please?"

Lwin opened the box and removed an object wrapped in a red silk cloth. He held it in the palm of one hand and carefully peeled back the flaps of the cloth with the other. Then I saw it, the most magnificent uncut ruby I'd ever seen in my life. Its crystalline edges were jagged, the color of dried blood. The size was absolutely incredible, staggering, larger than a golf ball but smaller than a baseball. I'd never seen a ruby so much as a quarter that size before. I was so stunned I couldn't breathe. I pictured Granddad grinning from ear to ear and saying, "Now, isn't that a dandy?"

"Colonel Lwin, this is the most amazing thing I've ever seen in my life."

"You like?"

"It's astounding."

"Here, you hold," he said. "My compliment."

He put the ruby in my hand. It was so heavy it felt like lead. I was awestruck, giddy. "My God, I can't believe this."

My reaction pleased him. "Beautiful like you, Miss Chandler."

I glanced up, only then realizing the shawl had slipped off my shoulders. He stared at my breasts with the same yearning I felt for the Heart of Burma. But I was so taken with the remarkable gemstone that I didn't care. This was a once-in-a-lifetime find, a once-in-a-lifetime experience.

"What it worth?" Lwin asked.

"Oh, I couldn't possibly say. I'd have to examine it carefully under proper conditions. Even then it would be a guess. There's nothing to compare it to."

"I think you very honest lady. Chung Lee say best in the world, just like Heart of Burma. So I agree to whatever price you say, if you are nice to me like Meg Ryan."

The comment got my attention. "What do you mean by that?"

"We take off clothes and have sex."

"Pardon me?"

"I say—"

"I heard what you said," I interrupted, indignant. "I can't believe you said it."

"Why not? You want something. I want something."

"But I'm not interested in having sex with you, Colonel. I'm here to do business."

"Me, also. You have your terms. I have my terms. Now take off dress. I been waiting all night."

"Some gentleman you are. Here, take your ruby."

I offered it, but Lwin grabbed my wrist, lunging at the same time, landing on top of me. He had my arms pinned, his grinning mouth was just inches from mine.

"I give you twenty thousand dollar, cash," he said.

"Get off of me, Colonel Lwin, before I get angry!" I said through my teeth. "Now!"

Either he didn't think I was serious, or he didn't care. In any case, the only movement he made was to grab my breast. That gave me the opportunity I needed to push him off me and over the side of the bed. He landed on the floor with a thud.

I jumped off the bed, the Heart of Burma still in my hand, and gave him the worst evil eye I could muster. "Give me the key to the door," I demanded.

"You serious, Miss Chandler?"

"Damned right, I'm serious. Give me the key, and I'll give you the ruby."

"Why you want to go?"

"Because I don't have that kind of interest in you. As a matter of fact, Mr. Bannon and I are romantically involved. We love each other and we plan to marry."

"What? This true?"

"Yes."

"He say nothing to me. Even when I get him woman."

"That's because I told him I wanted to keep our personal relationship private."

Lwin got to his feet. "This very unfortunate, Miss Chandler."

"What do you mean?"

"I think Mr. Bannon and Miss Woo in bed, trying to make baby this minute."

"Not Cole. Even if he wanted to, he couldn't. Did you see how sick he was?"

"Miss Woo change any man's mind."

"I don't believe it."

"Okay, we go see." He slipped his shoes back on, took the door key from his pocket and dangled it before me with one hand while holding out the other for the stone.

I reached for the key, but he snatched it back.

"First ruby."

"No. First, the key."

"Okay, same time."

We simultaneously snatched what the other held, ending up with what we wanted. Lwin chuckled. "Yes, I think you make very good wife. Mr. Bannon very lucky man . . . unless he already pillow with Miss Woo."

I unlocked the door and marched through the house. Lwin came running after me, buttoning his shirt as he went. The guards at the front door wouldn't let me leave until the colonel arrived and gave the order. Lwin, two guards, and I marched across the compound, headed for the guesthouse.

I led the way in and went directly to Bannon's room. There I found him naked on the bed with Miss Woo, also undressed, propped up on a pillow beside him, smoking a cigarette through a long black holder.

"Ayi!" she cried at the sight of us, snatching up the sheet to cover herself.

Cole remain motionless in his naked glory and appeared to be sound asleep.

"Mr. Bannon look pretty happy," Lwin said, sounding too pleased by a turn.

I wasn't so sure. I went to the bed for a closer look at Bannon. "Cole!"

He didn't so much as twitch a muscle. I shook his shoulder. "Cole!"

Nothing.

"What did you do to him?" I snapped at the woman, who has half cowering.

She was either too terrified to speak or didn't understand. I shook Bannon again and yelled his name. His eyes flickered open. Seeing me, he gave me a drunken smile.

"Lexie," he mumbled, "you were great."

Lwin laughed. "I tell you Miss Woo make him very happy."

Turning on my heel, I stomped from the room.

The next morning I'd showered, dressed, and had breakfast before Bannon put in an appearance, dragging himself into the sitting room in a robe. His face was puffy, his hair mussed. He looked like he'd gone a couple of rounds with Johnnie Walker.

"Well, if it isn't loverboy."

"Jesus," he said, leaning on the table as he dropped into the chair across from me. "What happened last night?"

"You're asking me? You should be addressing your question to Miss Woo."

"Who?"

"Your date, Cole. Were you too drunk to remember going to bed with her?"

"No way."

"Trust me, you did. When I got back the two of you were

sprawled on the bed, naked as a couple of jaybirds. She was having her post-coital cigarette and you were sawing wood like there was no tomorrow."

"Can't be."

"Well, you're wrong. Why would I lie about something like that?"

"I don't remember any of that," he protested. "They must have doctored my drink. When I got up to go to dinner, I couldn't see straight. Everything after that is a blank."

"You weren't so far gone you couldn't get it up for Miss Woo."

"I have no recollection of that at all."

"Yeah, sure."

"I swear to you."

"Cole, you missed your calling. You should have been a politician."

He rubbed his head, groaning. I was giving him a bad time because I was pissed, even though I half suspected they'd drugged him so that Miss Woo could distract him more easily. Their plan succeeded, but I still wondered how hard he'd resisted.

"My head feels like it's full of cement," he said, glancing up at me. "So what happened with Lwin?"

"He was more interested in sex than talking about the ruby."

"What?"

"The only way I could get him to show it to me was to go to his bedroom."

"You didn't."

"I did."

"Bullshit."

"He lured me onto his bed, then jumped me. I was so distracted by the stone that he caught me completely off guard."

"You're just saying that because of me and the woman . . . assuming what you said about us is true, which I'm now beginning to doubt."

"Oh, it was true all right. And what I said about the colonel is also true," I said, doing my best to piss him off. "Actually, what Chung Lee said about him is pretty accurate. Lwin's a lecher, but he's cultured. And he can be *very* charming." I punctuated the comment with a pert smile, one worthy of Meg Ryan.

"Don't give me that," he said, seeing I was pulling his leg. "You wouldn't do it."

"Why would you care anyway? You seemed pretty happy."

"I was delirious."

"Lwin was a bit too grabby, but I didn't mind too much," I said, continuing my act. "I think he really does like me, to be honest. And that's flattering. But the Heart of Burma, my God! Cole, I've never seen a gemstone so incredible in my entire life. Just to be able to hold it in my hand was worth everything I've gone through to get here, including last night with the colonel."

Bannon turned bright red. "Tell me you didn't have sex with him."

I laughed, having achieved what I intended. "If you'd feel better, fine. I didn't."

"And it's true, right?"

"Cole, I think it's better if we just move on. What's done is done."

He shook his head, groaning. "This is the cruelest, most bitchy thing you've done, Lexie. I thought you were a better person. And it especially hurts that you're kicking me while I'm down. How could the woman I love treat me like this?"

"Deal with it, Cole." I was enjoying this too much to let him off the hook. He looked at me like I'd ripped out his heart. I laughed again.

"You think it's funny?

"I think you're trying to divert the conversation away from the fact that you screwed another woman on the heels of professing your love for me."

"And what you did with Lwin is better? At least I was unconscious."

"Pour yourself some tea, and let's talk about the Heart of Burma. Lwin wants us at his office in . . ." I checked my watch. ". . . forty-five minutes. I'll thoroughly examine the stone, then give you a figure that you'll convert into bartered items. If we come to terms, then we can saddle up and be on our way."

"What? You aren't staying to become Lwin's concubine?"

"Actually, he proposed that. Sincerely."

"And of course you're stringing him along."

"Let's put it this way, the offer's open. But enough sex talk. We have an appointment, and we have to be prepared." I got up and headed for my room.

"Going in to put on more perfume?" he called after me.

"No. Than likes his women natural. He says I'm perfect just the way I am." Doing a little pirouette, I went through the door.

Chapter
54

Half an hour later Bannon came out of his room, looking more human, but he was still grumpy. "Ah, it's the Cole Bannon of old, the one before Miss Woo."

"Very funny."

"We both had a bad night, but we can't let that divert us from the task at hand."

"As soon as Lwin hands over the ruby, I'm going to deck the sonovabitch. I'm sure he drugged me."

"Well, it was for a good cause."

"I'm glad you're happy, Alexis," he groused. "Come on, let's get this over with."

We left the guesthouse and headed for Lwin's office, which was in a small building just beyond his home. The morning was overcast. It looked like rain.

"I do need to update you on one point," I said as we walked along, "just so we can keep our stories straight. All kidding aside, the colonel did get pretty aggressive, so to put a stop to it, I finally told him that you and I were engaged to be married."

"I don't believe it."

"It was an act of desperation, but I said it and now we've got to live with it."

"So even unconscious and with another woman, I still managed to save your butt."

"You were a convenient excuse, Cole. But I admit, the guy does creep me out."

Bannon started to say something, then stopped. I glanced over to see what was wrong and noticed him staring at a group of men coming toward us.

"Oh, shit," he said under his breath.

"What?"

He dropped to a knee and began re-lacing his boots, tucking his head as he did. The men passed by, staring curiously as everybody in the camp had since our arrival. *Farangs* were a rarity in these parts.

Once the group had gone, Bannon popped up and, taking my arm, hurried me along. "Sweetheart," he said, "we've got to kick this thing into high gear. When we see Lwin, do your thing with the ruby, let's make our deal, then get the hell out of here."

"Cole, what's the matter?"

"I recognized one of those men, and worse, I think he recognized me."

"Who was he?"

"I can't explain now. Let's just do this and go."

Colonel Lwin was not in his office when we arrived, but his aide told us he'd be arriving momentarily. That got Bannon muttering to himself as he paced, looking out the window. Why was it a problem that somebody recognized him? Had it not been for the presence of the colonel's aide, I would have insisted he tell me what was going on.

But then my would-be paramour, the Burmese Tiger, arrived accompanied by two guards. I quailed at the sight of him. I'd managed to keep him at bay the night before, but I feared not for long. Bannon was right; we had to get the hell out of there.

The colonel carried the gold box I'd first seen in his boudoir the previous night. The sight of it was enough to put color in my cheeks. Lwin probably thought it was him.

"So, good morning Miss Chandler and Mr. Bannon," he said, cheerily, giving us a gold-tooth smile. "You sleep well?"

Bannon grumbled, prompting me to chirp, "Very well, Colonel. Thank you."

"Me also," Lwin said, "but I could sleep better if Meg Ryan came last night."

He laughed heartily, amused by his own quick wit. I beamed my politic admiration. Bannon sat in a glum silence.

Lwin signaled for us to follow him into his private office, where he set the gold box on the blotter of his large teakwood desk, then sat in his high-back chair. Motioning for us to sit, he said, "Mr. Bannon, I think congratulations in order. I understand you marry Miss Chandler. Very lucky."

"Well," Bannon said with a thin smile, "she *is* lucky, you're right."

Lwin laughed. "Very good. But I tell you this. If you get tired of Miss Chandler, send her to me. I take her."

"That's good to know," Bannon replied. "I'll keep it in mind in case she gets out of line." He gave me a wink, showing his first spark of life all morning.

I gave him an I'm-not-amused look.

"So, Colonel," Bannon said, "Lexie says you've got quite a rock. Is it in the box?"

"Right here," Lwin said, patting the lid.

"Let's have a look at it then, shall we?"

Bannon wasn't kidding when he said he wanted to do this quickly, and I soon found out why. The colonel's aide en-

tered moments later and whispered something in his ear.
The dark look that came over Lwin was as ominous as anything I'd seen since our arrival. He sent the aide away,
picked up the box and put it in a desk drawer. When his
hands reappeared on top the desk, he was holding an automatic pistol. I flinched at the sight of it and heard Bannon
mutter "Oh, shit."

"Mr. Bannon, you are man of many surprise. You have
beautiful fiancée and lying heart. I should shoot you now.
Only reason I don't is respect for Miss Chandler."

"That's damned decent of you, Colonel."

I stared at the gun. I was at a loss as to what was going on,
but my heart pounded. "Would somebody please tell me
what this is about?"

"You don't know you marry rat?" Lwin said with disbelief.

"I know Cole's not perfect, but what reason would you
have to shoot him?"

I no sooner got out the question than the aide came charging
back into the office with four guards in tow. Lwin barked out a
command and the guards seized us by the arms and dragged
us from the room. I glanced back at the colonel as I went
through the door. His face was so red it looked like a tomato.

More guards waited outside the building, as well as a half-
ton truck. It was raining now, and the mood couldn't have been
more gloomy. We were handcuffed and led to the back of the
vehicle. It began to pour. I was soaked by the time they lifted
me up onto the bed of the truck and shoved me onto a bench
on one side. They put Bannon on the other side, across from
me. Guards joined us. I looked at Bannon and he looked at me.

"Not the best way to celebrate our engagement," he said.

"I'm waiting for an explanation, Cole."

"Remember the story you were told about me being an
arms merchant?"

"*Story?*"

"Yeah, well, it's not true."

"Dear God," I said, rolling my eyes. "You lied to me *again?* I can't believe it."

"Let me explain."

I hooted. "Let me guess. You're a serial killer."

"That might be better," he replied.

I groaned. "Why couldn't Lwin have shot me and put me out of my misery?"

"Sweetheart, it's not entirely bad."

"Entirely? Dammit, Cole, I finally started trusting you, and now you've done it *again*. How *could* you?"

"I was trying to protect you, Lexie."

"Protect me! Well, all I can say is you did one hell of a job. I can't even begin to tell you how safe I feel right now."

The truck's engine came to life, and we began to move.

Bannon said, "I tried to talk you out of coming, remember? I wanted to forget the whole thing and take off for Tahiti, just the two of us."

"You conveniently forgot to tell me why, didn't you?"

"I couldn't."

"What's keeping you from telling me now? Your parole officer?"

"Lexie, I'm a special agent on assignment with the Drug Enforcement Agency. I'm here to spy on Lwin. He's cranking up his drug operation again, and we're trying to nip it in the bud. I've been working with the Thai police. It's a joint operation involving the DEA, the CIA, and the FBI."

My jaw dropped. "Oh . . . my . . . God." I stared at him, searching his eyes, cursing them. But then a thought occurred, and I grew wary. "How do I know this isn't just another of your cock-and-bull stories?"

"It's the truth, believe me," he said as we bumped along.

"If I'm not mistaken, I've heard that before."

"Well, this time I mean it."

"Oh, really? Well, you know what? I need something more than your word. In fact, it just might take a joint resolution of the US Congress with the presidential seal attached before I believe anything you say . . . amazing as that may seem."

"I'm truly sorry, sweetheart. Sorry I've deceived you, sorry I couldn't level with you before now. But I want you to know I would have, if it had been possible."

I thought back over the events of the past several days. "Was Chung in on it?"

"No, he didn't know the whole story, but the Thai officials put pressure on him to work with me, to make sure I was included in the operation."

"How did you concoct the story about running an import-export business? And what about Sumgi and Dru and your wife?"

"That's all true, Lexie. Years ago, before I married, I worked with the DEA, but that was in the past. Then, a few months ago Elliot Webster, the guy you saw at the zoo, asked me to take on the mission. I have the background and the credentials they needed, and they couldn't find anyone else, so I agreed to do it."

"Was that business about Santa Noonwongsa a fabrication, too?"

"No, that was all real. The bastard damned near messed everything up."

"No kidding."

"Over and above almost killing you, I mean."

"Speaking of me, I was used—not just by you, but by my government, as well."

He looked sheepish. "There's more to it than that, Lexie. The campaign against Lwin has been going on for a long time. They tried repeatedly to infiltrate his organization, but kept coming up empty. Then, when word about the Heart of

Burma got out, it looked like the opportunity they'd been looking for. Chung had the connections we needed to make an overture to Lwin, so the decision was made to work through him."

"The ruby being the pretext."

"Exactly. The problem was, we needed a reputable expert. Since Chung Lee had to sell Lwin on the idea, we left that part of it up to him. In fact, the less we got involved in it, the more credibility the gemologist would have. When Chung gave us your name, the FBI checked you out to make sure you could be trusted not to try to pull something behind our backs."

"Oh, that's rich."

I was being sarcastic, but that did explain what had happened in New York. In fact, it explained why I'd been the object of scrutiny for days. The FBI, the DEA, the Thai authorities all had reason to keep an eye on me, which explained why I'd been watched and followed. The pieces were beginning to fit together.

"I personally didn't know anything about you," Bannon continued, "except your name. We were to team up, and you'd provide me the entrée I needed to get to Lwin."

"Like I say, I was used."

"We were perfectly willing to allow you and Chung Lee to take a profit on the ruby. In fact, the plan was to keep what you were doing and what I was doing separate."

I indicated the handcuffs. "Your plan seemed to have gone awry, Mr. Bannon."

"Only because we ran into that guy on the way to Lwin's and he recognized me."

"Who was he, anyway?"

"A Thai official. He wasn't involved in the operation. He's an administrator of some sort. I've seen him at police headquarters several times. My guess is he's on Lwin's payroll.

Probably ratted out the people who've been sent here in the past."

"Why would he be here in Myanmar?"

"Who knows? But it wouldn't be all that difficult to arrange. Instead of taking his mistress to Pattaya, he spent a few days here with Lwin. In any case, he saw me and obviously put two and two together. It was bad luck, that's all."

"Yeah, really bad luck."

"I'm not thrilled about this myself."

"So, here were are."

"Yes, Lexie, here we are."

I looked out the back of the truck at the rain as we sloshed and slid along. "What are they going to do to us?"

"I don't know, but my hope is Lwin will give you a kick in the butt and send you home. As for me, well, let's say the prospects are not so good."

"Will he kill you?"

"Let's not worry about that right now. First, let's solve your problem."

The truck lurched to a stop and Cole Bannon gave me a faint smile, one full of sadness and regret. At that instant I knew one thing with certainty. There was no way I'd let him die.

Chapter
55

The stockade was located near the
edge of the camp some distance from Lwin's offices. Bannon and I were thrown into separate cells at opposite sides of the building. I was soaking wet and as miserable as I'd ever been in my life.

The place was filthy and, by all appearances, little used. As best I could tell we were the only prisoners. I hoped that didn't mean they solved their disciplinary problems through executions.

The minutes after the cell door closed behind me were among the lowest I'd ever experienced. It was rare for me to feel powerless, but in this instance I did. The worst part was the uncertainty. The next worst thing was being alone. I had trouble believing I'd be blamed for what happened, though who could say what Lwin would think? Bannon, though, was in for a rough time, and that was the best that could be said about his prospects.

I leaned against the dank wall, hugging myself and wondering how this could have happened. Just twenty-four hours ago the Heart of Burma was within my grasp, Bannon's love for me seemed genuine, we were looking forward to celebrating our success and getting to know each other, only to have it all come tumbling down. How could things have so quickly gone from hope for the future to pending doom?

I walked in a circle, if only because I couldn't bring myself to sit or lie on the filthy burlap sack stuffed with rags which served as a mattress. I felt claustrophobic. There was no window in the cell, only air vents on the outside wall, below the ceiling. They were also the source of light. A single naked bulb hung overhead but it probably wasn't turned on until dark. I quailed to think of sleeping in the place. I was certain there'd be rats, mice, or, for that matter, snakes slithering in from the nearby jungle. I began shivering, as much because of my despair as my misery.

After a while it became too much and I lost it. Throwing myself against the door, I started pounding on it, desperate to get out. "Cole," I cried. "Can you hear me? Cole?"

"I hear you, Lexie," came a muffled reply.

"What are we going to do?"

"Hang tough," he replied. "Concentrate on surviving."

I thought about that for a moment, then yelled, "Easier said than done."

"You have to cooperate with them, sweetheart. Say or do anything you have to. You're innocent, and they can't torture a different story out of you."

"*Torture?*"

"Figure of speech, Lexie. Figure of speech."

I knew he was trying to be supportive, but my confidence was more fragile than my hope. I wanted to continue our conversation, but it was difficult to talk when you had to yell to be heard. We lapsed into silence out of necessity, but every once in a while the circumstances would get to me and I'd holler something to him, just to hear his voice.

Alternately squatting and standing, I struggled to hold it

together. Time hardly moved, and I found myself measuring things by the levels of my anxiety. That changed when I heard a commotion in the hallway. There were footsteps and voices. The sounds seemed to be coming from the other side of the building, where Bannon was being held.

I heard shouts, angry shouts, banging sounds, then cries of pain. I recognized Bannon's voice. It didn't take long to figure out they were beating him.

Listening to it was excruciating. They might as well have been raining their blows on me, crushing my bones, tearing my flesh. I tried covering my ears, but it did no good—each thud, each cry of pain, shot through my heart. Finally, in desperation, I began pounding on the door of my cell. "Colonel Lwin! I want to speak to Colonel Lwin!"

My pleas went unheeded. I prayed that Bannon would lose consciousness, if only so that they'd stop beating on him.

After a while, there was silence, and I figured my prayer had been answered. Ten minutes passed, and I heard a key turning in the lock. I backed against the wall, thinking maybe it was my turn to be beaten.

The door opened and a soldier with a rifle slung over his shoulder looked in. But he didn't enter. Instead, he stepped back and Colonel Lwin appeared. He glanced around as if assessing my conditions. I did not see compassion on his face.

"You call for me, Miss Chandler?"

"I want to know what you want so that they'll stop beating Cole."

His brow rose. "Nothing. He confess everything. I know whole story. Tomorrow he shot."

The word cut through me like a bullet into flesh. "Why do you have to kill him?"

"You beautiful, Miss Chandler, but you don't understand nothing about war. This war. They want to kill me, so I kill them first."

There was such utter finality to his words. I knew begging for mercy would do no good. Exceptional measures were called for if Bannon was to be saved. I had one resource at my disposal, and I realized employing it was his only chance. "Soldiers do more than fight, Colonel. I know that you, for example, are very fond of women. You were attracted to me, weren't you?"

"So?"

"I want to make a deal with you."

"I listening."

"You let Cole live, and I'll do anything you want."

"*Anything?*"

"Yes. And the better you treat Cole, the better I treat you. I may not be Meg Ryan, but I can be nice to men like Meg Ryan is in her movies."

A big smile filled his face. He pushed his glasses up off his nose. "You do this for Mr. Bannon because you love him?"

"Yes, to be honest. But if you'll give me what I want, then I'll make you very, very happy, Colonel Lwin."

"Easy to say."

"Just give me the chance to prove it."

"What if I say show me now?"

"Fine. But I want to see Cole first, and I want him to get medical treatment. I also want your word he'll never be beaten again. No more torture."

"You ask much."

"I'll give much, Colonel."

He thought. "How you know I don't take you to bed and shoot him anyway?"

"You kill him, and I'll never please you again. I'd rather die. Besides, I trust you to be good to your word. It's in your interest."

"How long you willing to come to my bed, Miss Chandler?"

"For as long as I please you. But you have to let me visit

Cole every day. If I see that he's been treated well, that night you can have me."

Lwin pointed at the door. "Go see him, then come to my house. We start now."

When I entered Bannon's cell, I found him on his back on the filthy floor, his face bleeding, one eye nearly swollen shut. He was semiconscious.

"Cole," I said, kneeling beside him, "can you hear me?"

He came to and looked at me through his good eye, trying to make sense of what he was seeing. "Lexie?"

"Yes, it's me," I said, leaning down and kissing his battered lips.

"You okay?" he asked.

"I'm fine."

I could tell that thinking was hard for him. He scrunched up his face.

"How'd you get in here?"

"I insisted."

He thought about that. "Yeah," he said upon reflection, "sounds like you."

"Cole, the camp doctor will be here soon. You'll be treated and you'll get a clean cell. Things will be much better."

He looked confused. "How'd this happen?"

"I can be very convincing. But don't worry about that now. Just relax. Would you like some water?"

He gave a half nod. I signaled to the guard that I wanted the water bottle I'd been given at Lwin's instructions. I was glad the colonel had left, because I didn't want Bannon to figure out what was going on.

Lifting his head, I helped him drink. We could hear them scrubbing the adjoining cell where he was to be moved.

"What's that sound?" he asked, growing more coherent by the moment.

"They're fixing up a cell for you so that you'll be more comfortable."

He pondered that, his eyes getting clearer. "What did you promise Lwin?"

"Less hostility."

He closed his eyes, wincing. He knew. "No, Lexie, don't do it."

I stroked his bloody cheek. "It's the only way I can keep him from killing you."

"I don't care. Just get out of here, any way you can. Forget me."

"I can't leave you, Cole, no matter what."

He looked at me beseechingly. "What good will it do if I live a few more days?"

I leaned close and whispered in his ear. "We're leaving here together, you and I both. I haven't figured out how yet, but we're going to Tahiti, Cole. I promise."

Tears formed at the corners of his eyes and ran down his cheeks. His expression was more eloquent than any words he could have spoken. I wouldn't let this defeat me. Bannon and I would have a future, whatever it took, whatever I had to do.

Chapter 56

Bannon was moved to his new clean
cell and with its fresh mattress while we waited for the doctor. The guards brought a table and chair for him as well. I sat on the mattress and was holding his hand when the doctor appeared at the door. He was a small man with thick glasses. After examining Bannon, he told me his injuries weren't serious. "Concussion, bruised rib and contusion," he said blandly. "Now you can go, miss."

They took me to a waiting jeep, making me sit in the rain, an armed soldier on either side of me. There was little need to guard me, since Bannon would certainly be executed if I tried to escape, but they couldn't rely on that.

Colonel Than Lwin's expectation was that I would become his sex slave. I would pretend to accommodate him until I figured out how to get out of this hell hole. If the best way was to kill Lwin, that's what I'd do. But I needed a plan and an opportunity to carry it out.

The trouble was, I didn't have the luxury of time. I'd do what I could to stall, but I had to prepare myself for the worst. One thing was beyond doubt: I could not and would not abandon Cole Bannon, no matter what.

The rain had slowed to a drizzle, the air was redolent with the smell of earth and vegetation. As I sat in the jeep looking across the compound, I realized how precious my freedom was, how important it was that Bannon and I survive so we could be together. The Heart of Burma was no longer important. The challenge I faced was infinitely more critical to my happiness and the future I wanted. But a tremendous obstacle stood in the way—the Burmese Tiger.

The driver came out of the building, got in the jeep, and we took off, making our way to Colonel Lwin's house. Because of the muddy condition of the road, we moved slowly, like a funeral procession, me a condemned prisoner on her way to the guillotine.

We no sooner pulled up in front of the colonel's house than Lwin himself came out the door. He was attired in battle fatigues, his side arm on his hip. Notwithstanding the jaunty angle of his beret, his expression was grim.

"Bad news, Miss Chandler," he said. "I must leave for important truce conference with enemy. This mean I can't pillow you now."

His words thrilled me, but I didn't let my happiness show. "I understand."

"Good news is I come back tonight," he said "We can have sex until morning." He flashed a gold-toothed smile. "But this way you have time to be all ready for me."

"Whatever pleases you, Colonel."

"What pleases me is go to bed now, but this is war. Soldier first, then lover." He appraised me. "You dirty, but still very pretty. I like you very much, Miss Chandler."

Lwin reached out and touched my chin with his fingertip, then dragged his finger down my chest to the V of my shirt. Pursing his fat lips, he unbuttoned the top buttons, exposing the swell of my breasts. He ran his finger over them. "You like?"

"I want to please you."

"Very good, Miss Chandler. Very good."

The hungry look on his face turned dark, making me wonder if he was going to throw me to the ground and take me right there in front of his men. A dozen of them stood watching us, their colonel marking his claim to the white *farang* concubine.

"I will think about you all day," he said. "Your mouth, your breast, but especially this." Stepping closer he lifted his hand between my legs, gritting his teeth through the half smile on his lips. Then he began stroking me. "You like this?" he asked.

I looked straight through the little toad and I saw Bannon's battered face. I saw the tears in the corners of his eyes and heard him tell me he loved me. "Yes, Colonel," I replied. "I like it very much."

"Miss Chandler," he said rubbing my mound, "I think we have sex many month, maybe many year."

"I hope so," I muttered.

Then Colonel Than Lwin brushed by, giving me a spirited pat on the butt before climbing into his jeep. "See you tonight."

I should have turned, smiled at him, and waved, but it took all my willpower to keep from pouncing on him and strangling him to death. This was only a taste of what was to come. I had to suck it up and find the strength to get through this. Enduring wouldn't be enough. I had to prevail and that meant finding a way to escape.

The houseboy, Han, ushered me inside where Kee waited, whether to serve me or keep an eye on me was hard to say. The room I was given was nicely furnished. How many women had occupied it before me I couldn't imagine. How long I would be the incumbent was easier—it wouldn't be for long.

My room had a private bath, which was modest but adequate. When I told Kee I wanted to take a shower, she shook her head. "Something better."

Taking my hand, she led me to the master bath. In light of the fact we were in the middle of the jungle, the fixtures and decor were amazingly opulent, worthy of the finest luxury hotel. Dominating the room was a large bath on an elevated pedestal. That suite at the Nakhon Spa where I met Bannon came to mind. The huge tub was very much like this one and intended for much the same purposes, I was quite sure.

I recalled the conversation I'd had with Bannon about the girls at the spa, his defending them and my condescension. He'd told me they freely prostituted themselves out of a desire to make things better for their loved ones. At the time it had seemed like a cynical rationalization, but now I saw it in a different light.

Kee filled the tub and left me to soak at my leisure, giving me a chance to think. Lwin's house was well guarded. Escape wouldn't be easy. But even if I could find a way to sneak from the house, I'd still have to get to Bannon and the stockade was well guarded, too. If I somehow managed to free us both, we still had to flee through the jungle, probably with Lwin's troops in hot pursuit. To make matters worse, I had no idea if Bannon was sufficiently recovered for an escape attempt. If not, there was no telling how long before he would be.

The odds were against us, but I had to be ready to act when the opportunity arose.

Kee returned after a while with a few sarongs for me to choose from, explaining in broken English that concubines did not serve their masters wearing jungle fatigues. I told her I still wanted my fatigues and that should I ever accompany the colonel into the field, I'd need them. She assured me that they would be placed in the wardrobe as soon as they were back from the laundry. I put on one of the sarongs, feeling like a geisha.

I resolved to make the best possible use of the time I had until Lwin's return. Though Han and Kee kept an eye on me, I had the run of the house. Looking out each window, I confirmed that the place was well-guarded, with half a dozen sentries posted around the perimeter. There would be no making a run for it in broad daylight. If I were to escape, it would have to be at night.

I would also need a weapon. There weren't any guns lying around, though Lwin had his sidearm which he probably kept with him, maybe at his bedside. I'd watch where he put it and look for an opportunity to grab it. It would be nice if I had something else as well, perhaps a knife from the kitchen.

But even if I managed to arm myself, it was unlikely I'd be able shoot my way out. Nor were the prospects good I could sneak away. Two possibilities came to mind. Since I would be close to Lwin, I might be able to get the drop on him, take him hostage, force him to order Bannon's release, the three of us fleeing the camp in a jeep, me holding a gun to Lwin's head. The other possibility was to create a diversion, something that would distract the guards long enough to make a run for it. If I were able to kill or injure Lwin, that might do the trick. Either way, a weapon was key.

Chapter
57

I spent most of the afternoon in the salon feeling like a nervous, unwilling bride. Han would look in on me from time to time, either to see if I wanted something or to make sure I was still there.

I was resigned to at least one night of sex with Lwin. Bannon would be in better shape if he had a day or two to recover, and there was no point in making a premature attempt to escape if it was doomed to failure. And yet my instinct was to fight. To give myself to a man I detested ran contrary to everything I believed in.

After thinking of the way Lwin touched me in front of his men, I couldn't sit still any longer and decided I had to find out what condition Bannon was in. I told Han that the colonel had promised me I could visit my friend. "I'd like to see him now."

"So sorry, Colonel say you can't leave house. Maybe you like something to eat?"

I could see that ploy wouldn't work. "Yeah, sure."

I followed him into the kitchen, thinking this might be my chance to snatch a knife. There weren't any lying about, which meant they were probably in a drawer. I leaned against the counter as Han prepared a light snack.

"If I can't go see Mr. Bannon, could I at least speak to the doctor?" I asked.

"Sorry, I forget, miss. Doctor send message. Say he much better. Not so dizzy."

"That's good to know."

"He very lucky that Colonel like you very much, miss."

Han opened a drawer and took out a knife to cut fruit. My heart leapt at the sight. "Have there been many women here?"

"Yes, very many."

When Han turned his back, I eased closer to the drawer. "Why do they leave?"

"To have baby. Colonel like girlfriend to get pregnant. He like make baby."

I reached my hand out to snatch a knife just as Han turned around. I picked up a little cake on the counter instead. He closed the drawer.

"Maybe you have baby, too."

"I don't think so," I said, shivering at the thought.

The snack prepared, Han said, "Come, please," and led the way back to the salon, setting the plate on the coffee table. I nibbled on fruit and cakes while he watched from across the room. All I could think of was the knives in the kitchen drawer.

Over the course of the afternoon and evening I made two or three visits to the kitchen but either Kee or Han followed. Resigned to the fact I wouldn't be getting a knife, I glumly awaited Colonel Lwin's return.

Around midnight I went to my room to sleep, buoyed by the fact that Lwin had not yet returned, though I knew he could arrive during the night and summon me to his bed. I had trouble falling asleep, but finally I drifted off.

I awoke three or four times during the night, my heart pounding with the anxiety of my dreams, but still nobody had awakened me saying Lwin had arrived. During the small hours, the house quiet, I decided it was the time to steal a knife.

I crept from my room and made it to the kitchen without seeing anyone. I found the knife drawer in the dark and removed a trimming knife with a four or five-inch blade. I'd just hidden it under my silk robe when the light came on. Han stood bare-chested at the door, looking suspicious.

"What you doing?" he demanded.

"I was thirsty and wanted a drink. I was looking for a glass."

"You ask, please."

He went to the refrigerator, and I quietly pushed the drawer closed. He got a glass from a cupboard and handed it to me along with a bottle of mineral water. Thanking him, I returned to my room. The knife clutched in my hand, I got into bed, wondering if, after all the setbacks Bannon and I'd endured, it was possible I'd suddenly gotten lucky.

When morning came with no tangible sign of the colonel, I wondered if fate had spared me. Desperate to know if he'd arrived during the night, I dressed in the sarong I'd worn the night before, hid my knife in the fabric and went to Lwin's bedroom. The bed was still made and there was no sign of him. Deciding that if I were to need the knife it would most likely be here, I stuck it under the mattress where I could get to it while we were in bed, then left the room.

A breakfast of fruit and tea and rice cakes was waiting in the dining room. I asked Han if there had been any word from the colonel.

"He call. Come back very soon."

Any hope of a reprieve went out of me like the air from a balloon.

For an hour Kee and I waited in the salon for the Burmese Tiger to make his appearance. When I heard the sound of vehicles out front, my stomach clenched. Han ran to open the door and the colonel came striding in. Seeing Kee, he sent her scurrying, then turned his attention to me. Taking off his glasses, he rubbed his eyes. He looked beat, but managed to smile.

"Your dress very nice. Beautiful lady." He dropped into a chair, exhausted, his legs splayed, his shoulders slumped. "Thinking of you naked keep me going last night."

"Did things go well?" I asked.

"No," he groused. "Bad negotiation. Much more fighting to come. Maybe I kill whole army before they leave me alone."

"I'm sorry to hear that, Colonel."

"You look better all clean now."

"Thank you." I smiled, even though I was awash in homicidal feelings.

"I am very tired, Miss Chandler. No sleep last night. I will go bed and rest before we pillow. In three hour you come to my bed. I feel much better then. Okay?"

Another reprieve! I was elated, but remained calm. "Whatever you wish."

He smiled and rubbed his eyes again, yawning. "I wish beautiful dream about you, Miss Chandler. Open dress now. Show me breast."

I managed not to flinch. I loosened the sarong, pulled back the fabric enough for him to see my breasts. Lwin stared for a long time, running his tongue across his lips.

"Come here," he commanded, pointing to the floor beside him.

Afraid of what was coming, I knelt by the chair. Reaching out, he cupped my breast, and stroked my nipple with his thumb, not stopping until it got hard.

Grinning he said, "Very nice. Yes, very nice." Then he yawned, shaking his head and getting to his feet. "Now I sleep. Three hour, Miss Chandler. When you come, bring bottle of champagne and two glass." Patting my cheek, he staggered off to bed.

When he was beyond hearing, I exhaled, hardly having breathed while he touched me. He had to be the most evil man I'd ever known. Gritting my teeth, I thought of the knife I'd hidden under the mattress and resolved to use it, hoping to hell Bannon was ready for a tough slog through the jungle.

Kee returned and offered to teach me Than Lwin's favorite game, a Burmese version of Chinese checkers, but I couldn't think about anything but him groping me and the knife I'd hidden under the mattress. I had never contemplated killing anyone in cold blood, but if there was a candidate for whom I'd make an exception, it was Colonel Lwin.

While my master napped, I alternately paced the house and lay on my bed, undecided about whether to fly into action as soon as I could get my hands on the knife or wait until dark, when my chances of escape would be better. The one thing I knew with certainty was that before this was over I would either gain our freedom or I would die trying. There could be no compromise.

Finally, it was time to awaken Lwin. Summoning my determination, I went to the kitchen, where Han had the champagne and glasses waiting. He must have been through this ritual dozens of times, but this time the outcome would be very different.

I carried the bottle and glasses to Lwin's bedroom and lightly rapped on the door. Hearing no response, I opened the door and peeked in.

Colonel Lwin was asleep on the bed, naked. He was snoring. I preferred not to look at his body, so I concentrated on his face. Asleep, he didn't look imposing. The Burmese Tiger seemed more like a plump house cat. Still, I felt utter contempt.

My hands shaking, I put down the bottle and glasses. If killing him was the thing to do, it would be easiest now. Too damn bad it was still day. Maybe if I didn't awaken him, he'd sleep until evening, when I'd have the cover of darkness going for me. On the other hand, if I could get his gun, I could take him hostage.

Much as I detested Than Lwin, I was not eager to kill him. The hostage scenario was more my style. I looked around but didn't see his sidearm. It was probably locked away. Unless I found it, I was back to killing him tonight and escaping in the course of the pandemonium that followed.

And so I sat on the chair in the corner and began counting the minutes. Scarcely half an hour passed before Lwin snorted and began to stir. I held my breath, but my worst fears were realized when his eyes fluttered open. Seeing me, he grinned.

"Miss Chandler, you come to pillow. You bring champagne?"

"Yes, it's there," I said, pointing.

"Good. Open and bring to me in bath."

I briefly considered going for the knife, but with him awake, I no longer had an advantage. During the period of lethargy after sex would be the next best time to get the drop on him, but that meant submission. Was there any way I could stall until dark? I doubted it.

Sliding over to the edge of the bed, he got up and waddled off to the bathroom. I realized I could get the knife now and stab him in his bath, but that was risky. A struggle and shouting could alert Han and the guards.

Moments later I heard the sound of running water. Girding myself, I removed the foil and wire cage from the bottle, then popped the cork. The sound brought a hoot of delight from the bath.

"Come, Miss Chandler."

Picking up the glasses, I went into the bath. Lwin sat on the edge of the tub, waiting for it to fill. I handed him a glass and filled it for him.

"So, did you sleep well?" I asked.

"Feel much better. Ready now. Wine, bath, and we have sex. You drink, too."

Resigned, I poured myself a splash of wine, intending not to have much, then went ahead and filled the glass. I put down the bottle. Lwin extended his glass toward me.

"To many month good sex with Miss Chandler," he said. "And maybe baby. Let's hope."

We clicked glasses, and he downed his like he was knocking back a shot of tequila. Seething, I took only a sip.

"No," he said. "More quick. It go to your head faster."

I guzzled it down, thinking maybe I was better off to deaden my feelings. I refilled the glasses, and we knocked them back again.

The tub was full, and I turned off the water. As I leaned over he stroked my ass.

"Time to take off dress," he said, stepping into the tub. "But very slow. I watch." Lwin motioned for me to move to where he could better see, then leaning back in the tub with a regal cant to his head and a gleaming smile, he motioned for me to begin.

Chapter 58

My heart pounding with agony, I unfastened the sarong and slowly unwrapped it. Kee had taken away my underwear, saying the colonel didn't like women to wear underthings when they came to his bed, so I had nothing on under the dress.

"Mmm," Lwin purred as the garment draped open, revealing my body. "Go on."

I lifted the sarong off my shoulders and let it slide very slowly down my back to the floor. Though the bathroom was warm, I shivered. The colonel's eyes were hard and full of lust.

"Dance for me," he said.

Bannon's two little friends at the Nakhon Spa came to mind. I'd been dutifully shocked when I'd seen them dancing nude, but I sometimes thought how the three of them had seemed to be having a good time. I didn't know if I was capable of losing myself that way—at least with a toad like Lwin—but the longer I stretched out the seduction, the better. There was no music, so I hummed to myself, closing my eyes as I began to gyrate, twisting and undulating my body as sensuously and provocatively as I could.

"Turn," Lwin commanded.

My eyes still closed, I turned my back to him, so he could watch my ass as I swayed. I no longer smiled because he couldn't see my face. Tears ran down my cheeks.

I heard the water slosh, and I turned to see Lwin stand, his penis pointing at me like a crooked finger. Stepping from the tub, he came toward me, his face flush. Without a word, he grabbed my wrist and pulled me into the bedroom where he virtually flung me onto the bed. He stared at my pubis. I resisted closing my legs, though every fiber of me yearned to do just that. I thought of the knife that was within reach. It took all my willpower not to lunge for it. Much as I wanted to, I couldn't kill him now. I had to wait till dark.

Lwin climbed onto the bed and pushed my legs wider apart, crawling between my knees. His teeth gritted, a flash of gold in the corner of his mouth, the Burmese Tiger pounced, landing on me, sinking his teeth into my neck. As I cringed he reached down between us to find his shaft and drive it to its mark. The Tiger was about to enter me when the house was shattered by a tremendous concussion. The roof seemed to lift from the walls, and the ceiling fell, coming down on me and my master like a giant hammer.

For a second I thought I was dead. The house had collapsed. All I could feel was the colonel's naked, inert body smashed against mine. We were in semi darkness with bits of daylight coming through cracks in the mound of debris. Plaster dust and smoke filled the air. I could hear explosions and cries in the distance, then the sound of automatic weapon fire. The camp was under attack!

I tried to move, but couldn't. Lwin seemed to be unconscious, which was a blessing. Now, if I could only make my escape before he came to . . . but the weight on me was so great I could hardly breathe.

Feeling around with my free hand, I realized that the ceiling had come down and the bed collapsed, driving the mattress to the floor. The bedframe had taken the weight of the falling structure and Lwin's body had cushioned me. As the moments passed with no sign of life, I began to wonder if he was dead. I couldn't detect breathing. I finally got my free hand to his neck and felt for his pulse. There wasn't one. He was dead.

Somehow I gathered myself, knowing I had to escape. With effort, I managed to get one leg out from under Lwin. I could feel empty space to one side, a gap between large sections of the fallen ceiling and roof. The dust having settled, I could now smell the outside air.

Continuing to struggle, I managed to slip from beneath Lwin's lifeless body, dropping into the gap beside the mattress. The space extended beyond the bed and I wiggled through it. More light angled through the rubble. Getting into a squatting position I managed to lift the larger pieces of ceiling panel and wall board, pushing them aside so I could stand. I looked around, finding myself virtually outdoors. Some of the walls still stood, but there was nothing overhead but the late afternoon sky.

After a brief lull there was another series of explosions. The small arms fire grew more intense. Naked, I was helpless. I needed to find something to wear. I climbed through the debris, working my way toward the door. As I passed the colonel's large chest of drawers, I saw that it had been knocked over and shattered by a large beam. The gold box containing the Heart of Burma lay nestled in the rubble like an egg in a nest. I snatched it up, looked inside to see if the ruby was there.

I found it intact and as astonishing as ever. If I were to survive the ordeal, it seemed to me I should come walking out of the jungle with the Heart of Burma in hand. True, it paled in importance aside freedom, but it was still a nice bonus, the missing piece in the Rutledge crown.

Tucking the box under my arm, I continued picking my way through the fallen structure. The sitting room, I discovered, was demolished, but the section of the house where my room was located wasn't as badly damaged, the roof still intact.

My fatigues and boots were in the armoire, where Kee had put them. My heart beating with excitement, I dressed, and took a pillowcase from the bed, figuring I could use it as a sack. I wrapped the gold box in a jacket and put it in the pillowcase along with a bottle of water and some fruit from a bowl on the table. I went to the window. Seeing no one, I pushed the shutters open, threw my leg over the sill and stepped out.

The compound was covered in a dense cloud of dust and gun smoke. I could see soldiers running in one direction or another and flashes of small arms fire. The battlefield lay between me and Bannon.

Mortar rounds were coming in hot and heavy. One had probably hit the house. It was not the ideal time to be running across the compound, but I had no choice.

Slinging the sack over my shoulder, I took off at a dead run. The fog of war, in both the literal and figurative sense, can cause confusion, pandemonium and chaos, but it also gave me the cover I needed for protection from all but the closest rifleman. It did not, however, protect me from the mortar and artillery fire that rained down on the compound.

Rounds exploded on all sides as I ran at full speed, dodging craters, bodies, and burned-out pieces of equipment. Nothing landed close until I was within sight of the stock-

ade. Then a mortar round slammed into the ground just beyond a nearby jeep. The blast knocked me to the ground, but
the vehicle shielded me from the spray of shrapnel. Still, a
hail of mud and dirt rained down, covering me.

My ears ringing, I got to my knees, disoriented by the
shock of the explosion. Ahead I saw the silhouette of the
stockade in the drifting smoke. I hoped to God I'd find Bannon there and that he'd be all right. The problem was the
smoke was acrid, burning my eyes and making them tear so
badly I could barely see. Stumbling along, I tripped over
what I thought was a log, until I looked and saw that it was a
dead soldier. An automatic rifle was clutched in the dead
man's hand.

Wrenching the weapon free, I continued on, reaching the
stockade under a hail of gunfire. Rounds chewed up the dirt
at my feet and whizzed past my head. Somehow I stumbled
through the door unscathed. There was nobody around, the
guards having fled.

"Cole!" I cried. "Cole!" I hurried to the end of the building where his cell was located, but with the interior of the
building full of smoke, I wasn't sure which one was his. For
all I knew they'd moved him again. I banged on each door.
"Cole! Cole!"

Then I heard his voice. "Lexie?"

"Yes, it's me! Are you all right?"

"Except for the fact that I'm locked up."

I looked around, not knowing how I was going to get the
door open. I had no idea where the keys were. My best hope
was to shoot the lock. "I've got a gun, Cole. Stand back and
I'll shoot." I aimed the weapon. "Are you clear?"

"Fire away, sweetheart."

I squeezed off a couple of rounds, then kicked the door
open. There, amid the smoke and the noise of the battle,
stood Cole Bannon. This image of him would endure in my

mind for all time. Dropping the gun, I rushed in and threw myself in his arms, desperate to hold him before an artillery shell blew up the building.

Bannon held me and I kissed his battered face. I'll never forget his smile.

"Will you be able to walk?" I asked. "How bad are your injuries?"

"I feel like I've been run over by a truck, but I'll walk to the ends of the earth, if that's what it takes to get out of here. How did you get away?" he asked, wiping the mud from my cheek with his thumb. "Did Lwin get preoccupied playing soldier?"

"Let's just say he didn't have much choice."

"You were that persuasive, huh?"

"No, more like that lucky. But we don't have time to talk about it now. We have to get the hell out of here."

We left the cell. Bannon snatched up the automatic rifle and I grabbed the pillowcase. We made our way to the entrance of the building. Kneeling in the doorway, he looked out at the battlefield.

"Jesus," he muttered, "how did you get through that?"

"I had to find you," I said simply.

He took my hand and kissed it.

"I still don't know who the hell you really are," I said, "but the one thing I do know is that I love you."

"I never thought I'd live to hear those words."

"Let's hope we both live to say them again."

Bannon stuck his head out the door and looked each way, then pulled back in. "The Myanmar army must have the camp surrounded. They've most likely cut off routes of egress and are pounding away with artillery, slowly tightening the noose."

"What are we going to do?"

"We're on the edge of the jungle. I think our best bet is to make a dash for the undergrowth. Let's go around the right side of the building and have a look at what's in back. If there's no gunfire coming from the jungle, we'll make a run for it."

Keeping low, we moved around the building and stopped at the back corner. Bannon had a pronounced limp, and I could tell he was in pain. He took a quick peek. "I'll go first and if they fire on me, you'll know not to come."

Giving me a quick kiss on the cheek, he took off, hobbling as fast as he could. No one seemed to fire in his direction, so I followed, keeping my head down. Reaching the edge of the jungle seconds behind him, I dove into the undergrowth, breathless. We each gave a silent cheer, exchanging high fives.

"They're all around us, I'm sure," he said of the government soldiers. "The question is, can we slip through their lines. Our chances would be better if it was dark, but we can't wait. They'll do a sweep as soon as they've suppressed return fire. We've got to get as deep into the jungle as we can."

"Then let's go."

We moved through the undergrowth cautiously, making slow but steady progress. The battle continued to rage behind us. From time to time we'd hear small arms fire as Lwin's escaping troops encountered government soldiers lying in wait. Once we had to change routes to avoid a mortar battery that was lobbing shells into the compound. Later we came across a prisoner collection point that we skirted only to encounter a passing patrol, which came within feet of where we lay in the mud.

When the coast was clear, we continued on, pushing our way through the jungle, the sounds of the battle beginning to fade into the background. For the first time I began to believe we might escape unscathed.

After a while we came to another trail, this one headed

south, toward Thailand. "This may be the road home," Bannon said.

"It couldn't be more beautiful if it was a four-lane highway."

"We still have to be careful, but the farther we get, the better our chances."

We moved smartly along the trail, putting as much distance between us and the battle as we could. Bannon was really hurting, his limp growing more pronounced. But he didn't complain. Finally we came to a stream and decided to stop and rest. Sitting on a log, I recalled the incident with the snake and turned to look up in the branches to make sure another wasn't lying in wait. Bannon saw. Understanding, he chuckled.

"It's not funny," I said.

"I'll never forget the look on your face when Myat swung that machete."

I shivered at the recollection, wondering what had happened to Myat. Kee's and Han's fates were also unknown. While I couldn't call any of them friends, they were human beings, and I did not like the thought of harm coming to any of them. Lwin might be the exception. I pictured him as I last saw him, dead in the rubble of his house. It wasn't a very dignified way for a soldier to die, yet it seemed just.

"What are you thinking about, Lexie?"

"Nothing."

"That isn't what your expression said."

"Let's find a different subject, Cole."

Bannon studied me, reading my thoughts. "What did Lwin do to you?"

I drew a breath, knowing the subject couldn't be avoided. "He humiliated me."

He colored. I knew what he was thinking. "Did the bastard hurt you?" he asked in a voice tremulous with rage. It was a euphemism, and it was obvious what he meant.

"He humiliated me."

"But did he—"

"Cole, he's dead. He died before anything happened. Okay?"

Bannon took my hand, his eyes shimmering. "I never should have let you come."

I leaned my head on his shoulder, pressing his hand to my cheek. "It's over now, and we're together. That's all that matters."

"You're finally able to let go of the ruby, huh?"

"Not exactly. It's in the sack."

"You're kidding."

"You didn't think I was willing to come out of this empty-handed, did you?"

He laughed and kissed the top of my head. It was the happiest either of us had been in days. I was beginning to think I could love life again . . . that is until I heard a click behind us, the metallic sound of a pistol being cocked.

Chapter
59

From the corner of my eye I could see
the muzzle of the automatic pointed at the back of Bannon's
head. Turning a bit more, I realized the hand holding it be-
longed to a rebel soldier. He said something in Burmese that
neither of us understood, then switched to broken English.

"Drop gun."

Bannon pushed the automatic rifle from where it had been
leaning on the log to the ground. A second man came out of
the nearby brush toward us. He appeared to be wounded, his
sleeve bloody. The wound must have been superficial because he seemed to have mobility. He was unarmed except
for a sheathed knife on his belt.

He looked at each of us in turn and said something to his
friend. I couldn't understand a word, but if I had to guess, it
was something like, "Hey, it's them, Colonel Lwin's concubine and the American traitor."

The man with the pistol stepped over the log and he, too,
checked us out. They, like we, were fleeing the battle, but I
couldn't tell if having that in common registered with them
or not. They exchanged more words, and the man with the

wounded arm picked up the pillowcase, which had been on the ground between my legs.

"Oh, shit," I muttered under my breath.

The man took out the fruit, seemingly pleased to see it. There went our dinner.

Then, when he pulled the jacket out of the pillowcase, my heart sank. There was more jabbering as he unwrapped it and found the box. This seemed to please him, too, but his reaction was nothing compared to what happened when he found the ruby. Both men stared at it, their mouths hanging open. Then they shrieked with glee.

"Can you believe this?" I said to Bannon, realizing the Heart of Burma was about to slip through my fingers.

"Sweetheart, maybe the time has come to let go of the damned thing."

At the moment I had little choice. I suppose I should have considered myself lucky if they simply bid us adieu and took off with the stone, but after all I'd been through I hated to wimp out while Granddad's dream went up in smoke.

During the conversation that followed, the men seemed to be debating what to do with us. It appeared the guy with the pistol wanted to shoot us; the wounded man seemed to be against it. Their words got more and more angry.

"We may have to decide this for them," Bannon said to me. "If the guy with the gun lowers if for just a second, I'm going to jump him. Can you handle the other one?"

"You kidding? I could take them both."

"I like your spirit, sweetheart."

The two men were arguing hot and heavy. My guy got so exercised he put the ruby back in the box, dumped it in the pillowcase with the other stuff and started to leave. When the gunman turned to object, Bannon leaped on him, the gun going off as he knocked him to the ground. As they tussled, rolling into the creek, the guy with the ruby plunged into the brush. I went after him, tackling him before he'd gone twenty yards.

As we rolled on the ground, my adversary pulled his knife. I grabbed his hand, and we struggled. He was not large, and he had a bad arm, which evened up any advantage he had being a man.

We continued to wrestle, rolling to the edge of the stream. Finally, I managed to wrench the knife away and press it to his throat. At the same moment there were more shouts back where the trail crossed the creek, and I realized somebody else had arrived, probably having heard the shot. Were they government troops or were they rebels?

Looking up, I saw Bannon crouched in the bushes across the stream, the pistol in his hand. He was dripping wet from his tussle in the stream. He mouthed the word, "rebel" to inform me who the men were. They were calling out, probably because they'd found the body of the man he'd killed. I clamped my hand over my adversary's mouth so he couldn't sound the alarm. Bannon signaled for me to slit the guy's throat.

I could see why it was necessary, but the guy was a human being. Sure, earlier I'd been prepared to stab Lwin to death, but this guy was hardly a villain of that ilk. To the contrary, he'd wanted to spare our lives. How could I kill him?

As I vacillated, my man reached in his shirt pocket and pulled out a tattered photograph of a child. A little girl like Dru.

I glanced up at Bannon. He again signaled for me to kill the man. But the picture of a little girl in her father's trembling fingers made it a whole new ball game. I thought of Dru and her stuffed elephant. Her trusting eyes. The Heart of Burma was in a pillowcase only a few feet away. The rebel soldiers continued calling. Bannon was desperate for me to kill the guy so we could escape. It all converged on me.

But this man's fate was in my hands. His life. His child's life. In a bizarre way, my life, as well. I could not kill him, nor could I let him go. Leaning close to his ear I whispered for him to be still, not to move. "If you're quiet," I said, "you'll live. We both will live. Trust me," I said, sending the same message with my eyes. "Trust me."

I knew he couldn't understand my words, but maybe he could understand my tone. Human kindness needed no language, after all. I took my hand from the man's mouth and put a finger to my lips. I could see he understood.

There was a final shout from the man's friends, then silence. I looked over at Bannon and he looked back at me. Then he turned and crawled through the undergrowth back toward the trail. A couple of minutes later he came up my side of the creek.

"They're gone," he said.

I got to my feet, stepped over and picked up the pillow-case. Reaching inside I removed a piece of fruit and tossed it to the man. He looked up at me with watery eyes and a smile of gratitude.

Bannon shook his head. "Lexie, you're amazing."

"I make a lousy soldier," I said.

"I won't argue with that."

While all the excitement was going on it had grown late and dusk was falling. I looked up through the trees at the pinky-orange sky.

"We're going to have to sleep in the jungle tonight with the snakes, aren't we?"

"I'm afraid so, sweetheart."

"How long will it take to get back to Thailand?"

"A day or two."

"Will we make it, Cole?"

"The question you need to ask is how badly I want to take you to Tahiti."

"How badly *do* you want to take me to Tahiti?"

Lifting my chin, he kissed me. Really kissed me. "That answer your question?"

The man at our feet beamed. But for my understanding of our common humanity, he could at that very moment be dead. He gave me a thumbs-up, which I returned.

I was free, I was my own person, and I had Granddad's ruby, having lived up to the Rutledge legacy. I was still Garnet Chandler's daughter, too, but I had a feeling that wouldn't be so much of a problem down the road. Mama, genteel Southern lady that she was, had fallen for Cole even before I did.

Bannon took my hand. "Come on, Sparkle, let's get out of here."

I slung the pillowcase over my shoulder, and he pulled me toward the trail. Before we disappeared into the jungle, I glanced back for a last look at my man. He was studying the photograph of his child while taking a bite of fruit.

It was an image I would never forget.

No fooling! The best in romance comes from Avon Books...

Promise Me Forever by Lorraine Heath

"Lorraine Heath steals your heart!"
—New York Times bestselling author Christina Dodd

A very proper lady rekindles the passion—and love—with the Earl of Sachse, a man she thought she'd lost in this latest by USA Today bestselling writer Lorraine Heath.

Sighs Matter by Marianne Stillings

"Marianne Stillings writes fun, sexy suspense!"
—New York Times bestselling author Carly Phillips

When Claire finds herself in danger she turns to a sexy detective she had vowed never to see again . . . even if they had engaged in a willing, mutual seduction.

The Viscount's Wicked Ways by Anne Mallory

"A fresh, vibrant talent who cannot be ignored."
—Romantic Times BOOKclub

The brooding Viscount Blackfield is a man any well-bred lady would shun. But Patience Harrington has never been a proper lady!

Angel in My Bed by Melody Thomas

"An author to watch!"
—USA Today bestselling author Karen Hawkins

Meg Farady believed her former life was behind her—until the man she believed had betrayed her came back into her life. And that man is...her husband!

Avon Romances

the best in

exceptional authors and unforgettable novels!